VISIONS IN DEATH

Titles by J. D. Robb

Naked in Death

Glory in Death

Immortal in Death

Rapture in Death

Ceremony in Death

Vengeance in Death

Holiday in Death

Conspiracy in Death

Loyalty in Death

Witness in Death

Judgment in Death

Betrayal in Death

Seduction in Death

Reunion in Death

Purity in Death

Portrait in Death

Imitation in Death

Divided in Death

Titles by Nora Roberts

Honest Illusions
Private Scandals
Hidden Riches
True Betrayals
Montana Sky
Born in Fire
Born in Ice
Born in Shame
Daring to Dream
Holding the Dream
Finding the Dream
Sanctuary
Homeport
Sea Swept
Rising Tides
Inner Harbor
The Reef
River's End
Carolina Moon
Jewels of the Sun
Tears of the Moon
Heart of the Sea
The Villa
From the Heart
Midnight Bayou
Dance upon the Air
Heaven and Earth
Face the Fire
Three Fates
Chesapeake Blue
Birthright
Key of Light
Key of Knowledge
Key of Valor

By Nora Roberts and J. D. Robb

Remember When

VISIONS IN DEATH

J. D. ROBB

DOUBLEDAY LARGE PRINT HOME LIBRARY EDITION

G. P. PUTNAM'S SONS
NEW YORK

This Large Print Edition, prepared especially for Doubleday Large Print Home Library, contains the complete, unabridged text of the original Publisher's Edition.

G. P. Putnam's Sons
Publishers Since 1838
a member of
Penguin Group (USA) Inc.
375 Hudson Street
New York, NY 10014

Published simultaneously in Canada

ISBN 0-7394-4582-0

Printed in the United States of America

Friendship cannot live with ceremony,
nor without civility.
—LORD HALIFAX

Is this a vision?
is this a dream?
do I sleep?
—WILLIAM SHAKESPEARE

VISIONS IN DEATH

I

She'd gotten through the entire evening without killing anyone. Lieutenant Eve Dallas, cop to the bone, figured the restraint showed enormous strength of character.

Her day had gone smoothly enough. A morning court appearance that had been as routine as it was tedious, paperwork both extensive and mind-numbing. The single case she'd caught had involved pals and their dispute over who had dibs on the last of the illegals—a party mix of Buzz, Exotica, and Zoom—they'd been toking on while lazing around on the roof of an apartment building on the West Side.

The dispute had been resolved when one of the afternoon partyers had taken a header off the roof, clutching the last of the illegals in his greedy fist.

He probably hadn't felt much, even when he'd splatted onto Tenth Avenue, but it sure as hell had broken the party mood.

Witnesses, including an uninvolved Good Samaritan from a neighboring building who'd called in the nine-one-one, all stated that the individual who'd been scooped off the sidewalk and into a bag had leaped of his own volition onto the roof ledge, danced an energetic keep-away boogie, lost his precarious balance, and taken flight with a giggling *wee-haw.*

Much to the surprise—and possible entertainment—of the afternoon passengers on an airtram who'd also witnessed the last dance of one Jasper K. McKinney.

One inappropriately delighted tourist had managed to capture the entire incident on his pocket vid.

It all jibed, and the books would close on Jasper as death by misadventure. Unofficially, Eve labeled it death by stupidity, but there wasn't a place on the sheet for that particular observation.

As a result of Jasper and his eight-story dive, she'd clocked out of Cop Central barely an hour past end-of-duty, only to get bogged down in ugly midtown traffic because the temporary vehicle some sadist in Requisitions had tossed at her limped along like a blind, three-legged dog.

She had rank, for God's sake, and was entitled to a decent ride. It wasn't her fault she'd had two units destroyed in two years. Maybe she'd forget strength of character and go maim somebody in Requisitions in the morning.

It sounded like fun.

And after she'd gotten home—okay, almost two hours late—she'd had to transform herself from kick-ass murder cop to fashionable corporate wife.

She was a good cop, she reminded herself, but more than a little shaky in the corporate wife arena.

She supposed she'd been fashionable, since her husband had the entire getup—down to the underwear—set out for her. Roarke knew clothes.

She just knew she was wearing something green with sparkles all over it, and where it wasn't green and sparkly, it showed a lot of skin.

There hadn't been time to argue about it,

but only to dive into the outfit and shove her feet into shoes—also green and sparkly. With high enough, needle-thin heels, she'd been nearly eye to eye with her man.

It wasn't a hardship to be eye to eye with Roarke. Not when his were that wild, unearthly blue in a face drawn by artistic angels. But it was tough being social with strangers when you were worried you might tip over and fall on your ass any second.

But she'd gotten through it. Through the quick-change, the quick shuttle trip from New York to Chicago, through the cocktail hour where her brains were nearly bored to suet despite truly excellent wine, and the corporate dinner with Roarke entertaining about a dozen clients, with her playing hostess.

She wasn't quite sure what kind of clients they were since Roarke had his fingers in every pie known to man or beast, so she didn't attempt to keep up. What she did know was that most of them could take the prize for most tedious during the four-hour ordeal.

But there had been no casualties.

Points for her.

What she wanted now was to get home,

get out of the sparkly green thing, and fall into bed to sleep for the six hours she'd have before the clock started ticking again.

The summer of 2059 had been long, hot, and bloody. Fall, with its cooler temperatures, was coming. Maybe people wouldn't be as inclined to kill one another.

But she doubted it.

She'd barely settled into her seat on the plush, private shuttle when Roarke lifted her feet into his lap and slipped off her shoes.

"Don't get any ideas, pal. When I finally get out of this dress, I'm not getting back in."

"Darling Eve." His voice was a purr that echoed of Ireland. "That's the sort of statement that gives me ideas. However lovely you look in that dress, you'd look even lovelier out of it."

"Forget it. No way I'm dragging this thing back on, and I'm surely not getting out of this shuttle wearing what you laughingly call underwear. So just . . . Oh, sweet baby Jesus."

Her eyes crossed, then did a slow roll to the back of her head when he pressed his thumbs into her arch.

"I owe you a foot rub, at the very least."

He smiled as she let her head fall back and moaned. "For services above and beyond. I know you detest the sort of thing we did tonight. And I appreciate you not pulling out your weapon and stunning McIntyre over the canapés."

"The guy with the big teeth who laughed like a donkey, right?"

"That would be McIntyre. He's also a very important account." He lifted her left foot, kissed her toes. "So thanks."

"It's okay. Goes with the package."

Hell of a package, she thought, studying him through barely open eyes. All gorgeously wrapped six feet two inches of him. Not just the lean, muscled build or the heart-stopping face framed with the sweep of black silk hair. But the brains, the style, the edge. The whole shot.

And best of all, he not only loved her, but he *got* her. Of all the things they fought about—and it was never hard to find something—they never butted heads over this.

He never expected any more of her in the corporate wife area than she could give. A lot of people would, and she got that. Roarke's enterprises included holdings, properties, factories, markets, and God knew, on and off planet. He was absurdly rich, with all the power that went with it. A lot of men in his position would expect a spouse to be at their beck, to drop everything and drape themselves over his arm at a moment's notice.

He didn't.

For every business event or social occasion she managed to attend as his wife, there were probably three she missed.

Moreover, there were countless times he arranged his schedule to suit hers, or put in time as consultant on a case.

In fact, when she thought about it, he made a much better cop's husband than she made corporate wife.

"Maybe I owe you a foot rub," she considered. "You're a pretty good deal."

He skimmed a finger down her foot, from toes to heel. "I certainly am."

"But I'm still not getting out of this dress." She scooted down in her seat, closed her eyes. "Wake me up when we land."

She'd only started to drift when the communicator in her evening bag signaled. "Oh, come *on.*" She didn't open her eyes but reached out, clamped a hand on the bag. "What's our ETA?"

"About fifteen."

With a nod, she pulled out the communicator and engaged. "Dallas."

Dispatch, Dallas, Lieutenant Eve. Report to Belvedere Castle, Central Park. Officers on scene. Homicide, single victim.

"Contact Peabody, Detective Delia. I'll meet her on scene. My ETA is thirty minutes."

Acknowledged. Dispatch out.

"Shit." Eve dragged a hand through her hair. "You can dump me and go on."

"I dislike dumping my wife. I'll go with you and wait."

She scowled down at the fancy dress. "I hate going to scenes in these getups. I hear about it for weeks."

It was worse because she had to put the shoes back on, and then navigate in them over the grass and onto the paths of the city's greatest park.

The castle sat at the highest point of the park, with its skinny tower rising up into the night sky and the rocky ground giving way to the lake at its feet.

It was a pretty enough spot, she supposed, for tourists to take their snaps and vids during the day. Once the sun set, areas like this were the natural habitat of the street sleepers, chemi-heads, unlicensed companions on the troll, and those with nothing better to do than look for trouble.

The current city administration made a lot of noise about keeping the parks and monuments clean. And to their credit they even tossed money at the process with some regularity. There would be volunteers as well as city workers combing the park for litter, blasting off graffiti, sprucing up gardens and such.

Then everyone would get cozy and comfortable and put their efforts into other matters until it all went to hell again.

At the moment it was in decent shape with hardly enough litter to make the predawn cleanup crews work themselves into a lather.

With Roarke beside her, she strode as best she could toward the barricades the cops had already put in place. The castle was lit up like day with crime-scene lights.

"You don't have to wait," she told him. "I can catch a ride."

"I'll wait."

Rather than argue, she shrugged and pulling out her badge, went through the barricades.

No one made any comments about the dress or shoes. She'd figured her rep for ass-kicking would have kept the uniforms quiet, but it surprised her not to detect a single grin or snicker behind her back.

It surprised her more when her partner stepped toward her without a smart remark on her wardrobe.

"Dallas. It's bad."

"What've we got?"

"Female, caucasian, about thirty. I got the scene recorded. I was about to run her for ID when they told me you'd arrived on scene." They walked together, Peabody in her comfortable airskids, Eve in the arch-killing heels. "Sexual homicide. Raped and strangled. But he didn't stop there."

"Who found her?"

"A couple of kids. Jesus, Dallas." Peabody stopped a moment, stood in her hastily thrown-on clothes, rubbing a hand over her tired face. “Snuck out of the house, thought they’d have a little adventure. Sure as hell got more than that. We’ve contacted the parents and child services. We’ve got them in a black-and-white.”

“Where is she?”

“Down there.” Peabody led the way, then pointed.

She lay on the rocks, just above the dark, still water of the lake. She wore nothing but what looked to be a red ribbon tied around her neck. Her hands were clasped together between her breasts, as if in prayer, or plea.

Her face was smeared with blood. Blood, Eve thought, that had spilled out of her when he’d taken her eyes.

She had to ditch the shoes or risk breaking her neck. Using the can of Seal-It from the field kit Peabody handed her, she coated her hands, her bare feet. Even so, it wasn’t an easy climb down in the party dress, and she imagined she looked completely ridiculous, completely uncoplike sparkling her way over rocks toward a body.

She heard something rip, and ignored it.

"Oh, man." Peabody winced. "You're going to ruin that dress, and it's totally iced."

"I'd give a month's pay for a goddamn pair of jeans and a normal shirt. A pair of fucking boots." Then she put it out of her mind, set her feet solidly, and turned to the body.

"Didn't rape her down here. There's going to be a secondary scene. Even a lunatic doesn't rape a woman on a heap of rocks when there's all this grass. Raped her somewhere else. Killed or incapacitated her somewhere else. Had to carry her down here. Had to have some muscle and bulk to manage that—unless there was more than one of them. She's what, maybe a hundred and thirty pounds anyway. Deadweight."

More to protect the scene than the dress, Eve hitched the skirt up. "Let's get an ID on her, Peabody. Find out who she is."

While Peabody used the Identi-pad, Eve studied the position of the body. "Posed her. Praying? Begging? Resting in peace? What's your message?"

She crouched to examine the body. "Visual evidence of physical and sexual assault. Facial bruises, torso, forearms—those look defensive. She's got some matter under her nails. Tried to fight, scratched at him. It's not skin. Looks like fibers."

"Her name's Elisa Maplewood," Peabody said. "Central Park West address."

"Not so far from home," Eve stated. "She doesn't look uptown. No pedicure. Hands aren't smooth and pampered. Got calluses."

"Lists employment as a domestic."

"Yeah, that's more like it."

"She's thirty-two. Divorced. Dallas, she's got a four-year-old kid. A daughter."

"Oh, hell." Eve drew it in, then set it aside. "Bruises on her thighs and the vaginal area. Red corded ribbon around her throat."

It was dug into her skin so the bruised flesh puffed around it, then the tails draped down to her breasts.

"Time of death, Peabody?"

"Getting it." Peabody drew back the gauge, studied the readout. "Twenty-two twenty."

"About three hours ago. And the kids found her?"

"Just after midnight. First on scene responded, dealt with the kids, took a visual from above, and called it in at quarter to one."

"Okay." Steeling herself, she took the microgoggles, slipped them on, then bent over the ruined face. "Took his time here. Didn't hack at her. Neat, precise cuts. Almost surgical, like he was doing a fucking transplant. So the eyes were what he was after. They were the prize. The beating, the rape, those were just the prelude."

She eased back and took off the goggles. "Let's turn her, check the back."

There was nothing but the darkened flesh from the settling of blood, and what Eve identified as grass stains on the buttocks and down the thighs.

"Came at her from behind, that's what he did. But it didn't matter to him if she saw him. Knocked her down—sidewalk or pavement. No, gravelly path. See the scrapes on her elbows? Smacks her around. She tries to fight him off, tries to scream. Maybe she does scream, but he's hauling her away, somewhere he can have his fun without anyone trying to interfere. Drags her, across the grass. Beats her into submission, rapes her. Ties the cord around her neck, kills her. When that part of the job's over, it's time for the real business."

Eve replaced the goggles. "Strip off

what's left of her clothes, take her shoes, anything else she was wearing. Jewelry, anything that individualizes her. Carry her down here. Pose her. Take the eyes—carefully. Check the pose, make any necessary adjustments. Wash off all that blood in the lake if you want. Clean up, take your prize, and be on your way."

"Ritual killing?"

"His ritual anyway. They can bag her," Eve said as she straightened. "Let's see if we can find the kill site."

Roarke watched her slide her feet back into the shoes. She'd have been better off barefoot, he mused, but that wasn't an option the lieutenant would consider.

Despite the heels, the glamorous dress—worse for wear now—the glitter of diamonds, she was every inch the cop. Tall, lean, steady as the rocks she'd just climbed on to view some new horror. You wouldn't see the horror in her eyes, those long, golden brown eyes. She looked pale in the harsh lights, and the glare of them only accentuated her sharp features. Her hair, nearly the same color as those eyes, was short, choppy, and mussed now from the breeze off the water.

He watched her stop, hold a brief conversation with a uniform. Her voice would be flat, he knew, and brisk, and reveal nothing of what she felt.

He saw her gesture, and saw the stalwart and more comfortably dressed Peabody nod. Then Eve was peeling off from the group of cops, and heading back to him.

"You're going to want to go on home," she told him. "This is going to take some time."

"I suspect it will. Rape, strangulation, mutilation." He lifted a brow when her eyes narrowed. "I keep my ear to the ground when it involves my cop. Can I help?"

"No. I'm keeping civilians—even you—out. He didn't kill her down there, so we need to find where he did. I probably won't make it home tonight."

"Would you like me to bring you, or send you, a change of clothes?"

Since even with his amazing powers, he couldn't just snap his fingers and put her in boots and trousers, she shook her head. "I've got spare stuff in my locker at Central." She glanced down at the dress, sighed at the smears of dirt, the small tears, the stains from body fluid. She'd tried to be careful, but there you go, and God knew what he paid for the damn thing.

"Sorry about the dress."

"It's not important. Get in touch when you can."

"Sure."

She struggled—knew he knew she struggled—not to wince when he skimmed a finger down the dent in her chin, when he leaned down and brushed his lips to hers. "Good luck, Lieutenant."

"Yeah. Thanks."

As he walked back to the limo, he heard her raise her voice. "Okay, boys and girls, fan out. Teams of two. Standard evidence search."

He wouldn't have carried her far, Eve deduced. What would be the point? The added time, trouble, the additional risk of being seen. Still, they were talking Central Park, so it wasn't going to be quick and easy unless they ran into incredible luck.

She did, inside of thirty minutes.

"Here." She held up a hand to stop Peabody, then crouched. "Ground's torn up some. Hand me the goggles. Yeah, yeah," she said after she'd strapped them on. "We got some blood here."

She went down on hands and knees, her nose nearly to the ground, like a hound scenting prey. "I want this area cordoned off. Call the sweepers. I want to see if they can find any trace. Look here."

She got tweezers out of the field kit. "Broken fingernail. Hers," she decided when she held it up to the light. "Didn't make it easy for him, did you, Elisa? You did what you could."

She bagged the nail, then sat back on her heels.

"Dragged her over the grass. You can see where she tried to dig in. Lost a shoe. That's why she's got grass stains and dirt on one foot. But he went back for it. Took her clothes with him."

She pushed to her feet. "We'll check bins in a ten-block radius in case he dumped them. They'll be torn, bloody, dirty. We'll see if we can get a description of what she was wearing, but even without it, we'll look. Kept them though, didn't you?" she murmured. "Kept them as a memento."

"She lives a couple blocks from here," Peabody commented. "Grabbed her close to home, dragged her here, did the job, then carried her over to the dump site."

"We'll canvass. Let's get this coordinated, then take her residence."

Peabody cleared her throat, studied Eve's dress. "You're going like that?"

"Got a better idea?"

It was hard not to feel a little ridiculous, striding in her ruined dress and mile-high shoes toward the night droid on door duty in front of Maplewood's building.

At least she had her badge. It was one of those things she never left home without. "Lieutenant Dallas, Detective Peabody, NYPSD. Regarding Elisa Maplewood. She lives here?"

"I'll need to scan your IDs to verify."

He looked pretty spiffy for so early in the morning, but that was a droid for you. He wore a natty red uniform with silver trim, and was designed to replicate a man in his mid-fifties, just a bit of silver at the temples to match the braid.

"These are in order. Mrs. Maplewood is a live-in domestic, employed by Mr. and Mrs. Luther Vanderlea. What's this about?"

"Did you see Ms. Maplewood tonight?"

"I'm midnight to six. Haven't seen her."

"We'll need to see the Vanderleas."

"Mr. Vanderlea is out of town. You'll need to clear a visit with the desk. Comp's on this time of night."

He unlocked the doors, walked in with them. "Secondary scan for ID," he informed them.

It irritated, but Eve passed her badge through the electronics on the fancy desk in the black-and-white lobby.

Your identification is verified, Dallas, Lieutenant Eve. What is the nature of your business?

"I need to speak with Mrs. Luther Vanderlea, regarding her employee, Elisa Maplewood."

One moment while Mrs. Vanderlea is contacted.

The droid hovered while they waited. Quiet music played. It had switched on when they'd started across the lobby. Set to activate, Eve assumed, when a human entered.

Why people needed music to cross a room, she couldn't say.

The lights were dim, the flowers fresh. A few good pieces of furniture—in case you wanted to sit down and listen to the recorded music—were arranged tastefully. There were two elevators in the south wall, and four security cameras to sweep the lobby.

The Vanderleas had a lot of bucks under the belt.

"Where's Mr. Vanderlea?" she asked the droid.

"Is this an official inquiry?"

"No, I'm just a nosy so-and-so." She waved her badge under his nose. "Yes, this is an official inquiry."

"Mr. Vanderlea is in Madrid on business."

"When did he leave?"

"Two days ago. He's due back tomorrow evening."

"What—" She broke off as the comp signaled.

Mrs. Vanderlea will see you now. Please take Elevator A to the fifty-first floor. You will find Mrs. Vanderlea in Penthouse B.

"Thanks." Even as they crossed the checkerboard floor, the elevator doors opened. "Why do we thank machines?" Eve wondered out loud. "They couldn't possibly give a shit."

"One of those innate human traits. That's why programmers have them thanking us, too, I guess. You ever been to Madrid?"

"No. Maybe. No," she decided. She'd been a lot of places over the last couple of years. "I don't think. Do you know who designs shoes like the ones I'm wearing, Peabody?"

"The shoe god. Those are magolicious shoes, sir."

"No, not the shoe god. These are the product of a man, a devious flesh and blood man, who secretly hates all women. By designing shoes like this, he can torture them for profit."

"They make your legs look a hundred feet tall."

"Yeah, that's what I want all right. A pair of

hundred-foot legs." Resigned, she stepped off on fifty-one.

The door to Penthouse B was wide as a truck, and opened by a petite woman in her thirties wearing a moss green dressing gown.

Her hair was long and sleep-tousled, and was a deep, dark red with subtle gold streaks streamed through it.

"Lieutenant Dallas? God, is that a Leonardo?"

Since she was goggling at the dress, it didn't take Eve long to conclude she was talking about it. "Probably." As Leonardo was not only the current darling of the fashionable set, but also the main squeeze of Eve's closest friend. "I was . . . at a thing. My partner, Detective Peabody. Mrs. Vanderlea?"

"Yes, I'm Deann Vanderlea. What's this about?"

"Can we come in, Mrs. Vanderlea?"

"Yes, of course. I'm confused. When they called from downstairs and said the police wanted to see me, my first thought was something happened to Luther. But I'd have gotten a call from Madrid, wouldn't I?" She smiled, uncertainly. "Nothing's happened to Luther, has it?"

"We're not here about your husband. This concerns Elisa Maplewood."

"Elisa? Well, she's in bed at this hour. Elisa can't be in any trouble." She folded her arms. "What's this about?"

"When did you last see Ms. Maplewood?"

"Right before I went to bed. About ten. I went to bed early. I had a headache. What *is* this?"

"I'm sorry to tell you, Mrs. Vanderlea, but Ms. Maplewood is dead. She was killed earlier tonight."

"That—that's just ridiculous. She's in bed."

The simplest, cleanest way, Eve knew, was not to argue. "You may want to check on that."

"It's nearly four in the morning. Of course she's in bed. Her suite is back here, off the kitchen."

She swept away, through the spacious living area, furnished in what Eve recognized as antiques. A lot of gleaming wood and curved lines, deep colors, complex patterns and sparkling glassware. It flowed into a media room, with the wall screen recessed, and the game and communication center housed in some sort of cabinet. Armoire, she corrected. That's what Roarke called those big-ass cabinets.

A dining room angled off to the side, with the kitchen behind it.

"I'd like you to wait here, please."

Snippy now, Eve noted. Irritated and afraid.

Mrs. Vanderlea opened a set of wide pocket doors and walked into what Eve assumed was Elisa Maplewood's personal area.

"This place is *huge*," Peabody whispered.

"Yeah, lots of space, lots of stuff." She looked around the kitchen. Everything was silver and black. Dramatic, efficient, and so clean she doubted even a team of sweepers would come up with a single mote of dust.

It wasn't that different a setup than the one in Roarke's house. She didn't think of the kitchen as hers. That was Summerset's province, and she was more than happy to let him rule there.

"I've met her before."

Peabody glanced back from her ogling of the massive AutoChef. "You know Vanderlea?"

"Met them, don't know them. One of the 'dos' I got dragged to. Roarke knows them. I didn't place the name, who the hell can remember all those *people*? But her face clicked."

She turned as Mrs. Vanderlea hurried back into the room. "She's not there. I don't understand. She's not in her room, or anywhere in her suite. Vonnie's sleeping. Her daughter, her little girl. I don't understand."

"Does she often go out at night?"

"No, of course she—*Mignon*!" With this, she dashed back into Elisa's suite.

"Who the hell is Mignon?" Eve muttered.

"Maybe Maplewood switched to girls. Might have a lover."

"Mignon's not here." Deann was sheet-white now, and her fingers trembled as she held them to her throat.

"Who is—"

"Our dog." She spoke quickly, the words jumping out of her mouth. "Really Elisa's dog, emotionally. A little teacup poodle I bought a few months ago—for company, for the girls, but Mignon bonded with Elisa. She—she probably took her for a walk. She often does that the last thing at night. She took the dog for a walk. Oh, God. Oh, my God."

"Mrs. Vanderlea, why don't you sit down? Peabody, some water."

"Was there an accident? Oh God, was there an accident?" There weren't tears, not yet, but Eve knew there would be.

"No, I'm sorry, it wasn't an accident. Mrs. Maplewood was attacked, in the park."

"Attacked?" She said it slowly, as if the word were foreign. "Attacked?"

"She was murdered."

"No. No."

"Drink a little water, ma'am." Peabody pressed the glass she'd poured into Deann's hands. "Sip a little water."

"I can't. I can't. How can this be? We were just talking, a few hours ago. We were sitting right here. She told me to take a blocker and go to bed. And I did. We . . . the girls were tucked in for the night, and she made me tea and told me to go to bed. How did this happen? What happened?"

No, Eve thought. It wasn't the time to make it worse with details. "Drink some water." She noticed Peabody going over to close the pocket doors.

The kid, Eve remembered. This wasn't a

conversation a child should hear, if she should wake.

When she did wake, Eve thought, her world would be changed, irrevocably.

2

"How long has she worked for you?" Eve knew the answer, but it would be easier to guide Deann over smooth ground before they moved to the rocks.

"Two years. Two years. I—we—my husband travels a great deal, and I decided I wanted live-in help rather than just the day staff and droids. More for company, I suppose. I hired Elisa because I liked her."

She ran a hand over her face and made an obvious effort to settle. "She was qualified, of course, but we just hit it off right away. If I were to hire someone who'd live in my house, be a part of my household, I wanted it to be someone I was comfortable with, on a personal level. The other deciding factor was Vonnie. Yvonne, her daughter. I have a little girl, I have Zanna. They're the same age, and I thought they'd be playmates. They are. They're like family. They *are* family. Oh God, Vonnie."

She pressed her hands to her mouth, and now the tears came. "She's only four. She's just a baby. How will I tell her that her mother's . . . How will I tell her?"

"We can do that, Mrs. Vanderlea." Peabody sat. "We'll talk to her, and have a counselor from Child Protection available for her."

"She doesn't know you." Deann pushed to her feet, walked across the room to a drawer, took out tissues. "She'd only be more frightened and confused if she heard . . . from a stranger. I have to tell her. I have to find the way to tell her."

She dabbed her cheeks with a tissue. "I need a second."

"Take your time," Eve told her.

"We're friends. Like Zanna and Vonnie. It wasn't . . . our relationship wasn't like employer and employee. Her parents . . ."

Deann drew in a breath, long, deep. Eve gave her top points for control when she came back to the table. "Her mother lives downtown, with Elisa's stepfather. Her father, ah, he's in Philadelphia. I can . . . I can get in touch with them. I think, they need to hear this from me first. They need . . . I have to call Luther. I have to tell him."

"Are you sure you want to handle this yourself?" Eve asked her.

"She would have done it for me." When her voice broke, she pressed her lips together, bore down. "She would have taken care of my baby, and I'll take care of hers. She would have . . . Oh, God, how could this happen?"

"Did she mention any problems to you? Speak of being concerned about someone who bothered her, or made threats?"

"No. No. She would have. People liked Elisa."

"Was she involved with anyone—romantically, socially?"

"No. She really wasn't dating at this point. She'd had a difficult divorce, and was interested in creating a stable home for her daughter, and just—as she put it—giving men a rest."

"Was there someone she rebuffed or discouraged?"

"Not that I . . . was she *raped*?" Deann's hands fisted on the table.

"The medical examiner has yet to determine—" Eve broke off when Deann's hand shot out, gripped hers.

"You know, and I won't have you holding back. She was my friend."

"The indications are she was raped, yes."

The hand tightened on Eve's, trembled once, violently, then released. "You'll find him. You'll find him and you'll make him pay."

"That's my intention. If you want to help me do that, I need you to think. If there's anything, however insignificant it seems to you. If she said anything, however casually."

"She would have fought," Deann stated. "Her husband was abusive, and she got counseling, she got help, and she left him. She learned to stand up for herself. She would have fought."

"She did. Where's the ex-husband?"

"I'd like to say he's sweating in hell, but he's in the Caribbean with his current bimbo. He lives there, runs some sort of dive shop. He hasn't seen his own child, not once, not ever. Elisa was eight months pregnant when she filed for divorce. I won't let him have that child."

A combative light glowed on her face now, and the heat of it toughened her voice. "I'll fight him if he tries to take custody. I can do that for her."

"When's the last time she heard from him?"

"A few months ago, I think, when his child support payment was late again. Bitching and complaining about having to give her his money when she had this cozy setup here." She drew that long breath again. "The money went directly into an account for Vonnie, for her education. Not that he'd think of that."

"Did you ever meet him?"

"No, I was denied that dubious pleasure. To my knowledge he hasn't been back to New York in four years. I'm not thinking very clearly yet," she admitted. "But I will. I can promise you, I'll think very clearly, very carefully, and do anything I can to help you. But I need to call my husband now. I need to talk to Luther—and to be alone, please. To be alone so I can find the right way to tell Vonnie when she wakes up. To tell Vonnie and my own little girl."

"We'll need to see her rooms, look through her things. Some time tomorrow. Is that a problem?"

"No. I'd let you do it now, but . . ." She looked back toward the door. "I want Vonnie to sleep, as long as she can."

Eve rose. "If you'd get in touch with me in the morning then."

"I will. I'm sorry, I've completely forgotten who you are."

"Dallas. Lieutenant Dallas. Detective Peabody."

"Right. Right. I admired your dress when you came to the door. It seems like years ago already." She got up, rubbing at her face as she studied Eve. "You seem familiar to me. I can't figure out if it's because it seems you've been here for years, or if you are."

"I think we met before, at some charity dinner or something."

"At a charity dinner? Oh, well, of course. Roarke. You're Roarke's wife. Roarke's cop, people call you. I don't have all my wits."

"No problem. I'm sorry to meet you again under these circumstances."

Her gaze sharpened now, and the warrior gleam still lit her face. "When people talk about Roarke's cop over their cocktails and canapés, they say she's a little scary, a little mean, and very relentless. Would that be a fair description?"

"Close enough."

"Good. Good." Deann held out her hand, took Eve's firmly. "Because you're my cop now, too."

"She's got a tough road over the next few days," Peabody commented as they rode down to the lobby. "She strikes me as the kind who'll handle it when she gets her balance."

"She's got spine," Eve agreed. "We'll look at the ex-husband. Could be he decided to come up to New York. Talk to the vic's parents, other friends. Get a clearer picture of her routine from the Vanderleas."

"It wasn't a chance kill. The mutilation takes it out of the box for me. The setup, the pose. If it wasn't personal, a one-on-one sort of thing, it was planned, at least."

"Agreed." They crossed the lobby, and headed out to the waiting black-and-white. "Maplewood walked the dog at night. A routine, a pattern. Killer notices her, notices the pattern, and lies in wait. Tells me he knew the dog wouldn't go for him, or had a way to incapacitate the dog."

"Have you ever seen one of those little poodles?" Peabody held her hands together to form a little cup.

"Still got teeth, right?"

She stood just outside the car, scanning the neighborhood. Well lit. Security droids would patrol regularly. Doormen on duty 24/7. There would have been some vehicular traffic that time of night, during the attack.

"She walked the dog into the park. Just the verges, probably, but she went inside. Felt safe. She lives here, knows the area. Probably stayed close to the street, but not close enough. He'd have to be fast. Have to be waiting, almost certainly."

She left the sidewalk herself, picturing it. "Let the dog sniff around the trees, do the dog thing. It's a nice night. She'd relax, enjoy it. She and Vanderlea might've been pals, but she still worked in there, and hard. You could see by her hands. She'd enjoy a little time out here with the dog, just walking, just hanging."

She played her light over the grass,

toward the grab spot that was surrounded by barricades. "He waited until she was out of sight of the street. Just far enough. Killed the dog or the dog ran off."

"Killed the dog?" Peabody's immediate distress had Eve shaking her head.

"A guy beats, rapes, strangles, and mutilates a woman, I don't think he's going to see offing a dog as crossing any lines."

"Jeez."

Eve headed back toward the car. She could go home, change. Home was closer than Central. It would save her the indignity of walking through Central in her current attire. A point that couldn't be over-valued.

"The black-and-white can take us to my place. We can put together what we've got, catch a couple hours' sleep and start fresh in the morning."

"I hear that. I also hear the unspoken. You don't want to go to Central in your party dress."

"Shut up, Peabody."

It was after five A.M. when Eve crept into the bedroom. She stripped off as she crossed to the bed, letting clothes lay where they fell, then crawled naked into bed.

She hadn't made a sound, had barely shifted the mattress, but Roarke's arm circled her waist, and drew her back against him.

"Didn't mean to wake you up. I'm going to catch a couple hours. Peabody's bunked in her favorite guest room."

"Turn it off, then." His lips brushed her hair. "Just sleep."

"Two hours," she murmured. And turned it off.

Her next, not quite coherent thought was: Coffee.

She could smell it. The seductive scent climbed into her sleeping brain like a lover up a flower-strewn trellis. Then she blinked her eyes open, and saw Roarke.

He was invariably up before her, and as usual was already dressed in one of his master-of-the-world suits. But instead of being in the sitting area of the bedroom, as was his habit, scanning the early stock reports and whatever over his breakfast, he was sitting on the side of the bed, looking at her.

"What's up? Something happen? Was there another—?"

"No. Relax." He pressed a hand to her shoulder to hold her down when she started to spring up. "I'm your wake-up call, complete with coffee." He moved the cup into her line of sight.

And watched her eyes glaze over with longing.

"Gimme."

He eased back, handed it over, waited while she took her first, desperate swallow. "You know, darling, if caffeine ever makes it to the illegals list, you're going to have to register as an addict."

"They try to make coffee an illegal, I'll kill them all, and it won't be an issue. How do I rate coffee in bed?"

"I love you."

"Yeah, you do." She took another gulp, grinned. "Sucker."

"That's no way to persuade me to get you a second cup."

"I love you back?"

"That would probably work." He rubbed a thumb along the shadows already dogging her eyes. "You need more than two hours, Lieutenant."

"It's all I can spare. I'll make it up. Eventually. Gonna grab a shower."

She was up, and took what was left of the coffee with her into the bathroom. He heard her call for jets on full, at one-oh-one. And only shook his head at her habit of boiling herself awake every morning.

He'd see that she got some fuel in her, and hopefully wouldn't have to tie her down and force-feed her. He'd just begun to program the AutoChef for breakfast, when he heard the quick padding steps behind him.

"I'd swear there was a chip in your head that signals any time anyone so much as thinks of food." Roarke glanced down at the pudgy cat rubbing hopefully against his leg. "I'll wager you've already been fed in the kitchen."

Galahad purred like an engine and rubbed harder. Ignoring him for the moment, Roarke selected French toast for Eve, something she had a hard time resisting. He added a couple rashers of bacon, knowing his own weakness where the cat was concerned.

Eve came out wearing a short white terry robe. "I'm just going to grab something at Central when . . ." She sniffed the air, spotted the plate of French toast. "That was low."

"Yes." He patted the seat beside him, then moved the cat when Galahad took him up on the invitation. "Not you. Sit down, Eve. You can spare fifteen minutes for some breakfast."

"Maybe. Besides, I should fill you in on a couple things. Two birds, time efficiency." She sat, poured syrup lavishly over bread.

She took a bite, nudged the cat back as he tried to belly toward her plate, then reached for the fresh coffee Roarke poured. "The victim worked for Luther and Deann Vanderlea."

"Of Vanderlea Antiquities?"

"That's what it said when I ran his data. How well do you know them?"

"I used Vanderlea extensively when furnishing this house, and others. Consulted with his father for most of it, but I know Luther and his wife. I wouldn't call them personal friends, but certainly friendly acquaintances. He's knowledgeable about his business, and very involved in the running of it at this stage. Pleasant enough people, and she's very bright and charming. Are they suspects?"

"Luther was in Madrid at the time of the murder. As far as I can confirm at this point. Wife's not on my list. In fact, unless she's an award-winning actress, she and the victim were as much friends as boss and domestic. More. She took it hard, but stood up to it. I liked her."

"I can tell you, from what I know of Luther, I can't see him raping a woman, much less murdering one and cutting out her eyes."

"He the type who might try to diddle with the maid under his wife's nose?"

"One never knows what a man might try to diddle with under his wife's nose, but it wouldn't be my call where he's concerned, no. They strike me as very happy together. I think they have a young child."

"Girl, age four. Same age as the victim's daughter. Deann Vanderlea's having a very hard morning."

"The victim have a spouse?"

"Ex. Lives in the Caribbean. Abusive history. We'll look at him close."

"Current lover?"

"Not according to Deann. Victim, Elisa Maplewood, purportedly went out, between ten and midnight, to walk the little foo-foo dog. We'll get the exact from building security. Strolled into the park where he grabbed her. Waited—had to be waiting—attacked, raped, strangled, then carted her over to the rocks to lay her out, finish his job. Are the eyes a symbol?" she wondered. "Windows to the soul, an eye for an eye? Or a twisted religious ritual? Maybe just a souvenir."

"You'll want Mira."

"Oh yeah." Eve thought of the city's top profiler. "I'm pulling her in this morning."

She'd cleaned her plate while she'd talked and got up now to dress. "We could get lucky, and this was a one-time deal."

"Why do you think it's not?"

"Too organized and precise. Too many symbols. The eyes, red ribbon, the pose. Maybe we find all these apply directly somehow to Elisa Maplewood, but I think they apply to the killer rather than the victim. They mean something to him, personally. Elisa may have been a type: physically, her location, her background, something of the sort. Or it may have been enough for her to be female and available."

"Do you want my help with the Vanderleas?"

"I might, at some point."

"Let me know. Darling, not that jacket." More resigned than appalled, he rose to take the one she'd yanked out of her closet, and after a quick study, drew out one with pale blue checks over cream. "Trust me."

"I don't know what I did before you were my fashion consultant," she told him.

"I do, but I don't like to think about it."

"I know a dig when I hear one." She sat to pull on her boots.

"Mmm." He slid his hands in his pockets, and fingered a small gray button. One that had fallen off possibly the most unattractive, ill-cut suit he'd ever seen. One she'd been wearing the first time he'd laid eyes on her.

"I've a 'link conference shortly, then I'll be in midtown most of the day." He leaned over, laid his lips on hers. Left them there for a long, satisfying moment. "Take care of my cop."

"That's my plan. You know, I hear your friends say your cop is scary, mean, and relentless. What do you say about that?"

"Lieutenant, *your* friends say the same. Give my best to Peabody," he added as he walked out.

"I'll keep your best," she called out, "and give her what's left over."

She heard him laugh, and decided that was every bit as good as coffee for setting her up for the day.

Setting up the appointment with Dr. Mira was her first task when she got to her office at Central. Peabody's to-do list included confirming Luther Vanderlea had been in Madrid, and ascertaining the ex-husband's whereabouts.

Eve fed the known data into her office computer and ran a check with IRCCA to search for any other like crimes.

The number of sexual homicides involving mutilation didn't surprise her. She'd been a cop too long. Even the number that involved damaging, destroying, or removing the victims' eyes didn't put a hitch in her stride.

She eliminated those where the perpetrator was in a cage, or in the ground, and spent her morning studying the unsolved or unconvicted.

Her 'link signaled a number of times—reporters on the scent. And these she easily ignored.

Letting accumulated data cook, she shifted back to the victim.

Who was Elisa Maplewood?

Standard public education, she read. No college. One marriage, one divorce, one child. Professional mother's stipend through first two years. Parents divorced when she was thirteen. Mother, also a domestic, stepfather a laborer. Father in the Bronx, unemployed and with a sheet, Eve mused. And looked more closely at Abel Maplewood.

Petty larceny, drunk and disorderlies, receiving stolen property, assaults—spousal assault, illegal gambling, public lewdness.

"Well, well, Abel, you're a little bit of a creep, aren't you?"

No sexual assaults on record, but there was always a first time. Fathers raped their daughters. She knew that only too well. They held them down, beat them, broke their bones and pushed themselves into their own flesh and blood.

She eased slowly away from the desk when she felt her heart begin to race. When she felt the memories, the nightmare of memories, begin to descend over her mind.

She went for water rather than coffee, drank it, slowly as well, standing at her single, narrow window.

She knew what Elisa had suffered during the rape—the pain, the terror that was more than pain—the degradation and shock. She knew, the way only another victim knew.

But she had to use that knowledge to find the killer, to find justice, or she was no good. If she let those memories come down too hard, blur her focus, she was no good.

Time to get back into the field, she told herself. Back in the field and do the job.

"Dallas?"

She didn't turn, and didn't ask herself how long Peabody had been there, watching her find her control. "You confirm Vanderlea?"

"Yes, sir. He was in Madrid, as advertised. He's on his way home now. Canceled his last day of business after his wife contacted him. He was at a breakfast meeting this morning—time difference, here and Europe—at seven Madrid time. Next to impossible for him to have zipped home, killed Maplewood, zipped back and made that meeting."

"The ex?"

"Brent Hoyt. He's clear. Seeing as he spent the night at the drunk tank on St. Thomas last night, he wasn't in New York."

"All right. Maplewood's father—Abel—has a sheet. We'll need to look at him. We're heading back to the Vanderleas first."

"Ah, there's someone here who wants to speak to you."

"Pertinent?"

"Well . . ."

"I don't have time to chat." Eve turned around. "We'll check in with Morris at the morgue, then head uptown. I have to be back here to meet with Mira."

"Yeah, well, she's very insistent. Claims to have information. She looks normal."

"As opposed to? If someone's come in with information regarding the current investigation, why didn't you just say so?"

"Because—" Peabody debated letting Eve find out for herself, or protecting her own skin. It was a short debate. "She says she's a psychic."

Eve stopped dead. "Oh, come on. Feed her to the liaison. You know better than to let the loonies in."

"She's registered and licensed. And she pulled the pal card."

"I don't have psychic pals. It's a firm policy."

"No, it's the mutual friend deal."

"Mavis has all kinds of looney friends. I don't let them into my office."

"Not Mavis. She claims to be a friend of Louise's. Dr. Dimatto. The really normal, upstanding Dr. D. And she's shook, Dallas. Her hands are trembling."

"Hell. We give her ten minutes." She checked her wrist unit, and as a buffer set it to signal in ten. "Bring her in."

Eve sat, brooded. This is what happened when you went and made friends. *They* had to go out and make friends, and then those friends somehow insinuated themselves into your life, or your work. Before you knew it you were hip-deep in people.

And half of them were crazy.

All right, she amended. Not all psychics were crazy or scamming. Some of them—a very few some of them—were legit. She was well aware that law enforcement sometimes used sensitives to good effect.

But she didn't use them. She believed in doing the job through investigative procedure, technological processes, evidentiary study, deduction. Then you tossed in instinct, luck, and some ass-kicking.

That worked just fine for her.

She went for coffee now.

She turned from the AutoChef, cup in hand as the woman came to the door with Peabody.

She looked normal. Her hair was long, waving past her shoulders in a perfectly normal shade of brown. A dark and glossy brown that looked as if it might have been the one God opted for when he put her together. Her skin was dusky and smooth, her eyes a clear and pale green that showed nerves, but seemed sane, as they met Eve's directly.

The face was strong and sexy with one of those lush mouths and a thin, aquiline nose. Mexican or Spanish blood, Eve assumed. Ancestors who'd baked in the heat and strummed guitars. Exotic.

Eve put her in the middle thirties. Judged her to be about five six, with a toned, disciplined build.

She wore casual and well-cut pants with a long shirt, both the color of summer poppies, a couple of rings with deeply colored stones, and dangles at her ears—slim drops of gold.

"Lieutenant Dallas. This is Celina Sanchez."

"Okay, Ms. Sanchez, have a seat. I'm pressed for time, so why don't we get right to it."

"All right." She sat, folded her hands tightly together on her lap. She breathed in and out once. "He took her eyes."

3

"Well, now that I've got your attention . . ." Celina unhooked her fingers to press two to her right temple, as if to compress a pain. "Could I have some of that coffee?"

Eve stayed where she was, sipping her own. They hadn't released the mutilation details to the media. But there were leaks, she knew. There were always leaks.

Her voice was shaky, and carried no accent. It was husky, a shade on the provocative side. "How did you get this information, Ms. Sanchez?"

"I saw it, and it's not an image I enjoyed."

"You saw the victim in Central Park?"

"Yes. But I wasn't in the park. I was in my

home. I'm here to explain it to you. I'd really appreciate the coffee."

Eve sent Peabody a brief nod. "You knew Elisa Maplewood?"

"No. Before we go any further, I've never worked with the police. It's not what I do and not something I aspire to."

She used her hands when she talked, lifting them, gesturing in a manner that told Eve it was habitual. Then she gripped them together in her lap as if to hold them still.

"I don't want to see what you see, Lieutenant. I don't want to live with those images in my head. Primarily, I do private consultations and parties. I'm not a lunatic or a glory-seeker, though from what Louise has told me about you, I imagine you think I am."

"How do you know Louise Dimatto?"

"We went to school together, and we've remained friendly since. Thanks." She took the cup of coffee Peabody handed her. "You're more open to extra-normal areas, Detective. Do you have sensitives in your family?"

"Ah, I—"

"Let's keep this about you," Eve interrupted.

"All right." Celina sampled the coffee, and smiled for the first time since she'd come into the room. "This is wonderful, and I can tell you, frankly, I need the jolt. I had a dream."

"Uh-huh."

Celina's smile only widened. "The snarkiness settles me down. Who knew? Louise also said I'd like you, Lieutenant Dallas. Oddly enough, I think she's probably right."

"That's real nice. Can we stay on line here?"

"Of course. In the dream I saw a woman. She was young, attractive, light brown hair, I think. Straight hair, just brushing her shoulders. It looked light brown in the streetlights. She came out of a building, leading a little white dog on a leash. She was wearing jeans and a T-shirt. There was a doorman, and they exchanged a few words. I couldn't hear; I was too far away.

"She crossed the street—wide street—with the little dog prancing in front of her. In the dream, my heart started pounding with fear. I wanted to shout at her to go back, to go back inside the building, but I couldn't speak. I watched her take the dog into the park. She rubbed her arm, and I thought that she was thinking she should've tossed on a jacket. The nights are getting cooler. She'll go back for a jacket, and maybe it'll be all right. But she didn't."

Celina's hands trembled again as she lifted the cup to her lips. "She kept walking, with the dog pulling on the leash. The shadow fell over her, but she didn't see, she didn't know. He came at her from behind. I couldn't see him, just shadows. He'd been waiting, watching, as I'd been watching. Oh, I could feel his excitement, the madness of it, just as I could feel her fear. His was red, dark, vicious red, and hers silver. Red shadows, silver light."

The cup rattled as she set it aside. "This isn't what I do. This isn't what I want."

"You're here. Finish it."

She'd lost all color, and her pale eyes were glassy. "He hit her, and the little dog ran away when he kicked at it. She tried to fight, but he was very strong. He hit her in the face, knocked her down. She tried to scream, but he kept hitting her. He kept . . ."

Her breathing went shallow as she rubbed a hand over her heart. "He kicked her and hit her, and he dragged her deeper into the shadows. She lost a shoe. He wrapped a ribbon, a cord, around her neck. Red for power. Red for death. Tight. She fought for air, she fought him, but he was too strong. He tore at her clothes. Bitch, whore, cunt. Hating her, hating her, he raped her. Tightened the cord, tighter and tighter until she was still. Until she was dead."

Tears tracked down Celina's cheeks. Her hands were back in her lap now, twisted together like wires. "He'd shown her what she was good for. Shown her who was in charge. But he wasn't done. He picked up her clothes, put them in a small bag. And he carried it, and her, deeper into the park. He's strong, very strong. He takes care of himself. Who's more important, after all?"

Her breath continued to hitch and jump. Her eyes stared.

"There's a castle, a castle on a lake. He's king of the castle. He's king of everything. He slings her over his shoulder, climbs down the rocks. And he lays her out, very carefully. She'll like it there. Maybe this time she'll stay."

Staring, Celina lifted her joined hands, pressed them between her breasts. "Rest in peace, whore. And he cuts out her eyes.

God, God, he cuts out her eyes and puts them in a little pouch, and the pouch into the bag. There's blood running down her face. Blood on his hands. And he, he leans down and kisses her. I woke up, I woke up from the dream with the chill of that bloody mouth on mine."

Eve's wrist unit beeped, and had Celina jolting.

"What did you do?" Eve asked her.

"What did I . . . Well, after I finished shaking, I took a tranq. I told myself it was a nightmare. I know better, but I *wanted* it to be a nightmare, not a vision. My gift has never taken me anywhere so dark, and I was afraid. I took a tranq and used it to block it out. Cowardly, but I don't claim to be brave. I don't want to be brave, not about something like this."

She picked up her coffee again. "But this morning, I turned on the screen. I tend to avoid the news channels, but I was compelled to check. I had to know. And I saw the report. They ran her picture—the pretty woman with the light brown hair. They said her name. I didn't want to come here. Most of the police are born skeptics. It's why you are what you are. But I had to come."

"You say you saw—in this vision—the victim. But you didn't see her attacker?"

"I saw . . . his essence, you could say. I saw a form." Her throat worked as she swallowed. "It frightened me, more than I've ever been frightened in my life. And, frankly, I wasn't going to come here. I was going to try to put it away. Knowing that about myself made me feel small and ugly."

She lifted a hand, toyed with a chain around her neck. Her nails were painted a deep and shiny red, with the half moons picked out in vibrant white. "So I came to you, because Louise has spoken of you. And I'll try to help."

"How do you intend to help?"

"I might see more if I had something of his, something he'd touched. I don't know." A flicker of irritation ran over her face. "This isn't my field. It's new ground for me, and you're not making this any easier."

"It's not my job to make it easy, Ms. Sanchez. It's my job to investigate."

"Well then, investigate me all you want," she shot out. "I can only tell you what I know. I know the man who did this is big, or thinks of himself that way. I know he's strong. Very strong. I know he's mad. And I know this woman, Elisa Maplewood, wasn't his first. He's done it before. He doesn't intend for her to be his last."

"How do you know?"

"I can't tell you so that you'd understand." She leaned forward now, urgently. "It's what I felt from him. He hated her, and the hatred thrills and frightens him. Hate and fear, hate and fear. Those are paramount. He's hated all of them, and feared all of them. I don't know why I saw her, saw him. Maybe she and I were connected in some other life, or will be in one to come. But I'm afraid. I'm more afraid than I've ever been, that I'm connected, somehow, to him. I need to help you stop him because I think I'll go mad myself if I don't."

"And your fee?"

Celina's lips twisted into a tense smile. "I'm very expensive, and well worth it. But I would do this pro bono. With one provision."

"Which is?"

"I don't want, under any circumstances, my name released to the media. I don't want anyone to know, beyond those who are absolutely necessary, that I'm involved. Not only because it's the sort of publicity I'd find irritating, not only because it's the sort of exposure that would generate an interest in the sort of clientele I avoid, but because I'm afraid of him."

"We'll let you know. Thank you for coming in."

On a half laugh, Celina got to her feet. "Are you always so hard?"

"You tell me. You're the psychic."

"I don't read minds." Celina's tone took on an edge as she tossed her hair back. "And I don't read people without their permission."

"I can promise you, you'll never get mine. I've got a job to do, Ms. Sanchez. I'll add what you've told us and your offer into the mix. We'll be in touch."

"Looks like Louise was wrong after all. I don't like you." She strode out.

"Well gee, she didn't have to go and hurt my feelings."

"You were a little rough on her," Peabody commented. "You didn't believe her?"

"I didn't say that. My verdict on her is reserved until we check her out. Run her."

"Sir, she can't be licensed if she's got a sheet."

"She can't be licensed if she's been convicted," Eve corrected, and headed out. "Run her. Thoroughly. And track down Louise Dimatto. I want to see what she has to say."

"Good thinking. Which, of course, goes without saying," Peabody added when Eve sent her a cool look. "If she checks out, will you use her?"

"I'd use a two-headed talking monkey if it helped nail this guy. But right now, let's just do our tedious cop business in our tedious cop way."

The morgue was her first stop. She could count on Chief Medical Examiner Morris to do the job, give her the data she needed, without a lot of bureaucratic bullshit attached.

She found him in autopsy, with his protective gear over a steel blue three-piece suit. On closer look, she saw the vest was decorated with abstract line drawings of naked women.

Morris wasn't considered a fashion plate without cause.

His long, dark hair was drawn back in a glossy braid that hung neatly between his shoulder blades. He still carried his vacation tan. At the moment, his sealed hands were smeared with blood and bodily fluids. He hummed a jaunty tune under his breath as he worked.

He glanced over when Eve and Peabody entered, and behind his goggles, his long, dark eyes smiled.

"You nearly cost me twenty."

"How'd I do that?"

"I bet Foster you'd be in before eleven. You cut it close."

"I got hung up by a psychic. What's your stand on that kind of thing?"

"I believe we're all born with innate gifts, skills, potentials, and some of those gifts are not easily explained. I also believe ninety percent of those who claim to see are dirty rotten liars."

"I'd up the last part a couple of percentage points, but that's about my take, too." She looked down at the body now. "What do you see?"

"A very unlucky young woman who, depending on your personal philosophies, no longer sees anything, or now sees everything. Severe trauma," he began. "Premortem. He wailed on her, Dallas. Sexual assault with none of his fluids left behind. He'd sealed up for the rape. Strangulation, cause of death. The ribbon's your murder weapon. Mutilation was postmortem. Clean cuts. Somebody's been practicing."

"How clean? Surgically?"

"If he's a doctor—a cutter—he didn't graduate top of his class. I'd say he used a laser scalpel and with good skill, but not exceptional skill. Several little jags." He gestured to a second pair of microgoggles. "Want to see?"

Saying nothing, Eve fit on the goggles, leaned over the body with Morris.

"See here? Here?" He nodded to the screen where the wounds were magnified so Peabody could study them as well. "Not precise. Little tremors in the hand, I'd say. And I found fluid. He nicked the left eyeball a bit, though we'll have Dickhead confirm that in the lab."

"Okay."

"I haven't found any trace of him on her. Grass, dirt, a few strands of hair, none of it human. You'll want Dickhead on that. Some could be canine, but that's a guess since she was a dog owner. All the blood's hers."

"That's too damn bad. Fibers?"

"A few, under her nails, on her person. She didn't go down easy. They're off to the lab, but I'd make them as cloth, most are likely from her own clothes. Some are probably from his shirt as there's some sealant on them, too."

Eve straightened, pulled off the goggles. "You see anything like this before?"

"From my lofty height, Dallas, you see every damn thing. But this precisely, no. You?"

"Not all the elements together."

But her gut told her she'd see them again.

"She's clean, Dallas. Sanchez. No arrests, no criminal." Peabody studied the readout as Eve drove uptown. "You want to hear the deal?"

"The highlights."

"DOB, February 3, 2026, Madison, Wisconsin. Brrr. Both parents living, in Cancun. That's more like it! No sibs. Private schools all the way. No marriage. One cohab, three-year stint that ended about fourteen months ago. No children. Registered and licensed as sensitive. Self-employed."

"How long's she had the license?"

"Fifteen years. Totally clean on it. A few civil suits brought against her, all judgment in favor of defendant. That's pretty normal for working psychics. People get pissed that something didn't work out the way they wanted, and they sue."

"People sue the clouds if it rains on their picnic."

"She does a lot of corporate work. Parties, conventions. Private consults. Makes a damn good living at it. About seven, eight times that of your lowly homicide detective. Resided current Soho address for twelve years. Also has a residence in Oyster Bay. Nice. Sounds legit to me."

"Uh-huh. You track down Louise?"

"She's at the shelter today."

"Oh." Eve had been hoping for the Canal Street Clinic. She'd yet to make a personal appearance at the women's shelter Roarke had founded. "We take the vic's residence first. If we clear enough time, we'll go by, talk to Louise."

"I've been wanting to see *Dochas* for myself," Peabody commented. "Charles says Louise is really juiced about it."

"You talk to Charles?"

"Sure, now and then."

As Charles, a professional and licensed companion, was Louise's guy, and had been Peabody's guy, minus sexual fun, it just struck Eve as weird.

But the ins and outs of relationships always struck her as weird. Her own included.

"Any luck with the ribbon?"

"If you call the fact that more than thirty retail outlets carry it in the borough of Manhattan alone luck, then yeah. Got the manufacturers, the distributors. It's a pretty common item, Dallas, in craft stores, party stores. Some of the better department stores carry it in their gift wrap department. It's going to be tough to find his source."

"If it was easy, everybody would be cops."

It was far from easy to question Deann Vanderlea again. The woman looked exhausted, ill, and weighed down with worry and grief.

"I'm sorry we have to intrude."

"It's all right. Luther, my husband, he's been delayed. Air traffic. I'd do better if he were here. I couldn't do much worse."

She gestured toward chairs in the living

area. The lounging robe had been replaced with slouchy black pants and a white, oversized shirt, but her hair was still tousled, her feet still bare.

"I haven't slept, and I'm holding on by the fingernails at this point. Do you have any news? Did you find the man who did this?"

"No. The investigation is ongoing, and we're using all resources."

"It was too much to hope for." She looked around, distractedly. "I should make coffee, or tea. Or something."

"Don't trouble yourself." Peabody spoke gently, a tone Eve never quite managed with the same ease. "If you'd like something, I'd be happy to get it for you."

"No. Thank you, no. Vonnie—she's sleeping again. She and Zanna. I don't know if she understands, really understands, her mother's not coming back. She cried. Cried and cried. We all did. She fell asleep, worn out from it, and I put her back to bed. Zanna, too. I put them together, so neither of them would wake alone."

"She'll need counseling, Mrs. Vanderlea."

"Yes." Deann nodded at Peabody. "I've already made calls. I'm making arrangements. I want, I need . . . God. Luther and I, we want to make arrangements for Elisa. For her memorial. I'm not sure who I need to speak with about it, or how soon, or . . . I need to keep doing." A shudder ran through her. "I'm all right as long as I keep doing something."

"We'll put someone in touch with you," Eve told her.

"Good. I've called our lawyers as well, to arrange for emergency custody of Vonnie. To start proceedings to make it permanent as soon as we can. She's not going to be ripped away from the only home she's ever known. I've spoken with Elisa's parents—well, her mother and stepfather. Her mother—"

Her voice broke again, and she shook her head fiercely as if to deny herself the luxury. "They're coming here later today, so we can sit down and talk about what's best. Somehow."

"Elisa would be grateful that you're taking care of her daughter. She'd be grateful you're helping us do our job."

"Yes." Deann squared her shoulders at Eve's words. "I hope so."

"What do you know about Abel Maplewood? Elisa's father."

"A difficult man, in my opinion. But he and Elisa managed to maintain a good relationship. I haven't been able to reach him to tell him. He's out West somewhere. Omaha, Idaho, Utah . . . I'm so scattered." She dragged both hands through her hair. "He's been out there a week or so, visiting his brother, I think. Probably sponging off him, to be frank. Elisa was always slipping him money. Her mother's going to try to reach him today."

"It would help if we had his whereabouts. Just routine."

"I'll see you get the information. And I know you need to look in her rooms. I put the girls in Zanna's room, so they won't be disturbed." She started to rise, but Peabody put a hand to her shoulder.

"Why don't you stay here, try to rest. We know where her rooms are."

They left her there. "Record on, Peabody."

They stepped into a small, cheerful sitting room done in bold colors. There were a few toys scattered around, and a little basket with a red cushion Eve assumed was a kind of bed for the dog.

She moved through it, and into Elisa's

bedroom. "Make a note to have EDD check out her 'links, her data units." She went to the dresser first, began to go through drawers.

She already had a sense of a settled, content, hardworking woman. The search of her quarters did nothing to change that. There were a number of framed photographs, most of the child. There were flowers and the little trinkets women enjoyed having around.

Her wardrobe was casual, with two good suits, two pair of good shoes. There was nothing in it that spoke of a man.

She checked the bedside 'link herself, pulled up the last incoming. It was from her mother, a chatty, affectionate conversation that included the child toward the end when the little girl ran into the room and babbled away at her *gamma.*

"Dallas, I think I found something." Peabody held up another basket. This was in the cupboard under the sitting room entertainment screen.

"What is it?"

"A craft basket. Handwork stuff. She did crafts." Peabody held up a skein of ribbon.

It wasn't red, but it was the same basic type as what had killed her.

Eve stepped forward to take it just as a little girl came into the sitting room. She was tiny, with curly hair so blonde it was nearly white spilling around a pretty, chubby-cheeked face. She was knuckling her eyes.

"That's my mommy's. You're not supposed to touch Mommy's sewing basket, 'less she says."

"Ah . . ."

"I'll take her," Peabody murmured, and handing off the basket to Eve, crouched down to child level. "Hi, are you Vonnie?"

The child hunched her shoulders. "Not supposed to speak to strangers."

"That's right, but it's okay to talk to the police, isn't it?" Peabody took out her badge, gave it to the little girl. "Did your mommy tell you about the police?"

"They help people and catch bad guys."

"That's right. I'm Detective Peabody, and this is Lieutenant Dallas."

"Whatsa Loonat?"

"It's a job," Peabody said without missing a beat. "It means she's a policeman who catches lots of bad guys."

"Okay. I can't find my mommy. Aunt Deann's sleeping. Can you find my mommy?"

Peabody's eyes met Eve's over the little girl's head. "Why don't we go find your aunt Deann?" Peabody suggested.

"She's sleeping." Her voice spiked, her lips began to tremble. "She said a bad man hurt my mommy and she can't come home. I want my mommy to come home *now.*"

"Vonnie—"

But she shook Peabody off, planted herself in front of Eve. "Did a bad man hurt my mommy?"

"You should come with me now, Vonnie."

"I want her to say." She pointed her little finger at Eve, poked out her bottom lip. "She's the Loonat."

Jesus, Eve thought. *Oh, Jesus.* She jerked her head, signaling Peabody to get Deann, then she sucked it in, crouched as Peabody had. "Yes. I'm sorry."

"Why?"

"I don't know."

Tears were gathering in big eyes the color of bluebells. "Did she go to the doctor?"

Eve thought of Morris, the steel table, the cold, clear lights of the morgue. "Not exactly."

"Doctors make you better. She should go to the doctor. If she can't come home, can you take me to her?"

"I can't. She's . . . she's in a place we can't go. All I can do is find the person who hurt her, so he can be punished."

"He'll have to stay in his room?"

"Yeah, so he can't ever hurt anyone else."

"Then she can come home?"

Eve looked over, helpless and weak with relief when Deann rushed in. "Vonnie. Come with me, baby."

"I want Mommy."

"I know, baby. I know." Deann gathered her up, snuggled her in as the child began to weep on her shoulder. "I fell asleep. I'm sorry."

"I know it's hard. I know it's bad timing all around. I need to ask you where she got the supplies in this basket."

"Her sewing basket? Here and there. She loved to make things. I went with her a few times. She tried to teach me, but I was hopeless. There was a place on Third—ah, God—um, Sew What. And a big supply house downtown, near Union Square. Total Crafts, I think. And the one at the Sky Mall. I'm sorry."

She rocked back and forth on her heels, stroking Vonnie's hair. "She'd go in to a shop if she was passing, rarely came out empty-handed."

"Would you know where she bought this, specifically?" Eve held up the ribbon.

"No, I don't."

"I'm going to arrange for her data and communication equipment to be taken in. Would all her transactions and transmissions have been made and received by the ones in these rooms?"

"She might have called her mother, say, from one of the other 'links. But she did all her personal work on her own unit. I need to settle Vonnie down."

"Go ahead."

Eve studied the ribbon. "It's a good lead," Peabody said.

"It's a lead." She put the ribbon in her evidence bag. "Let's run it down."

The main door of the penthouse opened as Eve walked back into the living area. The man who entered had a shock of gold hair, a pale, tired face. She saw Deann spring up from the couch where she was holding Vonnie, and with the child still in her arms, leap toward him.

"Luther. Oh, God, Luther."

"Deann." He enfolded both of them, dropped his head to his wife's shoulder. "It's not a mistake?"

She shook her head, and let go with the weeping Eve imagined she'd been holding in for hours.

"I'm sorry to intrude. I'm Lieutenant Dallas."

He lifted his head. "Yes. Yes, I recognize you. Deann? Sweetheart, take Vonnie in the bedroom." He kissed them both, and let them go.

"I'm very sorry for your loss, Mr. Vanderlea."

"Luther. Please. What can I do? Is there something I should do?"

"It would help if you answered a few questions."

"Yes. All right." He looked in the direction his wife had gone. "I couldn't get here sooner. It seemed to take forever to get home. Deann told me . . . I'm still not clear. Elisa—she went out to walk the dog, and she was . . . Deann said she was raped and murdered. Raped and murdered right over in the park."

"Would she have told you if she was being bothered by anyone, if she was concerned about anything?"

"Yes." He said it without hesitation. "If not me, certainly she would have told Deann. They were very close. We . . . We're family." He sat, let his head fall back.

"Were you and Ms. Maplewood close?"

"You're asking me if Elisa and I had a sexual relationship. I wondered if you would, and told myself not to be insulted. I'm trying not to be. I don't cheat on my wife, Lieutenant. I certainly wouldn't take advantage of a very vulnerable woman in my employ, a woman I liked very much, a woman who worked very hard to give her child a good life."

"I don't ask to offend you. Why do you characterize Ms. Maplewood as vulnerable?"

He pinched the bridge of his nose, dropped his hand. "She was a single parent who had been misused by her husband, who was dependent on me for her salary, for the roof over her head, come to that. Not that she couldn't have found other employment. She knew how to work. But she might not have found a situation that allowed her child to grow up in a home like this, with a playmate, with people who loved her. Vonnie's welfare was first for Elisa."

"Was she threatened by her ex-husband?"

He smiled, humorlessly. "Not anymore. She was a strong woman, who'd put him where he belonged. In the past."

"Do you know of anyone who'd want to hurt her?"

"Absolutely no one. That's the God's truth. I can't resign myself, not fully, to the fact that anyone did. I know you have a job to do, but so do I. My wife needs me, the children need me. Can we do whatever else needs to be done later?"

"Yes. I want to take this." She pulled out the roll of ribbon. "I can give you a receipt."

"Not necessary." He pushed to his feet, rubbed his hands over his face. "I've heard you're good at your job."

"I am good at it."

"I'm depending on you." He offered his hand. "We all are."

They hit crafts stores, crisscrossing Manhattan on the way downtown. Eve had no idea there was so much involved in the making of so many things easily available ready-made. When she expressed the opinion, Peabody smiled and fingered some brightly colored thread sold in hanks.

"There's a lot of satisfaction in making something yourself. Picking the colors, the materials, the pattern. Individualizing it, and seeing it come to life."

"You say so."

"A lot of craftsmen and artisans in my family. Goes with the whole Free-Ager philosophy. I'm pretty handy myself, but I don't have a lot of time for it. I still have the tea cozy my grandmother helped me crochet when I was ten."

"I don't even know what that is."

"What, the tea cozy or crocheting?"

"Either, and I find I have no interest in finding out." She studied the shelves and displays, full of supplies and finished products. "A lot of the clerks we've talked to remember Maplewood. Don't see a lot of men in these joints."

"Needlework remains primarily the work and/or hobby of the female. Too bad. It can be very relaxing. My uncle Jonas knits up a storm and claims it's one of the reasons he's a healthy, vital one hundred and six. Or seven. Maybe it's eight."

Eve didn't bother to respond but headed out of the shop. "Nobody, thus far, remembers any man bothering Elisa or any other customer for that matter. Nobody asking questions about her, loitering around. Same kind of ribbon. There has to be a connection."

"He could've bought it anywhere, any time. He might've seen her in one of the stores, then gone back later to buy his own. You know, they have these craft fairs, too. He could've bumped into her at one of those. I bet she'd go to the fairs, maybe take the kids."

"That's a good line. Check it out with the Vanderleas." She stood on the sidewalk, thumbs in front pockets, fingers tapping idly on her hips as people streamed or trudged around her. "Do that later. They need some space. We're only a few blocks from the shelter. We'll ask Louise about the witch."

"Sensitives aren't necessarily witches, just as witches aren't necessarily sensitives. Hey, a glide-cart!"

"Wait, wait!" Eve pressed a hand to her temple, stared at the sky. "I'm getting a vision. It's you stuffing a soy dog in your mouth."

"I was going to go for the fruit kabob and perhaps a small, walkaway salad. But now you've put the damn dog in my head and I have to have it."

"I knew that. Get me some fries, tube of Pepsi."

"I knew *that,*" Peabody replied. But she was too happy with the idea she'd actually get lunch to complain about paying for it.

4

It didn't look like a refuge, Eve thought. It looked, from the outside at least, like a well-maintained, modest, multiresident building. Middle-income apartments, sans doorman. The casual observer wouldn't note anything special about it, even if he bothered to look.

And that, Eve reminded herself, was precisely the point. The women and children who fled here didn't want anyone to notice.

But if you were a cop, you'd probably note and approve of the first-rate security. Full-scan cams, cleverly disguised in the simple trims and moldings. Privacy screens activated at all windows.

If you were a cop and knew Roarke, you could be certain there were motion pads at every access, with top-of-the-line alarms. Entrée would require palm plate identification, keypad code, and/or clearance from inside. There would be twenty-four-hour security—probably human and droid—and you could bet your ass the entire place would lock down like a vault at any attempt to break in.

Not just a refuge, but a fortress.

Dochas, Gaelic for "hope," was as safe—probably safer due to its anonymity—as the White House.

If she'd known such places existed, would she have fled to one instead of wandering the streets of Dallas, a child broken, traumatized, and lost?

No. Fear would have sent her running away from hope.

Even now, knowing better, she felt uneasy stepping up to the door. Alleys were easier, she thought, because you knew there were rats in the dark. You expected them.

But she reached up to ring the bell.

Before she could signal, the door opened.

Dr. Louise Dimatto, that blond bundle of energy, greeted them.

She wore a pale blue lab coat over a simple black shirt and trousers. Two tiny gold hoops glinted in her left ear, with a third in the right. There were no rings on her competent fingers, and a plain, serviceable wrist unit sat on her left hand.

Nothing about her screamed money, though she came from big green seas of it.

She was pretty as a strawberry parfait, classy as a crystal flute of champagne, and a born reformer who lived to fight in the trenches.

"About damn time." She grabbed Eve's hand and pulled her inside. "I was beginning to think I'd have to call nine-one-one to get you down here. Hi, Peabody. Boy, don't you look great."

Peabody beamed. "Thanks." After considerable experimentation, she'd found what she liked to think of as her detective look with simple lines, interesting colors, and matching airsneaks or skids.

"We appreciate you making time," Eve began.

"Time's constantly being made. My goal is to make enough so there's twenty-six hours per day. That should be just about right. How about a tour?"

"We need—"

"Come *on.*" She kept Eve's hand trapped

in hers. "Let me show off a little. Remodeling and rehab are finally complete, though Roarke's given me carte blanche for additional decorating or equipment. The man is now my god."

"Yeah, he likes that part."

Louise laughed, and hooked her arms through Eve's on one side and Peabody's on the other. "I don't have to tell you the security is flawless."

"No security is flawless."

"Don't be a cop," she complained and gave Eve a little hip check. "We have common rooms down here. Kitchen—and the food's great—dining area, library, a playroom, and what we call the family room."

Eve could already hear the chatter as Louise took them down a hallway, gesturing to rooms. Women and children chatter, Eve thought. The sort that always made her feel awkward and edgy.

It smelled like girls, too—mostly—though she caught sight of what she thought were a couple of young boys loping off toward what was likely the kitchen area.

There were scents of polish and flowers and what she thought might be hair products. Tones of lemon and vanilla and the hard candy smell she always associated with groups of females.

There was a lot of color in the place as well as a lot of room. Cheerful color, comfortable furniture, spots for sitting alone, spots for conversation.

She saw immediately that the family room was the popular spot.

There were about a dozen women of various ages and races gathered there. Sitting on sofas, on the floor with the kids, who were also of various ages and races. They were talking, or sitting in silence, watching the entertainment screen or juggling babies on their laps.

She wondered why people were forever bouncing babies when it seemed—from her wary observation—that the perpetual motion only caused whatever was in their digestive systems to come spewing out. Of either end.

Not all the babies appeared to appreciate it, either. One of them was burbling in what might have been contentment, but two others were making sounds very reminiscent of emergency vehicles on the run.

It didn't seem to bother anyone, particularly. Certainly not the field of kids on the floor, playing or bickering over their chosen activities.

"Ladies."

Conversation died off as the women looked toward the doorway. Children shut up like clams. Babies continued to wail or burble.

"I'd like to introduce you to Lieutenant Dallas and Detective Peabody."

In the moment's pause, Eve saw the reaction to the thought of *cops.* The drawing into self, the nervous flicker of eyes, the gathering closer of children.

The abuser might be the enemy and Louise the ally, but cops, Eve thought, were the unknown and could fall into either camp.

"Lieutenant Dallas is Roarke's wife, and this is her first visit."

There was relief for some—the easing of tension in faces and bodies, even tentative smiles. And for others, the suspicion remained.

It wasn't just a mix of ages and races. There was also a mix of injuries. Fresh bruises, fading ones. Mending bones. Mending lives.

She knew their apprehension; felt it herself. And hated that while Louise looked at her expectantly, her skin was going cold, and her throat shutting down.

"It's a nice place you've got here," she managed.

"It's a miracle." The woman who spoke stood up. She limped slightly as she crossed the room. Eve pegged her at around forty, and from the looks of her face, she'd taken a nasty and recent beating. She held out a hand to Eve. "Thank you."

She didn't want to take the hand offered. Didn't want the connection, but there was no choice as the woman looked at her with expectation, and horribly, with gratitude. "I didn't do anything."

"You're Roarke's wife. If I'd had the courage to come to a place like this, to go to the police, to look for help before now, my daughter wouldn't be hurt."

She turned slightly, gestured toward a girl with dark curly hair, and a skincast on her right arm. "Come say hello to Lieutenant Dallas, Abra."

The girl obeyed, and though she pressed her body against her mother's legs, she stared curiously up at Eve. "The police stop people from hurting you. Maybe."

"Yeah. They try to."

"My daddy hurt me, so we had to go away."

There would be a horrible snapping sound when the bone broke. A terrible and bright pain. A flood of greasy nausea. A red haze of shock over the eyes.

Eve felt it all again as she stood there, staring down at the girl. She wanted to step back, far, far back. Away from it.

"You're okay now." Her voice sounded thin and distant under the roaring in her ears.

"He hurts my mama. He gets mad and he hurts her. But this time I didn't hide in my room like she said, and he hurt me, too."

"He broke her arm." Tears flooded the woman's bruised eyes. "It took that to wake me up."

"You don't blame yourself, Marly," Louise said gently.

"We can stay here with Dr. Louise, and nobody hurts you, and nobody yells or throws things."

"It's a good place." Peabody hunkered down as much to take the focus off Eve as to speak to the child. Her lieutenant looked ill. "I bet there's lots to do."

"We have chores, and teachers. You have to do your chores and go to school. Then you can play. There's a lady upstairs, and she's having a baby."

"Is that so?" Peabody glanced back at Louise. "Now?"

"First-stage labor. We have full obstetric and natal facilities, and a midwife on staff full-time. Try to keep off that leg as much as possible for another twenty-four, Marly."

"I will. It's better. A lot better. Everything is."

"We really need to speak with you, Louise."

"All right, we'll just . . ." Louise trailed off as she got a look at Eve's face. "Are you okay?"

"Fine. I'm fine. A little pressed for that time, that's all."

"We'll head up to my office." Deliberately, she laid her fingers on Eve's wrist as they walked back toward the stairs. "Your skin's clammy," she murmured. "Pulse is rapid and thready, and you've gone pale. Let me take you into Exam."

"I'm just tired." She eased away. "We're running on two hours' sleep. I don't need a doctor, I need an interview."

"Okay, all right, but you don't get the interview unless you down a protein booster."

There was activity on the second floor as well. Voices behind closed doors. And weeping.

"Therapy sessions," Louise explained. "Sometimes they can get intense. Moira, a moment?"

Two women were standing outside of what Eve assumed was another therapy room or office. One turned, and her gaze skipped over Louise and fastened on Eve. She murmured something to her companion, gave her a long hug, then started down the hall.

Eve knew who she was. Moira O'Bannion, formerly of Dublin. The woman who'd known Roarke's mother, and after more than thirty years had told him that what he'd known of his beginnings was a lie based on murder.

Sickness curdled in Eve's belly.

"Moira O'Bannion, Eve Dallas, Delia Peabody."

"I'm so glad to meet you. I hope Roarke is well."

"He's good. He's fine." Sweat began to slide like cold grease down her spine.

"Moira's one of our treasures. I stole her."

Moira laughed. "Recruited, we'll say. Though dragooned wouldn't be far off. Louise is fierce. You're having the tour."

"Not exactly. It's not a social call."

"Ah. I should let you get to business then. How's Jana doing?"

"Four centimeters dilated, thirty percent effaced last check. She's got a ways to go."

"Let me know when she's ready, will you? We're all excited about the new baby." Moira smiled at Peabody. "It's good to meet you both, and I hope you won't be strangers. My very best to Roarke," she said to Eve and stepped out of their way.

"Moira's brilliant," Louise said as she led the way to the next level. "She's making a big difference here. I've been able to—ha—dragoon some of the best therapists, doctors, psychiatrists, and counselors in the city. I bless the day you stomped into my clinic downtown, Dallas. It was the start of the twisty path that led me here."

She opened a door, gestured them inside. "Not to mention leading me to Charles." Briskly, she walked to a cabinet, and opened it to reveal a minifridgie. "Which reminds me, we're setting up that dinner party

I keep trying to pull off. Night after tomorrow, Charles's place—it's cozier than mine—eight o'clock. Suit you and McNab, Peabody?"

"Sure. Sounds like fun."

"I've cleared it with Roarke." She handed both Eve and Peabody a bottled protein booster.

She'd have preferred ice-cold water and an open window so she could lean out, just breathe. "We're in the middle of an investigation."

"Understood. Doctors and cops learn to be flexible and live with canceled social engagements. Barring emergencies, we'll expect you. Now sit, drink your protein. Lemon flavored."

Because it was quicker than arguing and she could use a boost, Eve opened the bottle and chugged.

The office was a big step up from the one Louise kept at her clinic. Roomier, more fancily furnished. Efficient, as you'd expect, but with style.

"Swankier digs here," Eve commented.

"Roarke insisted, and I confess, he didn't have to twist my arm. One of the elements we're aiming for here is comfort. Hominess.

We want these women, these kids, to feel at ease."

"You've done a good job." Peabody sat and savored her drink. "It feels like a home."

"Thanks." Cocking her head, Louise studied Eve. "Well, you look better. Color's back."

"Thanks, Doc." Eve dumped the empty container in the recycler slot. "So. Celina Sanchez."

"Ah, Celina. Fascinating woman. I've known her for years. We went to school together for a couple of years. Her family's loaded, like mine. Very, very conservative, like mine. She's the black sheep. Like me. So, naturally enough, we're friends. Why are you looking into her?"

"She paid me a visit this morning. Claims she's a psychic."

"She is." Louise frowned, and got herself a bottle of fizzy water. "A very gifted sensitive, who practices professionally. Which is why she's the black sheep. Her family disapproves of and is embarrassed by her work. As I said, very conservative. Why did she come to see you? Celina specializes in private consult, and party work."

"She claims she witnessed a murder."

"My God. Is she all right?"

"She wasn't there. She had a vision."

"Oh. That must've been horrible for her."

"So you buy it. Just like . . ." Eve snapped her fingers.

"If Celina came to see you, told you she'd seen a murder, she saw one." Thoughtfully, Louise sipped at her water. "She doesn't hide her gift, but she keeps it all very professional, and well, you could say surface."

"Define surface," Eve prompted.

"She enjoys what she does—what she has, and she's geared it toward entertaining more than counseling, let's say. She keeps it light. I've never known her to get involved with anything like this. Who was killed?"

"A woman was raped, strangled, and mutilated in Central Park last night."

"I heard about that." Louise sat behind a glossy and feminine desk. "There weren't a lot of details. Your case?"

"Yeah. Celina had a lot of the details that weren't released. You're vouching for her?"

"I am. Yes, I'd believe her, no question. Can she help?"

"Yet to be determined. What do you know about her, on a personal front?"

Louise lifted the water bottle again, and

took her time drinking. "I don't like dishing about my friends, Dallas."

"I'm a cop. I don't dish."

Louise blew out a breath. "Well, as I said, she's from a wealthy, conservative family who doesn't approve of her. It takes considerable strength of character to buck your family." She toasted herself, drank. "Her father's side is aristocratic Mexico, though he moved to Wisconsin for several years for some business or other. They live in Mexico now, and Celina bolted for New York, made it her place while we were still in college. As much, I'd say, because she wanted the city as because this particular city was several thousand miles from her family, yet on the same continent."

She shrugged, considered. "I'd say she's a straightforward, goal-oriented type. She studied parapsychology in college, and related subjects. She wanted to know everything she could about her gift. For a sensitive, she's a logical, somewhat linear woman. She's loyal. It takes loyalty to keep friends for a decade or so. Ethical. I've never known her to intrude, psychically, or to use her talent to exploit. Did she know the woman who was killed?"

"Not, she said, in this particular life."

"Hmm. I remember having discussions with her about connections, past, present, to come. Not your style, I know, but a valid and accepted theory, even in some scientific circles."

"What about personal relationships?"

"Other than friendships, you mean. She was involved with someone for a few years. Songwriter, musician. Lovely man. They broke it off a while ago. Around a year ago." She shrugged. "Too bad. I liked him."

"Name?"

"Lucas Grande. Reasonably successful. He's had a number of songs published and produced, and works regularly as a session musician. He scores vids, too."

"Why'd they split?"

"That feels like dish. How does this relate?"

"Everything relates until I know it doesn't relate."

"Basically, things cooled off between them. They just weren't happy together anymore, so they went their separate ways."

"It was mutual?"

"I've never heard Celina trash him any more than a woman does when she splits with a guy. I don't see her all that often—not enough time—but from what I could see, she handled it well enough. They loved each other, then they didn't. They moved on."

"Did she ever mention Elisa Maplewood to you?"

"That's the woman who was killed? No. I never heard the name before this morning on the news."

"Luther or Deann Vanderlea?"

"Antiques?" Louise's eyebrows lifted in interest. "I know them a little. I think one of my uncles plays golf with Luther's father, something like that. It's possible that Celina knows them, socially. Why?"

"Victim worked for them. Domestic."

"Ah. You're reaching, Dallas."

"Yeah, but you never know just what you'll grab out there."

"You must be really proud," Peabody said as they got back into the car.

"Huh?"

"Place like that." She looked back toward Dochas. "What Roarke's done here."

"Yeah. He puts his money where a lot of

people can't even bother to put their mouths." As Eve started to pull out, Peabody laid a hand on her arm. "What?"

"We're partners now, right?"

"As you never fail to remind me."

"We're friends."

Dubious, Eve tapped her fingers on the wheel. "Is this going to get sloppy?"

"People have private stuff. They're entitled. But friends and partners are entitled to unload on friends and partners. You didn't want to go in there."

It shouldn't show, Eve thought. It wasn't allowed to show. "I went in there."

"Because you're aces at doing things you don't want. Things other people would walk away from. I'm just saying that if something gets over you, you can unload. That's all. And it wouldn't go beyond me."

"You see me doing anything that interferes with the job?"

"No. I only—"

"Some people have personal stuff that can't be cleared up with a nice little heart-to-heart and ice-cream sundaes." She whipped away from the curb, cut off a cab, and punched it through a yellow. "That's why it's personal."

"Okay."

"And if you're going to sulk because I'm not crying on your shoulder, you can just suck it up." She swerved down a side street without a thought to destination. "That's what cops do. They suck it up, do the job, and don't go around looking for somebody to pat their head and say, 'There, there.' I don't need you to play the understanding friend so I can dump my guts all over the floor for your perusal. So just . . . shit, shit, *fuck.*"

She yanked the wheel, double-parked, and ignoring the furious blasts of horns, slapped on the On Duty light.

"Out of line. Out of orbit. Way out. None of that was called for. None of it."

"Forget it."

"I'm tired," she said, staring out the windshield. "Beyond protein booster tired. And I'm edgy. And I just can't get into all the whys of it. I just can't."

"It's okay. Dallas, I'm not sulking. I'm not pushing."

"No, you're not." Hadn't been, Eve admitted. "And you're not taking a punch at me, even when I deserve it."

"You'd hit me back, and you hit harder."

With a short laugh, Eve rubbed her hands over her face, then made herself shift in the seat, meet Peabody's gaze. "You're my partner, and you're my friend. You're good in both areas. I've got . . . the shrinks would call them issues. I have to deal with them. If you observe something in my behavior that affects an investigation, I expect you to call me on it. Otherwise, I've got to ask you, as my partner and my friend, to leave it alone."

"Okay."

"Okay. Let's get moving before there's a riot, and they drag us out of the car and stomp us to death on the street."

"I'm for that."

She drove the next block in silence. "I'm going to drop you off at home," Eve said. "We need sleep."

"Does that mean you're going home to work on the case alone?"

"No." Eve smiled a little. "I'm going to take my meeting with Mira, then go home and crash for a while. I'll work some tonight. If you want to do the same, you could push at the ribbons some more. And verify Abel Maplewood's whereabouts on the night of."

"Can do. What are we going to do about Sanchez?"

"I'm going to sleep on it."

Since her head was messed up, Eve figured it was a really good time to see a shrink. Or a really bad time. Either way, it wasn't smart to miss or cancel an appointment with Mira.

Mira would take it fine, but her admin would punish you.

So instead of lying facedown on some flat surface, catching some much needed sleep, she was sitting in one of Mira's cozy scoop chairs, accepting a cup of tea she didn't want.

Mira had a soft, pretty face surrounded by soft, pretty hair the color of natural mink. She enjoyed attractive, monochromatic suits. Today's was the green shade of good pistachio ice cream. She wore a trio of beaded necklaces with it, in a darker shade of green.

Her eyes were the same blue as her scoop chairs, and while invariably kind, rarely missed a detail.

"You're exhausted. Haven't you slept at all?"

"Couple hours. I drank a booster."

"All well and good. Sleep is better."

"Next on my list. Tell me about him."

"Angry and violent, with that anger and violence targeted toward women. I don't believe his use of the red ribbon was accidental. Scarlet, the brand for whores. There's a duality in his view on women. Whores to be used and abused, yes, but the pose, the location, indicate an awe of them. A religious pose, a castle. Madonna, queen, whore. He chooses his symbols."

"Why Maplewood, specifically?"

"You believe she was specifically targeted. This wasn't random?"

"He lay in wait. I'm sure of it."

"She was alone and unprotected. She had a child, but no husband. This may play a part. She may also represent, by appearance, by lifestyle, by circumstances, the female in his life who influenced him. Sexual homicide with mutilation most often occurs when the perpetrator was abused or humiliated or betrayed in some fashion by a strong female figure. Mother, sister, teacher, spouse or lover. It's unlikely he has or has been able to maintain a long-term, healthy intimate relationship with a woman."

"And sometimes they're just fucking murdering bastards."

"Yes." Mira calmly sipped her tea. "Sometimes. But there is a root, Eve. There's always a root, whether real or fantasized. Rape is about power, more than it's about violence, certainly more than it's about sex. Penetration by force, for your own gratification while causing fear and pain. Not just forcing yourself on another person, but *into* them. Murder takes that power to another level. The ultimate control over another human being. The method, strangulation, is very personal, very intimate."

"I think he got off on it. He strangled her face-to-face. He watched her die."

"I'd agree. We can't know if he ejaculated as there was no semen, but I don't believe he's impotent. He may be so without the violence, but if he'd been unable to orgasm, we would see more injuries, pre- and postmortem."

"Cutting out her eyes is pretty injurious."

"A symbol again. He enjoys symbols. He blinded her. She has no power against him as she can't see him—or is allowed to see him only in a manner he directs. This is a powerful symbol to him, and possibly the most important. He took her eyes away from her—not destroying them, which would have been quicker and easier—and more violent—but with some care. Eyes are important to him. They have meaning."

She'd had blue eyes, Eve thought. Dark bluebell eyes, like her daughter. "Maybe he fixes them. Could be an eye doctor, a tech, a consultant."

Mira shook her head. "I'd be surprised if he could work with, treat, or interact with women on a day-to-day basis. It's most likely he lives alone, works at a job where he can work alone, or primarily with men. He's organized, but he's also a risk taker. And he's proud. He not only attacked and killed in a public place, but he left her there, displayed."

"Look at my work, and be afraid."

"Yes. If Elisa Maplewood was symbolic rather than target specific, his work isn't finished. He's organized enough to have his next victim in mind already. He'd study her habits, her routines, and strategize the best way to take her."

"Her father looked like a possibility, for about ten seconds. He's got a sheet, but reports are he's out of town. Verifying that, but it doesn't feel like it was personal on that level."

"Because of the symbols." Mira nodded. "Yes, I agree, unless you find those symbols relate between father and daughter. Probabilities would be he didn't know Maplewood on that personal a level, but only what she symbolized to him."

"I'm going to run probabilities. We're tracking down the ribbon. It's a good lead." But she brooded. "What do you think of psychics?"

"Well, as I have a daughter who's a sensitive . . ."

"Oh yeah. Right." She brooded a moment more while Mira waited patiently. "I had a visit this morning," she began, and told her of Celina.

"Do you have any reason to doubt she was telling the truth?"

"Other than a reluctance to believe in woo-woo, no. She's checking out. It's a little annoying to admit that she's the best lead I've got."

"You'll speak with her again?"

"Yeah. Personal prejudices and reluctance don't belong on the job. If she's a lead, I'll use her."

"There was a time you were nearly as reluctant to consult with me."

Eve flicked a glance up, shrugged. "Maybe for the same reasons. You always saw too damn much to suit me."

"Maybe I still do. You not only look exhausted, Eve, you look sad."

There was a time she'd have shrugged that off as well, and walked out. But she and Mira had come a long way. "Turns out Louise Dimatto knows the psychic. Old pals. I needed to talk to her about it. She's doing duty at Dochas today."

"Ah."

"That's a shrink trick. *Ah.*" She set the tea aside, rising to pace the office, to jingle loose credits in her pockets. "And it works. It's an amazing thing Roarke's done, and only more amazing—to me—when you get down to the reasons he did it. Some for himself, sure, seeing as he was kicked around plenty as a kid. Some for me—more, for me—because of what I went through. But altogether more for us. Because of who and what we are now."

"Together."

"Jesus, I love him more than . . . it shouldn't be possible to feel this way about someone. And still, knowing what he'd done there, knowing it was important to him I have some part in it, I've avoided going there."

"Do you think he doesn't understand why?"

"Another thing that shouldn't be possible is the way he understands me. It's a good place, Dr. Mira, and the name is right on target. And I was sick the whole time I was there. Sick in my heart, in my gut. Sick and shaky and scared. I wanted to walk out, away from those women with their bruises, those kids with their helpless faces. One of them had a broken arm. One of the kids. A girl, about six. I'm not good with kids' ages."

"Eve."

"I could feel the bone snap. Could hear it. And it took everything not to just go down to my knees and scream."

"And you're ashamed of that?"

Shame? She wasn't sure. Was it shame she felt, or anger, or some nasty brew of both? "You've got to get over it, sometime."

"Why?"

Stunned, Eve turned back, stared. "Well . . . because."

"Overcoming and getting over are two very different things." Mira spoke briskly now because she wanted to get up, to go over, to draw Eve into a hug that wouldn't be appropriate, or understood. "Yes, you should strive to overcome. To survive, have a life, to be happy, to be productive. You've done all that, and a great deal more. But no, you're not required to get over it. To get over being beaten and abused and raped and tortured. You ask more of yourself, Eve, than you ask of anyone else in the world."

"It was a good place."

"And in this good place you saw a child someone had tried to break. It hurt you. But you didn't walk away."

She sighed, sat again. "Peabody caught a drift. When we're out, she does the pal thing, offers to listen if I need to dump. So how do I respond to that?"

"Snap her head off, I imagine," Mira said with a little smile.

"Yeah. I ream her. Slap her up and down, mind-your-own-business kind of shit, stuff just jumping out of my mouth."

"You'll apologize."

"Already did."

"You work together, as a unit. And you have a friendship outside of the job. You may want to consider telling her, at least some of it."

"I don't see what good it would do either one of us."

Mira only smiled. "Well, something to think about. Go home, Eve. Get some sleep."

5

Since all Eve wanted was a few hours of oblivion, Mira's advice wasn't hard to take. She pulled through the gates of home.

Summer still reigned here, with perfect summer flowers in deep summer colors, with shimmering green grass that seemed to stretch for miles, and the tall leafy trees that spread cool shade.

The house with its towers and peaks and graceful terraces lorded over them: part castle, part fortress, all home.

The best part of it was there was a bed inside, with her name on it.

She left the car at the front steps, and realizing she'd neglected to call Requisitions and bitch, she gave the door an irritated boot when she got out. Then she forgot it and dragged up the steps and into the house.

He was lurking. Summerset was the universal champion of lurk. He stood in the foyer, bony in black, his snooty nose in the air and the fat cat at his feet. In Eve's opinion, Roarke's majordomo never missed the chance to give her the needle.

"You're earlier than expected, and appear to have gotten through the day without destroying any article of clothing. I must note this event down on my calendar."

"Bitch when I'm late, bitch when I'm early. You could go pro on the bitching circuit."

"Your current offensive mode of transportation has not been properly garaged."

"Your current offensive face hasn't yet been beaten to a pulp by my fists either. Mark that on your calendar, Creepshow."

He had a couple more in his pocket, but decided to save them since there were circles of exhaustion under her eyes, and she was already heading up the steps. Hopefully to bed. He glanced down at the cat.

"That should do for the moment." He wagged a finger toward the stairs, and Galahad trotted up them.

She thought about going to her office first, putting her notes and thoughts into a report, maybe checking in with the lab, running some probabilities.

But her feet took her straight to the bedroom where the cat streaked in just behind her. He bolted up the stairs of the platform, took a running leap, and landed, with considerable grace for a tub of lard, on the bed.

And sat, dual-colored eyes narrowed on Eve's face.

"Yeah, good idea. I'm right behind you."

She stripped off her jacket, tossed it on the sofa in the sitting area, peeled off her weapon harness, and dumped it on the jacket. Then she sat on the arm, pried off her boots, and decided that was good enough.

She didn't leap on the bed; it was more of a crawl. Stretching out on her stomach, ignoring the cat who slithered onto her butt and circled twice before settling, she ordered herself not to think. And dropped into sleep like a stone down a well.

She felt the dream coming. Felt it oozing out of her system like blood from a wound. In sleep she twitched, and her hands balled into fists. But she couldn't fight it off, and it took her.

Took her back.

It wasn't the room in Dallas, the place she feared most. It was dark, without the wash of dingy red light, without the icy air. Instead there were shadows, and a clammy kind of heat, the heavy smell of flowers going to rot.

She could hear voices, but couldn't make out the words. She heard weeping, but couldn't locate the source. It seemed like a maze, sharp corners, dead ends, a hundred doors all closed and locked.

She couldn't find her way out, or in. Her heart was thundering in her chest. She knew there was something else in the dark, something close behind her, something horrible waiting to strike.

She should turn and fight. It was always better to stand and fight, to face down what came after you and beat it back. But she was afraid, so afraid, and ran instead.

It laughed, low.

Her hand shook when she reached for her weapon, shook so hard she could barely draw it. She would kill it, if it touched her, she would kill it.

But she kept running.

Something stepped out of the shadows, and on a breathy scream she stumbled back and fell to her knees. Sobs clogged her throat as she brought her weapon up, sweaty finger poised to fire.

And saw it was a child.

He broke my arm. The little girl, Abra, held her arm close to her body. *My daddy broke my arm. Why did you let him hurt me?*

"I didn't. It wasn't me. I didn't know."

It hurts.

"I know. I'm sorry."

You're supposed to make it stop.

More shadows moved, circling her, taking form. She saw where she was now. In the room in the house called Hope, the room full of bruised and battered women, of sad-eyed, broken children.

They stared at her, and their voices filled her head.

He cut me.

He raped me.

He burned me.

Look, look at my face. I used to be pretty.

Where were you when he threw me down the stairs?

Why didn't you come when I was screaming?

"I can't. I can't."

Elisa Maplewood, blind and bloody, stepped closer. *He took my eyes. Why didn't you help me?*

"I am. I will."

It's too late. He's already here.

Alarms rang, lights flashed. The women, the children stepped back, stood like a jury at sentencing. The little girl called Abra shook her head. *You're supposed to protect us. But you can't.*

He strolled in, the big, terrifying smile on his face, the vile and vicious gleam in his eyes. Her father.

Take a look at them, little girl. Plenty of them, and there's always more. Bitches just beg for it, so what's a man to do?

"Stay away from me." On her knees, she lifted the weapon again. But her hands shook. Everything shook. "Stay away from them."

That's no way to talk to your father, little girl. He swung out, smashing her face with the back of his hand in a blow that sent her sprawling onto her back.

The women began to hum like bees trapped in a hive.

Gotta teach you a lesson, don't I? You never learn.

"I'll kill you. I killed you before."

Did you? He grinned, and she'd have sworn his teeth were fangs. *Then I'll just have to return the favor. Daddy's home, you worthless little cunt.*

"Stay back. Stay away." When she lifted her weapon, it was only a small knife held in a child's trembling hand. "No. No. Please, no!"

She tried to crawl away, away from him, away from the women. He reached down, as casually as a man might reach for an apple in a bowl. And snapped her arm.

She screamed, a child's terrified and baffled scream, as the white-hot pain flashed and burned.

There's always more of them. There's always more of us.

And he fell on her.

"Eve. Wake up. You wake up now." Her face was bone white, and her body had gone rigid when he'd rolled her over to gather her in. An instant before she'd screamed.

An icy tongue of panic licked up Roarke's spine. Her eyes were wide open, blind with shock and pain. He wasn't completely sure she was breathing. "I said *wake up*!"

Her body arched, and she sucked in air like a drowning woman. "My arm! He broke my arm, he broke my arm."

"No. It's a dream. Oh, baby, it's a dream. Come back now."

He trembled as much as she did as he rocked her. Catching a movement, he snapped his head up as Summerset rushed in. "No. I've got her."

"Is she injured?"

He shook his head, stroked her hair as she wept against him. "Nightmare. A bad one. I'll take care of her."

Summerset stepped back, then stopped at the door. "Get a soother in her, whatever it takes."

Nodding, Roarke waited until Summerset went out, shut the door behind him. "You're all right now. I'm right here."

"They were all there, all around me in the dark."

"It's not dark now. I've got the lights on. Do you want them brighter?"

She shook her head, burrowed into him. "I didn't help them. I didn't stop him when he came in. Like he always comes in. Her arm was broken, the little girl's arm was broken, just like mine. And he broke mine again. I felt it."

"He didn't." Roarke kissed the top of her head, eased her back even when she tried to cling. "Look here now. Eve, look here. Your arm's fine. You see?"

Though she tried to cradle it against her body, he drew it out, ran his hand gently from wrist to shoulder. "It's not broken. It was a dream."

"It was so real. I felt . . ." She bent her arm at the elbow, stared at it. Echoes of that phantom pain still rolled through her. "I felt it."

"I know." Hadn't he heard her scream? Hadn't he seen the glassy shock in her eyes? He kissed her hand, her wrist, her elbow. "I know. Lie back down now."

"I'm okay." Would be. "I just need to sit here a minute." She looked down as the cat wormed his way between them. Her hand wasn't quite steady when she stroked along his back. "Guess I scared the shit out of him."

"Not enough to make him bolt. He was with you, banging his head against your shoulder. Doing what he could, I'd say, to wake you."

"My hero." A tear plopped on her hand, but she was beyond being embarrassed by it. "I guess he rates some fancy fish eggs or something." She breathed deep, looked up into Roarke's eyes. "You, too."

"You're having a soother." Even as she opened her mouth to argue, he cupped her chin in his hand. "Don't argue, and for Christ's sake, don't make me pour it in you. We'll compromise this time, and split one. I damn well need it as much as you, or close to it."

She could see it now. He was so pale his eyes were like blue fire against the white of his skin. "Okay. Deal."

He got up, went over to the AutoChef, and ordered two short glasses. When he came back, she took the one he handed her. Then switched them. "Just in case you got sneaky and tranqed mine. I don't want to go out again."

"Fair enough." He tapped his glass to

hers, then downed his portion. After she'd done the same, he set both glasses aside.

"I might point out, that I know you, every suspicious and cynical inch. And if I'd tranqed one of the glasses, I'd have held onto it, knowing full well you'd switch them."

She opened her mouth, shut it again. "Damn it."

"But I didn't." He leaned forward, kissed her nose. "Deal's a deal."

"Scared you. Sorry."

He took her hand again, just held onto it. "Summerset said you got home a bit before five."

"Yeah, I guess. Needed the zees." She glanced toward the window. "Must've gotten some. It's going dark. What time is it?"

"Nearly nine." He knew she wouldn't sleep again, not now. He'd have preferred it if she would. If he could just lie beside her, holding her close, while they both slept off the dregs of the nightmare.

"You could use a meal," he decided. "And so could I. Want to have it in here?"

"That works for me. I could use something else first."

"What do you want?"

She laid her hands on his face, eased up to her knees to press her lips to his. "You're better than a soother. You make me feel clean. And whole, and strong." She slid her fingers into his hair when his arms came around her. "You make me remember, and you help me forget. Be with me."

"I always am."

He kissed her temples, her cheeks, her lips. "I always will be."

She slid into him, swaying a little as they knelt on the wide bed in the half light. The storm had passed, but something inside her still quaked from it. He would calm that. He would make it right again. She turned her head, her lips brushing his throat as she sought the taste, the scent of mate.

And finding it, she sighed.

He understood her needs, what she sought from him, sought to give him. Slow, tender, thoughtful love. There were after-shocks trembling inside him yet, but she would quell them.

His lips skimmed a line along her jaw, found hers, then sank dreamily in. Deep and quiet. And she, his strong, troubled woman, melted against him. He held her there so they drifted together into the peace, mouth to mouth, heart to heart. This time, he knew, the flutter of her pulse signaled contentment.

When he eased her back so their eyes met, she smiled.

Watching her, he unbuttoned her shirt, felt her hands, steady again, loosen his. He slid it off her shoulders so he could trace his fingers over her. Skin, pale and smooth, surprisingly delicate over such disciplined strength. A low sound of pleasure hummed in her throat as she spread her hands over his chest.

Then she leaned down, pressed her lips to his ear. "Mine," she said.

It shook him, down to the soul.

Taking her hands in his, he turned them palms up and laid his lips in the center of each. "Mine."

They slid down together to lie facing one another, to touch, to explore as if it were the first time. Long and lazy caresses that both stirred and soothed. Unhurried passion that lit low fires.

She was warm now, and sure.

His lips brushed her breast and made her sigh again. Closing her eyes, she floated on the bliss. She stroked his hair—all that glorious black silk; his back—hard strength.

She heard him murmur *aghra*—my love. And thought, *Yes, I am. Thank God.* And arched to offer him more.

Arousal was a long, slow climb up, gradually up until sighs became moans and pleasure became a quiver of anticipation. When he brought her to peak, it was like being lifted up on the rise of a warm blue wave.

"Fill me." She drew his head down until their mouths met again. "Fill me."

He could see her eyes, open now, dark and drenched. So he slipped inside her, was surrounded, welcomed. Then enfolded.

They moved together, a gentle rise and fall in an intimacy so complete it squeezed his heart. He laid his lips on hers again, would have sworn he breathed her soul.

And when she spoke his name, the tenderness shattered him.

She watched the night sky through the window over the bed. It was all so still she could almost believe there wasn't a world out there. That there was nothing beyond this room, this bed, this man.

Maybe that was one of the purposes of

sex. To isolate you, for a little while, from everything but yourself and your lover. To allow you to focus in on your body, its needs, the gratification that was physical, and if you were lucky in that lover—emotional as well.

Without those pockets of solitude and sensation, you might just go mad.

She'd used sex before Roarke, for the release, the physical snap. But she'd never known, or understood, the intimacy of the act before him, the complete surrender of self to another. She'd never experienced the emotional peace that followed until he'd loved her.

"I have things to say to you," she said.

"All right."

She shook her head. "In a little while." If she stayed like this much longer, saturated with him, she'd forget there was a world out there, one she'd sworn to protect. "I've got to get up. Don't much want to, but I have to."

"You're going to eat."

She had to smile. He hadn't finished taking care of her, she thought. He never finished. "I'm going to eat. In fact, I'll get dinner for both of us."

He lifted his head, and those eyes, those brilliant blue eyes, narrowed thoughtfully. "Will you?"

"Hey, pal, I can work a stupid AutoChef as well as the next guy." She gave him a light slap on the ass. "Roll over."

He complied. "Was it the sex or the soother?"

"Was what the sex or the soother?"

"That put you in a domestic frame of mind?"

"A smart mouth won't get you dinner."

Smart mouth or not, he figured he was probably getting pizza.

She hooked a robe out of her closet, then while he watched her with some surprise, took one out of his and brought it to him. "And a smart mouth isn't always verbal. I can see sarcastic thoughts in your head."

"Why don't I shut up and get us some wine?"

"Why don't you?"

He left her contemplating the AutoChef and opened the panel to the wine rack. He assumed she needed to keep busy, keep the nightmare at bay. Thinking pizza, he selected a bottle of chianti, opened it, and set it aside to breathe.

"You'll be working tonight."

"Yeah. I have to do some stuff. I've got Mira's profile, and I want to walk through that again. Put together a progress report. I haven't done any probabilities yet either. Plus I have to scan the eye banks, transplant facilities, that sort of thing. A time waster since he didn't take them to sell them. But it's got to be eliminated."

She brought two plates over to the sitting area, set them down on the table.

"What've you got there?" he asked her.

"Food. What does it look like?"

He cocked his head. "It doesn't look like pizza."

"My culinary programming skills run beyond pizza."

She'd chosen chicken sautéed in wine and rosemary, with wild rice and asparagus.

"Well fancy that," he murmured, flummoxed. "I've opened entirely the wrong wine."

"We'll live with it."

She went back for a basket of bread. "Let's eat."

"No, this won't do." He opened the wine rack again, found a bottle of Pouilly-Fuissé in the chilled section. He opened it, brought bottle and glasses to the table. "Looks lovely. Thanks."

She sampled a bite. "Pretty good. Doesn't quite measure up to the soy fries I had at lunch, but it's not bad." When he winced, as she'd intended, she laughed.

"Hopefully you'll be able to choke down whatever Charles and Louise serve when we go to dinner."

She stabbed more chicken. "Don't you think it's weird? You know, Charles and Louise, Peabody and McNab, all having a cozy dinner at Charles's place. I'm pretty sure the last time, the only time, McNab was ever over there was when he and Charles punched each other out."

"I doubt it'll come to that again, but if it does, you'll be there to break it up. And not weird, darling, no. People find each other. Charles and our Peabody were, and are, friends."

"Yeah, but McNab thinks they did the mattress rhumba."

"Whatever he thinks, he knows they're not dancing now."

"I still say it's going to be weird."

"A few awkward moments, perhaps. Charles and Louise love each other."

"Yeah, about that. How can they cruise along this way? He's out there boinking other women professionally, then boinking her for love. What's with that?"

An amused smile curving his lips, Roarke sipped his wine. "You're such a moral creature, Lieutenant."

"Yeah, we'd see how open-minded and sophisticated you are if I decided to turn in my badge and become a licensed companion. I'd have a hard time working up a client list because you'd smash all their faces in."

He merely inclined his head, in agreement. "But you weren't an LC when I met and fell for you, were you? A cop, and that took some considerable adjusting on my part."

"Guess it did." And that, she thought, was as good a segue as she could ask for, considering what she wanted to say. "I know it did. But I think, under all that, you'd already done considerable adjusting. Meaning you weren't just after the main chance, however you could get it. I don't think you ever were."

"In my misspent youth, Lieutenant, you'd have hunted me down like a dog. Not that you'd have caught me, but you'd have tried."

"If I'd been hunting . . ." She trailed off, waved it away. "Not where I was going." She picked up her wine, took a long sip, set it down. "I went to Dochas today."

"Oh?" His gaze sharpened on her face. "I wish you'd contacted me. I'd have made time to go with you."

"It was work related. I needed to talk to Louise about this psychic chick, and Louise was there today."

He waited, but she said nothing. "What did you think?"

"I think—" She set down her fork, clasped her hands together in her lap. "I love you more than I can say. I don't have the words to tell you how much. How much I love you, how proud I am of you for what you're doing there. I was trying to come up with them, but I can't."

Moved, he reached across, waited until she unclasped her hands to take his. "What's being done there wouldn't be if you weren't part of it. Part of me."

"Yes, it would. That's the thing. Maybe you did it sooner because of me. Because of us. But it was in you to do it. It always was. I'm sorry I haven't gone before."

"Doesn't matter."

"I was afraid to. Some part of me I didn't want to look at was afraid to go there. It hurt to go." She released his hand. She had to do this, say this, on her own. "To see those women, those kids. To feel that fear. Even more to feel the hope. Even more than that. It brought it back."

"Eve."

"No, you just listen. There was this girl—you know, sometimes I think fate just slaps something down in front of you and makes you deal. Her arm was in a skincast. Her father had broken it."

"Oh, Christ."

"She talked to me; I talked back. I can't remember exactly. My head was buzzing and my stomach was clenched. I was afraid I'd be sick right there, or just fucking pass out. But I didn't. I got through it."

"You don't ever have to go back again."

She shook her head. "Just wait. I dropped Peabody at home, saw Mira, came here. I needed sleep. I thought I would just sleep, but it caught up with me. It was bad, you know it was bad. But you don't know that in the nightmare, I was back there, in the shelter. With all those battered women, all those broken kids. And they're asking me why I didn't stop it, why I let it happen."

She held up a hand so he wouldn't interrupt, though she saw her own pain reflected on his face. "He was there. I knew he'd come. He said there'd always be more. More of him, more of them. I couldn't stop it. When he reached for me, I wasn't me anymore. I mean not who I am now. I was a kid. He broke my arm, just like before, and he raped me, just like before."

She had to pause, had to wet her throat with wine. "But here's the thing. I killed him, just like before. And I'll keep killing him, as long as it takes. Because he's right. There's always more of them—the brutal and the battered. There's always more, and I can't stop it all. But I can damn well do the job and stop some of it. I have to."

She let out a breath. "I can go back there. I want to go back there, because I know when I do I won't be scared or sick—or if I am, it won't be as much, as bad. I'll go there because I can see what you've done, what you're doing, is another way to stop it. Her arm was broken, but it'll heal. So will she, because you've given her a chance."

It took him a moment, a long moment, before he could speak. "You are the most amazing woman I've ever known."

"Yeah." She gave his hand a squeeze. "We're a hell of a pair."

6

Eve took a detour to edd. it was always a culture shock for her to walk into a division where cops dressed like partygoers or weekend loafers. Lots of airboots and neon hues, and as many people walking or trotting around talking on headsets as manning cubes and desks.

Music blatted out, and she actually saw a guy dancing, or she assumed it was dancing while he worked with a handheld and porta-screen.

She made tracks through the bull pen and directly into Captain Ryan Feeney's office, where she expected to find sanity.

She lost the power of speech when she saw him, the reliable Feeney, with his fading vacation tan, his wiry ginger hair threaded with gray. His face was comfortably creased and droopy, but instead of one of the rumpled shirts he habitually wore, he was decked out in a stiff and spotless one the color of raspberry sherbet.

And he had on a tie. A tie. The closest she could come to describing the color was what you might get if you electrocuted grass.

"Jesus Christ, Feeney. What're you wearing?"

The look he sent her was that of a man bearing up under a hideous emotional weight. "Wife said I needed to start wearing color. Bought this getup then hung over me, nagged my ears off until I put it on."

"You look . . . you look like a manager for street LCs."

"Tell me. Look at these pants." He shot out a leg so Eve was treated to the sight of that skinny limb wrapped in modified skin-pants in the same electric shade as the tie.

"God. I'm sorry."

"Boys out there think I look iced. What're you going to do?"

"I don't honestly know."

"Tell me you've got a case for me, something that's going to take me out in the field where I can get bloody." He lifted his fists, a boxer's pose. "Wife can't bitch if these glad rags get ruined on the job."

"I've got a case, but I've got no fieldwork in the E area. Wish I could help you out. Can't you at least take that noose off?"

He tugged at the tie. "You don't know the wife like I do. She'll call. She'll be doing a damn spot-check on me all through shift to make sure I'm suited up. It's got a jacket, Dallas."

"You poor bastard."

"Ah well." He let out a heavy sigh. "What're you doing in my world?"

"The case. Sexual homicide with mutilation."

"Central Park. Heard you caught that one. We're doing the standard on the 'links and comps. You need more?"

"Not exactly. Can I close this?" She gestured toward his door, got the nod. When she'd shut it, she went over to sit on the corner of his desk. "What's your stand on consulting with psychics on the job?"

He pulled his nose. "Not much call for it in my division. When I worked Homicide, we'd get calls now and then from people claiming they had visions, or information from the spirit world. You know that."

"Yeah, still do. We waste time and manpower following them up, then go along and investigate with our measly five senses."

"Got some genuines out there." He pushed away from the desk to program for coffee. "Most departments these days have a sensitive attached as civilian consultant. More than a few carry badges, too."

"Yeah, well. We were partnered up for a long time."

He handed her a mug of coffee. "Those were the days."

"We never used a sensitive."

"No? Well, you use what you use when the tool fits."

"I've got one claims she saw the Central Park murder in a dream."

Feeney sipped contemplatively. "You check her out?"

"Yeah, and she jibes. Licensed and registered. Got a reference from Louise Dimatto."

"Doc's not an asshole."

"No, she's not. If you were me, would you bring her in?"

He lifted a shoulder. “You know the answer to that.”

She frowned into her coffee. “You use what you use. Yeah, I know. I guess I just wanted to hear it from somebody who’s got his feet planted. Thanks.”

She set the nearly untouched coffee down. She was getting spoiled, she thought. She was finding it easier and easier to walk away from the stuff if it wasn’t real coffee. “Thanks.”

“No sweat. Let me know if you need somebody to dig in, get his hands, and personal attire, dirty.”

“Will do. Ah, you know somebody could spill coffee on that getup. Wouldn’t be your fault.”

He sent her a pitying look. “She’d know. Ain’t nobody more psychic than a wife.”

She rounded up Peabody. If she was going to consult with a psychic, she was going to run the possibility by her commander first.

Whitney listened as she gave her oral to back up the data she’d already sent to his attention. He didn’t interrupt, but sat quiet at his desk, a big man with dark skin and close-cropped silvering hair. Years of riding a desk hadn't wiped the cop out of him. It reached right down to the bone.

The only change in his wide, sober face was a quick lift of eyebrows when she mentioned Celina Sanchez. When her report was complete, he nodded, then eased back.

"Psychic consultant. Not your usual style, Lieutenant."

"No, sir."

"The media liaison is handling the public information front for now. We'll continue to omit the exact nature of the mutilation, as well as the description of the murder weapon. If you decide to consult a sensitive, that data will also be omitted."

"She's firm on that, Commander. If I consult with her, I wouldn't feel comfortable giving her name to the liaison, or anyone beyond the active investigative team."

"Understood. The name of your sensitive sounds familiar to me. I may have met her at some time or other. Socially. I'll check with my wife, who has a better memory for that sort of thing."

"Yes, sir. Do you want me to wait to speak

with Ms. Sanchez again until you've done so?"

"No. This is your call. Detective, your opinion on this matter?"

Peabody's spine snapped straight. "Mine, sir? Ah . . . I might be more open to extrasensory gifts, Commander. We have sensitives in my family."

"Would you be one of them?"

She relaxed enough to smile. "No, sir. I just have the basic five. I believe, as Lieutenant Dallas believes, that Celina Sanchez is worth at least a follow-up interview."

"Then talk to her. If and when the eyes leak to the media, we'll see this case blasted on and through every media outlet. We need to close it before the circus comes to town."

Celina lived in a section of SoHo that ran to high-end art, trendy restaurants, and tiny one-room boutiques. It was the land of young, well-heeled, well-dressed urbanites who liked to hold intimate, catered brunches on Sunday mornings, voted Liberal Party, and attended esoteric plays they only pretended to understand, much less enjoy.

Street artists were welcome, and coffeehouses were abundant.

Celina's two-story loft had once been part of a three-story sweatshop that had produced massive amounts of cheap, designer knockoff clothing. It, like other similar buildings in the sector, had been revitalized, rehabbed, and reclaimed by those who could afford the real estate.

From the street, Eve noted the windows were as wide as shuttle ports, and a long, narrow terrace with an ornate iron railing had been added to the third floor.

"You sure you don't want to call for an appointment?" Peabody asked.

"She ought to know we're coming."

Peabody approached the sidewalk-level front entrance beside Eve. "That's sarcasm, sir."

"Peabody, you know me too well." Eve rang the buzzer for Celina's loft. Moments later, Celina's voice drifted through the intercom.

"Yes?"

"Lieutenant Dallas and Detective Peabody."

There was another sound. It might have been a sigh. "Please come up. I'll release the door and the elevator. Just ask for two."

The little security light over the door went from red to green. Locks snicked open. Eve stepped inside the entryway, scanned and observed three first-level apartments. To her left, an elevator door opened. They stepped in, requested two.

When the door opened again, Celina stood on the other side of an ironwork gate. Her hair was up today, in some twisty coil that was secured by what looked like a couple of fancy chopsticks.

She wore skin-pants that were cropped a few inches above the ankle and a snug tank that left her midriff bare. She wore no shoes, no facial enhancements, no jewelry.

She opened the gate, stepped back. "I was afraid you'd come. We might as well sit down."

She gestured behind her to a wide space furnished with a generous S-shaped sofa the color of good red wine. There was an oversized table on each curve, and on one stood a long, shallow bowl filled with what appeared to be rocks. Beside it, a tall pillar candle rose out of a hammered cup.

The floor was the original wood, by Eve's guess, and had been sanded, sealed—whatever people did with old, original wood—to turn it into a glossy, honey-toned sea. Brightly patterned rugs were scattered over it, as brightly patterned art was scattered over the pale green walls.

Through archways, she spotted the kitchen, a party-sized dining area. There were open-tread, metal steps, painted a deeper green than the walls and boasting a railing that was fashioned to resemble a slim, slithering snake.

"What's that?" Eve nodded toward the only door, shut and secured.

"My consultant space. It has another entrance. I like the convenience of working at home when I can, but I also value my privacy. I don't take clients in this part of my house."

She gestured again, toward the sofa. "Can I get you something to drink? I cancelled my consults today. I don't think I'd do anyone any good. You caught me in the middle of a yoga session. I'd like some tea myself."

"No, thanks," Eve responded.

"I wouldn't mind. If you're making it anyway."

Celina smiled at Peabody. "Have a seat. It won't take long."

Rather than sitting, Eve wandered. "You've got a big space here."

"Yes. I need open spaces. I'd go crazy, for instance, in your office. You spoke with Louise?"

"She contacted you?"

"No. But you strike me as a thorough woman. I assume you checked my license, my record, my background, and spoke with Louise before deciding to talk to me again. You'd consider it necessary."

"Louise said you were the black sheep."

Celina came out, carrying a tray with a squat white pot and two fragile-looking white cups and saucers. She shot Eve a wry smile. "Yes, that's accurate. My family disapproves, and is mildly embarrassed not only by my gift but that I choose to make a living from it."

"You don't need the money."

"Not for financial security." She crossed the room to set the tray on the table. "But for personal satisfaction. In your circumstances, Lieutenant, you hardly need the salary the police department pays you. But I imagine you collect it just the same."

She poured two cups of tea, passed one to Peabody. "I can't stop thinking about Elisa. I don't want to think of her. I don't want to be part of this. But I have to."

"The NYPSD may hire and attach, at the primary's request, expert consultants, civilians."

"Mmm-hmm." Celina arched one dark eyebrow. "And did I pass the audition?"

"So far. If you're willing and able to serve as such on this matter, you'll be required to sign a contract. The contract will include a gag order, preventing you, by law, from discussing any aspect of the investigation."

"I've no desire to discuss any aspect of the investigation. If I agree to do this, I require you to sign a document insuring that my name, my association with the investigation, will not be given to the media."

"So you said before. You'll be paid a fee—standard rate." Eve held out a hand to Peabody, waited while Peabody took documents out of her bag. "You'll want to read these over. You're free to consult a lawyer or legal representative before signing."

"You're giving your word, I'm giving mine.

I don't need a lawyer for that." But she crossed her legs, settled back, and read each document carefully. "I don't have a pen."

Peabody pulled one out, offered it. Celina signed both documents, handed the pen off to Eve.

"Well, that's that, isn't it?" Celina let out a breath after Eve scrawled her name on each contract. "That's that. What do I do?"

"Tell me again exactly what you saw." Eve laid a recorder on the table. "For the record."

She went through it again, closing her eyes from time to time as she repeated details. Her hands didn't shake, and her voice stayed strong and steady, but Eve watched her pale, degree by degree as she recounted the murder.

"And where were you when you saw this happen?"

"Upstairs. In bed. My security was on, all night, as always. I have full alarms, and cameras on all doors. You're welcome to take the discs into evidence, check them."

"I will. It covers both of us. Have you had any visions since night before last?"

"No. Just a . . . a sense of dread, and a

feeling of anticipation. That could be my own nerves."

"Peabody? Evidence bag."

Saying nothing, Peabody took out a length of red corded ribbon, sealed. "Do you recognize this, Ms. Sanchez?"

"Celina." Even her lips had gone white. "It looks like what he used on her."

Eve unsealed the bag, held the ribbon out. "Take it. Tell me what you see."

"All right." Celina set down her cup, then rubbed her palms nervously on her thighs. She breathed slowly, then took the ribbon.

She ran it through her fingers, kept her gaze fixed on it. "I don't . . . nothing comes, nothing clear. Maybe I need time to prepare, maybe I need solitude." Baffled frustration ran over her face. "I thought . . . I expected more. I was so sure that I'd get something since I had this connection. I know he used this to kill her. They both touched it, but I get nothing."

Eve took the ribbon, resealed it, handed it back to Peabody. "Why do you think you didn't see his face that night? You saw hers."

"I don't know. My connection must be

with the victim. Maybe Elisa didn't see him clearly."

"Possible. Maybe you could try again, with the ribbon."

"I don't know what difference it would make. Maybe if you left me alone with it," she began as Peabody took out an evidence bag.

"I can't do that. Chain of evidence."

"It doesn't give off anything. Not for me, in any case." Still, Celina reached out for it when Eve unsealed the bag.

When her fingers closed over it, her eyes went huge and blind. She dropped it to the floor, as if it had burst into flame. And her hand closed over her own throat as she choked.

While Eve only eyed her narrowly, Peabody sprang up, took Celina firmly by the shoulders and shook. "Snap back!" she ordered.

"Can't breathe."

"Yes, you can. It's not you. Take the air in, let it out. There, in and out again."

"Okay. Okay." She let her head fall back, closed her eyes as a single tear slid down her cheek. "Give me a minute." She kept breathing, kept her eyes shut. "You're a cold bitch, Dallas."

"Yeah, I am."

"Testing me. The first ribbon was a blind, meant nothing. Just a test."

"Bought it yesterday. Sealed up before I bagged it."

"Smart. Thorough." She had her breath back, and her color—and what might have been respect in her eyes. "Well, I suppose if I'd been murdered, I'd want a cold bitch looking for my killer." Frowning, she looked at the ribbon Eve had picked up off the floor. "I wasn't prepared. That's why it hit so hard. I can prepare myself, to an extent anyway."

She held out her hand, and Eve let the ribbon flow into her palm.

"She suffered. Terror and pain. She doesn't see his face, not really. She's dazed and afraid and hurt, but she fights him. God, he's strong. Big, tough, strong. It's not his face. I think it's not his face. The rape is quick, almost mercifully quick. He's in her, panting, pounding, when she feels this tighten around her neck. She doesn't know what it is, but she knows she's going to die. And she thinks: Vonnie. She thinks last of her child."

"Tell me about him."

She sat straighter, breathed slower. "He hates her. Fears her. Reveres her. But not her. So much rage, so much hate, rage, excitement. It's hard to get more than that. It's like blows raining down on my psyche. It's hard to get through the madness. But I know he's done this before."

"Why does he take her eyes?"

"I . . . She needs to be in the dark. I don't know, except he wants her in the dark. I'm sorry." She handed the ribbon back to Eve. "It's hard, and I can't handle the ribbon for long. It's too much. I can do it in short sessions."

Eve nodded, noting the sheen of perspiration covering Celina's face. "I see that. I need you to come with me to the crime scene."

Celina pressed a hand to her belly. "I'd like to change first."

"We'll wait."

After Celina had gone upstairs, Peabody let out a low whistle. "You gotta admit, she's got stones."

"Yeah. She stands up."

"And from where I'm sitting, she's the real deal."

"Looks like."

Restless, Eve got up. She liked the space, not just the amount of it, but the use of it. She admired the way Celina had held out her hand for the murder weapon.

"Is it the civilian or the psychic aspect you don't like?"

Eve flicked a glance over her shoulder at Peabody's question. "Little of both. I don't like attaching civilians to an investigation, and don't bother reminding me how often Roarke ends up that way. It's bad enough he does, bad enough I'm getting used to it. And the psychic thing. How much good is that really going to do?"

She turned back to Peabody. "What did she tell us? He's big and strong and out of his fucking mind. That's no bulletin."

"Dallas, it's not like she's going to give us a name and address. This stuff doesn't work that way."

"Why the hell not?" Irritated, she jammed her hands in her pockets. "If you can *see* stuff, why can't you see salient details? The killer is Murdering Bastard who resides at 13 Homicide Drive. *That* would be useful."

"Frosty. Just think of how quick we'd close a case. Then the department would hire a whole team of psychics—the, ah, the SDD—Sensitive Detective Division—and . . . You know what, I don't like it after all. We'd be out of a job."

Eve shot a dark glance toward the stairs. "And I don't like the idea that she could start poking around in my head."

"She wouldn't do that, Dallas. Legitimate sensitives respect privacy. They don't intrude."

Peabody's father had, Eve remembered. Inadvertently, but all the same. And there, she admitted, was the core of her bias.

"I like her," Peabody added.

"Yeah. She's okay. We'll take this little field trip, see what comes of it. Then you and me? We're going back to straight cop work."

Celina changed into a pair of black pants and a blue, scooped-necked blouse. She wore several crystal drops on a chain around her neck.

"For protection, intuition, the opening of the third eye." She held them up as they stood at the edge of Central Park. "Not everyone ascribes to their benefits, but under the present circumstances, I'm willing to try anything."

She adjusted the enormous sunshades that hid half her face. "Pretty day," she said. "Warm and sunny. The sort of day that brings people outside. I love New York this time of year. And I'm stalling."

"The applicable areas have been searched, swept, recorded," Eve began. "From what we've learned, the victim walked the dog in this direction, and entered the park approximately at this point."

Eve started into the park.

"So many people have been through here, I don't know what I'm going to get. Truthfully, my gift is more direct, contact with someone or something. Usually."

About ten yards into the trees, Eve stopped. There was no one around, she noted after a sweep. People were at work, in school, at the shops, in restaurants.

It was too close to the street, this tony street, for chemi-head gatherings or illegals transactions.

"It was here, wasn't it?" Celina took off her shades, pocketed them, stared at the ground. "Where he grabbed her, dragged her deeper into the woods."

Her breathing was slow and even as she walked. A very deliberate sound.

"Struck her, in the face, knocked her down, dazed her. I can see the ground's torn up, so this must be where he . . ."

She took another breath, then squatted down and ran her hands over the grass and dirt. Yanked them back again. "God!"

Eve could see her clench her jaw as she touched the ground again. "He raped her here. Control, humiliate, and punish. There's a name in his mind—not hers. I can't see it, can't quite . . . but it's not her name, it's not Elisa he's punishing."

She drew her hands back again, tucked them under her arms as if to warm them. "It's difficult for me to get past her, and what was done to her. She's my connection, and she doesn't know him. She doesn't know why this is happening. He's just . . ."

She lifted her head, looked at Eve. "I can see you."

Eve felt a chill in her belly. "I'm not why you're here."

"You're a very strong presence, Dallas. Strong mind, strong feelings. Strong instincts. You layer over it all."

With a half laugh, Celina straightened,

stepped carefully back and away from the scene. "I'm surprised you're so resistant and suspicious of sensitives when you have a gift yourself."

"I don't."

Staring, Celina huffed out an impatient breath. "Bull. Do you think what you see and feel and *know* is just instinct? Only instinct?" Then she shrugged. "Whatever you call it, it's a gift."

She rubbed her arms. "He carried her from here. It's dim because she was already gone. Some part of her is still with me, but it's thin."

"She weighed about a hundred and thirty. Deadweight now."

"He's very strong."

"Have to be."

"Prides himself," Celina murmured as she began to walk. "Yes, there's pride. In his body, in his strength. She's so much weaker than he is now."

"Not the victim." Eve fell into step with her. "But who the victim symbolizes."

"Possibly. Probably." Celina brushed stray hair away from her face. A trio of interlinked gold circles swung at her ears. "You probably see him more clearly than I do. You're not as afraid of him as I am."

She paused to study the castle. "I wonder why he picked this spot. It's fanciful. A landmark. He could have left her anywhere. It would've been easier."

Eve had her thoughts on that, but kept them to herself. "How tall is he?"

"Well over six feet. Well over. Closer to seven. Thick-bodied, but hard—not fat. Not hard fat. Muscular. I could feel that, when he raped her."

She sat on the grass. "Sorry. I'm getting the shakes. I'm not used to this kind of work. It's draining. How do you do it?"

"It's what I do."

"Yes. Both of you." She opened her purse, took out a pretty box. "Blocker," she said when she selected a pill from it. "Vicious headache. I can't do anymore today. I'm sorry. Tapped out."

To Eve's surprise, Celina stretched out full length on the grass. "Do you know what I'd normally be doing now?"

"Can't say."

Idly, Celina checked the time. "Oh, yes. Francine. Right about now I'd be settling down to a consult with Francine. I give her a weekly, because I'm fond of her. She's a lovely, foolish, wealthy woman with a terminal case of husbanditis. She just keeps marrying them. She's about to take on husband number five, though I've advised her against it. Just as I did with numbers three and four."

Lazily, Celina drew the pair of stylish sunshades back out of her pocket. She slipped them on. "She'll get teary during our hour together, and protest that she must follow her heart." Her lips quirked as she patted a hand on her breast. "That *this* time it's going to be different. She'll marry the opportunistic son of a bitch who will then cheat on her—he already has, but she'll refuse to believe it—make her miserable, then walk off with her pride, her self-esteem, and a nice chunk of her portfolio."

She shook her head, pushed herself up to sitting. "Poor gullible Francine. And that, Lieutenant Dallas, Detective Peabody, is about the most tragic case I allow myself to deal with."

"How do you know when you talk to a client that you won't see something tragic?" Eve asked, and Celina smiled.

"It's my job to know. And if I miss something, then see it, I do what I can, then I step back. I don't believe in suffering, particularly when it's me doing the suffering. I don't understand why people insist on causing it or enduring it. I'm a shallow creature," she said, stretching like a cat in the sun. "But until a couple of nights ago, a damn contented one."

Peabody offered a hand to help her up. Celina studied it, grinned. "Can I take a peek? Just surface. Not deep probe, no secrets. You both interest me."

Peabody wiped her hand on her trousers, then offered it again. "I guess so."

Celina clasped hands, continued to hold it after she'd gained her feet. "You're a dependable woman. Sturdy shoulders, and a loyal streak that encompasses every area of your life. You're proud of your badge, and the work you do. Careful," she said with a laugh, and released Peabody's hand. "You open like a door. I didn't intend to peek into your personal life. But he's a cutie." She winked. "She-Body."

Peabody flushed. "We're, ah, moving into a new place together. Going to cohabitate."

"Congratulations. Ain't love grand?" Smiling, she turned to Eve. Raised her eyebrows.

"No."

Laughing, Celina tucked her hands into her pockets. "One of these days, I predict, you'll trust me enough. Thanks," she said to Peabody. "You cleansed my palate. I'll catch a cab in a bit. I want to walk off this headache before I go home."

She started to walk, directing herself away from the path they'd taken. Then she stopped, turned. There was none of the easy humor on her face now. "It's going to be soon. The next. I don't know how I know that, but I do. It's going to be very soon."

Eve watched her go, and gift or no gift, knew she was right.

7

"She's really interesting." Peabody waited a beat, then slid her gaze toward Eve as they cut west, then south toward Central. "Don't you think?"

"She's not a yawn. But tell me, in specifics, what did we get from this?"

"Okay, not a lot that we didn't already know or believe or suspect."

Peabody shifted in her seat and regretted the tea. Now she had to pee, and she knew damn well Eve wouldn't stop at a handy restaurant where the flash of a badge would get her toilet privileges. She crossed her legs tight, and tried to concentrate.

"Still, the fact is it's interesting to consult with a sensitive, one as obviously gifted as Celina. I am dependable and loyal, after all."

"Just like the family schnauzer."

"I prefer cocker spaniel 'cause they've got those cute, floppy ears." She recrossed her legs. "And, in my experience, if a sensitive's made this sort of connection, they can get more if they focus and keep open. I think she will. She's hooked in, and wants to see it through."

Eve glanced in the rearview at the blast of siren. She recognized the subtle difference in tone and identified an emergency medical vehicle an instant before the spinning red light of the medical tech wagon came into view.

She eased toward the curb, and the rattrap she was currently stuck with driving vibrated like gelatin in the wake of the speeding wagon.

"I want you to call Requisitions, the minute we get back to Central. Beg, bribe, threaten, offer sexual favors of any nature, but get us a decent ride by the end of shift."

Peabody had her teeth clenched and did her best to speak through them. "Who's going to perform the sexual favors, should it come to that?"

"You, Detective. I outrank you."

"The sacrifices I make for the badge."

"Health clubs."

"What?"

"We're going to start checking out health clubs."

"Sir, I don't think I can tone up appreciably before dispensing sexual favors if you want the vehicle by end of shift."

"Jesus, Peabody, get your face out of the gutter."

"Well, you put it there."

Eve jockeyed through traffic. "Let us return to our sworn duty and our current investigation. If we're after a solo—and there's no evidence to lead us to suspect this was a duet or gang killing—this is one strong son of a bitch. Not just in shape, not muscle-bound, but a seriously strong guy. Guy who can carry one-thirty the distance from the kill site to the dump site, and haul that much deadweight down a small cliff of rocks, probably works out regularly and seriously."

"Could have his own equipment. Somebody really serious usually does."

"And we're going to try tracking that, too. Full-scale home gyms to start. But if we're going to use what the psychic queen gives us, she said he was proud—proud of his body. He'd want to show it off, wouldn't he? Show what he can do."

"Health club."

"Health club."

"Dallas, just offhand, would you care to guess how many health clubs we have in our fair city?"

"We start with ones who cater primarily to men. He doesn't like women. So you scratch off the girly gyms where ladies prance around in their skin-suits and drink veggie juice or nibble nutribars before their massage. No day spa attached, no salons on premises. Forget the social clubs where guys go to play on the machines and pick up dates. Scratch off the facilities that cater primarily to same-sex orientation. The gay pickup cathedrals. We look for traditional, serious bodybuilder spots. The kind that pull in the sweaty guys with big necks."

"Oooh. Sweaty guys with big necks. Hubba. Lifting face out of gutter immediately, sir."

"Too late now," Eve muttered. "We can try another canvass of the victim's neighborhood. This guy surveilled her, got her routine. We go at it asking about an unusually tall, beefy guy. After you tackle Requisitions, contact the Vanderleas. See if either of them remembers seeing someone like that around."

"Check." Just a few more blocks, Peabody thought. Then she'd be able to pee. She squirmed, crossed her legs the other way.

"We run down home gym equipment: weight machines, virtual systems with bodybuilding programs. We check out subscriptions to magazines that— Squirming isn't going to help, you know. You shouldn't have downed all that tea."

"It's really nice of you to point that out now," Peabody shot back with some bitterness. "And squirming does too help. Oh, thank all the gods and goddesses," she breathed when they drove into Central's garage.

"Free-Ageism pop out when your bladder's full, Detective?"

"That's not all that's going to pop out." Peabody bolted from the car the instant it stopped, and ran/waddled to the elevator.

* * *

In her office, Eve glanced at her 'link, noted several messages. She ordered them to play while she set up a murder board for Elisa Maplewood.

As they ran, she ordered some to delete, some to save. Then stopped what she was doing to turn around and grin at the screen as Mavis came on.

"Hey, Dallas! We're back in town, my honey lamb and me. Maui is just *iced.* Totally TPD—tropical paradise deluxe. Everything was mag. The concert, our roll-on-the-sand-naked vacation part. And guess what? The belly's completely poking out now. Honest to God, I am so knocked up. You gotta see. I'll jet by, soon as I can."

Which was always a treat, Eve thought when the message ended. But if Mavis's belly really was poking out now, she wasn't entirely sure she wanted to see. Why pregnant women wanted anybody to see their poked-out bellies was another mystery, and one she had no desire to solve.

She turned to the AutoChef for coffee when Nadine Furst, Channel 75's on-air ace, clicked on.

"Dallas. I know you're going to give me the usual yaddah-yaddah blah, but I really want to talk to you re the Maplewood case. If I don't hear from you, I'm just going to show up at your office. I'll bring you a cookie."

Eve considered. It might be smart to give a short on-air, especially with the bribe of baked goods. A brief one-on-one, and woman-to-woman. His profile indicated he hated and feared the female, so wouldn't it burn his ass to be discussed on screen by two women? It might push him into making a mistake.

She'd think about it.

The thought of cookies made her hungry. With a glance at the door, she reached behind the AutoChef, under the slight lip, and tugged off the candy bar she'd taped there.

It was an obvious hiding place to her mind, but it had foiled the insidious candy thief who plagued her.

She bit righteously into chocolate, dropped down at her desk, and engaged her computer.

Your authorization code and password are not recognized. Access denied.

"What the hell are you talking about?" She gave the machine a quick boot with the heel of her hand. "Dallas, Lieutenant Eve." She read off her badge number for authorization, repeated her password.

The computer gave a cheerful little beep, then a long grinding buzz. The screen flickered.

"Don't you start on me. First my vehicle, now this. Don't you even start."

Acknowledged. Operations shutting down.

"No! Damn it, you bitch, you son of a bitching bastard whore, you know that's not what I meant." She smacked it again, set her teeth, and repeated the start-up process.

After a series of mechanical hiccups, it hummed.

"That's better. Okay. Open case file 39921-SH. Maplewood."

Acknowledged.

What flashed on-screen wasn't a case file. It wasn't police business unless the various naked couples writhing in athletic and impressive positions were a bunch of Vice cops undercover at an orgy.

Welcome to Fanta-Cee! Your virtual garden of sexual pleasure. You must be twenty-one to enter. Your debit account will be charged at the rate of ten dollars per minute during your one-week trial membership.

"Mother of God. Computer, close and delete current area."

Incomplete command.

"Like hell. Close this file."

Acknowledged.

The cavorting figures disappeared.

"Now you listen to me. This is Dallas, Lieutenant Eve. I *own* you. I want case file 39921-SH, and I want it now."

The screen jumped, filled with text. In what was possibly Italian.

The sound Eve made was somewhere between a scream and a bellow. She rapped the machine with her hand, punched it with her fist, and considered just ripping it out of the network and tossing it out her window.

Maybe, just maybe if her luck was in, there'd be a Maintenance guy strolling by under it. Two birds, one stone.

As satisfying as that would be, she calculated she could expect a replacement unit sometime near the end of the current century.

She swung to her 'link, intending to contact Maintenance and ream whoever was unfortunate enough to answer.

"And where will that get you, Dallas?" she asked herself. "Those puss-faced jerks in Maintenance, they live for moments like this. They'll sit around down there and laugh and laugh until you're forced to go down and kill every last one of them and spend the rest of your life in a cage."

She punched the computer again, just for the hell of it. And inspired, tried another angle.

"EDD. McNab. Hey, Dallas!"

Peabody's main squeeze grinned at her from her 'link screen. His narrow, pretty face was surrounded by bright blond hair that sported a couple of skinny temple braids.

"I was just about to shoot you the report on the e-work."

"Don't bother. My unit's funky. It's giving me grief, McNab. How about doing me a favor and taking a look at it?"

"You call Maintenance?"

When she merely growled, he gave a heh-heh-heh sort of laugh.

"Delete that. I can give you thirty in about fifteen."

"Good."

"Or if you officially requested I report to your office at once, to bring you a disc and hard copy of the e-work, I could come now."

"Consider yourself officially requested."

"Allying op."

"What?" But he'd already broken transmission.

Annoyed, she dug out her pocket unit and set to work trying to transfer the data she wanted from the desk unit to the PPC. She wasn't an e-geek, but she wasn't stupid, she told herself. She knew how to handle basic tech.

She was pulling her hair when McNab

bopped in. He was wearing a purple shirt with a green placket down the center. It reached the thighs of baggy green pants with purple racing stripes. Both colors were picked up in his checked airsneaks.

"E-Man to the rescue," he announced. Today's complement of silver ear hoops dangled with purple and green beads. "What seems to be the problem?"

"If I knew the problem, I'd have fixed it myself."

"Right." He dumped a little silver toolbox on her desk, plopped into her chair. Rubbed his hands together. "Wow. Chocolate." He widened his grin, wiggled his brows.

"Shit. Go ahead. Consider it payment in advance."

"Uptown!"

"What?"

"Uptown." He bit into the candy. "You know, like . . . excellent. Let's have a look. I'll just open it for a standard diagnostic."

He gave a series of commands that might as well have been in Venutian to Eve's ears. A lot of codes and symbols and strange little shapes spilled on-screen, and the computer's voice responded in a kind of gasping croak.

"See! See!" Eve sprang to lean over McNab's shoulder. "That's not right, is it? That's not good."

"Well, hmmm. Just let me—"

"It's sabotage, isn't it?"

"You expecting sabotage?"

"You don't *expect* sabotage. That's why it's sabotage."

"There's a point. I need to look around some. Why don't you, ah, take a break maybe."

"You want me to leave my own office?"

He gave her a pained look. "Lieutenant."

"Okay, okay." She stuffed her hands in her pockets. "I'll be in the bull pen."

She heard his long, relieved sigh as she strode out.

She marched straight to Peabody's desk.

"Comp woes?" Peabody asked. "McNab stopped by for a second on his way in to you."

"They sabotaged it."

"Who are they?"

"If I knew who they were, I'd hunt them down and peel the skin off their bones while they begged for mercy."

"Uh-huh. Okay, so I got a hold of Deann Vanderlea. Somebody found the puppy."

"Huh. The dog?"

"Yeah, Mignon. She was nearly on the other side of the park, and a couple joggers found her, checked her collar ID. They brought her back."

"Was it injured?"

"No, just scared. Having the pup back will give them a little comfort. Anyway, she and her husband and the vic all used Total Health Fitness and Beauty for workouts and such, by the way. Not the kind of spot we're looking for as regards the killer's habits."

"It was good to check."

"She doesn't remember seeing anyone suspicious around the neighborhood. Doesn't recall noticing a big guy at any point, but she's going to ask her husband and some of her neighbors. The doorman."

"We'll canvass again anyway."

"Yeah. Father's out of the picture. Alibied by a couple thousand miles, and he doesn't fit the physical type we're after."

"He'd have been too easy. How about my vehicle?"

"I've got a line on that. Give me a little time."

"Everybody wants time today. Let's do a

search on the health clubs. Manhattan-based to start."

Eve watched, with some irritation as Peabody's unit responded smoothly to her commands.

"How come the detectives and uniforms in this division have better equipment than I do? I'm the boss."

"You know, there's a theory that some people have a kind of mechanical . . ." The term *deficiency* sprang to Peabody's mind, but she was too concerned with her own health and safety to speak it. "Like an infection or something. And it affects the machines they operate."

"That's bullshit. I don't have any trouble with my home equipment."

"Just a theory," Peabody said, and hunched her shoulders. "Do you have to lurk there while this is running?"

"I have to lurk somewhere." Disgusted, Eve strode out. She'd get a tube of Pepsi, that's what she'd do. She'd cool off with a drink, then go back and hassle McNab.

She wanted to sit in her own damn office and do her own damn job. Was that too much to ask?

She approached a vending machine, then just stood there, staring at it resentfully. It would probably spit the Pepsi all over her, or send her some health drink just for spite.

"Hey, you." She signaled to a passing uniform, then dug out credits.

"Get me a tube of Pepsi."

The uniform looked down at the credits Eve dumped in her hand. "Ah, sure, Lieutenant."

The credits were plugged in; the machine responded with a cheerful and polite announcement of the selection and its contents. The tube slid quietly out of the slot.

"Here you go."

"Thanks."

Satisfied, Eve drank as she walked back toward the bull pen. That's how she'd handle this deal, she decided. She'd have other people screw with the machines whenever possible. She was rank, after all. She was supposed to delegate.

"Lieutenant?" McNab signaled her, and though she tried not to see it, watched him purse his lips toward Peabody.

"No kissy faces in Homicide, Detective. Is my unit up and running?"

"Good news, bad news. How about the bad first?" He gave her a come-with-me head signal and went back to her office. "Bad news. You got a dink system here."

"It was working fine before."

"Yeah, well, see it's got some internal problems. That's the easiest way to explain it. Some of its guts, we'll say, were designed with planned obsolescence in mind. Only so many operating hours before they start to fail."

"Why would anybody build something that's programmed to fail?"

"So they can sell new ones?" Because she looked like she needed it, he risked patting her shoulder. "Administration and Requisitions buy cheap most times, I guess."

"Bastards."

"Absolutely. But the good news is I've got it up for you. Replaced some things. It's not going to last more than a few days the way you use it. But I can get my hands on some parts. I've got connections. I can basically rebuild it for you. Meanwhile, if you could try not to smack it around, it should hold."

"Okay, thanks. I appreciate the quick work."

"No prob. I'm a genius. See you tomorrow night, right?"

"Tomorrow night?"

"Dinner? Louise and Charles?"

"Right. Right. Don't blow kisses in my bull pen," she called when he pranced out.

She sat, drank Pepsi, and stared at the machine. Dared it to give her trouble. Since Peabody was running Manhattan, Eve decided to expand to the Bronx for gyms.

The machine responded to her search request as if nothing had ever happened between them. It gave her enough confidence to turn her back on it while the search ensued, and study her board.

"Where'd he see you, Elisa?" she asked aloud. "Where did you come into his radar? He saw you, and something about you clicked in that sick mind of his. So he watched you and studied you and laid in wait for you."

A domestic. A single parent. Liked to make things with her hands. Divorced. Abusive husband.

She didn't need the file to remember the details on Elisa Maplewood.

Early thirties, slightly less than average

height, average build. Light brown hair, long. Pretty face.

Standard education, lower-middle-class upbringing. Native New Yorker.

Liked nice clothes in simple styles. Nothing too trendy, nothing too provocative. No current personal partner or romantic entanglement. Minimal social life.

Where did he see you?

The park? Take the kids to the park. Walk the dog. The shops? Buy your craft supplies, window shop.

She grabbed the hard copy of the report McNab had left on her desk. 'Link transmissions to her parents, to Deann's pocket unit, to Luther's office, to the craft store on Third to check on an order. Incomings ran along the same lines.

Her web activity ran to parenting sites, craft sites, and chat rooms. Downloads of magazines showed crafts again, parenting again, and some home decorating stuff, some online shopping. Downloads of a couple books tagged as current best-sellers.

Nothing popped from the search of the Vanderleas' equipment.

Chat room might be worth checking out,

she thought, and made a note of it. But it was tough for her to see this big, muscular guy knitting . . . whatever people knit. More than that, Elisa struck her as being too sensible, too savvy to give personal information to anyone in a chat room. He hadn't tracked her through her discussions on making blankets or the like.

He's done it before.

She thought of Celina's words. And she agreed with them.

What he'd done to Elisa had been well planned and well executed under risky conditions. Quick and efficient, and to Eve that meant practice.

She hadn't hit all the elements with her search for similar crimes. Maybe he'd added or adjusted. Maybe one or more of those hits had been his work.

Pride. Celina had spoken of his pride. She wasn't sure she liked depending so heavily on the opinion of a psychic, but it was another point she agreed with. There'd been pride, arrogant pride, in the way he'd displayed his victim.

Look at what I've done, what I can do. In the city's great park, so close to the home of the wealthy and privileged.

Yeah, he was proud of his work. And what did a man with pride in his work do when that work didn't reach the standards he wanted?

He buried the mistakes.

Her blood began to hum. It was the right track. She knew it. And she swung back to her machine. She saved and filed the results of her initial search, then brought up Missing Persons.

She started with a twelve-month search, stuck with Manhattan, and keyed in Elisa's basic description to narrow the parameters.

"Dallas—"

"Wait." Attention focused on her screen, Eve shot up a hand to stop Peabody. "He had to practice. He had to. Guy builds his body up, stays strong and fit, it takes discipline. Takes practice. He lives and walks and exists day after day, holding in that kind of rage, it takes discipline, it takes willpower. But you have to let it out some time, you have to let go. You have to kill. So you practice until you get it just right."

Search complete. Two results that match parameters given. First image on-screen.

"What is it?" Peabody demanded.

"Potentially? His practice sessions. Look at her. Same physical type as Maplewood. Same age group, same coloring, same basic build."

Peabody came in, mirroring Eve's earlier position by leaning over her shoulder. "No resemblance—beyond surface I mean—but yeah, same basic type."

"Computer, split screen for second image, list date on each."

Working . . . Task complete.

"Thumbs-up for McNab," Eve mumbled.

"Don't look like sisters," Peabody commented. "Cousins, maybe."

"Marjorie Kates," Eve read. "Age thirty-two. Unmarried, no kids, midtown address. Employed as restaurant manager. Reported missing by fiancé, April second of this year. Didn't come home from work. Lansing and Jones caught this one. Second is Breen Merriweather. Age thirty. Divorced, one child—son, age five—Upper East Side. Employed as a studio tech, Channel 75. Reported missing by childcare provider, June ten, this year. Didn't return home after her shift. Polinksi and Silk caught it.

"I need these files, Peabody. I need to talk to these detectives."

"On it."

Since Lansing and Jones worked out of Central, it only took trips on three glides and one elevator to get to their division.

She found them both at desks, facing each other.

"Detectives Lansing and Jones? Lieutenant Dallas, Detective Peabody. Appreciate the time."

"Lansing." The bull-chested, redheaded cop of about fifty stuck out a hand. "No problem, Lieutenant. You think one of yours is connected to one of ours."

"I need to check it out."

"Jones." The petite, thirtyish black woman shook Eve's hand, then Peabody's. "Fiancé, Royce Cabel, came in to make the report. She was only missing overnight, but the guy was a mess."

"Last seen when she left the restaurant—Appetito on East Fifty-eighth—at closing, about midnight, April first."

"She lived about three blocks away, usually walked back and forth. Guy's expecting her home by twelve-thirty, he says, but he falls asleep. When he wakes up, about two, she's not there. He flips, calls around to everybody he can think of. Then he's here, bright and early next morning to talk to the cops."

"She poofs three weeks before the wedding," Lansing continued. "So you look at a couple things. Maybe her feet got cold and she took off. Maybe they had a fight and he offs her, comes in to report to cover it up."

"But it doesn't play." Jones shook her head. "We got copies of the reports, our notes, witness statements, interviews for you. You can see everybody we talked to said Kates was hip-deep in wedding plans. She and Cabel had been cohabbing for about eighteen months. Got nothing on him that points to violence."

"Took a Truth Test. Didn't even blink when we suggested it."

"She got dead," Jones said. "That's my gut on it, Lieutenant."

"And we got nothing, until you buzzed us up."

"I don't know if we've got anything now.

Any problem if I talk to some of the people on your list?"

"Nope." Lansing pulled his lip. "How about a clue?"

"We're on the sexual homicide/mutilation in Central Park. Our vic's the same physical type as your MP. I'm pursuing the theory that he's done some practicing."

"Well, shit," Jones said.

"We can go by Polinski's and Silk's station on the way to see this Royce Cabel."

"How about the gyms with sweaty guys with thick necks?"

"We'll move on it."

Because it was faster, they squeezed on an elevator to ride down to garage level. Eve did her best to ignore the elbow wedged in her ribs. "I want us to give Nadine an interview."

"Because of the 75 connection?"

"Not just. I'm thinking it might grate our big, strong man to see three women dissing him on-screen. To know two women are heading the investigation."

"There's a thought."

Several people pushed their way off when

the doors opened. Eve glanced up, noted she had three levels to go. "Why don't we see if we can set up the interview later today?"

"At Central?"

"Yeah. Central Park. At last." Eve all but leaped out of the doors when they hit the garage.

"Dallas, wait!" Peabody grabbed her arm, dug in her heels. "I have something to tell you."

"Make it snappy."

"I want to say first, that in just a few moments, you're going to be overcome with a powerful urge to kiss me on the lips. I won't think less of you for it."

"Peabody, why, even in your wild, perverted dreams—dreams I want no part in or of—would I ever have the least compunction to kiss you on the lips?"

"Close your eyes."

Eve spoke quietly, almost casually. "Have you lost your fucking mind?"

"Okay, okay." Peabody pouted a little. "You're no fun." She crossed over to Eve's parking slot, spread her arms with a flourish and said: *"Voilà!"*

"What the hell is that?"

"That, Lieutenant, is your replacement vehicle. Pucker up."

Eve goggled. It was a rare thing to see the lieutenant goggle, and Peabody celebrated the moment with a snappy little tap dance.

Slowly, Eve walked around the sleek, navy blue sedan. It shone under the hard garage lights like a dignified jewel. The tires were big, black, and clean. The glass and chrome sparkled.

"This is not my vehicle."

"Is too."

"This is my vehicle?"

"Uh-huh." Peabody bobbed her head like a puppet on a happy string.

"Get out." Eve smacked her in the shoulder. "How'd you pull this off?"

"A little fast talk, some slight exaggeration, a lot of prevarication, and a little assistance from an e-fairy who knows how to hack."

"You got it through unethical and possibly illegal means."

"Damn straight."

Eve set her hands on her hips, looked Peabody square in the eyes. "This is such a proud moment for me. A proud, proud moment."

"Are you going to kiss me on the lips?"

"Not that proud."

"How about a peck on the cheek?"

"Get in the car."

"Your codes, Lieutenant." She handed them over, strolled around to the passenger side. "And you know what, Dallas? This bitch is *loaded.*"

"Oh yeah?" Eve slid into a seat, grinned when she didn't get the sensation of sitting on bumpy rock. "Well, let's see what she can do."

8

It rocked. not only was everything operational, but it *moved.* She could zip into vertical and down again, stream instead of muscle her way through traffic.

All comp systems were go, as she was told, politely, by a computerized voice before she even thought to ask. The voice addressed her as Lieutenant Dallas, informed her the outside temp was a pleasant seventy-eight degrees with winds from the south, southwest at a mild twelve per hour.

It offered to calculate the most convenient route to her destination, or destinations, with projected traffic patterns and ETAs.

It was a fricking miracle.

"You love this car," Peabody said with a smug little smile on her face.

"I do not love a vehicle. I appreciate and expect efficient machines and tools, machines and tools that assist me in doing my job rather than inconveniencing and hampering me."

She whipped around a trudging maxibus, threaded through a mired mass of Rapid Cabs, and for the hell of it, executed a quick vertical maneuver that shot them east.

"Okay. I *love* this car!"

"Knew you would." Peabody all but sang it.

"If they try to take it from me, I'll fight them. To the death. To the bloody death."

She smiled all the way to her destination.

Since Polinski was out on personal time, she dealt with Silk, a stubby fireplug of a man who sat at his desk munching on no-fat soy chips while he gave her background on the Missing Person's investigation.

Breen Merriweather had been reported missing by her neighbor and childcare provider on June tenth. She'd left the studio between midnight and twelve-fifteen. And vanished without a trace.

No serious romantic relationships, no

known enemies. She'd been in good health and good spirits and had been looking forward to an upcoming vacation—she'd planned to take her son to DisneyWorld East.

Eve took copies of files and notes.

"Tag Nadine," Eve told Peabody. "Let's do this setup at the castle. In an hour. Make it ninety minutes."

They met Royce Cabel at his apartment. He opened the door before they knocked, and looked at them with what Eve recognized as terrified hope.

"You found out something about Marjie."

"Mr. Cabel, as I told you when I contacted you, we're conducting a follow-up. I'm Lieutenant Dallas. This is my partner, Detective Peabody. Can we come in?"

"Yeah, sure. Yeah." He dragged a hand through his long, wavy brown hair. "I just thought—I wanted to meet you here instead of at work because I thought maybe you'd found something. Found her. And didn't want to tell me over the 'link."

He glanced around the room, blankly, then shook his head. "Sorry. I guess we should sit down. Ah, aren't Detectives Lansing and Jones still working?"

"They are. We're pursuing another angle. It would help us if you'd tell us what you know."

"What I know." He sat on a deep green sofa heaped with pretty pillows.

The apartment was painted a dull gold, and struck Eve as being female—the pillows, the soft, fancy throws, the sudden splashes of reds and dark blues.

"I feel like I don't know anything," he said after a moment. "She was working nights. That was going to change in June, when she took over as day manager. We'd be on the same schedule again."

"How long had she been working nights?"

"For about eight months." He rubbed his hands on his thighs as if he didn't know what else to do with them. "It was okay. She liked the work, and the restaurant's only a couple blocks away. I'd go in and have dinner at least once a week. And having her days free gave her lots of time to handle the wedding stuff. She was doing almost everything herself. Marjie loves planning."

"Did the two of you have any problems?"

"We didn't. I mean we did—everybody does—but we were in a real up phase. The wedding. Hell, I didn't have to do anything but show up because she had everything organized. We talked about starting a family."

His voice shook, and he cleared his throat, stared hard at the wall.

"Did she ever mention anyone coming into the restaurant who disturbed her? Anyone coming by here, or anywhere else?"

"No. I told the other detectives. If somebody'd been bothering Marjie, she'd have told me. If somebody'd pissed her off at work, she'd have told me. We talked all the time. I always waited up for her, and we'd hash out the day. She just didn't come home."

"Mr. Cabel—"

"I wish she'd just walked off." Emotions pitched into his voice. Traces of anger now, anger circling around the fear. "I wish she'd gotten freaked or fallen out of love with me or found somebody else or just got a goddamn wild hair. But she didn't. It's not Marjie. Something happened to her, something terrible. And I don't know what I'm going to do."

"Mr. Cabel, do you or Marjie belong to a health club or gym?"

"Huh?" He blinked, sucked in a breath. "Yeah, who doesn't? We, ah, we go to Able Bodies. We try to make it two, three times a week. Sundays for sure since we're both off. We'd do a couple hours, maybe, then have brunch in their juice bar."

Brunch in the juice bar didn't fit, Eve thought, and decided on another tack. Before she could speak, Peabody lifted one of the couch pillows.

"These are really beautiful. Unique. They look handcrafted."

"Marjie made them. She was always making something." He ran his hand over one of the pillows. "Used to call herself a craft addict."

Pop, Eve thought. "Would you know where she bought her supplies?"

"Her supplies? I don't get it."

"It's details, Mr. Cabel," Peabody told him. "Details help."

"It was one of the things we didn't do together." He mustered up a smile. "She'd dragged me along a few times, on her hunts, but I made her feel rushed, she said, because I was so obviously bored. She's got a little studio set up in the second bedroom. There's probably some record of where some of the stuff came from."

Eve rose. "Can we take a look?"

"Sure." He got up quickly, the enthusiasm for the new angle clear on his face. "It's right in here."

He led them into a small room, full of material and threads and ribbons. Fringes and framing and objects Eve couldn't begin to identify. It all appeared to be meticulously organized into groups. There were a couple of small machines, and a mini data and communication center.

"Can we turn this on?"

"Sure. Let me get it for you." He walked over to the d and c, booted it up.

"Peabody." Eve tipped her head toward the unit.

"She could make anything," Cabel continued, and wandered the room, touching fabrics. "The quilt on the bed, the folk art scattered around the apartment. The sofa out in the living area? She picked it up off the street, hauled it home, fixed it up, recovered it. One day, she's going to start her own business, do home decorating, or maybe run her own craft school. Something."

"Lieutenant? There's a transaction here for supplies, February 27, another March 14. Total Crafts."

Eve nodded, continued to riffle through wide baskets, painted boxes. And lifted out three rolls of corded ribbon. One in navy, one in gold. And one in red.

"He trolls the craft shops." Again, Eve crossed the park, her focus on the castle. "Why does a guy like that troll the craft shops?"

"He could have spotted them somewhere else, followed them there."

"No. Two women, their only known connection a hobby. One dead, one missing and presumed. I guarantee you when we finish with Nadine and go talk to Breen Merriweather's baby-sitter, we're going to find she did crafts. We're going to find she bought supplies, at one time or another, from Total Crafts, or one of the other locations either Maplewood or Kates used. He sees them there, they fit his requirements. He stalks them, studies them."

She tucked her thumbs in her pockets. "Then he lays in wait, and takes them. If he did Kates, he almost certainly had to have his own transpo. There's nowhere between the restaurant and the apartment where he could have raped, murdered, mutilated her, then hid the body. He had to do a snatch and grab, then take her somewhere."

"If we're right about Kates, then he changed his method for Maplewood."

Eve shook her head. "Not changed. Perfected. Kates was one of his trial runs. Might have been more before her. Sidewalk sleepers, runaways, junkies, whatever. Someone who wouldn't get reported missing, or was reported months before the grab. He had it down to a science when he killed Elisa Maplewood. He might have been working up to that for years."

"Happy thought."

"They represent somebody: mother, sister, lover, a woman who rejected him, refused him, abused him. Dominant female figure."

Why, she wondered, did the twisted tree of a murderer so often go back to the mother root? Did the gestation and birthing process come with the power to nurture or destroy?

"When we get him," Eve continued, "it's going to come out that she—this symbol—knocked him around or boo-hoo broke his heart or made him feel weak and helpless. So his defense lawyers will come along saying: Oh, he was damaged, poor sick son of a bitch. He's not responsible. And that's a pile of shit, that's a big, smelly pile of *bull*-shit. Because nobody's responsible for choking the life out of Elisa Maplewood but him. Nobody."

Peabody let the rant run, waited until she was sure it was over. "Preaching to the choir."

Eve drew it back in. "Yeah. Where the hell is Nadine? She doesn't show in five, we cancel. We need to follow up on Merriweather."

"We're a couple minutes early."

"I guess we are." Eve sat on the grass, drew her knees up, and studied the castle. "You ever skip around parks when you were a kid?"

"Sure." Glad the storm had passed, Peabody sat beside her. "Free-Agers, you know. I was a regular nature girl. You?"

"No. Couple of stints in what you could call summer camp." Run by state-hired Nazis, Eve thought, who regulated every breath. "This one's not so bad. You know it's still in the city, so it's okay."

"Not looking to make nature girl?"

"Nature'll kill you, just for the hell of it."

Eve glanced over and watched Nadine and her camera operator crossing to them. "Why would she wear those skinny heels when she knew she'd be hiking over grass?"

"Because they're jazzed, and make her legs look mag."

Eve supposed everything about Nadine looked mag, from her sweep of streaky blonde hair to the toes of her jazzed shoes. She had a foxy, angular face, observant green eyes, and a slim body that curved appropriately in her on-camera suit of power red.

She was smart, she was sneaky, she was cynical.

And for reasons Eve imagined neither of them fully understood, they'd become friends.

"Dallas. Peabody. Don't you two look relaxed and pastoral. Why don't you set up there?" She gestured to the camera. "I want the castle in the background. You got any real juice," she said to Eve, "I can take this live."

"No. And we're keeping it short. We could even say pithy."

"Pithy it is." Nadine took out a small compact to check her face, lifted a paper-thin sponge and dabbed her nose. "Who's leading off?"

"She is." Eve jerked a thumb at Peabody.

"I am?"

"Let's get to it." Nadine nodded to the camera, angled her body. Gave her shoulders a roll, her hair a little shake. And her easy smile turned into a cool, serious look.

"This is Nadine Furst, in Central Park with Lieutenant Eve Dallas and Detective Delia Peabody of the New York City Police and Security Department, Homicide Division. Behind us is Belvedere Castle, one of the city's most unique landmarks, and the site of a recent, violent murder. Elisa Maplewood, a woman who worked and lived only a short distance from here, a single mother of a four-year-old child, was assaulted near the very spot where we're standing. She was brutally raped and murdered. Detective

Peabody, as a key member of the investigative team handling Elisa Maplewood's murder, can you tell us what progress you've made in finding her killer?"

"We are actively pursuing all leads and utilizing all the resources at our disposal."

"Are you confident you'll make an arrest?"

Don't screw up, Peabody ordered herself. Don't screw up. "The case remains open and active. Lieutenant Dallas and I will continue to work toward identifying Ms. Maplewood's assailant, gathering evidence that will result in an arrest in order to bring this individual to justice."

"Can you tell us what specific leads you are pursuing?"

"I'm unable to discuss specific details of this investigation as such might taint the case we're building or affect the progress of said investigation."

"As a woman, Detective, do you feel this particular crime more personally?"

Peabody started to deny, then remembered part of the purpose of the interview. "As a cop, it's imperative to remain objective in every investigation. It's impossible not to feel, on a personal level, compassion and outrage for any victim of any crime, but that compassion and outrage can't be allowed to overcome objectivity and interfere. Because the victim must be our priority. As a woman, I feel that compassion and outrage on Elisa Maplewood's behalf. Like Lieutenant Dallas, I want the individual responsible for her suffering and pain—for the suffering and pain of her family, her friends—identified and punished."

"Do you agree, Lieutenant Dallas?"

"Yes, I do. A woman stepped out of her home, intending to walk her dog in the city's greatest park. Her life was taken from her, and that's enough for outrage. But it was taken viciously, violently, deliberately. As a cop, as a woman, I will pursue the man who took Elisa Maplewood's life, however long it takes, until he's brought to justice."

"How was she mutilated?"

"At this point, that detail of the crime and investigation is not for public consumption."

"Don't you believe in the public's right to know, Lieutenant?"

"I don't believe the public has a right to know everything. And I believe the media has the responsibility to respect the department's decision to hold certain details back.

We don't do so to deprive or deny the public of their rights, but to preserve the integrity of an investigation.

"Nadine," she said and had Nadine blinking. Eve never referred to her by her first name on-air. "We're women in what could be considered high-powered professions. However much a crime like this disturbs us, a crime in this case specifically targeted at women, we have to maintain that professionalism in order to do the job we've signed up to do. And in this case, the case of Elisa Maplewood, it will be women who stand for her, and who work toward seeing that her killer is punished to the fullest extent of the law."

Nadine started to speak again, but Eve shook her head. "That's it. Camera off."

"I have more questions."

"That's it," Eve repeated. "Let's take a walk."

"But—" Nadine only sighed as Eve was already hiking away. "Slow it down. Heels here."

"Your choice, pal."

"You wear a weapon, I wear heels. Tools of our respective trades." She hooked her arm through Eve's to slow her down. "So, what was that last bit about? *Eve.*"

"A personal message to the killer. Off-record here, Nadine."

"Tell me how he mutilated her. Off-record, Dallas. It's driving me crazy."

"He cut out her eyes."

"Jesus." Nadine breathed in, stared off into the trees. "Oh, Jesus. Was she already dead?"

"Yeah."

"Thank God for that. So you've got some psychotic out there who has a big hate on for women? Not Maplewood specifically."

"That's my working theory."

"And the reason you suggested the interview. Us three girls. Clever of you."

"Tell me what you know about Breen Merriweather."

"Breen?" Nadine's head snapped around. "Oh God, oh God, did you find her?" She gripped Eve's arm now. "Is she dead? Did this bastard kill her, too?"

"No, she hasn't been found. I don't know if she's dead, but I suspect she is, and I believe it might be connected. What do you know about her?"

"I know she was a nice, hard-working

woman who adored her son . . . Jesus, is he targeting single mothers?"

"I don't think so, no."

"Let me take a second." She walked a few feet away, hugged her arms. "We weren't best pals or anything like that. More a working friendship. I liked her, and appreciated her efficiency. I saw her, evening shift, the night she disappeared. I left the station about seven. I know she was on till midnight, handling the eleven o'clock. Everything I've heard is secondhand, but it's reliable."

She turned back. "She clocked out, left the station just after her shift ended. She would have taken the subway home, that's what she always did. It's just three blocks east. One of the guys saw her heading out, yelled good night. She waved to him. As far as I know he's the last one in the station who saw her. He said she was walking east, toward the subway."

"Did she do crafts?"

"Crafts?"

"You know what crafts are, Nadine."

Interest, keen, replaced the sorrow. "As a matter of fact, she did. She did a lot of handwork, always had a bag of supplies with her, and some project going. She used to work on it during breaks or wait time. Is that the connection?"

"It's looking that way. You know any big, bodybuilder-type guys? Anybody like that at 75?"

"We're desk jockeys and faces." She shook her head. "We on-air types work out, body-sculpt, whatever it takes to keep trim, but the public doesn't want their news and entertainment from big bruisers. We got some burly techs, and some overweight drones, but none of them would qualify as bodybuilders. Is that your line on him?"

"Another working theory."

"I need a full interview when this is wrapped, Dallas. If Breen was part of this thing, I need to do a full interview with you and Peabody for the station. She was one of ours."

"You'd want one anyway."

"I would." Nadine smiled a little. "But if this hits home, I need it. Fuck objectivity. It's personal."

"I hear that."

* * *

To save time, Eve requested Breen Merriweather's childcare provider meet them at Breen's apartment. Eve used her master to gain access, and stepped into a small, cheerful set of rooms with air stale from disuse.

"Her family's paying the rent." Annalou Harbor, the sixtyish provider, looked around the apartment with sad eyes. "I still come in once a week, water her plants. Aired it out a couple times, but . . . I live upstairs."

"Yes, ma'am."

"Her husband took Jesse, her little boy. I miss that baby. Such a sweetie." She gestured to a framed photo that showed a grinning little boy in a sideways ball cap. "Breen would never have left him. Not while there was breath in her body. So I know there isn't. I know she's dead. That's why you're here. You're Homicide. I recognize you. I've seen you on-screen."

"We don't know, Mrs. Harbor. But we're pursuing—"

"Don't pad it for me, Lieutenant Dallas." The tone was firm, and just a little prim. "I'm not a gossip, and I'm not looking for some sort of twisted excitement. I loved that girl like she was my own, and I can help you more if you don't try to dance around it."

"We believe it's highly possible that she's dead, Mrs. Harbor, and that her death may be connected with another case we're investigating."

"The murder in Central Park, the rape-murder. I keep up." She pressed her lips together until they turned white, but she didn't crumble. "What can I do to help you?"

"Where does Ms. Merriweather keep her craft supplies?"

"In here." She led the way into a tiny room equipped with two counters, several hand-painted cabinets, and the machines Eve was now accustomed to seeing in such places.

"See, she set it up as an activity room, for her and Jesse. His toys and games over there, her supplies here. That way they could be together when they had leisure time. Breen liked making things. She knit me a beautiful throw last Christmas."

Eve opened cupboards while Peabody tackled communications and data. There were several samples of the corded ribbon.

"I got hits on Total Crafts, and a couple of the others on the list," Peabody announced.

"Mrs. Harbor, we're going to need to take her 'links and computer, and some other items into evidence. Can you give me the contact number for her next of kin?"

"Take what you need. Her mother told me to cooperate with the police in any and every way. I'll get in touch with her."

"My partner will give you a receipt."

"All right. It'll be easier for them, for all of us, to know." She looked around the room, and though her lips trembled once, she firmed them. "However bad it is, it'll be easier to know for certain."

"Yes, ma'am, it will. I realize the other detectives interviewed you, but I'd like to ask you some questions."

"That's fine. Can we sit down? I'd like to sit down."

"It's hard to think," Peabody began when they were back in the car, "that if these three women are linked, that nobody connected to them saw this guy. If he's the physical description we believe, you wouldn't see him blending."

"He's careful."

"Are we going to try another push with Celina?"

"Not yet. I need think time."

She settled down to it in her office, her feet on her desk, her head back. She visualized the pattern. He wouldn't have expected them to recognize the pattern so quickly, because he wouldn't have expected the police to link the murder with the disappearances.

But if—when—he killed again, he'd know they'd see the connections between victims. It didn't worry him.

Why?

The murder weapon was available at the shops the murder victim, and the suspected victims, had frequented. It wouldn't take much longer for the exact location to be identified. Did he think, because it was a fairly common item, the cops couldn't nail the source through basic lab work? Possibly.

But even so, he'd have to believe the investigation would include the point of purchase. Even if someone else had bought the ribbon, he'd been inside or within sight of the store or stores, in order to select his victim.

But he wasn't worried about it any more than it seemed he'd worried about being seen or caught assaulting Elisa in a public park.

Because, like many psychopaths, he believed he was invulnerable? That he wouldn't be caught, or because a part of him was begging to be caught?

Stop me. Find me, catch me.

Either way, wasn't he enjoying the risk factor? Wasn't he aroused by the chances he took?

Arousal: in the selection, in the trolling, in the stalking. All that anticipation building.

Gratification: physical violence, sexual violence, murder committed with an item considered more traditionally female, then left on the victim like a decoration.

Enjoyment: possessing the strength to overpower and control and kill. And more, the strength to bear the weight of the dead, more than the average man could manage.

Final satisfaction: removal of the eyes. *Owning* the eyes, Eve thought. Arranging the body in a specifically chosen manner and location.

He'd be back to the arousal stage again. If not now, soon.

She swung her legs off, wrote up her daily, then gathered what she needed for an evening session at home.

She went out to Peabody's desk. "I'm hitting some of the gyms, working my way uptown toward home. If you're with me, you'll have to get yourself back downtown when we call it a day."

"I'm not missing a chance to ogle and interrogate big, sweaty guys. I might cut out at six, though, unless we've got something. McNab and I have a packing date tonight."

"A packing date?"

"Yeah, we've got to get some serious packing done at my place. We'll be moving into our place in a few days. Our place." She patted her belly. "Still gives me a little bit of the jitters."

"You can't imagine what it gives me," Eve said, and walked away when Peabody snorted.

9

They spent a couple of hours talking to men with big pecs and tree-trunk legs in workout facilities that carved out the frills and concentrated on the testosterone.

Peabody's main complaint was that a large percentage of the members seemed to be more interested in ogling themselves or each other rather than a certain police detective.

It was a fishing expedition, Eve thought as she swung toward home. And she didn't feel any appreciable tugs on her line. Yet.

She'd start running names, that's all. The few hundred of them she'd compiled from membership and subscription lists. See if she got any pops on sex crimes. He hadn't started down his current path yesterday.

He'd be single, so that would eliminate more. He wasn't gay, or hadn't recognized himself as such. He didn't work nights; that's when he killed.

No human hair recovered on the victim or from the murder or dump sites. Had he sealed up that thoroughly, or did he—like some of the obsessive body guys she'd seen today—regularly remove his head and body hair?

She could almost, almost, get a picture of him in her head.

Trying to define it, she turned toward the gates of home. Then was forced to stomp on the brakes when they remained shut.

"Summerset, you prick."

She lowered the window, barked into the intercom. "Open the damn gates, you rat-faced, pointy-assed—"

"One moment, please. Your voice print is being identified."

"I'll give you my voice print. I'll give you my voice print all over your—"

She broke off again, hissing as the gates slid open. "Thinks he's got a new trick up his sleeve to bust my chops. Thinks he's going to keep me stewing outside the gates now while he runs his little game. If he had balls, I'd kick them into his throat."

She slammed out of the car, jogged up the steps and burst into the house ready to rumble.

"If you wish automated entry, Lieutenant," Summerset said before she could spew, "you'll need to inform us when you intend to arrive in a strange vehicle. One not yet scanned and cleared for security. Otherwise, as you know, you're required to announce yourself so the system can read and verify your voice identification or access codes."

Shit. He had her there.

"It's not a strange vehicle. It's my vehicle."

He gave her his sour smile. "Come up in the world, have we?"

"Just blow me." Annoyed at the missed opportunity to pound on him, she started up the stairs.

"You have guests. Roarke is entertaining Mavis and Leonardo on the west terrace, first level. I'm about to serve canapés."

"Goodie." But since the half candy bar was now a far, fond memory, she could admit, privately, that anything involving food sounded fine to her.

She wound her way through the house, and found everyone sipping drinks. Not exactly, she corrected. Mavis was gesturing with her glass as she bubbled, more frothy than the lemon fizz in her hand.

She stood on the patio in a pair of shimmering green boots that ran up to her knees like a thin coat of paint where they met equally tight pants in red, no blue, no red.

Eve narrowed her eyes as the pants changed hues every time Mavis wiggled, which was always. The shimmering green top floated down to her hips where a lot of beads dangled.

Her hair was red today, and to Eve's relief stayed that way even when she danced in place. She'd left it down so it trailed along her butt with the ends picking up that same shimmering green, as if they'd been dipped in paint.

The two men watched her, Roarke with a bemused and affectionate smile, and Leonardo with open adoration.

Roarke shifted his gaze, winked at Eve.

Rather than interrupt, Eve crossed over to where a wine bottle and glasses were set up. She poured herself a drink, then crossed the patio to sit on the arm of Roarke's chair.

"Dallas!" Mavis threw out her arms, and somehow didn't spill a single fizzing drop. "Did you just get here?"

"Just."

"I didn't know if we'd get to see you. But we wanted to come by so I could give Summerset a smoochie."

"Please, you're going to make me sick."

Mavis only laughed. "Then Roarke came in right behind us, so we're having a little hang. We're getting snacks."

Her eyes, green to go with the shimmer, danced.

"So I hear." Eve leaned around Roarke. "How's it going?" she asked Leonardo.

"Couldn't be better." He beamed at Mavis. He was a giant of a man, with skin of coppery gold. A wide face with dark eyes that were currently accented with a sweeping line of silver studs at each corner.

He wore boots as well, pale blue that rode up his calves. There his loose sapphire pants sort of poofed into them, reminding Eve of pictures she'd seen of—she thought—Arabia.

"Oh, boy, here's food!" Mavis made the dash over as Summerset rolled out a two-tiered trolley, laden with trays of fancy appetizers and sweets. "Summerset, if it wasn't for Leonardo, I'd scoop you right up and make you my love slave."

He smiled, a wide, toothy smile. Fearing nightmares, Eve turned away and stared into her wine.

"I believe I have several of your favorites here. You're eating for two."

"Tell me! I'm like an oinker every five minutes. Oooh, that's the salmon thingy with the stuff! This is just mag."

She popped it into her mouth. "I just love eating."

"You sit down now, honeypot." Leonardo walked over, rubbed her shoulder. "I'm going to fix you a plate."

"Cuddle bear," she cooed. "He totally spoils me. This pregs business is the top deal of the day. You gotta look."

Even as Mavis reached for the hem of her shirt, Eve was curling into herself and wincing. "Oh, Mavis, I don't . . . oh well."

There was the belly, in all its glory and accented by an interlinking trio of belly-button rings.

"Now check this." Still holding the shirt up, Mavis turned to the side. "See? It's poking. I know I said it was poking before. You know like five seconds after I found out I was knocked up, but now it completely is."

Eve tilted her head, pursed her lips. There was a little bit of a slope in that area. "Are you pushing it out?"

"No. Feel."

Eve wasn't quite quick enough to whip her hand behind her back. "I don't wanna. Don't make me touch it again."

"You can't hurt it." She pressed Eve's hand to her belly. "Solid baby."

"That's good, Mavis." Her palm was going to go damp any second. "Really good. You're feeling okay?"

"At the summit. Everything is totally uptown."

"You look beautiful," Roarke told her. "And cliché or not, you glow."

"I feel like I'm sending off waves." She laughed and bounced to a chair. "I still get the weepies sometimes, but they're happy weepies mostly. Like Leonardo and I were talking a couple days ago about how Peabody and McNab are moving into the building soon, and we're going to be neighbors, at least until we get a bigger place, and I just flooded."

She took the plate Leonardo brought her and cuddled up with him on the padded love seat. "So what do you think they want for, like, a housewarming?"

"Don't they have regulation temp control?"

"Jeez, Dallas." With a giggle, Mavis popped something else in her mouth. "Housewarming. You know, where people move into a new place and you get them a gift."

"Hold on. You have to give them a gift for moving?"

"Uh-huh. Plus they're shacking, so it should be a couple thing." She ate another canapé, fed one to Leonardo.

"Why does there have to be a gift for every damn thing?" Eve complained.

"Retail conspiracy." Roarke patted her knee.

"I bet it is," Eve said darkly. "I just bet it is."

"Anyway." Mavis waved it all away. "We really came by—and we're all pumped that you're both here—because we wanted to talk to you about the baby."

"Mavis, since you got pregnant, when haven't you wanted to talk about the baby?" Eve leaned over, took a canapé from her plate. "Not that there's anything wrong with that."

"Yeah, but this is a specific thing, that involves you."

"Me?" Eve licked her thumb and decided to steal another loaded cracker from Mavis's plate.

"Uh-huh. We want you to be my backup coach."

"You're taking up baseball?" Eve bit into the salmon thingy with the stuff, and decided it wasn't half bad. "Shouldn't you wait until you get the kid out of there?"

"No. Labor and delivery coach. You'd back up Leonardo when I have the baby."

Eve choked on the canapé and turned white.

"Take a drink, darling," Roarke said with a laugh in his voice. "Put your head between your knees if you feel dizzy."

"Shut up. Are you talking about . . . like, *being* there? In the actual place at the actual time? In the same room as . . . it."

"You can't coach me through it if you're in Queens, Dallas. You gotta have a backup coach, somebody who takes the class, learns about the breathing and the positions and the . . . stuff. Daddy Bear's first string, but you have to have one on the bench."

"Can I just stay on the bench? Outside?"

"I need you there." Tears swam into her eyes until they shimmered brighter than her boots. "You're my best friend in the whole universe. I need you with me."

"Oh man. Okay, okay. Don't flood. I'll do it."

"We feel," Leonardo said, and offered Mavis a green cloth to dab at her eyes, "that first for friendship there's no one who we want to share this miracle with more. Added to that, you're the most steady and solid people we know. In a crisis, you'd keep your heads."

"Our heads?" Eve repeated.

"We want Roarke there, too." Mavis sniffed into her cloth.

"Me? There?"

Eve turned her head, and saw—with pleasure—the rare sight of utter panic on his face. "Not so damn funny now, is it, ace?"

"We're permitted, even encouraged, to

have family present," Leonardo explained. "You're our family."

"Ah, I'm not sure it's quite proper for me to be . . . to see Mavis in that condition. Under those . . . circumstances."

"Get out." Sniffles forgotten, Mavis giggled and tapped Roarke playfully on the arm. "Anybody with a vid player's seen me mostly naked. And this isn't about the proper. It's about family. We know we can count on you. Both of you."

"Of course." Roarke swallowed a great deal of wine. "Of course, you can."

When they were alone, sitting in the soft light of dusk with the candles Summerset had lit flickering, Roarke reached out, gripped Eve's hands in his.

"They could change their minds. It's still months away, and they could easily change their minds and want this . . . event to be a private one between them."

She looked at him as if he'd sprouted a second head. "Private? Private? This is *Mavis* we're dealing with."

He shut his eyes. "God pity us."

"And it's just going to get . . . more." She

pulled away, sprang up. "Before you know it, before you know it she's going to want *us* to deliver the thing. They'll want to do it here, in our bedroom or something, with cameras—live feed to her fans. And us pulling the thing out of her."

Utter and genuine horror leaped into his eyes. "Stop it, Eve. Stop it now."

"Yeah, live feed, that's Mavis to the ground. And we'll do it." She spun back to him. "We'll do it because she's just sucking us in. Sucking us in like some . . ." She windmilled her arms. "Like some big sucking thing. Some big pregnant sucking thing."

"Let's just calm down." With the images Eve painted playing in his head, Roarke took out a cigarette. Lighting it, he ordered himself to think rationally. "Surely you've done this sort of thing before. You're a cop. You must have at least been on hand during a birthing."

"Uh-uh. Nope. No. Once, when I was still on patrol, we had to take this woman into a health center. Jesus, she was screaming like somebody was ramming steel spikes into her crotch."

"Merciful Jesus, Eve, could you dispense with some of the imagery?"

But she was wound up now. "And something gives way in there, and stuff's pouring out of her. Fluids, you know?"

"I don't, no. And I don't care to."

"Made a hell of a mess in the cruiser. But at least she had the decency—the common courtesy—to wait until she was inside, with the doctor or midwife or whoever the hell before she pushed it out."

For a moment, Roarke pressed his fingers to his temples. "We can't think about this anymore. We'll go mad if we do. We have to think about something else." He stabbed the cigarette out. "Entirely."

She drew one long, shaky breath. "You're right. I've got work."

"Murder. Much better. Let me help. I beg you."

She had to laugh. "Sure. It's the least I can do. Step into my office."

She took his hand, filling him in as they went inside and up.

"How much do you intend to use this Celina Sanchez?"

"I'd like to keep it minimal." She sat at her desk, kicked back to prop her feet on the edge. "She's got the Dimatto seal of approval, and she's even likable enough. I'd even call her steady. But it's not a good fit for me. Still, she's cued in to this, so I can't ignore what she can give me."

"I knew a man who kept a sensitive on staff and wouldn't make a decision without her. Worked well enough for him, as it happened."

"You got any?"

"I do. Precogs, clairvoyants, sensitives. I don't dismiss what they've been given, or what they can offer. But I prefer making my own decisions in the final run. You'll do the same."

"So far, her—let's call it intel—isn't adding much to my basic, nonsensitive cop work. But it matches it."

She frowned, mentally picking her way through the data and speculation. "Impressions we could pick up at the kill site, and the ones we got leading to the dump site indicate a size fifteen shoe. We may be able to make the tread, or at least a partial if Dickhead in the lab works some magic. Ground and grass were dry, but when he added her weight, he left some impressions."

"Well, that's a large foot you've got there, but not all men with big feet are big men."

"Big enough to leave impressions on dry grass, strong enough to lift and carry a hundred and thirty pounds of deadweight. You've got to speculate, do the probabilities. And when you do, you come up with a man between two hundred and seventy and eighty pounds. My guess would be a height of between six four and six eight."

He nodded, imagined he was building a picture in his mind similar to the one in hers. "And if you take it further, you assume that kind of strength and body type comes from discipline and dedication."

"Body sculpting procedures can give you the build, but they can't give you the strength."

"Hence, your foray into the world of musclemen."

"Reminded me I like my guys more on the lanky side."

"Lucky for me."

"I can't find any connection between the two missing and presumed and my vic, other than their predilection for fussy stuff and frequenting at least some of the same outlets for supplies."

"I could spare you time and look deeper there."

"That's what I was thinking."

"You can't buy a fifteen shoe just anywhere," Roarke continued. "You'd have to special order, or use a specialty outlet. For that matter, if your man is as described, he wouldn't be able to buy anything off the rack."

"Right. He'd need Enormous Guys 'R' Us, or the like."

"Catchy," Roarke mused. "I'll keep it in mind if I ever open a specialty retail outlet of that nature."

"I'm going to do a search and locate on specialty retail outlets of that nature," she said, mimicking his accent and making him grin. "Tonight."

"Well then, we should both be busy enough to keep our minds off things best not thought about. Before we go to our respective corners, tell me this: Why does he do it?"

"Control. Abuse is always about control. Rape is about control, and at its core, so is murder. Even if the motive for murder is greed, jealousy, self-preservation, rage, or entertainment, it still comes down to control."

"All crime comes down to it at its base, don't you think? I'll take this from you, be it your wallet or your life, because I can."

"Why did *you* steal when you did?"

A hint of a smile played around his mouth. "All manner of selfish and entertaining reasons, Lieutenant. Certainly to possess something I hadn't had, before I took it for myself. And the pleasure of doing so successfully."

"To punish the person who possessed it first?"

He inclined his head, acknowledging the point. "No. They were, in most cases, purely incidental to the goal."

"There's the difference. Doesn't paint the thief white, but murder often roots in punishment. I think it does here. Someone controlled him, punished him. A female, and now he's showing her who's boss. That's why he left her naked. She probably wasn't naked when he raped her. Tore her clothes—fibers still on her indicate—but he wouldn't have bothered to strip her down. He bothered after because it added humiliation."

She paused, considered. "He didn't mutilate the female part of her, which expresses another kind of rage and control. It wasn't sexual, but it was personal. He strangles, not with his hands—and odds are he could have snapped her neck like a twig—but he uses the ribbon. So it means something to him. The red cord is also personal. He takes her eyes, carefully, so he can blind her. Naked and blind, more humiliation. But he takes them so he can have that part of her. Does she watch him? I think, somehow, he wants her to watch him. Because he's in charge now."

"Endlessly fascinating," he replied.

"What?"

"Watching you work." He came around the desk, lifted her chin, kissed her lightly. "And there's nothing nonsensitive about it. I'll just put together a meal before we settle in."

"That'd be good."

While he went into the kitchen off her office, she set up a second murder board. To this one she added pictures of Marjorie Kates and Breen Merriweather.

She was standing, studying them when

Roarke came back in. He set a plate on her desk. "They're yours now, too."

"Yeah. I'm afraid they are."

"Attractive women. Comfortably attractive rather than stunning. It'll be the hair, won't it? It's the hair that's the greatest similarity."

"Build's close, too. Average build. Caucasian women around thirty with a nice average build and long light brown hair. That's a big pool for him to fish in."

"Not so big when you add in the other factors."

"No, that shrinks it. They have to poke around craft shops, and they have to be out, alone, sometime at night. He works them at night. Still gives him plenty to choose from."

She stepped back. "I'd better get to it before he picks another one."

When she went to her desk, she was delighted to see he'd brought out a burger and fries—even though there were a few little broccoli trees alongside them. She could ditch the broccoli—how would he know? But then she'd feel guilty. Since she was more ambivalent toward broccoli than guilt, she ate it first, to get it out of the way, while she started a search for retail shops that specialized in large men.

More than she'd expected, Eve noted as she poured coffee from the pot Roarke had set beside her plate. Upscale—well, think about it, she reminded herself—where else did the Arena Ball players, the basketball dudes, and tall or porky rich guys drop their fashion bucks?

There were midline and discount and, she discovered, design and tailoring services offered by a couple of the major department stores and a number of boutiques.

Didn't exactly narrow the field.

When she altered the search to shoes, it bounced a few out, and tossed a few new sources in.

He could buy primarily or even exclusively online, she thought as she bit into her burger. A lot of people did. But wouldn't he—a man who worked hard to build his body, who was proud of the results—want to select his clothes in real life? Check himself out in the mirror, have some fawning clerk tell him how good he looked?

A lot of projection, she admitted, out of a scarcity of solid facts.

But when she did a geographic run, she

found a shop called The Colossal Man was two crosstown blocks from Total Crafts.

"Isn't that interesting?" She nabbed a fry. "Computer, list any gyms currently in this case file located within a six-block parameter of Total Crafts."

Working . . .

She ate another fry.

Health and fitness facilities in that sector include Jim's Gym and Bodybuilders.

"Display map on wall screen, applicable sector. Highlight locations of retail shops and gyms."

She rose, the burger in one hand, to walk closer to the wall screen. Sometimes, she thought, you saw a pattern because you wanted to, and sometimes it was just there.

He'd walked those streets, she was sure of it. Walked from gym to shop to shop. Because he lived or worked, or both, in that sector. This was his neighborhood. People saw him there, knew him there.

And so would she.

She walked into Roarke's office where he sat at his desk enjoying what looked like seafood pasta while he worked. His laser fax was humming, and his comp signaled an incoming.

"You've got stuff coming in."

"Project reports I'm expecting," he said without looking up. "They can wait. I don't have anything for you yet."

"Put that on hold a minute, come take a look at this."

He brought his coffee with him, went with her into her office.

Eve gestured to the wall screen. "What do you see?"

"A sector of the West Village. And a pattern."

"So do I. I want to start with residences in this sector. Before you say anything, no, I can't even guess how many there must be. It's a long shot, a really long shot, but . . ."

"He may live there. So you start with residential, get owner and tenant lists, eliminate families, couples, single women, and fine-tune it down to men who live alone."

"You should've been a cop."

He shifted his gaze from the screen to her face. "Don't I have enough horror in my head with potential midwifery without you heaping more in there?"

"Sorry. It'll take a lot of time. He may live a block outside my parameter. Hell, he may live five blocks out and work inside it. Or work one block out. Or he could just do his shopping and bodybuilding there and live in fricking New Jersey."

"But you go with the percentages, and the percentages say here."

"It'd go quicker if you gave me a hand with the runs."

Nodding, he continued to study the screen. "Your place or mine?"

When Eve crawled into bed just after one in the morning, she knew she was on the scent. And hoped, could only hope, he waited long enough for her to track him down.

"Two months between Kates, Breen, and Maplewood. If he sticks with that schedule, I'll have him before he kills another one."

"Shut it down, Lieutenant." Roarke drew her in so her head settled against his shoulder. She rarely had the dreams when he kept her close. "Shut it down, and sleep."

"I'm close. I know I'm close," she murmured and drifted off.

He was waiting for her. She would come. She always walked this way. Briskly, her head down, her steps nearly soundless in her gel-soled shoes. She'd have put them on after her shift, after she'd taken off the whore shoes she wore to serve the men who leered at her over their drinks.

Whatever she wore, she remained a whore.

She'd walk by, head down, and the streetlights would shine on her hair. It would look almost gold. Almost.

People would think: That's a pretty woman, a nice, quiet pretty woman, going about her business. But they didn't know. He knew what was inside the shell. Bitter, black, and dark.

He could feel it rising in him now as he anticipated her. Rage and pleasure, fear and joy. You'll look at me now, you bitch.

And we'll see how you like it, see how you like it.

Thought she was so pretty. Liked to parade and pose in front of the mirror without her clothes. Or parade and pose for the men she let touch her.

Won't look so pretty when I'm done.

He slipped a hand into his pocket, felt the long length of ribbon.

Red was her favorite. She liked to wear red.

He saw her, as he once had. Screaming, screaming, naked but for the red ribbon she'd worn around her throat. Red as his blood when she'd beaten him. Beaten him until he'd passed out.

Only to wake in the black. In the dark, in the locked room.

She'd be the one to wake in the black now. Blind in hell.

There she was . . . there she was now, walking along in her brisk way, head down.

His heart thundered in his chest as she came closer.

She turned, as she always did, through the iron gates and into the pretty park.

For an instant, just one trip of that heart, her head came up. And there was fear and shock and confusion in her eyes when he leaped out of the shadows.

She opened her mouth to scream, and his fist broke her jaw.

Her eyes rolled back to white, to blind, as he dragged her away from the lights.

He had to slap her several times to bring her around. She had to be awake for it, awake and aware.

He kept his voice down—he was no fool—but he said what he needed to say as he used his fists on her.

How do you like it now, bitch? Who's the boss now, whore?

And there was both shame and unspeakable delight in ramming his body into hers. She didn't fight, only lay limp, and that was a disappointment.

She'd struggled before, and sometimes she'd begged. That was better.

Still, when he pulled the cord around her neck, when he yanked it tight and saw her eyes bulge, the pleasure was so keen he thought he, too, might die of it.

Her heels drummed, soft little thumps on the grass. Her body convulsed, and brought his—at last, at last—to completion.

"Go to hell." He panted it out while he stripped off her clothes. "Go to hell now, where you belong."

He stuffed her clothes in the bag he'd

brought with him, then hooked the strap crossways over his massive chest.

He picked her up as if she weighed nothing. And he reveled in his strength, in the power it gave him.

He carried her to the bench he'd selected, so lovely under the big, shady tree, so close to the dignified fountain. There he laid her out, carefully bringing her hands together, tucking them up between her breasts.

"There now. There now, Mother, don't you look nice? Would you like to see?"

He was grinning, a mad grin that all but burst through the thick layers of sealant he wore. "Why don't I help you with that?"

So saying, he took the scalpel from his pocket, and set to work.

10

When her bedside 'link signaled, Eve rolled toward the sound, said: Shit, crap, damn it, when she fumbled in the dark.

"Lights on, ten percent," Roarke called out.

Eve dragged a hand through her hair, shook her head to clear sleep. "Block video," she ordered. "Dallas."

"He's killing her. He's killing her."

The voice was so thin and breathy, Eve needed the readout to identify. "Celina. Pull yourself together. Pull it together and give me a clear report."

"I saw . . . I saw like the other. Oh, God. It's too late. It's already too late."

"Where?" She leaped out of bed, tossed

her voice toward the 'link as she raced for clothes. "Central Park? Is he in the park?"

"Yes. No. A park. Smaller. Gated. Buildings. Memorial Park!"

"Where are you?"

"I—I'm at home. I'm in bed. I can't stand what's in my head."

"Stay there. Understand me. Stay where you are."

"Yes. I—"

"End transmission," Eve snapped, and cut off Celina's wild weeping.

"Will you call it in?" Roarke asked.

"I'll check it out myself first. I should say we'll check it out," she amended as he was up and dressing as she was.

"Celina?"

"She'll have to deal." Eve strapped on her weapon. "We all have to deal with the stuff in our heads. Let's move."

She let him drive. It might have irked that he handled a vehicle—any vehicle—with more skill than she, but it wasn't the time to quibble about it.

It wasn't the time, she admitted, to quibble about psychics either. She yanked out her communicator and requested a patrol to report to Memorial Park to check out a possible assault.

"Look for a male, between six four and six eight, muscular build. Approximately two-seventy. If found, detain only. Consider said individual armed and dangerous."

Eve leaned forward, as if to give them more velocity as they streaked toward southern Manhattan. "She could be seeing something that's going to happen, not that has. It could be—what do you call it?"

"Precognition."

"Yeah." But there was a heaviness in her belly that told her otherwise. "I'm close. Goddamn it, I know I'm on the right track."

"If he's killed tonight, he didn't wait two months."

"Maybe he never has."

They chose the west entrance, off Memorial Place, and pulled up behind the black-and-white snugged to the curb.

"How many ways in and out of this?" Eve asked. "Three, four?"

"About that, at a guess. I don't know for sure. It's only about a block square, I think. One of the smaller and more tasteful of the original WTC memorials."

She crossed the sidewalk and, drawing

her weapon, moved through the stone archway that led into the green.

There were benches, a small pond. Big trees, plots of flowers, and a large bronze statue depicting firefighters raising a flag.

She moved past it, and heard the retching.

Swiveling toward the sound, she walked quickly south and saw the uniform on his hands and knees, puking into a bed of red and white flowers.

"Officer—" But she saw the bench a few feet away, and what was on it. "Deal with him," she told Roarke and walked to the second uniform who was holding his communicator.

She had her badge up. "Dallas."

"Officer Queeks, Lieutenant. Found her just a minute ago. I was about to call it in. We didn't see anyone. Just her. To ascertain death, I checked her pulse. She's still warm."

"I want this scene secured." She glanced back. "Is he going to do us any good?"

"He'll be okay, Lieutenant. Rookie," he added with a small, pained smile. "We've all been there."

"Get him on his feet, Queeks. Secure the

scene and do a sweep of this park. Carefully. This isn't where he killed her. There'll be another site. I'll call it in."

She drew out her communicator. "Dispatch, this is Dallas, Lieutenant Eve."

"Acknowledged."

"Homicide, single victim, female. Location Memorial Park, southwest sector. Contact Peabody, Detective Delia, and crime scene."

"Acknowledged, Dallas, Lieutenant Eve. Dispatch out."

"You'll want this," Roarke said from behind her, and offered her a field kit.

"Yeah. I need you to stay back." She sealed up, hooked on a recorder.

He watched her approach the victim, begin to record the scene visually and verbally.

It was fascinating to watch her work, he thought again. And sometimes it was unspeakably sad.

There was pity in her eyes, and there was anger. She wouldn't know it showed, and he doubted anyone but himself could see it. But it was there, inside her as she put a madman's latest work on record.

She'd study the dead, he thought, and the details. She'd miss nothing. But it wouldn't only be murder she'd see. She'd see the human. That made all the difference.

A little more slender than the others, Eve thought. Not as curvy. More delicate, and maybe just a bit younger. But still in the ballpark. Long, light brown hair—a little bit of a wave, but nearly straight. Had probably been pretty, too, though you wouldn't know it now. Not now that her face was ruined.

The beating she'd sustained was more severe than Maplewood's. He was enjoying that part more, she thought. He was less able to control himself.

Punish her. What she stood for.

Destroy her. What she stood for.

Whoever this woman was, it hadn't been she he'd killed. Whose face had he seen when he'd tightened the cord around her neck? Whose eyes had stared back at him?

When the position of the body, the visual injuries were on record, she drew the hands apart to run prints.

"Lieutenant!" Queeks called from her right. "I think we've got your kill site."

"Secure it. Block it off, Queeks. I don't want anyone walking around on my scene."

"Yes, sir."

"Victim is identified through fingerprints as Lily Napier, age twenty-eight. Listed address is 293 Vesey Street, apartment 5C."

You had been pretty, Lily, Eve thought as she studied the ID picture on her screen. Soft, slight. A little shy.

"Employed O'Hara's Bar and Grill, Albany Street. Walking home from work, weren't you, Lily? It's not very far. Saves the transpo fare, and it's a warm night. It's your neighborhood. You'd walk through the park, and then you'd be home."

She fit on goggles, examined the hands, the nails. Death hadn't yet leeched all the heat from her body.

"Looks like dirt, some grass. We can hope for fibers or skin. Broken wrist, looks like a broken jaw. Multiple contusions and abrasions on face, torso, shoulders. Did a number on you, Lily. Appearance of sexual assault. Some evidence of vaginal bleeding. Contusions, abrasions on thighs and genital area. Removing some fibers into evidence."

She worked meticulously, plucking tiny fibers from the body, never flinching as she took them from the genital area.

She sealed them, tagged them, logged them.

And if part of her system revolted, much as the rookie's had, if part of her wanted to scream at the visions of rape, she refused them, and continued on.

Still wearing the goggles, she leaned down into the dead face and studied the bloody holes where the eyes had been.

"Smooth, clean cuts, similar to those inflicted on Elisa Maplewood."

"Dallas."

"Peabody." She didn't look around, and thought only briefly that she missed, for some reason, the telltale clomp of Peabody's uniform shoes. "We've got the kill site just south. First on scene is Queeks. Verified that scene's secured."

"Crime scene's right behind me."

"Take part of the team with you, have them start looking in a direct path from that scene to this for impressions in the grass. But don't let anybody mess with that scene until I've seen it."

"On that. Uniforms found her?"

"No." Eve straightened now. "Celina Sanchez had another vision."

Eve finished her exam of the body and the dump site, then walked to where Roarke stood, just behind the crime scene sensors Queeks had set up.

She'd remember that, she thought. Remember that Officer Queeks worked quick and quiet and didn't annoy the primary with a lot of chatter and questions.

"You don't have to wait."

"I'll wait," Roarke said. "I'm in it now."

"Guess you are. Well, come with me. You've got good eyes. Maybe you'll spot something I miss."

She took a wide circular route to the second scene. If he'd left impressions in the grass again, she didn't want to disturb them.

She nodded to Queeks. "Good work. Where's the rookie?"

"I got him out securing the entrances with a couple of the guys. He's okay, Lieutenant, just green. Only been on the job three months, and this was his first body. It was a tough one, too. But he maintained until he was well away from the scene."

"I'm not writing him up for hurling, Queeks. You see anything I should know about other than the body?"

"We came in the same entrance as you. Got one on all four sides. We headed south, intending to make a circle. Saw her pretty quick. Didn't observe anyone else. Not in the park or on the street. We were just coming out of a double D on Varick when the call came through on this. Some street people out, some die-hard LC's trolling, but no one that fit the description we were given."

"How long have you worked in this sector?"

"About a dozen."

"You know O'Hara's?"

"Sure, Mick place down on Albany. Decent place, food's tolerable."

"What time does it close?"

"Two, earlier if it's slow."

"Okay. Thanks. Peabody?"

"Some blood. Some of the grass is ripped up, some's tamped down. Got a couple of small scraps of cloth. Might be from an article of clothing."

"I can see all that, Peabody. What do you see?"

"Well, I think he took her just inside the south entrance as she'd started in to cut across the park. Could've grabbed her outside, but more likely she cut in. He took her down here, assaulted, overpowered, tore some of her clothes in the struggle, though there's no indication she put up much of a fight. Raped her here. I haven't examined the body, but it looks like maybe she dug her fingers into the grass. As it appears to be the same MO as Maplewood, he would have strangled her at this point, taken her clothes, then carried her to the other location where he could pose her and remove her eyes."

"Yeah, that's what I see. Inside, though. She cut through, shortcut home. Patrols go by here regularly. Park stays pretty clean. Safe. He'd have to work fast, but that's no problem for him. He's got the routine knocked now. Time of death was oh two hundred, almost on the dot. First arrived two hundred twenty minutes. You factor in the time it took him to undress her, carry her, pose her, mutilate her, he cut it close this time."

"He could've still been in the park when they arrived."

Eve glanced back at Roarke, lifted her eyebrows.

"He could have heard them. Car pulls up, doors slam. He moves off, out of the lights, behind any number of trees. Wouldn't he, if he could, enjoy watching her be discovered?"

"Yeah. Yeah, he would."

"He'd only just finished with her. And wouldn't he need a moment to pat himself on the back for the fine job he'd done?" Unable to help himself, Roarke glanced back to where Lily Napier lay on the bench. "He hears someone coming, and nips back. He'd kill them if he had to, that would be his thinking. But how gratifying it must have been to see cops find her, so quickly, so fresh, with him able to see. Then he's out, the opposite direction, with a nice bonus to his evening."

As she'd speculated along the exact same lines herself, she nodded. "You're getting good at this. I want a thorough sweep of the entire park, every blade of grass, every flower petal, every tree."

"He seals up, Lieutenant," Peabody reminded her. "We don't have his DNA, his blood type, his hair, nothing to match if they could find anything in an area this size."

"He seals up." Eve held out a hand, turned it over so the smears of blood shone in the light. "Me, too. We're not looking for his DNA. We're looking for hers."

Again, she stepped back, but this time she gestured to Roarke. "Let's take a little walk."

"You're hoping to be able to see his direction. Where he moved, how he moved."

"Anything that adds a line to his picture's good." She needed to get away from cop eyes, from cop ears, and kept going until they were out of the park again, on the sidewalk. "I think, geographically, he's closer to home here than he was with Maplewood. But it doesn't matter to him. He'll go where he needs to go."

"And you didn't come all the way out here to tell me that."

"No. Look, there's no point in you waiting. We're going to be at this awhile, then I've got to go into Central."

"Déjà vu."

"Yeah. This guy likes night work."

"You haven't had more than an hour's sleep."

"I'll catch some in my office." She started to wipe her hand absently on her trousers, but he caught her wrist.

"Hold on." He opened her field kit, took out a rag.

"Right." Cleaning the blood off her hands,

she stared back through the stone arch. The park was brilliant with light now. The sweepers, in their protective suits, moved through it like silent images on a screen. The media would pounce soon—they always did—and would have to be dealt with.

Before much longer, lights would go on in the windows of surrounding buildings. Some would glance out, see and wonder. Then civilians would have to be dealt with.

She was going to shut down the park. So the mayor would have to be dealt with.

The fun never quit.

"What's on your mind, Lieutenant?"

"Too many things, and I've got to start lining them up. I'm going to be calling Celina into Central, get a detailed report of her . . . vision. I'm going to have a couple of soft-clothes cops escort her in. Eight hundred."

She stuck her hands in her pockets, pulled them out again when she remembered she'd wiped off the blood but hadn't cleaned off the sealant. "Here's the thing."

When she said nothing else, only continued to stare into the park, Roarke cocked his head. "And that thing would be?"

"She said she was home in bed when she

contacted me. I'd just like to verify that, that's all. Just like to nail that down."

"You don't believe her?"

"I don't *not* believe her. I just want to verify, so it's off my mind. So I don't find myself wondering. That's all."

"And if someone could . . . gain access to her bedroom when she was elsewhere, check her 'link, you wouldn't find yourself wondering."

"Yes." She looked at him then. "And I can't believe I'm standing here asking you to commit a crime. I know if she was home in bed when she contacted me, she couldn't have been here when the murder took place—not when she called minutes after Napier's death. I could request a check of her 'link, send an e-man to her place with her permission, but—"

"It seems rude."

She rolled her eyes. "I don't give a rat's ass about seeming rude, but I do about making an ass of myself. I do about potentially alienating a valuable source."

"Eight o'clock then."

She was torn between relief and worry. "Listen, I'll contact you when she comes in.

Just to make sure it's clear. If you get caught—"

"Darling Eve." There was a deliberate wealth of patience in his tone. "I love you more than life itself, and have, I believe, demonstrated that regularly throughout our relationship. So I can't understand why you persist in insulting me."

"Me neither. Just in and out. Just the 'link. Don't go poking around. If it checks out, don't contact me. If it doesn't, tag me on my personal."

"Shouldn't we have code words?"

She sent him a withering look as he grinned at her. "Yeah. Bite me."

Laughing, he jerked her forward and did just that, giving her a quick nip on the chin before brushing his lips over hers. "I'll find my own way home. Get a little sleep."

Eve turned back toward the arch, back toward death, and didn't see how she could.

Notifying next of kin was always hideous, but it was worse, somehow worse, when it had to be done in the middle of the night. She depressed the buzzer on an apartment on the Lower West Side and prepared to take a slice out of someone's world.

There was a wait, long enough she was preparing to ring again when the intercom blinked on.

"Yes? What is it?"

"Police." Eve held up her badge, stood with it in view of the peep. "We need to speak with Carleen Steeple."

"It's four in the fricking morning. What's this about?"

"Sir, we need to come inside."

The intercom clicked off, followed by an irritated rattle of chains and locks. The man who opened the door wore nothing but a pair of loose cotton pants and an annoyed expression. "What's this about? Some of us are trying to sleep, and I don't want you waking up the kids."

"We're sorry to disturb you, Mr. Steeple." The brother-in-law, Eve thought, according to the data. "I'm Lieutenant Dallas. This is Detective Peabody. We need to speak to your wife."

"Andy?" A woman with short, curly, sleep-ruffled hair poked her face out of a doorway. "What's going on?"

"Cops. Look, we reported the illegals

deals we saw, and the junkies roaming around in the broad fricking daylight. We did our civic duty, and don't appreciate getting hassled in the middle of the night."

"We're not with Illegals, Mr. Steeple. Carleen Steeple?"

The woman eased out, tugging at the belt of a robe. "Yes."

"Your sister is Lily Napier?"

"Yes." There was a flicker over her face. That first dawning of fear. "Is something wrong?"

"I'm sorry to inform you, your sister's dead."

"No." She said it quietly, the single sound on the verge of a question.

"Oh Jesus. Jesus." Andy Steeple transformed from pissed-off man to concerned husband in a snap. He walked quickly to his wife, gathered her against him. "Oh, honey. What happened?" he asked Eve. "What happened to Lily?"

"No," Carleen said again. Just: No.

"Can we sit down, Mr. Steeple?"

He gestured toward a seating area with comfortably worn chairs, a sofa cheerfully covered in bright, overblown flowers. "Come on, honey. Come on, sweetie." With his arm around his wife, he led her to the sofa. "Let's just sit down."

"Daddy?" A little girl, all curls and sleepy eyes padded into the room.

"Go back to bed, Kiki."

"What's wrong with Mommy?"

"Go on back to bed, baby. I'll be there in a minute."

"I'm thirsty."

"Kiki—"

"Would you like me to take care of her?" Peabody asked.

"I . . ." He looked undone for a moment, then nodded.

"Hi, Kiki, I'm Dee." Peabody walked over, took the little girl's hand. "Why don't we get a glass of water?"

"My partner's good with kids," Eve told him. "She'll be fine."

"Could there be a mistake?"

"No, sir."

"An accident?" Carleen turned her face into her husband's shoulder. "An accident?"

"No. Your sister was murdered."

"Junkies," Steeple said. Bitterly.

"No." Eve studied Carleen's face, the pallor, the tears, the plea in her eyes. "I know this is difficult. It's going to get more so. It appears that your sister was attacked on her way home from work. In Memorial Park."

"She always cut through the park." Carleen groped for her husband's hand. "It's quicker. It's safe."

"A mugging?"

Get through it, Eve told herself. Get it done fast, so they don't suffer in the speculation. "She was raped and strangled."

"Lily?" Carleen's teary eyes went huge in shock. *"Lily?"* She would have slid to the floor if her husband hadn't held her. "No, no, no."

"The city should be safe." There were tears in Steeple's eyes now as he rocked his wife. "A woman should be able to walk home from goddamn work and be safe."

"Yes, sir. She should. We're going to do everything we can to find who did this to her. We need your help. I need to ask you some questions."

"Now?" He tightened his hold on his wife. "Can't you see we're grieving?"

"Mr. Steeple." Eve leaned forward so he met her eyes, so he saw what was in them. "Did you care for your sister-in-law?"

"Of course I did. Jesus."

"Do you want the man who did this to her punished?"

"Punished?" He spat out the word. "I want him dead."

"I want to find him. I want to stop him. I will find him, and I will stop him. But with your help, I may be able to do it faster. I may be able to do it before he does this to someone else's sister."

He stared at her for a long moment. "Could you give us a minute? A minute alone?"

"Sure."

"You could go in the kitchen over there." He gestured.

Eve left them alone, walked into a galley-style kitchen with a bump out for eating. There were benches for seating covered by cushions with zigzagging patterns of yellows and blues. Yellow curtains with blue borders framed the windows. Place mats, she supposed you called them, lay on the table at each space, and matched the bench cushion.

Eve picked one up, fingering it.

"Lieutenant Dallas?" Steeple came to the doorway. "We're ready now. I'm going to make some coffee. I think we could all use some."

They sat in the living area, and with the little girl settled down, Peabody joined them. Carleen's eyes were stark and damp, but she was making an effort to compose herself, Eve saw.

"Nothing about this is easy," Eve began. "We'll be as brief as possible so we can give you some privacy."

"Can I see her?"

"Not at this time, no. I'm sorry. Your sister worked at O'Hara's Bar and Grill?"

"Yes. Five years now. She liked it there. It's a friendly place, and close to her apartment. She made good tips. She liked working nights and having most of her afternoons free."

"Was she in a relationship?"

"Not right now. She dated some, but she's been a little shy of men since the divorce."

"And the ex-husband?"

"Rip? He's remarried and lives in Vermont. I think, really, he was the love of her life, but she wasn't his. Things just fell apart. It wasn't ugly. It was just sad."

"Don't go looking at him for this." Temper spiked in Steeple's voice. "Some junkie maniac did this, and you waste time hassling a decent guy. A moron, but a decent guy, while the bastard who—"

"Andy." With a muffled sob, Carleen gripped his hand. "Don't. Just don't."

"I'm sorry. I'm sorry. But whoever did this is out there running around right now, and we're just *sitting* here. Next thing, she's going to ask where I was, and shit like that. Oh, goddamn." He lowered his head to his hands. "Oh, goddamn."

"The sooner questions are asked and answered, the sooner we can leave you alone. Do you know if anyone's been bothering her?"

"No." Carleen stroked her husband's hair as she spoke. "Some of the guys at the bar tease her, but it's not like that. She's shy. Lily's shy, but she's comfortable there. They're nice people. We go in sometimes. She never hurt anyone. I have to tell our parents. They live in South Carolina now. On a houseboat. They . . . how do I tell them Lily's gone? How do we tell Kiki?"

"Don't think about that yet," Steeple said before Eve could speak. He lifted his head, appeared to have regained some composure. "One step at a time, sweetie. Is this like the other woman?" he asked Eve. "I saw it on the news. I saw you. Is this the same?"

"We're pursuing that probability."

"She was—"

Eve saw it in his eyes. *Mutilated.* But he stopped himself from saying the word, and drew his wife closer. "She was killed uptown."

"Yes. Mrs. Steeple, did Lily do crafts?"

"Crafts? Lily?" A smile trembled onto her lips. "No. She didn't like to play house, as she called it. It was part of the problem between her and Rip. He wanted a homebody, and Lily just wasn't."

"You have what look like handcrafted pieces in the other room."

"Kiki's room, too," Peabody added. "It's a lovely quilt on her bed."

"That's my work. When I got pregnant with Drew, our son, I decided—well, we decided," she amended, linking her fingers with her husband's, "that I'd try the professional mother route. I wanted to be able to stay home with the children. Then I realized, pretty quickly, I'd need something to do. I started quilting, then that expanded to needlepoint, macramé. I enjoy it."

"Where do you get your supplies?"

"What does this have to do with Lily?"

"Mrs. Steeple, where do you get your craft supplies?"

"A number of places." She named several on Eve's list.

"Did Lily ever go with you, when you shopped for supplies?"

"Well, yes. We often shopped together, for a lot of things. She liked to shop, to spend time with me and the kids. We shopped together at least once a week."

"Thank you for your help."

"But . . . Isn't there something else?" Carleen asked when Eve got to her feet. "Isn't there something more we can do?"

"There may be. We'll stay in touch, Mrs. Steeple. You can reach either Detective Peabody or myself through Central, any time. I'm very sorry for your loss."

"I'll show you out. Carleen, you should check on the kids."

He walked them to the door, waited until

he was sure his wife was out of earshot. "Look, I'm sorry I shot off like that."

"No problem."

"I want to know. Was she mutilated—like that other woman? I don't want Carleen to see her if . . ."

"Yes. I'm sorry."

"How?"

"I'm not going to give you those details, not at this time. They're confidential to the investigation."

"I want to know when you find him. I want to know. I want—"

"I know what you want. But what you need to do is take care of your wife, of your family. You need to leave the rest of it to us."

"You didn't know her. You didn't know Lily."

"No. But I know her now."

II

It was after five A.M. when Eve walked into Homicide. The skeleton squad from the graveyard shift was handling the 'links, catching up on paperwork. Or sleep. She gestured a come-ahead to Peabody so her partner would follow her into her office.

"I've got to contact Whitney."

"Better you than me."

"While I do, you tag Celina. Inform her we're sending a couple of plainclothes to bring her in for a statement. I want her here at eight hundred hours. Then find me two cops to take the detail. When you get that set, you should catch a couple hours in the crib."

"Don't have to tell me that twice. Gonna join me?"

"No, I'll stretch out in my office."

"Where?"

"Just get this set up and close the door behind you."

Alone, Eve stared at the 'link, and recited a little mantra in her head.

Let the commander answer and not his wife, let the commander answer and not his wife. In the name of all that's holy, let the commander answer and not his wife.

Then, sucking it up, she sat down and made the call.

She nearly let out a cheer when Whitney's tired face popped on screen.

"I'm sorry to wake you, sir. There's been a homicide in Memorial Park. Single victim, Caucasian female, age twenty-eight. Sexual homicide with mutilation. The same MO as Maplewood."

"Scene secure?"

"It is, sir. I've closed the park and have men at every entrance."

"Closed it?"

"Yes, sir. It's necessary, for the next ten to twenty-four hours."

He let out a long, long sigh. "Which

means it's necessary for me to wake up the mayor. I want a full report on my desk by eight hundred hours. I'll see you in my office at nine hundred."

"Yes, sir."

Eve looked at the blank screen. No, she didn't see how she was going to manage sleep.

She input her notes and the record from on scene. Preparing for the long day ahead, she programmed a full pot of coffee, then sat to refine her report.

She read it over, searching for any missed details. Finding none, she ran standard probabilities, included the results. Then she saved it, filed it, and copied her commander, her partner, and Mira.

Rising, she pinned Lily Napier's photos, alive and dead, to her board.

At seven-fifteen, she set her wrist unit, stretched out on the floor and slept, restlessly, for twenty minutes. Primed with another cup of coffee, she took a shower in the facilities off the locker room. Briefly, she considered popping some Stay-Up, but it always made her feel jittery and strange.

If she was going to be heavily caffeinated, she preferred doing it with coffee.

She opted to use a conference room rather than her office for her session with Celina, and since Peabody didn't appear to be up from her nap, scheduled it herself.

Then she called down to the desk sergeant on duty, and requested to be informed when Celina Sanchez checked in.

Rather than tolerate the swill the department offered, she culled another pot of coffee from her office, and carried it to the conference room.

The desk sergeant beeped her just as Peabody came in. She sniffed the air. "God. Just pour it in a saucer and I'll lap it up."

"Get us some bagels or something from vending first," Eve told her. "Charge them to the squad budget."

"You're actually thinking about food. I must be dreaming."

"Sanchez is on her way up. So get your ass moving."

"That's the Dallas I know and love."

When the door was shut again, Eve pulled out her personal 'link and beeped Roarke's.

He answered quickly.

"Okay, she's . . ." Eve narrowed her eyes. "Where are you?"

"About to continue my little adventure in Daytime Breaking and Entering."

"I told you to wait until I contacted you."

"Hmm." He smiled and continued to work on Celina's bedside 'link. "It appears I've disobeyed, once again. I expect to be roundly punished at the first opportunity."

"Damn it—"

"Would you like to continue this chat, or let me get on with things?"

"Do it."

In Celina's bedroom, Roarke smiled to himself. He had a habit of irritating his wife, and was afraid he was just small enough to enjoy it.

He'd watched the cops pull up, go into Celina's building. Casual shirts and trousers aside, he'd have made them as what they were at two blocks, heading in the opposite direction.

Cops looked like cops, especially to the eye of a criminal. Even a former criminal.

And though he trusted his cop implicitly, he preferred casing a job personally.

Ten minutes after Celina had come out and driven off with her escort—it was always best to make certain the mark didn't turn around and go back for something forgotten—he jammed her security cameras with a remote. And strolled across the street.

Under three minutes later he was through the outside locks and alarms, and strolling inside.

A short time later, he'd verified the source of the transmission and was replacing the 'link. Celina had made the call exactly as she'd claimed. From her own bedside unit, moments after two A.M.

His cop could stop wondering.

It was hard to resist that poking around Eve had warned him against. It was, after all, in his nature. She, his cop, would never understand the hum in the blood that came from simply being where you were not allowed to be.

He gave himself a moment of it, admiring the art on the bedroom walls—fanciful, sensual, evocative. The color scheme that was richly and confidently female.

And if he wandered the second level of the loft, he was, technically, on his way out.

He liked the style, the openness of space, and again what he saw as the confidence of a woman who knew how she wanted to live, and did so.

He thought it might be interesting to hire her for some business event down the road.

He strolled out, as he'd strolled in. And with a check of the time, calculated he'd be in midtown in plenty of time for his first meeting of the day.

He didn't beep her. Eve knew Roarke and his clever fingers. When her personal 'link hadn't signaled by the time Celina was brought into the conference room, she knew the transmission was verified as being made from the bedroom 'link as stated.

No need to wonder, she thought. And no mistaking the emotional state of the stricken and exhausted woman who came into the room.

She looked drawn and sallow, like someone who was recovering from a long and severe illness.

"Dallas."

"Have a seat. Have some coffee."

"I will." She sat at the conference table and used both hands to lift the mug. Her rings clinked lightly against the cheap stoneware. "I took a soother after we spoke last night. Didn't help very much. I took another right before I came in. That doesn't seem to be doing the job either. What I'd like to do is tranq myself into a coma. But I'm not sure that would help either."

"It wouldn't help Lily Napier."

"That's her name?" She drank. Paused. Drank again. "I didn't turn on the media reports this morning. I was afraid I'd see her."

"You saw her last night."

Celina nodded. "It was worse than the last one. What I mean is, for me. I'm not equipped for this."

"It's very difficult for someone with your gift to witness or experience violence," Peabody said, and was rewarded with a grateful smile.

"Yes. God, yes. It's not that I experience the same extent—the full physical extent of the violence as the victim, but enough. And if . . . when you're linked, psychically, the emotions reverberate in you. I know how she suffered. I'm alive. I'm alive and whole and drinking coffee, while she's not. But I know how she suffered."

"Tell me what you saw," Eve ordered.

"It was . . ." Celina held up a hand, as if halting everything until she gathered herself. "The other time, it was like a dream. A vivid and disturbing dream, but something I could dismiss as just that. Until I saw the media reports. This was more. I wouldn't have, couldn't have mistaken it for anything but a vision. One of the most powerful I've ever had. It was like being there. Walking alongside her.

"She walked quickly, with her head down."

"What was she wearing?"

"Ah, dark skirt—black, I think—short. A white shirt. Long sleeves, open collar, and a little cardigan-style sweater over it. Flat shoes with thick soles. Gel-soles, perhaps. She barely made a sound. She had a bag. A small purse she wore on a strap over her shoulder."

"What was he wearing?"

"Dark. I don't know. She didn't know he was there, waiting, inside the park. In the shadows. He was dark, everything about him is dark."

"Skin? Is he black?"

"No . . . I. No, I don't think. I see his hands when he strikes at her. They're white. Glossy and white and big. Very big. He struck her in the face. There was horrible pain. Horrible, and she fell, and the pain went away. She . . . passed out. I think. He hit her, kept hitting her even when she was unconscious. In the face, in the body.

" 'See how you like it. See how you like it.' "

Celina's eyes went glassy, the pale, pale green of the irises nearly translucent. " 'Who's the boss now? Who's in charge now, you bitch?' But he stops, he stops beating her, slaps her cheeks lightly with those big hands. Bringing her around. She needs to be awake for the rest. There's such pain! I don't know, don't know if it's his or hers, there's so much pain."

"It's not your pain," Peabody said quietly and shook her head before Eve could speak. "You're a witness, and you can tell us what you see. It's not your pain."

"Not mine." Celina breathed in deep. "He tears her clothes. She can't fight, barely struggles. And when she tries to push at him, he yanks her hand away. Something in her breaks. She's confused, the way an animal's confused when it's caught in a trap. He rapes her, and it hurts. It hurts deep inside. She can't see him. It's too dark and the pain is overwhelming. She goes under again. It's safer there, there's no pain there.

She doesn't feel when he kills her. Her body reacts, convulsing. And that . . . there's a thrill in that for him. Her death throes bring him to orgasm.

"I'm sick." Celina pressed the back of her hand to her mouth. "I'm sorry. I'm sick. I need to—"

"Here, come on." Peabody was up, drawing Celina to her feet. "Come with me."

As Peabody helped her out of the room, Eve pushed away from the table. She walked to one of the windows, shoved it open so she could lean out. Lean out and breathe.

She understood the nausea all too well. What it was like to see, again and again. To feel, over and over. And the sickness that came with it.

She let the air, and the noise, the *life* of the city push it out of her again. She watched an airtram, crammed with commuters streak by, and an ad blimp hover, spewing out its announcements for sales, events, tourist packages.

Her legs felt watery yet, so she stayed where she was, listening to the click of chopper blades, the blast of horns from the street below, the rattle of an airbus.

It all teemed together, a cacophony that was a kind of music to her. A song she understood, and one that gave her a sense of place.

She was never really alone in the city. Never helpless with her badge.

Remembering pain, knowing its source, could make her stronger. It was good to know that.

Steadier, she closed the window, walked back to the table, and poured more coffee.

Some of the color had seeped back into Celina's cheeks when Peabody brought her back in. She'd fussed with her face a little—bright lip dye, eye gunk to cover the worst of the damage. Women, in Eve's opinion, could worry about the strangest things at the strangest times.

Once Celina was seated, Peabody went over to get a bottle of water.

"You're better off with this than the coffee," she said, setting it on the table.

"Yes, you're right. Thanks." She held out a hand, gave Peabody's a squeeze. "Thank you for staying with me, helping me pull myself back together."

"No problem."

"You must think me very weak," she said to Eve.

"You're wrong. I don't think anything of the kind. I . . . We . . ." she amended. "We come to them after it's done, and we see, day after day, the results of what people can do to each other. The blood, the gore, the waste. It's not easy. It should never be easy. But we don't see it happening—how it happens. We don't feel what the victim feels and have to take it in."

"Yes, you do." Celina wiped her fingers under her eyes. "You've just found a way to handle it. Now, I have to."

She steadied herself with more water.

"He undressed her after. I think. There was a part of me, by now, resisting the vision. Fighting it. But I think he took her clothes; they were torn from the rape. He carried her . . . Not her—damn it."

She sipped water, took three long breaths. "What I mean is she's someone else to him. He sees someone else, and he's punishing someone else. Someone who punished him. In the dark. He's afraid of the dark."

"He kills at night," Eve pointed out.

"He has to. He has to overcome it?"

"Possibly. What else?"

"I broke out of the vision. I broke out because I couldn't stand it. And I called you. I know I should have let it run its course. I might have seen something that could help. I was panicked, and I fought it until I broke out."

"We got to her, to the scene, quicker because you contacted me. We were able to preserve the scene because we were able to get there so fast. That matters."

"I hope to God it does. Are you any closer to him?"

"I think we are."

Celina closed her eyes. "Thank God. If you have anything of his, I can try to see him."

"We have the murder weapon."

Celina shook her head. "I'll try, but it's bound to be like it was before, so what I see—feel—is the act itself, and the emotions raging through it. I need something he's touched with his bare hands. Something he's worn or held to really see him, to add to what you already know."

Eve laid the cord on the table. "Try anyway."

Celina wet her lips, then reached out, touched the ribbon.

Her head snapped back, and her eyes rolled up so only a slice of green showed in the white. As she started to slide out of the chair, her fingers went limp and released the ribbon.

Eve leaped up, caught her before she hit the ground.

"All him. Nothing of her. She's gone. Hidden away when he puts it around her neck. There's just his rage and fear and excitement. It's all over me like—like insects biting at my skin. Horrible."

"What does he do when he's done with her?"

"Goes back to the light. He can go back to the light. I don't know what it means. My head. My head's splitting."

"We'll get you something for it, and have you taken home. Peabody?"

"Let's get you a blocker. Do you want to rest before you go home?"

"No." She leaned against Peabody. "I just want to go."

"Celina." Eve covered the red ribbon with her hand so when the woman turned she didn't see it. "You might want to talk to Dr. Mira, a little counseling."

"I appreciate the thought, I really do, but counseling—"

"Her daughter is Wiccan, and a sensitive."

"Ah."

"Charlotte Mira. She's the best, and it might help you to talk to someone who'd understand your . . . situation."

"It might. Thanks."

When she was alone, Eve lifted the red cord, studied it. She didn't need to hold it to see, or to feel. Gift? she wondered. Or curse?

Neither, she decided, and sealed the ribbon again. It was a tool, nothing more or less.

She was trying to find the energy just to stand when the door opened, and Commander Whitney came in.

She rose immediately. "Sir. I've just finished interviewing Sanchez, and was on my way to your office."

"Sit. Where's that coffee from?"

"My office, Commander."

"Then it'll be well worth it." He got himself a mug, poured, then sat across from her. Saying nothing, he scanned her face while he drank. "How much sleep you bank?"

"A couple hours." Less, but who was counting?

"Looks it. And the fact of that occurred to me when I came in and read your report. You've been eleven years, give or take a few months, under my command, haven't you, Lieutenant?"

"Yes, sir."

"That length of time, and your rank, and you don't feel it would be justified—even reasonable—to inform me that you're not only running on fumes but have a vital interview scheduled for eight hundred hours when I ordered you to report to my office at nine hundred?"

Since he seemed to want an honest answer, she took a moment to consider the question. "No, sir."

He rubbed the bridge of his nose. "I thought as much. You eat any of those?" He jerked his chin toward the bagels.

"No, sir, but they're fresh from vending. Well, as fresh as we get from vending."

"Eat one now."

"Sir?"

"Eat, Dallas. Indulge me. You look like hell."

She picked one up. "Matches how I feel."

"I spoke with the mayor, and have a meeting with him and Chief Tibble in about thirty. Your presence was requested."

"At the mayor's office, sir, or The Tower?"

"Mayor's office. But I will inform His Honor and the Chief that you're unable to attend as you are in the field."

She didn't speak, but something must have run over her face. Something that made him smile. "Tell me what just went through your mind. And don't clean it up. That's an order."

"I wasn't thinking anything, actually, sir. But I was mentally kissing your feet."

He laughed, picked up half a bagel, broke that in half, and bit in. "You'll miss some fireworks. Shutting down a public park."

"I need the scene preserved while the sweepers comb it."

"And the mayor will counter, after all the political malarkey, that according to all reports, this perpetrator seals, and therefore you're wasting public funds, police man-hours, and denying the citizens of New York access to public grounds while you chase the wild goose."

Politics weren't her forte, but she'd already gotten there on her own. "The timing.

In all probability he was still inside the park, very likely still with the victim at the dump site when the first officers on scene arrived. He had to have her blood on him. If the timing was that close, he might not have had the time or the inclination to clean up. I know he didn't. We found blood trails already. From kill site to dump site, and from there heading east. If I can mark his trail, his movements—"

"Do you think because I've sat at a desk I don't remember how it works in the thick? Every piece you find is another piece, simple as that. And while the mayor may not understand that, Tibble will. We'll handle it."

"Thank you, sir."

"What's your next move?"

"I want to bring in EDD. I've been compiling a list, residents in a sector that rays out from the craft shop that each of the vics frequented, and a couple of gyms I need to check out that may apply. I need to juggle it down, cross-check. We find names. We find matches—residents, members, customers. We match and we eliminate and we find him. Feeney can cut through it faster, faster than I can, and then I can stay in the field instead of at a comp."

"Get it started."

She walked out with him, and parted ways to go back to her office.

It was easy to brief Feeney. He understood her shorthand, her direction.

"Won't be quick," he warned her. "But we'll get on it as soon as you get us the data."

"I'm going to pressure the customer lists from the craft shop. Actually, two of them. One's out of the parameter, but not by much. I'll do the same at the gyms for membership lists. I'll feed you what I get as I get it, and shoot the data we gathered last night to your office unit."

"Works for me."

"I've been running eye banks. Donors and receivers. I think it's a time waster, but it has to be factored in. I'm going to give you what I've got on that, so you can add it to the mix."

"Give me all you got. You're looking pretty peaky there, Dallas."

"Peaky? Jeez."

She cut transmission. She zipped files, lists, even her work notes to Feeney. Despite the peaky remark, she thought, he had a cop's brain. Maybe outside of the e-work, he'd see something she'd missed.

She grabbed the jacket she'd forgotten to put back on after her shower. Striding into the bull pen, she gave Peabody a come-ahead.

"Let's roll out."

12

"What does *peaky* mean?"

Peabody wrinkled her brow. "I dunno. Ah, a little look-see—you know, peekaboo?"

"No." Eve idled at a light. "As applies to someone's appearance. They look peaky."

"Beats me, but it doesn't sound good. Want me to try to look it up?"

"No. I asked Feeney to do the matches, looking for names that come up residentially, and in consumer and/or employee lists from the area we've outlined, the shops and fitness facilities within. We need to get the lists."

"Feeney will find matches quicker than either of us. But it's still going to take time, considering the size of the area and the number of people we're dealing with. Then there's the number of matches to wade through. People tend to do at least some of their shopping and business in their own neighborhoods."

"Then we profile them. Unmarried males to start."

"I can follow the detecting dots. He likely lives alone, is between thirty and fifty."

"Closer to thirty," Eve interrupted. "Close, I think, to the ages of his victims."

"Why?"

"I don't know, just feels right. It could be a kind of trigger, couldn't it? The age. The age he is himself, the age he sees her—the one he's really killing. He's grown up, he's on equal ground now. He can punish her." Eve jerked a shoulder. "I sound like Mira."

"Some. And like Mira, it sounds plausible. So, we assume he's around thirty. We know he's strong, has big feet. According to our civilian consultant, he also has big hands and is well over six feet in height. But we can verify through evidence, the strength and the feet."

While negotiating traffic, Eve glanced at her partner. "Doesn't sound like you're convinced by our civilian consultant."

"I believe her, but her visions aren't hard fact. We work with the facts, and consider the rest."

"Now that's the kind of cynicism I like to hear."

"She isn't making this stuff up, and she didn't fake her reaction to the murder weapon. Dog-sick in the bathroom. Another couple of minutes I'd have called an MT. But visions can be tricky."

"Can they?"

"You know, when it comes to sarcasm, you have perfect pitch. What I'm saying is, visions often twist around reality."

Interested, Eve glanced over. "For instance?"

"For instance, Celina may see the killer as unusually big—tall, large hands, and so on—because he's powerful. Not only physically, which we can determine by the MO, but in some other way. Professionally, say, or financially. Or she sees him this way because he kills, and that's frightening to her. The boogie man's a big guy."

"Okay." Eve nodded as she began the hunt for parking. "Keep going."

"We know his shoe size, and that it's considerably larger than average. From this we can extrapolate that he is probably taller than average for a man. We know he's strong enough—powerful enough, you could say—to carry a woman, the dead weight of that woman, nearly fifty yards, and down a short but fairly steep cliff. It's cop work that's giving us the most likely picture of his physical type, not visions."

"Does the cop work confirm her visions, or do her visions confirm the cop work?"

"It's both, isn't it?" Peabody held her breath when Eve utilized the vertical and lateral modes to squeeze into an empty slice of space at a curb. Then let it out when it actually worked. "Civilian consultants are tools, but we have to know how to use them."

Eve eyed the traffic, waiting for a break in it where she could get out of the car without being slammed into the pavement. "She doesn't see his face."

"Could be he wears a mask. Or it could be she's too afraid to look, that she blocks it."

Eve stepped onto the sidewalk. "Can she do that?"

"If she's strong enough, and scared enough. And she's plenty scared. She's not a cop, Dallas," Peabody continued as they walked. "She's seeing murder, and it's not her choice the way it is ours. We don't want to see it, we don't pick up the badge. We sure as hell don't work in Homicide. I chose this because I wanted to live and work in New York, always did. I wanted to be a cop, and the kind of cop who found the big answers to the big questions. Who worked for people who'd been victimized, and against the ones who'd made them victims. You?"

"Close enough."

"Okay, but Celina didn't choose. She didn't decide, hey, I want to be a psychic, that'd be frosty. But she took what was laid on her and made her life work with it."

"Gotta respect that." Eve gave a brief glance at the sidewalk sleeper with his grimy license hung around his neck who was happily posing for tourists.

"Now, this comes along," Peabody added. "And I think one of her biggest fears is that this new deal isn't a one-shot. That she's afraid murder is going to be something she sees, even after this one's over. It's weighty."

"That must've been some puke session."

Peabody snorted out a laugh. "Gold metal status. But what I'm saying is she's trying, and it's costing her. She may help us, but in the end, it's our job, not hers."

"Agreed." Eve stopped outside the craft shop. "Using sensitives is problematic under the best of circumstances—the best being the sensitive is cop-trained and elects to be part of the investigative team. We've got neither of those things in this case. But she's linked into this, locked in. So none of us has a choice. We'll use her, ask the questions, follow up on her visions. And you hold her head when she barfs."

She reached for the door, stopped. "Why New York, Peabody?"

"Big, bad city. Hey, you want to be a crime fighter, you want to fight big, bad crime."

"Lots of big, bad cities out there."

"None of them is New York."

Thoughtfully, Eve studied the traffic jammed on the streets. Horns blasted in arrogant defiance of city ordinances. On the corner, a glide-cart vender shouted out colorful insults to the retreating back of a customer who'd obviously annoyed him.

"You got that right."

* * *

"Well. Well. This is a very unusual request."

The store manager dithered in her tiny office where the single chair was covered in what looked to Eve to be a lot of scraps stuck together in a pattern that worshipped some demanding and possibly psychotic god of color.

She was a fortyish woman with apple cheeks and a constant smile. She continued to use it even as she stood wringing her hands together and looking confused.

"You do keep a customer list, Ms. Chancy?"

"Well, of course. *Of course,* we do. Most of our clientele repeat, and they appreciate being notified of specials and sales and events. Why, just last week we had—"

"Ms. Chancy? We just want the list."

"Yes. Well, yes. Lieutenant, is it?"

"It sure is."

"You see, I've never had a request of this nature, and I'm unsure how to proceed."

"Let me help you out with that. You give us the list, and we say thank you for your cooperation."

"But our customers. They may object. If they feel I've, somehow, infringed on their privacy, they may object, you see. And shop elsewhere."

It wasn't difficult in the confined space, for Peabody to nudge Eve. "We can assure you of our discretion, Ms. Chancy," she said. "This is a very serious matter we're investigating, and we need your help. But there's no reason for us to reveal to any of your customers how we obtained their name."

"Oh, I see. I *see.*"

But she continued to stand, biting her smiling lip.

"What a beautiful quilt chair." Peabody ran her hand over it. "Is this your work?"

"Yes. Yes, it is. I'm particularly proud of it."

"I can see why. It's exceptional work."

"Thank you! Do you quilt?"

"A little. I do a little of this, a little of that. I'm hoping to make more time for my handwork in the future, especially since I'm moving to a new apartment shortly. I'd like to have it reflect my interests."

"Well, of *course,*" Ms. Chancy said, enthusiastically.

"I noticed how well supplied and how organized your shop is. I'll certainly be back, in an unofficial capacity, as soon as I've settled into my new place."

"Wonderful! Let me give you our store information. We hold classes, you know, and have monthly clubs for any interest." She plucked a disc out of a box covered with fabric daisies.

"Great."

"You know, Lieutenant, handcrafting not only gives you the opportunity to create beautiful things that reflect your own style and personality while honoring centuries of traditions, but is very therapeutic. I imagine anyone in your line of work needs to be able to relax and cleanse the soul."

"Right." Peabody swallowed the tickle of laughter at her field promotion by the shopkeeper. "I couldn't agree more. I have a number of friends and associates who could use the same."

"Really?"

"If we could have your customer list, Ms. Chancy." Peabody gave her a bright, toothy smile. "We'd very much appreciate your cooperation, and your support of the NYPSD."

"Oh. Hmm. When you put it that way." She cleared her throat. "But you'll be discreet?"

Peabody kept the smile plastered on her face. "Absolutely."

"I'll just make you a copy."

Back on the street Peabody's smile turned smug, and there was a little bounce to her step as she walked. "Well?"

"Well what?"

"Come on." She jabbed Eve with her elbow. "Spread a little glory."

Eve stopped at a glide-cart. Caffeine was going to be an essential part of the day. "Couple tubes of Pepsi," she ordered.

"One straight, one Pepsi Fitness. Watching the weight," she said to Eve.

Eve shrugged, dug out credits. She took the first hit and decided there was hope left in the world. "You did a good job. Maybe a longer dance than the one with me smashing Chancy's face into her desk, but not as messy."

"See, now that we're partners, I can be the one with the voice of reason."

"Uh-huh. What was up with that chair?"

"Quilt chair. They can be a real focal point—homey or amusing or striking. And it's a clever way to recycle scraps from other projects. I didn't like her choice of fabrics, but the workmanship was first class."

"Gee, the things you learn," Eve said. "That have absolutely no use. Pick up the pace, Peabody, it's a quicker way to ditch the weight than drinking PFs."

"But see, I'm drinking the PF *and* exercising. Which means I can have dessert at the dinner party tonight. So, what are you wearing?"

"What am I . . . oh shit."

"I don't think that's appropriate attire for a casual dinner. We have to go," she continued before Eve could speak. "Unless things heat up, we have to. A couple, three hours—after shift—socializing and recreating with friends isn't going to hamper the investigation, Dallas."

"Jeez." She chugged Pepsi as she strode the half a block north toward the first fitness center. "It's weird enough, this whole cozy gathering, but now I have to do it on no sleep and with bodies piling up. My life used to be simple."

"Mmm."

"It did. Because it didn't have all these people in it."

"If you need to shove somebody out, you

know, to simplify? Could you give Roarke the push? See, McNab and I have this understanding. If Roarke's clear, I get to take my shot at him. McNab gets one at you."

When Eve choked on the last swallow from the tube, Peabody gave her a helpful thump on the back. "Joking. Just sort of joking."

"You and McNab have a sick, sick relationship."

"We do."

Peabody beamed. "It makes us very happy."

Jim's Gym was a hole in the wall down a dingy flight of stairs and through a muscular iron door. Eve assumed if a prospective member couldn't handle the door, he was laughed back up to the sidewalk where he could slink away holding his puny biceps.

It smelled male, but not in a flattering sense. It was the kind of odor that hit you dead center of the face, like a fist wrapped in a sweaty jock strap.

Paint was peeling from the walls that had been tuned up to an industrial gray around the time she'd been born. There were rusty splotches in the ceiling from water damage and a grimy beige floor so soaked with sweat and blood the fumes of both rose up like fetid fog.

She imagined the men who frequented the place breathed it in like perfume.

The equipment was elemental—no frills. Weights and bars, a couple of heavy bags, a couple of speed bags. There were a few clunky machines that looked to have been manufactured in the last century. A single spotted mirror where a man built like a cargo shuttle was doing biceps curls.

Another was bench-pressing what looked like your average redwood, without a spotter. She imagined the concept of spotters would be spat upon in such facilities.

A third man pummeled one of the heavy bags like it was an adulterous ex-wife.

All were stripped down to baggy gray sweatpants and shirts with the arms ripped off. Like a uniform, she thought. All that was missing were the words *Bad Ass* emblazoned over the chest.

When Eve and Peabody stepped in, all movement stopped. Biceps Curls held his fifty-pounder suspended, Bench Press clanked his redwood in the safety, and

Heavy Bag stood, pouring sweat, with his fist laid into the bag.

In the silence, Eve heard the echoing thuds from the next room, and the encouraging: "Lead with your left, you stupid fuck!"

She scanned the faces, then went with Heavy Bag because he was the closest. "Place got a manager?"

To her amazement, he flushed scarlet—all two hundred twenty-five pounds of him. "Ah, just Jim. He's, um, he owns the place. He's, um. Um, he's got Beaner sparring over in the ring. Ma'am."

She started across the room. Bench Press sat up, eyed her with open suspicion and considerable dislike. "Jim, he don't take no females in here."

"Jim must be unaware that it's illegal to discriminate due to sex."

"Discriminate." He barked a laugh and sneered. "He don't discriminate. He just don't take no females."

"A fine distinction. What you got there? Two seventy-five. That be about your weight?"

He swiped sweat from his wide, cocoa-colored face. "Guy can't bench his weight, he's a girl."

With a nod, Eve unlocked the weights, adjusted them. "That's my weight." Then she wagged a thumb, inviting him to rise.

Heavy Bag stepped over as she positioned herself on the bench. "Ma'am. You don't want to hurt yourself."

"No, I don't. Spot me, Peabody."

"Sure."

Eve curled her hands around the bar, set. And did ten slow, steady reps. She replaced the bar, slid off the bench. "I ain't no girl."

She nodded to Heavy Bag, who blushed again, then strolled toward the next room.

"I can't bench my weight yet," Peabody said in an undertone. "I guess I'm a girl."

"Practice."

She stopped to watch the sparring match.

There was a bruiser in the ring with black skin so glossy it looked oiled. He had tree-trunk legs, abs that looked like ridges of steel. A punishing right, she noted, but he telegraphed it by dropping his left shoulder.

His opponent was in the Nordic god style, and quick on his feet. When she stepped closer, she made it as a droid.

The trainer was wrapped in gray sweats and jogged to different spots outside the ring to shout instruction and insult with equal fervor.

He was about five eight, Eve judged, and on the shady side of fifty. From the looks of it, his nose had had the occasion to meet someone's fist with some regularity. When he peeled back his lips to spew abuse on his fighter, Eve caught the glint of a silver tooth.

She waited until the end of the round and watched the black guy—heavyweight division—hang his head as the flyweight berated him from outside the ropes.

"Sorry to interrupt," Eve began.

Jim's head whipped around. "I don't like women in my place." He heaved a towel at his fighter, then rolled toward Eve like a small tank. "Out."

Eve took out her badge. "Why don't we start over?"

"Female cops. Worse than a regular female. This is my place. Man oughta be able to do what he wants to do in his own place and not have some female cop come around telling him he has to cater to women."

He was working up a good head of steam, eyes bulging, head bopping like a pigeon's, feet dancing in place. "I'll shut down before I have females prancing around here and asking me where's the fucking lemon water."

"Aren't we both lucky I'm not here to bust your chops about your overt violations of discrimination laws."

"Discrimination, my ass. This is a serious gym, not some froufrou palace."

"So I see. I'm Lieutenant Dallas, this is Detective Peabody. We're Homicide."

"Well, I sure as hell haven't killed anybody. Lately."

"That's a big relief to me, Jim. You got an office?"

"Why?"

"So we could go there and have a discussion instead of me cuffing you and hauling your disagreeable ass into Central to have the discussion there. I'm not interested in shutting you down. I don't give a rat's skinny ass if you block women from your membership list or if you haul them in by the bargeload to dance naked in the showers. Providing you have shower facilities, which from the smell of things, you don't."

"I got showers. I got an office. This is my place, and I run it my way."

"Fine and good. Your office or mine, Jim?"

"Goddamn females. You." He jabbed a finger at his fighter who continued to stand, gloves dangling, head down. "You do an hour with the rope till you learn what to do with your damn clumsy feet. I gotta go have a *discussion.*"

He marched off.

"Things started going downhill," Peabody commented as they started after him, "as soon as they gave us the vote. Bet he has that sad day circled in funeral black on his perpetual calendar."

They had to climb a set of rusty iron stairs to a second level. The amazing stench of body odor, mildew, and flatulence identified the shower facilities. And made the eyes water.

Even Eve who didn't consider herself overly fussy was forced to agree with Peabody's whispered: gross.

Jim turned into a room identified as his office by the desk buried under sparring gloves, mouth guards, paper, and used towels. The walls were decorated with photos of a younger Jim in boxing trunks. In one he held a title belt aloft. Since his right eye was swollen shut, his nose bloody, and his torso black-and-blue, she assumed it hadn't been an easy victory.

"What year did you take the title?" Eve asked him.

"Forty-five. Twelve rounds. Knocked Hardy into a coma. Took him three days to come out of it."

"You must be proud. We're conducting an investigation into the rape and strangulation of two women."

"Don't know nothing about it." He tossed what might have been a pile of dirty laundry off a chair and sat. "Got two ex-wives. Gave up on women after the second one."

"Wise choice. We believe the killer lives, works, or frequents this area."

"Which is it? Typical female, can't make up your mind."

"I can see why you have those two ex-wives, Jim. You're such a charmer. Two women are dead. They were beaten, raped, strangled, and mutilated, for no reason other than they were women."

The cocky grin faded from his face. "That's why I don't watch nothing but the sports channels. You think I go around beating and raping and killing women? I gotta get me a damn lawyer now?"

"That's up to you. You're not a suspect, but we believe the man who killed these woman, who may have killed others, is serious about his body maintenance. He's big, and he's very strong. You'd get that type in here."

"Well, Jesus H. Christ, what am I supposed to do? Ask a guy when he comes in to lift if he's going out to strangle some woman after?"

"You're supposed to cooperate with the authorities and give me your membership list."

"I know laws and shit. I don't have to do that unless you slap me with a warrant."

"Try this instead." Eve reached into Peabody's bag and took out Elisa Maplewood's ID photo. "This is what one of his victims looked like. Before. I won't show you the after. You wouldn't recognize her, not after what he'd done to her. She had a four-year-old daughter."

"Jesus H. Christ." He looked away from

it, glowered at the wall. "I know the guys who come in here. You think I'd let some crazy woman-killer use my place? I'd sooner have females."

"The membership list."

He puffed out his cheeks. "I don't hold with rape. Man's got a hand, doesn't he? Plenty of LCs around if he's got to stick his dick in something. I don't hold with rape. Worse than killing, you ask me."

He shoved at the debris on his desk until he unearthed an ancient portable computer.

Peabody heaved out a breath when they were back on the street. "That was an experience. My olfactory sense is still in shock. It may take a week to recover. Some of the places we hit yesterday were a little ripe, and you could say colorful. But that wins the trophy."

"We've got another one to go. Second craft place is two blocks west. We'll hit that, double back, and take the next gym."

Peabody calculated the distance already hiked, the distance yet to go. "I get two desserts tonight.

* * *

It took more than two hours. It would've taken longer, but they caught an assistant manager at the craft center who was so excited at the prospect of being even a peripheral part of a murder investigation she would have given them every scrap of data at her fingertips.

The second gym was cleaner, more crowded, and a great deal less pungent. But the manager insisted on speaking with the owner, who refused any cooperation until he, himself, could come in to deal with the situation.

He was a hard-bodied six three, a light-skinned Asian with a skullcap of salt-and-pepper hair. He offered Eve a hand and took hers in the careful way of a big man who was aware of his size and strength.

"I've heard about these murders. It's a terrible thing."

"Yes, sir, it is."

"Why don't we sit down?"

His office wasn't any larger than Jim's, but it looked to have been cleaned and outfitted not only within the last quarter century, but perhaps within the last week.

"I understand you want a list of our members."

"That's right. Our investigation indicates the killer may use facilities such as this."

"I don't like to think I'm acquainted with, or doing business with, anyone who could do something like this. It's not that I don't want to cooperate, Lieutenant, but it seems I should consult with my lawyer first. Membership lists are confidential."

"You're free to do so, Mr. Ling. We'll get a warrant. It'll take some time, but we'll get one."

"And the time it takes may give him the opportunity to kill another woman. I hear the subtext, loud and clear. I'm going to give you the list, but I'm going to ask if you need anything else, to come directly to me, rather than my manager. I'll give you my private number. Men gossip, Lieutenant, the same as anybody. I don't want our members put off by the idea they may be pumping iron or showering off next to a homicidal maniac."

"That's no problem." She waited a moment while he ordered his computer to access the membership list and copy to disc. "You don't cater to women?"

"Female members are welcome," he said

with a hint of a smile. "Otherwise I'd be in violation of federal and state statutes regarding discrimination. But oddly enough, you'll see we have no women on our membership list currently."

"Surprise, surprise."

"We'll let Feeney run with this awhile and grab a couple hours' sleep," Eve said when she and Peabody walked back toward Homicide. "We're going to need follow-ups with Morris and Mira, and if there's no report from the lab by fifteen hundred, we need to kick Dickhead."

"Want me to set them up?"

"No, I'll . . ." She stopped when she saw the big man rise from a bench outside her division. "Yeah, go ahead. Then take the two hours of personal."

Eve hung back until Peabody moved off into the bull pen, then, dipping her hands in her pockets, walked forward.

"Hey, Crack."

"Dallas. Good thing you came along when you did. Cops, they get nervous when a big, beautiful black man hangs around."

Big he was. Black he was. But beautiful,

not even close. He had a face even a besotted mother would have a hard time loving—and that was before the tattoos. He wore a skintight silver T-shirt under a long black leather vest. Snug black pants followed the acreage of his legs. Thick-soled black boots added another inch to his already impressive height.

He owned a sex club called the Down and Dirty where the drinks were next to lethal, the music was hot, and many of the patrons had spent as much time in a cage as out of one.

They called him Crack as he claimed that was the sound he made when he knocked people's heads together. And that summer, Eve had held him while he'd wept like a baby beside the body of his murdered sister.

"You just here to scare cops?" she asked.

"Nothing scares you, white girl. You got a minute? Maybe some place without so many ears."

"Sure." She led the way into her office, shut the door.

"Cop shops," he said with a glimmer of a smile. "Don't know as I've ever been in one in what you might call a voluntary capacity."

"Want coffee?"

He shook his head, shifting his bulk to look out the window. "Ain't much of a place here, hot stuff."

"No, but it's mine. You going to sit?"

Again, he shook his head. "Ain't see you in a while."

"No." The silence hung a moment, as they both thought of the last time they'd seen each other.

"Last time I did was when you come by my place to tell me face-to-face that you got the bastard killed my sister. I didn't have much to say to you."

"Wasn't much to say."

His shoulders lifted, fell. "No. Too much to say."

"I went by your place a couple weeks ago. Barman said you were out of town."

"Couldn't stay here after what happened to my baby. Had to get away awhile. Did me some traveling. Big-ass world out there. Took a look at some of it. Never thanked you for what you did for me and my baby sister. Couldn't get the words out before."

"You don't have to get them out now."

"She was beautiful."

"Yes, she was. I've never lost anybody really close to me, but—"

He turned back to her now. "You lose people every day. Don't know how you get through one and into the next." He drew a deep breath. "I got the letter from your man saying how the two of you had a tree planted in the park for my girl. That was a fine thing to do. I went by to see it, and it's a fine thing. Want to thank you."

"You're welcome."

"You did right by her, I wanted to say that. Wanted to say I know you took care of her, and I won't forget it. The living's got to live, no matter what. So now I'm gonna try to do that, best I can. You come down to the D and D now, I'll be there. Kicking ass and cracking heads, like always."

"I'm glad you're back."

"You need anything from me, you just ask. Now, I gotta tell you, hot lips, seen you look better."

"Long couple of days."

"Maybe it's time you got out of town awhile."

"Maybe." She angled her head as she considered him. "You're a big guy."

"Sweetcheeks." He patted his crotch. "I got written testimony to that effect."

"Bet. But just keep that big dog on the leash." She was thinking of geographics again. "Big, beautiful black man wants to maintain his big, beautiful build he goes to the gym regular."

"I got me some equipment of my own." He winked lasciviously. "But I use a place a couple times a week. Keeps mind and body disciplined."

"You know Jim's Gym?"

"Shithole."

"I hear that. What about Bodybuilders?"

"Ain't no ladies there. Why I want to waste this body on a buncha men? 'Sides, man with my attributes gets hit on in a place like that. Then I have to be busting somebody's face, and I use up my valuable time. Me, I use Zone to Zone. Man can get himself a full massage—a *full* massage after his workout if he's inclined."

"But you know the other places, and you could check them out from the inside, if you were so inclined?"

His grin spread. "Could, if a skinny white girl cop asked me to."

"I'm looking for a guy, between six four

and six eight, around two-seventy. Light-skinned. Woman hater. Loner. Seriously strong."

"Maybe if I moseyed into those places, like I was maybe considering changing my fitness allegiance, I'd see somebody like that."

"Maybe you would. Then you could tell me."

"See what I can do."

13

Eve banked an hour's sleep at her desk. When she woke, she was almost disappointed to find the lab reports holding in her incoming. There would be no way to justify trouncing the chief lab tech.

She read them over, listened to the interoffice memo from Peabody clearing the follow-ups, then scanned her voice and e-mail.

A message from the commander's office informed her she was required at a media conference at sixteen hundred. She'd seen that one coming. And she was going to be both unprepared and late if she didn't get her butt in gear.

She scrubbed her hands over her face,

and put through a call to Morris at the morgue.

He was at his desk, and answered himself.

"What can you tell me?" she asked him.

"I'm about to send you the report, but I can tell you Lily Napier had a short life, that it was ended in the same manner as Elisa Maplewood's, and in my opinion by the same individual. There was more violence to the face and body, which would lead me to believe his rage is increasing."

He shifted, and she could see him bring up a file. "Your on-site was thorough, as always. To that I can add she consumed some pork-fried rice four hours prior to her death, and was mildly anemic. There was no semen. I found fibers inside the vagina. My guess would be they're from her panties, and were carried inside during the rape. There were other fibers that will likely be identified as textile, and almost certainly be from her own clothing. Grass and dirt under her nails, in accordance with your observation. She dug them into the ground. No hair, other than her own."

"Hair from Maplewood turned out to be from the dog, and a squirrel," Eve told him.

"Dog's obvious, and it's probable she picked up the squirrel hair on the grass in the park. Dickhead's report IDs the fibers under Maplewood's nails as man-made, black. Ubiquitous black cloth. We'll match it when we get him, but for now we've got nothing from him."

"Lunatics are, unfortunately, rarely stupid."

"Yeah. Thanks, Morris."

She was about to try Mira's office when she felt her blood sugar bottom out. Since her chocolate supply was tapped for the moment, vending was her only choice. She walked out to the hallway and stared at a snack machine with pure dislike.

"Problem?"

She glanced over, saw Mira. "No. I was just going to grab something, then tag you."

"I had a consult in this section. Thought I'd come to you."

"Good, fine." After a brief hesitation, Eve pulled credits out of her pocket. "Do me a favor? Get me a Booster Bar."

"All right." But she waved Eve's credits away. "My treat."

"Thanks." Eve stuck them back in her pocket, jiggled them. "I'm avoiding contact with machines unless absolutely necessary. It's an experiment."

"Hmm. Fake fruit or fake caramel?"

"Fake caramel. Did you have time to read the report on Napier?"

"Only to scan it, I'm afraid." Mira made the selection, and the machine—in what Eve considered particularly snotty tones—raved about the Booster Bar's delicious flavor, energy snap, and on-the-go convenience before reciting the ingredients and nutritional data.

"There ought to be a mute feature on these things. There really should." Eve ripped the wrapper, bit in. "Do you need more time to study the case file?"

"I'll certainly take it, but I can tell you what you've probably already concluded. He's escalating. Since he killed again so quickly, it's logical to assume he's already selected and stalked more targets. Your on-site indicates no defensive wounds, and a more violent beating premortem."

"She was smaller than Maplewood. Sort of delicate. And he clocked her in the face first off, I'd say. Broke her jaw. Didn't have any fight in her."

"From the premortem injuries, my conclusion would be he was more angry, more frustrated by the fact this victim didn't fight. He can only truly demonstrate his superior strength and power if his victim struggles."

"Beating on somebody's not much fun if they can't feel it."

"In this case, I'd agree with that. She would have been somewhat of a disappointment to him."

"If he's disappointed, he may kill again more quickly. He may need the satisfaction." Eve took another bite of the bar, paced up and down the corridor while Mira waited patiently.

"I've got a media conference coming up. Do I tell women with long brown hair to stay off the streets after dark? Jesus. I feel like I'm building a box around him. I feel that, but I haven't got all the sides steady in place yet. While I'm getting them, while I'm looking for the goddamn lid, he's going to get another one."

"Yes, he probably will." Mira spoke with complete calm. "He may very well kill more than one before you finish the sides of that box and close the lid. And those deaths will be his doing, his responsibility. Not yours."

"I know that, but—"

"But it's hard for you to think there's a woman out there, going about her day, her life, unaware that someone's planning to end it, violently. Horribly. It's hard for you to know he may succeed despite everything you're doing."

"While he's planning it, I'm going to a fricking dinner party tonight."

"Eve." Mira took her arm, eased them a little farther away from the traffic pattern in the corridor. "There was a time you did nothing but the work."

"Dinner party." Eve held her hands out like scales, juggled the right. "Stopping a killer." And dropped the left as if with great weight. "No-brainer."

"It's not that simple or clear-cut, and you know it." The stubborn set of Eve's jaw had her pushing the point. "I'll tell you now that I estimated you had two, maybe three more years before you burned out. Before you couldn't stand over another body and keep your sanity. That would've been a tragedy, for you, for this department, for the city."

Even the thought of it rolled ice into Eve's gut. "I wouldn't have let it happen."

"It's not a choice. Two years ago February," Mira said quietly. "You came in for standard Testing after terminating a suspect."

"Suspect's a little vague description-wise when the guy was holding the bloody knife with the kid he'd just ripped apart in the blood pool at his feet."

"You almost didn't make it through Testing. Not because of the termination, which was justified and necessary, but because of the child. You got through it on sheer will. You know it, and so do I."

She remembered. She remembered perfectly the way she'd raced up the stairs, the screams tearing through the air, tearing through her head. And what she'd seen when she'd broken in the door. Too late.

She'd looked like a doll. A tiny, staring doll in the hands of a monster.

"I can still see her. Her name was Mandy." Eve eased out a breath. "Some hit you harder than others."

"I know it." Unable to prevent herself, Mira laid a hand on Eve's arm, rubbed lightly from elbow to shoulder. "You did the job, but couldn't save the child. And it hit you, very hard. You've had others, will have others that hit you equally. And the fact that you've opened your life, that you will go to a dinner party tonight, even if the job is still circling in part of your mind, may or may not make you a better person, a better cop, but I can promise you it's given you more years. A great many more years on the job."

"There was a time what you're saying would've just pissed me off."

A smile quirked Mira's lips. "Something else I know."

"Since it doesn't—much—maybe you're right. It's just dinner. You gotta eat." She looked down at the wrapper in her hand, gave a half laugh. "Eventually."

"I'll read the case file more thoroughly. If there's anything else, I'll contact you right away. And I'm going to red-flag this investigation. I'll be available to you for consult anytime. Day or night."

"Thanks." She rolled the wrapper into a ball, pitched it into a recycler. "And thanks for the boost. All around."

She stopped off in the bathroom to splash ice water on her face. And pulled out her communicator as she dried off.

"Peabody."

"Sir!"

Eve could see her white face, her startled eyes in the dim light of the crib. "On your feet, soldier. Media conference in fifteen. One Police Plaza."

"Got it. Just let me slap myself around and wake up. I'm on my way."

"Get there now. I'll slap you around."

"You sweet-talker."

Eve's lips twitched as she broke transmission. Maybe it wasn't such a hardship to open up her life—here and there.

In the grand scheme, Eve considered media conferences more of an ache in the ass than an actual pain. It was an annoyance, like a mild digestive disorder.

She could see the politics of the setup—using the steps of Central to make it a cop deal, rather than a mayoral one. Having the mayor make a brief statement before stepping back and giving the podium to the chief.

Tibble was terse and to the point, as she expected from him. He looked powerful and concerned and angry. All the traits you'd want in the city's top cop when a killer was brutalizing innocent women in the public parks. He wore a dark gray suit with a somber blue tie, and a small gold NYPSD badge in the form of a pin glinting on his lapel.

A formal and distinguished look, Eve supposed, that fit him like a glove. He took no questions, but like the mayor, issued a statement.

We're in charge, Eve concluded. *But we're not in the trenches. We work for order, and send our soldiers out to maintain it.*

It was a good theme, a strong stand, and a wise move to yield the podium to Whitney.

It all took time, and though no new information was really dispensed, it gave the media bones to gnaw on, and let the public know their top officials were on the job.

It was a good city, tightly run, Eve thought. For all its dark corners and jagged edges, it was a good city. That was important to remember. You didn't want to lose sight of the value and the strengths because you spent too much time wading through the wastes.

So she could stand here, in the bright light of a September afternoon on the steps of her house and know there was murder and meanness and casual cruelties, and still it was a good city.

A good city, and the only home she'd ever had.

"As primary on this investigation, Lieutenant Dallas will take more questions." Whitney turned to her. "Lieutenant."

Pecking order, Eve thought, and on impulse, took Peabody's arm, ignored the shocked jerk from it, and drew her to the podium.

"My partner, Detective Peabody, and I have little to add to the previous statements and the answers Commander Whitney has already given. This investigation is our priority. It is ongoing and active and we are pursuing any and all leads."

Questions spewed out like a geyser of hot air. She let them wash over her, then picked one out of the flood.

Both victims were mutilated. Do you believe these to be cult killings?

"None of the evidence we've accumulated during this investigation indicates cult involvement. We believe Elisa Maplewood and Lily Napier were both killed by one individual, acting alone and on his own volition."

Can you give us the nature of these mutilations?

"Due to the nature of the investigation, our desire to apprehend this individual with dispatch, and the necessity of building a strong case to bring said individual to justice, we can't reveal specifics as pertains to said investigation."

The public has a right to know.

Did they never tire of swinging that splintered bat? Eve wondered.

"The public has a right to be protected, and we're doing everything in our power to do so. The public has a right to be confident that its police force and city officials will work diligently to identify, apprehend, and prosecute the person responsible for the deaths of Elisa Maplewood and Lily Napier. The public does not have a right to all the salient and sensitive details of this case."

And you, she thought, don't have the right to clock up your ratings by slathering over the dead.

What connection is there between the two victims?

"Peabody," Eve murmured, and heard her partner gulp.

"They were both killed by the same method," Peabody stated. "They were both female, in the same age group, the same racial group. They were both in public parks at the time of the attacks."

What other connections? What are your leads?

"We're not able to disclose or discuss specific details of the investigation for reasons already stated."

Do you consider him a sexual predator?

"Two women," Eve began with what she considered Herculean patience, "were brutalized, raped, and murdered. I think you can draw your own conclusions."

Do you believe he'll kill again?

Can you describe the murder weapon in more detail?

Do you have any suspects?

Do you expect to make an arrest soon?

Will you close more parks?

Was the mutilation sexual in nature?

"I wonder." Her eyes had been flat and cold, but now hints of temper glinted in them. Eve interrupted the barrage of questions, and this time there was an edge in her voice. "I sincerely wonder which part of 'we will not disclose or discuss specifics' you fail, as a group, to comprehend. I wonder why you insist on wasting your breath and our time asking questions we cannot and will not answer. So let me save us all the effort and tell you what I know."

They quieted, as if she were about to reveal a new set of commandments. "Two women, and let me repeat their names in case you've forgotten them. Because I haven't forgotten who they were, nor has my partner, nor has any member of this department forgotten them. Their names are Elisa Maplewood and Lily Napier. These women's lives were violently and unrightfully taken. They were taken near their own homes, in our city. It is their rights that were violated in the most heinous way. It is their rights we will seek to defend as we continue our investigation. We will continue this investigation, with all the resources available, until such time as the individual who violated them is identified, apprehended, and incarcerated. I work for Elisa Maplewood and Lily Napier, and now I'm going to get back to it."

She turned away, strode back into Central, and ignored the questions hurled at her back.

The moment she was back in, a handful of cops, drones, and civilian liaisons broke into applause.

"Shit" was all Eve said, and that was under her breath.

"I thought you were brilliant," Peabody said from behind her. "Sincerely."

"Doesn't do any good to get pissed off, or to preach."

"I think you're wrong. I think Maplewood's and Napier's friends and families will appreciate what you said, and how you said it. Aside from that, I think it sends a message to the killer. Loud and clear. We're hunting him, and we're not going to stop."

"Yeah. Well, there's that."

"And since I enjoy watching you tear a small strip off the more assholey reporters, I can forgive you for tossing me into the deep end of the pool, without so much as a 'Hold your breath.'"

"You did fine."

"I did," Peabody agreed. Then closed her mouth quickly when Tibble and Whitney entered.

"Lieutenant, Detective." Tibble nodded to both of them. "You had considerable to say this afternoon, Lieutenant. Not your usual taciturn self."

"No, sir."

"Well said. Commander?"

Whitney paused as Tibble strode off. "Mayor's closing it down. A moment of silence for the victims." Whitney glanced toward the doors, cynicism in every pore. "An inspired touch and a good visual for the evening reports. Chill down a little," he suggested, "and get back to work."

"I'm as chilly as I'm going to get," Eve decided after he'd moved off to join Tibble. She checked the time. "It's early for anyone who was on Napier's shift, but let's take a shot at O'Hara's."

Her pocket 'link signaled. "Hell," she muttered when the readout warned her it was Nadine.

"I've made my statement, answered the questions. I'm done, Nadine."

"I'm not calling as a reporter. Give me five minutes."

She'd sneak, Eve thought, she'd prevaricate, but she wouldn't lie.

"Heading down to the garage. Can you get in there?"

The smirk twisted her lips. "Please."

"Level One, Section Three. I don't have time to wait for you."

She didn't have to wait. Nadine was already there, and the fact that she was idly buffing her fingernails told Eve she wanted to rub it in a little.

"I know this is your slot," Nadine began. "But since when is this your ride?"

Eve skimmed a hand over the fender of the shiny blue vehicle. Soon, when she was absolutely sure of privacy, she might just kiss it.

"Since my devious partner used the right bribe on the right person."

"Go, Peabody."

"It was nothing. A couple vids of Dallas naked in the shower, and we're cruising."

"Very funny. What do you want, Nadine? I'm on a tight schedule."

"Breen Merriweather." There was no smirk now.

"You have information?"

"I don't know that I do. I've very carefully asked some questions," she added before Eve could speak. "I know how to ask questions, and I comprehend all manner of things, including we will not discuss or disclose. Asking questions with the idea that Breen was one of this bastard's targets puts a different complexion on the answers. She made an offhand comment, a few nights before she disappeared, to some of the tech crew."

"What comment?"

"Coffee-break talk, some of the girl techs. One of them man-hunting. No good men left in the city. No big strong heroes, blah, blah. And Breen said she should come ride home with her some night. There was this big, silent type starting to ride her train. She made some joke about that old horse—you know, the size of a man's thumbs indicating the size of his equipment. Said this guy must be hung like a bull because his hands were the size of turkey platters."

"That it?"

"No." She pushed at her hair. "They were joking around, just chilling. So there was a lot of how big is he, Breen, and your expected lewd conversation. She—Breen—she said she'd pass him to one of the other girls, because he wasn't her type. She liked men with hair, and he was probably an asshole anyway, because he always wore sunshades. Middle of the night, and he's wearing sunshades."

"Okay."

"It had to be him."

"A lot of people ride the subway at night,

Nadine. Some of them are men. Some of the men are large. But yeah, it's possible."

"Trains have security cams."

"Yeah, they do." It was hard to look at hope, insistent hope, in the eyes of a friend. "And the discs are recycled every thirty days. She's been gone a lot longer than that."

"But you could—"

"I'll look into it."

"The sunshades, Dallas. He's got a thing for eyes."

"I comprehend things, too. I'm going to follow up on it."

"All right." She backed off though Eve could all but see her quiver to say more, to ask more. "You have to promise to let me know."

"Soon as I can."

Nadine nodded, then shook herself and looked back toward the vehicle. "So, how long you figure before you trash this one?"

"Shut up."

To discourage further conversation, she got in the car. She started it up, reversed around Nadine, and drove out of the garage.

And immediately contacted Feeney.

"I've got a tip."

"Me, too. Let a smile be your umbrella and you're gonna get your dumb ass wet."

"Huh. I'll remember that. Merriweather, Breen, missing and presumed. She commented to a coworker a couple days before she poofed about a big guy who started riding her train. Made a lot of comments regarding his size. Also described him as bald and wearing sunshades."

"Discs are recycled by now, if not destroyed." He pulled his lip. "We can go to the Transit Authority, cull through until we find discs, if they still exist, for that time period. We can pick through the images, try to find echoes of previous images. Lot of luck involved there, but we might find him."

She noticed—tried not to, but couldn't avoid it—that today's shirt was the color of lime juice. "I can ask Whitney for the extra manpower and OT you need."

"I can do my own begging, thanks. I'll send a couple of boys down to get started. Got the train route in the file."

"Keep me in the loop."

"McNab's eyes are going to bleed," Peabody commented when Eve ended transmission. "That's what he gets for being an e-man."

"We get a visual of this guy, we nail that visual, we nail the box."

It was going to take time, Eve thought. Not just hours, but days. And more than luck, it was going to require a small miracle.

O'Hara's was as advertised: a small, reasonably clean Irish-style pub. More authentic in that area, Eve noted, than some billed as such in the city that attempted to prove it by slapping up shamrocks everywhere and requiring the staff to speak with fake Irish accents.

This one was dimly lit, with a good, solid bar, deep booths, and low tables scattered around with short stools bracketing them rather than chairs.

The man working the stick was wide as a draft horse, and pulled pints of Harp, Guinness, Smithwick with an easy skill that told her he'd likely been doing so since he could stand.

He had a ruddy face, a thatch of sandy hair, and eyes that skimmed and scanned the room like a cop's.

He'd be the man to see.

"I've never had a Guinness," Peabody commented.

"You're not having one now."

"Yeah, on duty and all. But I'm going to have to try one sometime. Except they look a little scary and they cost beyond."

"Get what you pay for."

"Huh. Yet another tip."

Eve stepped up to the bar. Its tender pushed pints into waiting hands, then worked his way down. "Officers," he said.

"You've got good eyes. Mr. O'Hara?"

"I'm O'Hara. My father was on the job."

"Where?"

"In merry old Dublin."

She heard it in his voice, the same lilt that crept into Roarke's. "When did you come over?"

"When I was but a green and cheery twenty, off to seek my fortune. And did well enough."

"Looks like."

"Ah well." His face sobered. "You're here about Lily. You want my help, or that of any here, to find the bastard who murdered that sweet girl, you've got it. Michael, take the stick. We'll sit down a moment," he said to Eve. "Will you have a pint?"

"On duty," Peabody said, a little morosely, and he grinned.

"Beer's next thing to mother's milk, but I'll pour you out something soft. Take that booth down there. I'll be right along."

"Pretty nice place." Peabody settled in the booth, looked around. "I'm going to come back with McNab, try the Guinness. Does it come in light?"

"What would be the point?"

O'Hara brought two soda waters and a pint to the booth, and slid his bulk in across from them.

"To our Lily then." He lifted his glass. "Bless her sweet soul."

"What time did she leave here that night?"

He sipped. "I know you're cops, but I haven't your names as yet."

"Sorry." She pulled out her badge as she spoke. "Lieutenant Dallas, Detective Peabody."

"Roarke's cop. I thought so."

"You know Roarke?"

"Not in a personal manner of speaking. I've a few years on him, and we ran in different circles back in the day. My father knew him," O'Hara said with a twinkle.

"I bet."

"Did well for himself, too, didn't he now?"

"You could say. Mr. O'Hara—"

"I don't know him personally," O'Hara interrupted, and leaned in, his eyes keen on hers. "But I know of him. And one of the things I know is that he's a man who tends to want and have the best. Would that include his cop?"

"I'm sitting here, Mr. O'Hara, as Lily's cop. And I'm going to make damn sure she's got the best."

"Well." He sat back, lifted his pint again. "Well now, that's a fine answer. She left about half-one. It was a slow night so I scooted her along a bit early. I should've had someone walk her home. I should've thought of that after what happened to that uptown woman. But I never thought of it."

"You've got good eyes, Mr. O'Hara. Did you notice anyone in here that made you look harder?"

"Girl, doesn't a week go by someone doesn't make me take a harder look. I run a pub, after all. But not what you're meaning.

There was nobody I saw who made me think I'd need to worry for my girls."

"He'd be big," Eve continued. "A big man, strong-looking. He'd keep to himself, wouldn't socialize or make conversation. He might have worn sunshades. He wouldn't sit at the bar, unless there was no choice. He'd want a table—in Lily's section—and he'd make it clear he didn't want company."

"I'd remember someone like that." He shook his head. "But I don't. I'm here most nights. But not every."

"We'd like to talk to whoever worked Lily's shift."

"There'd be Michael, there at the bar now. And Rose Donnelly, Kevin and Maggie Lannigan. Ah, Pete, back in the kitchen at the dishes. Peter Maguire."

"Regulars?"

"Ah well. Why don't I write some of this down for you, get you addresses where I can. You can talk to Michael now, for he's a clever enough lad and can work the bar and talk at the same time."

"Thanks."

"Let me tell you something about Lily. She was a shy thing, and we teased her about it. She had a kind and quiet nature, and worked well. When she got to know you, got comfortable so to speak, she was easier. She had a smile for you, and she remembered your name and what you ordered. She didn't shine, but she was steady and sweet. We won't forget her."

"Neither will we."

14

The interviews took them past end-of-shift. And, Eve thought, unless she was going to screw up her personal life, she had to set the rest aside and head uptown.

"We could manage Rose Donnelly, that would finish it off." Peabody gestured west. "She doesn't live far."

"If it wasn't her night off, we might've caught her here. We can swing by, then I'll dump you and . . . Hold that thought." She dragged out her signaling 'link. "Dallas."

"I'm hoping I could speak to you." Celina's tired face filled the screen. "I can come to you."

"Something new?"

"No. Just . . . I'd like a few minutes."

"I'm downtown anyway. I'll come by now."

"Good. Thanks."

"I'll take Sanchez," Eve told Peabody. "See if you can link up with Donnelly, get her statement."

"Works for me. I'll see you later, at dinner. Walking another two blocks." Peabody rubbed her hands together. "I get to eat everything that's not nailed down."

Eve jumped back in the car, headed for SoHo. And called Roarke. "Hi. I'm running a little late."

"Shock and amazement."

"Everybody's got a joke today. I'll be there. I've just got to make another stop first."

"Don't worry about it. If little becomes very, do you prefer to go straight to Charles's, meet me there?"

"I'll let you know, but I hope to hell not. I want a goddamn shower. I think I can make it in an hour. Probably. Around."

"Close enough. I saw your press conference. They ran its entirety, and are following up with various sound bites."

"Goodie."

"I was very proud of you."

"Well . . . jeez."

"And I thought, if I were the man this woman with the cold and tired eyes was after, I would tremble."

"You wouldn't tremble if I was holding my weapon at your throat, but thanks. I'm going to take this last meet, then I'm heading home."

"Me, too."

"Oh." She brightened a bit. "You're still at work, didn't realize. That's good, that's better. I'm not the only one scrambling. See you."

Pleased with the situation, she pulled up in front of Celina's loft. Even as she crossed to the entrance, Celina's voice came through the intercom.

"I've cleared locks. Come right up."

Anxious, Eve thought as she went inside and entered the elevator. When it reached level two Celina was waiting to open the gate.

"Thanks for coming. Thanks for being so quick."

"I wasn't that far away. What's going on?"

"I need to . . . can I get you something? Tea? A glass of wine?"

"No. I'm heading home. I've got a thing."

"Oh." Distractedly, Celina brushed a hand through her hair. "Sorry. Let's sit down anyway. I made tea. Needed to keep busy while I waited for you."

Tea, Eve noted, along with little cookies, some neat wedges of cheese. Looked like girl-chat time to her, and she didn't have the time or the inclination. "You said there wasn't anything new."

"I haven't had another vision." She sat, poured tea for herself. "I kept some of my appointments today. Thought I should try. But I ended up cancelling the rest after taking the first two. I just can't concentrate."

"Tough on business."

"I can afford the time off. The regulars understand, and as for new clients . . ." She moved her shoulders, elegantly. "It adds to the mystique. But that's not the point."

"And the point is?"

"I'm getting to it." Celina tilted her head. "Not much on small talk, are you?"

"I figure there's a reason it's called small."

"Suppose you're right. To begin, I watched your media conference. I wasn't going to, but I felt, I thought, I should."

She curled up her legs. "And it made me think."

"It made you think what?"

"I can do more. I should do more. There's a reason I'm getting these visions. I don't know what it is, not specifically, but I know there's a purpose. And while I'm doing the minimum I feel is required of me, I could do more."

She sipped tea, then set the cup down. "I want to discuss going under hypnosis."

Eve lifted her eyebrows. Just when you're ready to bail, she thought, something interesting comes along. "How would that help?"

"There's a part of me that's blocking." Celina touched her hands to either side of her head, then her heart. "Call it a survival mechanism, which I like better than yellow-bellied cowardice. Something in me that doesn't want to know, to see, to remember, so I don't."

"Blocking the way you block picking up impressions or whatever you call them from people without their consent?"

"Not really. That's a conscious act, though it becomes as elemental as breathing. This is subconscious. The human mind is a powerful and efficient tool. We don't use it to its capacity. I don't think we dare."

She picked up one of the little golden cookies she'd set out with the tea, and nibbled. "We are able to block. Trauma victims often do. They're unable or unwilling to remember the trauma, or details of it, because they can't or won't face it. You must see this sort of thing in your work."

And in herself, Eve thought. In all the years she'd blocked out what had happened in that room in Dallas. "Yes."

"Under hypnosis, those blocks can be removed or lowered. I may see more. I know there's more, and I may see it. With the right practitioner . . . I'd need someone—I'd insist on someone very skilled not only in hypnosis, but in dealing with sensitives. I'd want a medical doctor present as well. I'd want Dr. Mira to do it."

"Mira."

"After you gave me her name, I did some research. She's very qualified in all the areas I'd need. She's also a criminologist, so it seems to me she'd be more cognizant of what to ask me, where to guide me while I was under. You trust her."

"Absolutely."

Celina gestured with the cookie. "And I trust you. I don't put myself in just any hands, Dallas. To be honest, I'm afraid of this. But I'm more afraid of doing nothing. And you know what's worse?"

"No."

"I'm terrified I've been pushed into a new arena. That what I have, what I am, is moving down a path I never wanted for myself." She hugged her right arm, rubbing it gently as if to soothe a spasm. "That I'm going to spend the next phase of my life seeing murder and violence, linking with victims. I liked my life the way it was. It makes it harder to realize it may never be just that way again."

"And still you want me to contact Dr. Mira?"

She nodded. "The sooner the better. If I stall, I might lose the courage to follow it through."

"Give me a minute," Eve said as she pulled out her 'link.

"Oh. Right." Celina rose, picked up the tea tray. She carried it into the kitchen.

With slow, deliberate moves, she put the clean cup and saucer away, set her own in the sink.

Then she laid her hands on her face, pressed her fingers to her closed lids. And hoped, with everything she was, that she was ready for what was coming.

"Celina?"

"Yes." On a quick jerk, she dropped her hands, then turned to the doorway where Eve stood.

"Dr. Mira can see you tomorrow, at nine. She'll need to do a consult first, and a physical exam before she agrees to hypnotherapy."

"Yes, good." She squared her shoulders as if adjusting to a weight, or shrugging one off. "That makes sense. Will you—could you be there?"

"If and when the hypnosis is approved, yes. Up until you're set to go under, you can change your mind."

Clasping a hand over the crystals dangling from her neck chain, Celina shook her head. "No, I won't. I thought this through, up and down and sideways before I contacted you. I won't change my mind. We're going to move ahead. I can promise you, I won't turn back now."

Eve dashed in the house, slammed the door at her back. "I'm late," she snapped before

Summerset could speak. "But here's the thing, I'm not always late, but you're always ugly. Who's got the real problem?"

Since she finished the question at the top of the stairs and kept going, she wasn't annoyed with any reply he might have made.

She stripped off her jacket as she hit the bedroom door. Released her weapon harness and tossed it on the sofa. Yanked off boots by hopping one-footed toward the bathroom, and had her shirt off when she heard the water running.

Damn, he'd beaten her home after all.

She peeled off the rest. "Turn that water temp up."

"Done. I adjusted when I heard the graceful patter of your delicate feet stomping about in the bedroom."

Knowing Roarke wasn't above being hysterically amused by having her scream after jumping into cold water, she stuck her hand in the spray first.

"Trusting soul," he said and grabbing her hand hauled her in. "Let's stay home and make hot, wet love in the shower."

"Forget it." She elbowed him aside, pumped soap into her hand. "We're going to dinner. We're going to sit around somebody else's house and make stupid conversation and eat food we don't even get to pick for ourselves and pretend not to wonder exactly where in the apartment McNab and Charles punched each other out."

"I can hardly wait." He pumped shampoo and began to lather it into her hair.

"What are you doing?"

"Saving you time. What have you done here?"

She hunched her shoulders. "Nothing."

"You have. You've been whacking at your hair again."

"It was in my eyes."

"Back here?" He tugged. "Fascinating. Does the NYPSD know they have a cop with eyes in the back of her head? Has the CIA been notified?"

"I can do this myself." She pulled back, scrubbed vigorously at her hair while glaring at him. "Don't tell Trina."

He smiled, wolfishly. "And what would my silence be worth to you?"

"You want a quick hand job?"

"See, you're being deliberately crude to put me off." He tapped her chin. "Oddly enough, it doesn't work."

"She'll know anyway," Eve muttered, and

stuck her head under the jets. "She'll know, the next time she gets her hands on me. And she'll make me pay. She'll pour goo all over me, and lecture, and paint my nipples blue or something."

"What an interesting picture that creates in my fevered brain."

"I don't know why I did it." She jumped out and into the drying tube. "I couldn't help myself."

"Tell it to the judge," Roarke advised.

They weren't very late, Peabody thought. And when you had two cops—two currently overworked, sleep-deprived cops—being on time wasn't even in the realm.

Besides, she'd wanted to take as much time as she could squeeze out to make sure she looked her best. Since McNab had given her a big, "Oh, baby!" she figured she'd pulled it off.

He looked pretty adorable himself. His hair was all shiny and slick, and his cute little butt was nice and snug against the seat of black pants—saved from being too conservative by the fluorescent silver stripe running down each leg.

She had her hostess gift—a clutch of fairly fresh tiger lilies she'd snagged from a vender near her subway stop—and they'd been cleared through the lobby to the elevator.

"Now, you're going to play nice, right?"

"Of course I'm going to play nice." He fiddled with the collar of his silver shirt and wondered if he should've added a tie. Give Monroe a run for his sophisticated money. "Why wouldn't I?"

She rolled her eyes at him as they stepped into the elevator.

"Then. Now. Then you were sleeping with him, and I was drunk and pissed off. Now you're not and neither am I. Drunk and pissed off," he qualified.

She ordered Charles's floor, fluffed at her hair, and wished she'd had time to curl it, just for a change. "Neither was I."

"What did you have to be drunk and pissed off about?" he asked.

"Sleeping with him. You sure my ass doesn't look fat in these pants?"

"What?"

"My ass." She craned her head around to try to see for herself. "It feels like it looks fat."

"What do you mean you weren't sleeping with him? After Louise? You mean after Louise."

"I mean ever. There ought to be a mirror in here so I could check my fat ass."

"Your ass isn't fat, and shut up. You were going around with him for months."

She gave the flowers she carried a little sniff. "You sleep with everybody you go around with?"

"Pretty much. Now just a damn minute."

"We're going to be late," she said as she stepped off the elevator and into the hall.

"We're going to be later. You telling me you never boinked the LC? *Ever?*"

"Charles and I were, are, friends. That's it."

McNab grabbed her arm, hauled her back a step. "You let me think you were boinking him."

"No, *you* let you think I was." She poked a finger into his chest. "And made an ass of yourself, which is a pretty short walk, really."

"You—he—" He paced down the hall and back again. "Why?"

"Because we were friends, and because I was boinking you, moron."

"But we broke up because . . ."

"Because, instead of asking what was going on, you accused and you ordered, and took that short walk to Assville."

"And you tell me now, a minute before we walk in his door."

"Yeah."

"That's cold, Peabody."

"Yeah." She patted his cheek. "I wait for payback, and I deliver. You were a jerk coming over here toasted and punching him, but I like that part. Which is why I was magnanimous enough to forgive you for sleeping with the twins."

"I didn't." He tapped a finger on her nose. "Gotcha."

"You didn't?"

"I was going to, and I could have because we were on the breakup shuttle. But I didn't want the twins."

"You bragged about it."

"Hey, I've got a dick. Man's got a dick, he's gotta have pride in it."

"You *are* a dick," she said, but with a sloppy grin. "Now I forgive you for thinking I was bouncing back and forth between you and Charles like some sex bunny."

"She-body, you're my little sex bunny."

"Aw." She flung her arms around him to

exchange the sloppy grin for a big, sloppy kiss.

The elevator doors opened behind them. "Oh God! There goes my appetite."

"Dallas." Peabody sent a dreamy look over McNab's shoulder. "We're making up."

"Next time make up in a dark, locked room. McNab, your hands are in violation of several civil codes."

"Whoops." Still, he gave Peabody's butt a final squeeze.

"You start on the transit discs?"

"Eve." Roarke laid a hand on her shoulder, aimed her toward Charles's apartment. "Let's at least try to make it through the door before you grill the detectives. Peabody, you look charming."

"Thanks. This is going to be fun."

They answered together, Charles Monroe, the urbane LC, and Louise Dimatto, the blue-blooded doctor dedicated to the downtrodden. Eve had to admit, they looked good together. He with his handsome vid king looks, and she with her polished-gold beauty.

It didn't mean she didn't consider it one of the oddest couplings of her acquaintance, but they looked good together.

"Everyone at once." Louise laughed and reached for Eve, the closest. "Come in. It's so good to see everybody when none of us is working."

She kissed Eve's cheek, then made a fuss over the flowers Peabody offered.

"Lieutenant Sugar." Charles went for the hello kiss as well, but he aimed for the mouth. There was a twinkle in his eye shot in McNab's direction, as he gave Peabody the same greeting.

It was going to be, Eve decided, a really weird evening.

The wine Roarke brought was welcomed, and opened. Conversation, Eve realized after ten minutes, wasn't stilted or sparse. Everyone appeared to be in a party mood. She'd just have to tuck the case into another area of the brain and get into the personal game for a few hours.

There was Louise, looking happy and picture pretty perched on the arm of Charles's chair, and wearing the casual gear of a dark pink sweater and black pants. Bare feet with pink toenails. And to Eve's considerable surprise, a little gold toe ring.

Charles kept touching her in that absent and intimate way a man touched a woman who was his focus. A brush on the arm, a stroke on the knee.

Didn't she wonder about the women who paid him to touch them and a hell of a lot more? Apparently not, Eve decided, by the gooey looks they sent each other every five minutes.

And there were McNab and Peabody, snuggled together on the cushy leather couch laughing and talking without any sign of awkwardness. Just one big happy family.

As a trained observer, she could safely say she was the only one weirded out.

Even as she thought it, Roarke leaned toward her, laid his lips close to her ear. "Relax."

"Working on it," she mumbled.

"Louise has been fussing half the day," Charles commented.

"I have." Louise shook back her cloud of hair. "It's the first time we've entertained friends together. And I like to fuss."

Fussing, Eve concluded, ran to putting small arrangements of color-coordinated flowers in little clear vases and positioning them in strategic spots throughout the apartment, and marrying the flowers with lots of white candles in different shapes and sizes so the light was subtle and gold.

She'd probably selected the background music, too. Something muted and bluesy that suited the lighting. The table was already set with lots of candles and flowers there, too. And glassware that glinted.

Put it all together with the wine and predinner finger food, and you had a cozy, relaxing atmosphere for an intimate gathering of friends.

How did people *know* how to put it together? she wondered. Did they take classes? Punt and hope for the best? Buy instruction discs?

"It was worth it," Peabody commented. "Everything looks mag."

"I'm just glad we're all here." Louise sent her smile around the room. "I wasn't sure you'd be able to make it—you particularly, Dallas. I've been following the case in the media reports."

"People keep telling me I need an actual life outside the job." Eve shrugged. "I figure if you get away from it for a little while, maybe you'll come back fresh."

"A healthy attitude," Louise said.

"Yeah, that's me." Eve leaned over and

plucked one of the colorfully topped crackers from a canapé tray. "My 'tude's always healthy."

"Especially when she's kicking your ass." With a grin, McNab ate a tiny stuffed shrimp.

"Skinny as yours is, pal, it doesn't take much."

"Do you ever get your skinny ass back to Scotland?" Louise asked him.

"Not really. I was born here and all that. Went back and forth a lot when I was a kid. My parents decided to roost back there, outside Edinburgh about five years ago, I guess. I was thinking, maybe next time Peabody and I have some real time, we could go check it out."

"Scotland?" She goggled at him. "Really?"

"They've got to meet my girl."

Her cheeks pinked. "I always wanted to go over and see Europe. You know, the countryside. Tromp around in fields and gawk at ruins."

Conversation turned to travel.

"Dallas," Louise said in an aside. "Give me a hand in the kitchen?"

"The kitchen? Me?"

"For a minute."

"Ah. Okay."

Eve followed her in, looked around. "We're not going to actually cook or anything?"

"What, do I look simple? Everything's stocked from a very nice restaurant around the corner. It's just a matter of putting it together for the table, which I'll take care of in a minute."

Louise sipped her wine, studying Eve over the rim. "Are you taking care of yourself?"

"What? Why?"

"Because you look tired."

"Well, shit. I spent a good five minutes slapping goop on my face. What's the point?"

"Your eyes look tired. I'm a doctor, I know these things. And I would've understood if you'd needed to cancel tonight."

"Thought about it, but the fact is I couldn't do anymore. Maybe I needed a break from it. Maybe I've got to learn how to take a break from it."

"That's good. But we'll make this an early evening."

"We'll see how it goes. You and Charles . . . things cruising there?"

"They are. He makes me awfully happy. No one has, in just that way, in a very long time."

"You look happy. Both of you."

"Funny, isn't it, how you find someone when you've stopped looking."

"I don't know. I never looked."

"Now that hurts." With a laugh, Louise leaned back against the counter. "You don't even bother to look, and you end up with Roarke."

"He just got in my way. Couldn't get around him, so I figured I might as well keep him." And oddly, she realized, it wasn't small talk when it was with a friend. It was just . . . talk.

"We're thinking about taking a little holiday together, maybe next month. Go up to Maine or Vermont, look at the fall foliage and stay in some quaint little inn."

"You're going to go look at trees?"

Laughing, Louise brushed Eve aside to set up the salads. "People do, Dallas."

"Yeah." Eve drank. "Takes all kinds."

* * *

Bitches. Whores.

All but consumed with rage, he stormed around the apartment. He had the screen on repeat, playing the Channel 75 interview and the media conference over and over and over.

He couldn't help himself.

They'd sent women out after him. Women discussing him, analyzing him, condemning him. Did they think he was going to *take* that?

Look at them. Pretending to be so good, so clean, so *righteous.* But he knew better. He'd seen, and he knew. Underneath they were cheap and vicious. Weak and vile.

He was stronger. Look at him now. Just look.

He did, turning to one of the walls of mirrors to admire his body. The sheer shape and strength. The perfection he'd worked so hard to achieve. He was a *man.*

"Do you see? Do you see what I am?"

He turned, holding out his arms, and a dozen pairs of eyes stared back at him as they floated in their jars.

They could see him now. She could see him. She had no choice but to look at him. Forever.

"What do you think now, Mother? Who's in charge now?"

They were all hers. All those staring eyes. But she was still out there, judging him, ready with her punishing hand, her slashing belt. Ready to lock him in the dark so he couldn't see. So he wouldn't know.

He'd take care of that. Oh, yes, he would. He'd fix her little red wagon. He'd show her who was boss. He'd show all of them.

They'd pay. This mother's son would make them pay, he thought as he stared back at the screen. He'd show them what he could do.

These three. He moved closer to the screen, gritting his teeth as he looked at Eve, at Peabody, at Nadine. They'd have to be punished. Sometimes you had to deviate from the plan, that's all. So they'd have to be punished. You were punished when you were bad. You were punished when you were good.

He'd save the top bitch for last, that's what he'd do. He smiled fiercely at Eve.

It was always smart to save the best for last.

* * *

It was a good meal, with good company. For nearly two hours, murder didn't play in her head. She enjoyed, particularly, watching Roarke relate. The way he slid, so smoothly, between Charles's urbane sophisticate and McNab's street-smart wiseass. How he mixed with the women, flattering without being oily, flirting without being obnoxious.

Effortlessly. Or it seemed effortless. But wouldn't he have things on his mind, too? The big wheels and complex deals that made up his work and a large part of his life. He would've spent the day buying and selling God knew what, coordinating and supervising projects she couldn't begin to imagine. Taking meetings, making decisions, contemplating the enormous chessboard of his empire.

Then he could sit, over coffee and dessert, telling a story about some bar fight from his youth to make McNab roll with laughter, or exchanging opinions about great art with Charles.

On the way home, he reached over, brushed a hand over hers. "That was a very nice evening."

"It didn't even nearly suck."

"High praise indeed."

She laughed at herself, stretched out her legs. Somewhere along the line she'd taken his advice. She'd relaxed. And after she'd relaxed, damn if she hadn't enjoyed. "I mean it."

"Darling Eve, I know you do."

"You're a layered guy, Roarke."

"I'm nothing if not."

"I don't know why I'm surrounded by smart-asses."

"Birds of a feather."

"Anyway," she said after a beat. "It was educational to watch you schmooze."

"I wasn't schmoozing. Schmoozing is business, or business-related. This was personal and friendly conversation."

"Ha. The things you learn." She leaned her head back. She was tired, but she realized, she wasn't weighed down by fatigue. "There was a lot of conversation. And it wasn't even boring or irritating."

"God." He picked up her hand, pressed it to his lips as he drove through the gates. "I adore you."

"Lot of that going around tonight, too."

"It was pleasant to spend time with two couples so obviously in love."

"Hard to miss it with all the gooey looks and pats and strokes. Sex sizzling in the air and all that. You ever think how it'd be if you switched them around?"

"Sizzling looks, gooey sex? I think of little else."

She snickered as they got out of the car to walk to the door. "No. The people. You put Peabody with Charles and McNab with Louise. It'd be totally screwed up."

"You could put Peabody with Louise."

"Sick. You're a sick man."

"Just playing the game." He took her hand as they walked upstairs to the bedroom. "You seem to have your second wind, Lieutenant."

"I think it's my third, maybe fourth of the day. I actually feel pretty good." She booted the door shut behind her. "In fact, sitting around in all that sizzle's got me hyped. How about some gooey sex?"

"Thought you'd never ask."

Hooking an arm around his neck, she jumped so he could catch her in his arms. She calculated her weight, his, narrowed her eyes. "How far do you figure you can carry me?"

"To the bed would be my first guess."

"No, I mean how far do you think you could haul me like this? Especially if I'm . . ." She went limp, dropped her weight, let her arms dangle.

She felt him shift and adjust, not quite stagger. "Tougher this way, right?"

"I still think I can manage the bed, where I certainly hope you plan to revive a bit."

"You're in good shape, but I bet you'd feel it if you had to carry me, say, twenty, thirty yards like this."

"Since I haven't strangled you, yet, I won't have to."

She boosted back up as he climbed the platform with her. "Sorry. No murder in the bedroom tonight."

She kept her arms locked around his neck when he lowered her to the bed. "You touch me."

Obviously amused, he nipped at her chin and that wonderful hair brushed her cheeks like strands of silk. "That's definitely on the agenda."

"No." She laughed again, then rolled over on top of him. "When we're just hanging out, when you don't even think about it. I like it."

She leaned down to rub her lips over his,

and linking fingers, stretching sinuously down, slid his arms over his head. "I like this."

"Enjoy yourself," he invited.

"Probably should make it fairly quick, in case I lose this third, fourth wind." She closed her teeth over his jaw, nipping lightly.

Keeping his hands locked with hers, she ran her lips down his throat, traced them back to his. Then she curled back like a cat to unbutton his shirt.

"Yeah." She rubbed her hands over his chest. "You're in shape." Then her lips.

She could feel his heartbeat pick up, drum lightly under her hands and lips. He wanted. Wasn't it amazing he always wanted her?

The muscles of his belly quivered when she tasted there, and jumped when she ran her tongue under his waistband. She slid down the zipper, freed him. Tormented him.

Then uncurling, she watched him as she peeled off her shirt, as she took his hands and pressed them to her breasts.

On a low hum of pleasure her head fell back. His hands were hard and smooth and skilled. The long, liquid tugs began, from heart to belly, from belly to loins, when he used them on her.

"Let me. Let me have—" He reared up, clamped his mouth on her, and the hum became a sob, the tugs a burn.

Now it could be desperate, now it could be urgent. Slick body straining to slick body, hands and mouths greedy for more. The sharp nip of teeth, the quick bite of nails, the hot slide of tongues.

She was trembling when she straddled him. Once again their hands and eyes locked. She took him in, took him deep. And cried out.

Breathless, she lowered her brow to his, fought for breath, for sanity. "A minute," she managed. "It's too much. Wait a minute."

"It's not too much." His mouth seared over hers. "It's never too much."

Never would be. She rose up, and rode.

15

While Eve was curled in dreamless sleep against Roarke, a woman named Annalisa Sommers split her part of the check and said good night to a few friends.

Her monthly post-theater club had broken up a little later than usual as everyone had a lot of news to share. The club was just an excuse, really, for her to get together with some of her friends and have a bite to eat, a few drinks—and talk about men, work—men.

But it also gave her the benefit of several opinions on whatever play they'd seen. She used them, as well as her own, for her weekly column in *Stage Right Magazine.*

She loved the theater, and had since she'd

played a yam in her first-grade Thanksgiving Day pageant. Since she couldn't act—though she'd pulled the yam off well enough to have her mother cry a little—had no skill for design or direction, she'd turned hobby into career by writing observations, rather than straight reviews, on plays on and off—and way, way off—Broadway.

The pay was lousy, but the benefits included free seats and regular backstage passes as well as the buzz of being able to make a semblance of a living doing something she enjoyed.

And she had a good feeling that the pay was going to improve, very soon. Her column was growing in popularity for the very reasons she'd hyped when talking herself into a job with *Stage Right.* Regular people wanted to know what other regular people thought about a play. Critics weren't regular people. They were *critics.*

After ten months on the job, she was beginning to get recognized on the street and enjoyed having people stop her to discuss, to agree or disagree, it didn't matter.

She was having the time of her life.

Everything was going so well. With work, with Lucas. New York was her personal playground, and there was no place else on earth she'd rather be. When she and Lucas got married—and her friends agreed things were definitely heading in that direction—they'd find a mag apartment on the West Side, throw fun and quirky little parties, and be ridiculously happy.

Hell, she was ridiculously happy now.

She tossed back her hair, and hesitated at the northwest corner of Greenpeace Park. She always cut through the park, knew the route through like she knew the route from her own kitchen to her own bedroom.

A very short walk, she admitted, until that pay raise.

But two women had been killed in city parks in the last week, so a shortcut at one in the morning might not be a smart move.

That was ridiculous. Greenpeace was practically her backyard. She'd be through it in five minutes, and home safe, tucked into her own little bed and counting sheep before two.

She was a native New Yorker, for God's sake, she reminded herself as she veered off the sidewalk and into the leafy shadows. She knew how to handle herself, how to stay aware. She'd taken self-defense courses, stayed in shape. And she had Anti-Mugger spray *with* panic alarm in her pocket.

She loved this park, day or night. The trees, the little play areas for kids, the co-op gardens for vegetables or flowers. It showed, to Annalisa, just how diverse the city was. Concrete and cucumbers, spreading within feet of each other.

The image made her laugh as she walked quickly along the path toward home.

She heard the kitten mewing before she saw it. It wasn't unusual to find a stray cat, even a feral one in the park. But this one, she saw as she walked closer, wasn't a cat. It was just a kitten, a little ball of gray fur, curled on the path and crying pitifully.

"Poor little thing. Where's your mama, you poor little thing?"

She crouched down, picked it up. It was only when she held it she realized it was a droid. She thought: Weird.

The shadow fell over her. Her hand dived into her pocket for the spray even as she started to spring back to her feet.

But the blow to the back of her head sent her sprawling.

The droid continued to mew and cry as blows rained down on her.

At seven hundred and twenty hours the next morning, Eve stood over Annalisa Sommers. The park smelled green. Verdant—she thought that was the word. Sort of alive and burgeoning.

You could hear the morning traffic, on the street and overhead, but here, there was a small slice of countrified with a vegetable patch spread out in tidy rows behind a screen of pest and vandal fence. She didn't know what the hell was growing in it. Leafy stuff and viney stuff and things that sprawled over small, neat hills.

Part of that verdant smell was probably fertilizer or manure or whatever the hell these people mixed in the dirt to grow things they'd eventually put in their mouths and call natural.

Well, come to think of it, there wasn't anything much more natural than shit.

Except blood and death.

At the end of the patch, behind the odd little vertical triangles where vines grew, behind the screen to keep dogs and street people out, was a statue of a man and a woman. Each wore a hat. He carried some sort of hoe or rake, and she a basket loaded with what was meant to be the fruits of their labor. A harvest.

Harvest was the name of the statue, she knew, but everyone called it Ma and Pa Farmer. Or just Ma and Pa.

Annalisa lay at their feet, like an offering to the gods with her hands clasped between her naked breasts. Her face was bloody and ruined, her body covered with bruises.

"Crappy way to start the day," Peabody commented.

"Yeah. A lot crappier for her."

Eve fixed on her goggles, got out her gauges. "Get her ID."

She began to recite what the recorder could already see.

"Victim is Caucasian female. Evidence of violence on face, torso, limbs. Broken clavicle. No defensive wounds evident. Red corded ribbon at the throat apparent murder weapon. Strangulation. There is evidence of sexual assault. Bruising and lacerations on the thighs and genitals."

"ID'd as Annalisa Sommers, age thirty-two. Resides Fifteen West Thirty-first."

"Identification now on record. Victim's eyes have been removed in a manner similar to previous victims Maplewood and Napier. Manner of assault, death, mutilation, location type, and position of body all in accordance with previous victims."

"He doesn't vary much from pattern," Peabody said.

"Not much. Why mess with success? Got some hair fibers. On her right hand, adhering to the dried blood."

She tweezed them off, bagged them. And sat back on her haunches.

"What was she doing in here, Dallas? Walking through here in the middle of the damn night. They four-walled the media conference. She had to know this guy trolls the parks."

"Not going to happen to her. People always think it can't happen to them, instead of thinking it's going to happen to somebody, why *not* me."

She studied the body. "She lives close. That fits with the others, too. Odds are she had a pattern, coming through here, on her way home, or away from home. She cuts through, knows her way around. Hair's not right," Eve muttered.

"A little shorter than the others, a little darker. But still in the ballpark."

"Yeah."

"He'd have to be a little flexible, wouldn't he?"

"Apparently."

With the scene on record, the body's position logged, she turned the victim's head, lifted it. "Took a blow to the back of the head. Hard blow. Maybe he comes up behind her, comes up, hits her, takes her down. She's got some scrapes at the knees, grass and dirt in the cuts. She goes down, hands and knees."

She lifted one of the hands, showed the abrasions on the heels. "Then he lays into her. Beating, kicking. Violence is escalating each time. More premortem violence. Losing it. Rapes her, carts her over, finishes the job."

"We didn't hear from Celina on this one."

"Noticed that?" Eve pushed to her feet. "We'll tag her in a few minutes. Let's look at the kill site."

It wasn't far this time, just on the other end of the vegetable patch, along the path.

Traces of blood were in splotches or sprinkles or smears, over grass and dirt.

Made it easier for him, Eve thought. He only had to carry this one about eight feet.

"Lieutenant?" One of the sweepers held out an evidence bag. "Found this at point three there. Standard pocket-sized Anti-Mugger. Might be hers. Didn't do her a lot of good."

"We'll check for prints."

"Got some hair, too. Few strays on the path, point one. Gray, so they aren't hers. Eyeballing, they don't look human."

"Thanks."

"Probably squirrel again," Peabody said.

"Maybe. What was her employment, Peabody?"

"Columnist, *Stage Right Mag.*"

Eve nodded. "Coming home then. Walking home. Oh-one hundred's late for theater. A drink after, maybe, or dinner. A date. Shortcut it through the park. It's her neighborhood. She's got her spray in her pocket just in case, so no worries. Quick breeze through and you're back on the street and almost at your own doorstep. He's waiting for her. Got the spot picked out, knows she'll walk right by. Takes her down from behind."

She frowned at the slight impression on the grass one of the sweepers had already marked. "Carts her over to lay her under Ma and Pa. Finishes the job." She shook her head again.

"Get what else you can on her. Next of kin, spouse, cohabit partner. I'm going to try Celina before we look at the vic's residence."

She moved away from the crime scene areas, put in the call.

Impatient, she jammed her hand into her pocket. The 'link had just switched to voice mail when Celina answered. "Cancel answering system." Celina pushed at her hair. "Sorry, I was asleep. I barely heard the signal. Dallas? Shit, shit! Am I late for my appointment?"

"You got time. Get a good night's sleep, Celina?"

"I did. Tranq'd the hell out of myself." Her eyes were a little dopey, a little vague. "Still groggy. Look, can this wait until I get some coffee?"

"We had another one."

"Another what?"

Eve saw the realization seep in, widen Celina's heavy eyes. "Oh God. No."

"I want some time with you. I'll meet you at Mira's office."

"I'll . . . I'll get there as soon as I can."

"Just keep the nine o'clock. I can't get there sooner."

"I'll meet you there. I'm sorry. Dallas, I'm sorry."

"Me, too."

"Got a mother and a sister in the city," Peabody told Eve. "Father's remarried and lives in Chicago. No spouse. Never married. No kids."

"Let's take the apartment, then the mother."

It was a small place—dramatic and messy, as Eve thought was often the case with single women. Playbills and theater posters were her decorator's choice. A playback of her 'link transmissions turned up several in just the last twenty-four hours of her life.

"Chatty girl," Eve commented. "We've got the mother, the sister, coworkers, gal pals, and a guy called Lucas who's apparently her romantic interest. All this chatter tells us she went to see a play at the Trinity last night, then out for supper and drinks with friends. Let's run the friends, and see if we can ID this Lucas."

"I'll see what I can get from the neighbors."

When Peabody went out, Eve continued to look around. Lived alone, she decided, but entertained men—or a man—from time to time. Date underwear in the drawers, along with a few standard sex toys. There were a few photos and holos, and two of them showed the victim with the same man.

Coffee-light skin, dark hair, neat goatee with soul patch, big smile with lots of teeth. Nice-looking guy, she thought, and she'd bet the bank his name was Lucas.

She took the photo into evidence. If they didn't get a last name, she'd run the picture for an ID match.

A gregarious, sociable woman who liked the theater, Eve mused. Kept up a friendly relationship with her mother and sister, had several pals, and from the conversations on the 'link had a monogamous romantic relationship with a man named Lucas.

And was dead because she cut through the park to save herself three blocks.

No, Eve corrected. She was dead because someone selected her, stalked her, and killed her. If she hadn't cut through the park last night, there'd have been another time or another way.

She'd been a target. Mission accomplished.

"Lucas Grande." Peabody came back in. "Songwriter and session musician. They've been seeing each other for a while. Neighbor said six months, or a little more. She saw the vic on her way out last night, about seven. Just waved at each other, but the neighbor thinks she was wearing jeans and a blue sweater, short black jacket."

"Get an address for Grande. We'll take him after we see her mother."

Eve wasn't sure which was worse, telling a mother her daughter was dead and watching her shatter, or telling a man his woman was dead and watching him dissolve.

They'd woken him. He'd come to the door sleepy-eyed, rumpled, and mildly annoyed.

"Look, I turned the music down. I don't play it loud after ten o'clock. Nobody complains on this floor. I don't know what bug's up the ass of that guy upstairs. He's so freaking hyped, he can spring for soundproofing."

"This isn't about a disturbance or complaint, Mr. Grande. We're going to need to come in."

"Well, shit." He backed up, gestured impatiently. "If Bird got busted for Zoner again, it's got nothing to do with me. We do sessions together. We're not joined at the damn hip."

"We're here about Annalisa Sommers."

"Annalisa?" His mouth quirked. "Did she and her girlfriends get polluted and do something stupid last night? I gotta bail her out or something?"

"Mr. Grande, I'm sorry to tell you, Ms. Sommers was killed last night."

The tickled smile dropped off his face. "That's not funny. What the hell's wrong with you to say something like that?"

"Mr. Grande, her body was found this morning, in Greenpeace Park."

"Come on. Come on." He retreated as he said it, his hands coming up as if begging her to stop.

"Let's sit down."

"Annalisa?" Tears flooded his eyes. "Are you sure it's Annalisa? It could be somebody else."

Anybody else, he'd be thinking, Eve knew. Anybody but mine.

"I'm very sorry, Mr. Grande. There's no mistake. We need to ask you some questions now."

"I just saw her yesterday. Grabbed lunch with her yesterday. We've got a date Saturday. How can she be dead?"

"We're going to sit down now." Peabody took his arm, led him to a chair.

The room was crowded with instruments. Some sort of keyboard, a music comp, a couple of guitars, sound boxes. Eve snaked between them to sit across from him. "You and Annalisa were seeing each other."

"We're going to get married. As soon as I ask her. I was going to ask her at Christmas. Wait until Christmas, make it special. What happened to her?"

"Mr. Grande, tell us where you were last night."

He had his hands to his face, and the tears were trickling through his fingers. "You think I could hurt her? I couldn't ever hurt her. I *love* her."

"No, I don't think that, but I need to ask."

"I had a session, ran until midnight, maybe later. After we hung around the studio, had some brews, some pizza, jammed. Got home, I don't know, around three. Jesus, did somebody hurt her?"

"Yes, somebody hurt her."

His face was already splotchy from weeping, but now it went white under the stain. "You said the park. Oh, my Jesus Christ. You said the park. Those other women. It was like those other women? Annalisa?"

"Tell me where you had your session, and who was there, and we'll get that out of the way."

"Tunes, on Prince. Um. Bird. God, God." His hands were all over his face, into his hair, fingers trembling. "John Bird, and Katelee Poder and I can't think straight. Her mother, have you told her mother?"

"We've just come from there."

"They're tight. Really tight. Gave me the once-over about five times. But she's okay. We get along good. I gotta go over there."

"Mr. Grande, do you know if anyone was bothering Annalisa? Someone you noticed, someone she mentioned."

"No. She'll mention if her nose itches, so

she'd say if there was. I've gotta go see her mom. I've gotta go be with her family. We need to go see Annalisa together. We need to do that together."

She'd had a solid seven hours' sleep, Eve thought, and had ended the previous day with a nice dinner with friends, and very satisfying sex. Despite all that, she carried a vicious headache with her into Mira's section.

Mira's admin informed her, with more amiability than usual, that the doctor was in session with Ms. Sanchez, but she would let them know Lieutenant Dallas had arrived.

"Let them finish," Eve told her. "It's better I'm not in there anyway. I've got some things I can take care of while I wait."

She checked her messages first, and found one from Berenski in the lab, gleefully relating that he'd nailed her shoe from the imprint.

"My genius knows no borders or boundaries. Took your pathetic imprint on grass, worked my magic, and reconstructed the tread. Matched the tread. Big foot was in a size fifteen Mikon, style called Avalanche.

It's a modified hiking boot, and there's not a lot of wear on this one. Retails at about three-seven-five. Eleven outlets in the city deal with that brand and carry it in that size. Got your list attached. You can come in and plant a big, wet one on me later."

"Yeah, that'll happen."

But she appreciated the magic, and scanned the attachment. After highlighting the outlets inside or bordering her downtown parameter, she spent the rest of her wait time writing her preliminary report.

She glanced up when the door opened.

"Dallas." Celina hurried out. Her eyes were swollen from a recent crying jag.

"Eve, why don't you come in." Mira gestured. "Celina, why don't you both come back in for a moment."

"I let you down." Celina closed a hand over Eve's arm as they walked toward Mira's office. "I let myself down."

"You didn't."

Eve sat, prepared to accept flowery tea, then sniffed like a hound when she smelled coffee.

"I knew you'd want it, and probably need it," Mira said as she offered a cup. "It's station house, but it's coffee."

"Thanks."

"I didn't check the media reports this morning. Thank you," Celina said to Mira, and took the tea. "I wanted to hear it from you. I've cried all over Dr. Mira and gotten the worst of it out. I won't break down again. But first, I want to tell you. I never even considered that he'd be out . . . that he'd hurt anyone last night. I was so damn tired, Dallas, and I wanted to get a good night's sleep before my appointment this morning. I just wanted to close everything out, so I took a couple of tranqs."

"That sort of thing block visions?"

"It can." Celina glanced toward Mira, got a nod. "The drug suppresses. I might have seen something, but I'd have been under so deep I wouldn't know. Hypnosis could bring it out. Just as it could lower the blocks on the others, so I would see in more detail. See what I hadn't allowed myself to see."

"Quite possibly," Mira confirmed. "Just as it can take a witness to an event back to the event, and bring more details, focus them in, through the practitioner's direction, to specifics. The things you see," she continued, "that you don't consciously recall."

"I get that," Eve said. "When can you do it?"

"We haven't done the physical exam as yet. If I don't find any problems, we could begin the sessions tomorrow."

"Sessions? Tomorrow?"

"It will almost certainly take more than one, Eve. And I prefer to wait twenty-four hours, to make certain the drugs are completely out of Celina's system, and that she's settled emotionally."

"Can't we start sooner? I'll meditate and cleanse. I'd like to start as soon as possible. I feel . . ."

"Responsible," Mira finished. "You feel responsible for the woman who was killed last night. But you're not."

"If she clears the physical, does the meditation thing, can you go sooner?"

Mira looked at Eve, sighed, then rose to check her calendar. "We could begin at four-thirty today. You may not get your answers, Eve. It depends on how receptive Celina is to the technique, and how much she actually saw and can bring back."

"Will you be here?" Celina asked her.

Don't depend on me, Eve wanted to say. *Don't look at me as your anchor.* "If I can.

I've got a line I've got to follow, and a lot of routine to deal with on the latest victim."

"If you can."

"Anything I should know?" Mira came back to sit. "As applies to profile?"

"Close to the same pattern. It looks like this Annalisa Sommers was cutting through—"

She broke off as Celina's tea cup shattered on the floor.

"Annalisa?" She pressed her hands down as if to push herself from the chair, then simply fell back again. "Annalisa Sommers? Oh, dear God."

"You knew her."

"Maybe it's someone else, with the same name. Maybe it's . . . of course, it's not. This is why. This has to be why I'm linked to this." She stared down at the broken china. "I'm sorry."

"No, sit still. Don't worry." Mira crouched down, laid a comforting hand on Celina's knee before picking up the shattered pieces. "Was she your friend?"

"No. I mean, not really." She pressed her hands to her temples. "I knew her a little. I liked her. You had to like her, she was so bright and full of life." She dropped her hands, and her eyes went huge and dark. "Lucas. Oh, my God, Lucas. He must be out of his mind. Does he know?" She reached out, grabbed Eve's hand. "Does he know what happened?"

"I've talked to him."

"I didn't think it could get worse, but it can. It does when it's someone you know. Why would she be in the park?" She thumped a fisted hand on her leg. "Why would any woman go near a park now? After what's already happened?"

"Because people do what they do. How did you know her?" Eve asked.

"Through Lucas." She accepted the tissue Mira gave her, stared at them as if unaware tears were sliding down her cheeks. "Lucas and I were involved. We lived together for a long time."

"Right." Eve nodded. "He's your ex."

"My ex-lover, yes, but not my ex-friend. It wasn't a nasty breakup. We just drifted apart, and moved on. We cared about each other, very much, but we weren't in love anymore." Finally, she pressed the tissue to her eyes. "We've kept in touch. We even see each other now and again for lunch, for a drink."

"For sex?"

She lowered her hands, slowly. "No. I suppose you have to ask something like that. No, we weren't intimate anymore. And some months ago, almost a year ago, I think, he and Annalisa began seeing each other. I know, because I could see it, and because he told me, it was serious between them. They were happy together, and I was happy for them."

"Broad-minded of you."

"Oh, for—" She broke off, swallowed whatever angry remark she'd been about to make. Took a calming breath. "Haven't you ever had someone in your life you loved, then you didn't—not in the same way?"

"No."

Celina gave a kind of sobbing laugh. "Well, people do, Dallas. And still manage to care about each other. Lucas is a good man. He must be devastated."

"He is."

She squeezed her eyes shut. "Should I go see him? No, not now, not yet. My being part of this would only make it worse, for everyone. Can we start sooner?" She reached for Mira again. "Couldn't we start right after the physical?"

"No. You need this time, particularly now. If you want to help, you need to take this time."

"I'm going to help." She balled her hands again. "I'm going to see his face. I swear it. When I do . . ." Her eyes burned as they lifted to Eve's. "When I do, you'll find him. You'll stop him."

"I'll stop him."

16

"She knew the Vic?" Sympathy rippled over Peabody's face. "Lucas, Lucas Grande, her ex. Didn't click before. Man, that's got to be rough. Especially rough. Must've been the trigger all along. It's the kind of logic in paranormal elements."

"You can't use *logic* and *paranormal* in the same sentence."

"Sure you can, oh stubbornly grounded one."

They were going to check out shoes, Eve thought. *That* was logical.

"When can I drive the new ride?"

"When you learn that a yellow light means haul ass to get through it before it turns red instead of slowing down to a crawl a half a block away."

"You force me to point out that you drive offensively rather than *de*fensively."

"Damn straight. You drive like one of those prissy ladies at lunch who won't take the last cookie in case somebody else wants it. No, please, please," Eve said in a high, satisfyingly prissy voice, "you go ahead. Hell with that. I want the cookie, I eat the cookie. Now, give me a for instance and stop sulking."

"I get thirty seconds of sulk time when my driving abilities have been so brutally and unjustly insulted. Besides, taking the last cookie is rude."

"And you and your prissy lady pals end up letting the waiter chow down on it after he takes the plate back to the kitchen."

With a huff, Peabody folded her arms over her chest because she realized that was probably true. And there were many cookies she'd missed due to manners. "For instance what?"

"Say you're shacked up with this guy."

Her mood lifted instantly. "I am shacked up with a guy," she said, proudly.

"Peabody."

"Yeah, yeah, this is a hypothetical." She sulked a little more as Eve plowed through a yellow light. "Is he really cute and sexy, and does he bring me cookies and let me eat the last one to show his love and devotion?"

"Whatever. So you and this guy call it off."

"Aw. I don't like this part."

"Who does?"

"Was it because I ate all those cookies and my ass got fat?"

"Peabody!"

"Okay, okay. Sir. I'm just trying to understand the motivation. Like who called it off, and why, and . . . never mind," she said when she saw Eve bare her teeth.

"You call it off, go your separate ways. You still pals?"

"Maybe. Depends. Don't bite through my jugular or anything, because it really does. Did the breakup involve calling each other unflattering names and hurling small, breakable objects, or was it sad, yet reasonable, a mutual decision. See?"

Eve didn't see it, but stayed the course. "No, but we'll say, for this case, it was sad, yet reasonable. So later this guy hooks up with another skirt. How would you feel about that?"

"Depends again. Am I hooked up with a guy? Is the other woman thinner than me, or better looking, or rich or something? Does she have perkier boobs? These factors play in."

"Goddamn it, why does it have to be so complicated?"

"Because it is."

"No, you're with the guy, then you're not, then he's with somebody else. Simple, straightforward. Are you all chummy?"

"Okay, let's see. I was hot for this guy before I moved to New York. We weren't cohabbing, but we were pretty involved. Stuck together, in every sense, for nearly a year. Then it fizzled. I wasn't wrecked or anything, but I was pretty, well, moony for a while. You get over it, though. We stayed friendly, you could say, and I used to see him around."

"Is this going to take much longer? Will I need a hit of Stay-Up to get through the rest?"

"You asked. Anyway, he hooked up with this skinny blonde with big tits. IQ of a rabbit, but hey, his choice, right? I felt a little pissy about it, but I got over that, too.

Maybe, in some dark recesses of my soul, I wouldn't mind so much if he got a mild case of genital warts, but his dick doesn't have to actually fall off or anything. And if me and McNab ever take a spin out West, I can show him—McNab—off. And so there. No big."

She waited a beat. "Still awake?"

"Barely."

"If you're thinking Celina's got some mojo vengeance thing going because of Grande and Sommers, I don't see it. Doesn't work that way anyhow."

"What doesn't work that way? You just said *depends* about six million times."

"The psychic angle doesn't work that way. It's not like she could put a spell on some guy, have him go around whacking women and make sure one of them was Sommers. Second, she came to us. If she hadn't, she wouldn't have made a blip on the investigative radar when Sommers got dead. Third, all evidence points to the fact that Sommers went into the park voluntarily and alone. Then there's the profile. Guy's a loner, a woman hater, and a predator."

"You're right, all the way down the line. I

guess I don't like paranormal logic, which smacks mightily of coincidence."

"I think there's another factor working in your head."

Eve said nothing for a long moment. "Okay. I don't like the whole setup. Depending on psychic visions or hypnosis. And I don't like Sanchez depending on me to bolster her up or hold her hand."

"No more room at the Dallas Inn for another friend?"

"Full up. Maybe if one of you moved off planet or met with a tragic accident I could juggle another one in."

"Come on. You like her."

"Yeah, so what? Do we have to be pals just because I like her? Does that mean we have to start hanging? Am I supposed to give her the last damn cookie now?"

Peabody laughed, patted Eve's arm. "There, there. You'll get through this trial. You had a good time last night."

Now Eve wanted to sulk, but she put her energy into scouting for a parking space. "Yeah, yeah. And don't think I don't know how this stuff works. Now we have to have everybody over to our place. Then you're going to have to have us over to yours, and—"

"We're already planning on having a housewarming party."

"See? See?" She zipped, with a deliberate recklessness she knew would have Peabody's heart stuffed into her throat, up to a second level, curbside. "It never ends. Once you start, you can't get off the friendship ride. You just keep circling around and around and around, with more people trying to cram on. Now I have to buy you a goddamn present just because you're shacked up in a new place."

"We could really use some nice wineglasses." She was laughing as she climbed out of the car. "You know, Dallas, you're pretty lucky in your friends, of which I am one. They're smart and fun and loyal. And diverse. I mean, could Mavis and Mira be any more different? But they both love you. Then the chilly thing happens, and your friends get to be friends."

"Yeah, and they go out and make other ones, and I get stuck with somebody like Trina." Self-consciously, she ran a hand over the back of her hair.

"She's unique." They walked down to

street level. "And you've got a man like Roarke, so you'll never lack for cookies."

Eve blew out a breath. "Wineglasses?"

"We don't have any nice ones, like for company."

Eve had felt more at home in Jim's Gym than she did in the high-end clothing store for the discerning king-sized man.

The shop was three floors: the main with one up and one down. Since the one down dealt with foot apparel—couldn't they just call it shoes and socks?—they headed down.

It seemed, she discovered, foot apparel didn't just mean shoes and socks. It included house slippers, boots, something called leg slickers—with or without belly control panels. There were shoe protectors, shoe boxes, heating inserts, foot and ankle jewelry, and any number of products that dealt with foot care or decoration.

Who knew there was so much involved dealing with a guy's feet?

The salesman she approached gave her the usual hem and haw before striding off to contact the store manager.

Eve zeroed in on the shoes in question while she waited.

Sturdy, she decided, hefting one. Practical and efficient, and well made from the look of it. She wouldn't mind having a pair herself.

"Madam?"

"Lieutenant," she corrected and turned with the shoe in hand. And had to take a step back, angle her head up to make eye contact.

He was seven feet if he was an inch, and skinny as the beanpoles she'd seen in Greenpeace Park. His skin was dark as a new moon so that the whites of his eyes, his teeth, gleamed like ice. As she gave him the once-over, his mouth quirked in a little smile that told her he was used to it.

"Madam Lieutenant," he said, very smoothly. "I'm Kurt Richards, the store manager."

"Power forward?"

He seemed pleased. "Yes. For the Knicks once upon a time. Most people automatically ask if I played basketball, but rarely guess the position."

"I don't get the chance to follow much

round ball. I bet you moved over the boards."

"I like to think so. I've been retired nearly eight years now. It's a young man's game, as most are." He took the shoe from her. His palms were so wide, his fingers so long, it no longer looked outsized. "And you're interested in the Mikon Avalanche?"

"I'm interested in your customer list for purchases of this model in size fifteen."

"You'd be Homicide."

"You're good at guessing positions, too."

"I saw a clip of yesterday's media conference, so have to assume this has to do with the Park Murders."

"That what they're calling them?"

"In large, red letters, yes." Lips pursed, he turned the shoe over in his hand, studied it. "You're looking for a man who wears this particular model in that particular size?"

"It would be of help to me if I could have your customer list for those specifics."

"I'd be happy to be of help." He replaced the shoe on its stand.

"And the names of any employees who purchased same."

That stopped him. "Well. I'm going to consider myself fortunate that I wear a seventeen in footgear. Would you like to come up to my office while I get that data for you, or browse the store?"

"We'll come up. Peabody—"

She broke off, frowning as she scanned the area and spotted Peabody with a handful of colorful socks. "For God's sake, Detective!"

"Sorry. Sorry." She hustled over. "Ah, my brother and my grandfather. Both big feet. I just figured . . ."

"No problem." Richards gestured to a clerk. "I'll have them rung up and boxed for you. You can pick them up at the main-level counter on your way out."

"You know, Christmas isn't that far away." With the business done, Peabody scrambled out of the store, purchases in hand, behind Eve.

"Oh please."

"Really. Time zips, and if you pick up stuff when you see it, you don't get that holiday crazy look in your eyes. Besides, these are really nice socks, and they were on sale. Where are we going? The car's—"

"We're walking. Next stop's only six or seven blocks. Hike'll do your ass good."

"I *knew* it looked fat in these pants." Then she stopped, squinted at Eve. "You just said that to pay me back for buying the socks. Right?"

"You'll just never know, will you?" She kept walking, digging out her communicator when it signaled. "Dallas."

"Got your first matches," Feeney said over a mouthful of nuts. "We're starting the next level, eliminating females, families, and those outside the profile parameters."

She wound and swerved through foot traffic. "Shoot the initial matches to my office unit, in case I need to backtrack. Appreciate the rush job, Feeney."

"My boys put in the time."

"How about the discs from Transit?"

"Slow going there. No promises."

"Okay. Lab ID'd the shoe. I've got a customer list from the first outlet. I'll send it to you. You get a bang from that, I need to know ASAP."

"On that. How many outlets altogether?"

"Too many, but we'll knock them down."

She paused at the intersection and ignored the steam from a nearby glide-cart that carried too much rehydrated onion, the pedestrian beside her who muttered under his breath about hell-demons, and the chatter, ladened with the Bronx, from the two women behind her that appeared to center on the purchase of an outfit that was going to make one of them look like a freaking goddess.

"He's a New York guy," she told Feeney, and strode into the street along with the horde an instant before the signal changed. "And I'm banking he does his buying in the city. We have to go outside—'burb, out of state, Net, it's going to take days, if not weeks. And he's stepped up the pace."

"Yeah, so I hear. We'll keep to the grindstone here. You need more feet in the field, let me know."

"I will. Thanks."

They hit two more retail outlets before Eve took pity on her partner and grabbed soy dogs at a glide-cart. It seemed like a good day to eat outdoors, to take advantage of the balmy weather.

So she sat on the grass of Central Park and studied the castle.

It hadn't begun there, but it was her jumping point.

A king-sized man. King of the castle. Or was that just stretching things?

He'd placed the second victim on a bench, near a memorial that honored heroes. Men, particularly men, who'd done what needed to be done. Manly men. Men who were remembered for their actions in the face of great trauma and adversity.

He liked symbols. King of the castle. Strength in adversity.

The third laid out near a garden, under a statue of farmers.

Salt of the earth? Salt purified, or it flavored. And that was bullshit.

Making something grow. Using your own hands, your sweat, and muscle to bring life? To bring death.

She blew out a breath. It could play in with the crafts. It could. Self-reliance, then. Do it yourself.

Parks meant something to him. The parks themselves. Something had happened to him in a park, something he paid back every time he killed.

"We could go back," she muttered. "Look back, see if there were any sexual assaults on a male in one of the city parks. No, a kid, that's the key. He's big now, nobody's going to mess with me now. But when he was a kid, helpless, like a woman. How do you fight back when you're a kid? So you've got to get strong, so it can't happen again. You'd rather be dead than have it happen again."

For a moment, Peabody said nothing. She wasn't entirely sure Eve was speaking to her. "Could be he got beat up, or humiliated rather than assaulted sexually. Humiliated or hurt in some way by the female authority figure."

"Yeah." Eve rubbed absently at a headache at the base of her skull. "Most likely the female he's killing symbolically now. And if it was his mother or sister, something along those lines, it probably wasn't reported. We'll check anyway."

"If a woman who had charge of him, control of him, abused him—physically, sexually—it would have twisted him from a young age, and later, the trigger gets pressed and he pays her back."

"You think getting knocked around as a kid is an excuse?"

The snap in Eve's voice had Peabody

speaking carefully. "No, sir. I think it's a reason, and it goes to motive."

"There is no reason for killing innocent people, for bathing yourself in their blood because someone messed you up. No matter how, no matter when, no matter who. That's a line for the lawyers and the shrinks, but it's not truth. Truth is you stand up, and if you can't, you're no better than the one who beat and broke you. You're no better than the worst. You can take your cycle of abuse and your victim as victimizer traumatized bullshit and—"

She stopped herself, tasted the acrid flavor of her own rage in the back of her throat. So she pressed her forehead to her updrawn knees. "Fuck it. That was over the top."

"If you think I sympathize with him, or find any excuse for what he's done, you're wrong."

"I don't think that. That rant came to you courtesy of personal neuroses." It was hard, it would be bitter. And it was time. Eve lifted her head.

"I expect you to go through the door with me, without hesitation. And I know you will, without hesitation. I expect you to stand with me, to walk through the blood, to handle the shit, and to put your personal safety and comfort second to the job. I know you will, not only because it's who you are but because, by God, I trained you."

Peabody said nothing.

"It was different when you were my aide. A little bit different. But a partner's got a right to know things."

"You were raped."

Eve simply stared. "Where the hell did that come from?"

"Conclusion drawn from observations, association, logical speculation. I don't think I'm wrong, but you don't have to talk about it."

"You're not wrong. I don't know when it started. I can't remember everything."

"You were abused habitually?"

"*Abuse* is a clean word, Peabody. Really, it's a soft word, and you—people—tend to use it so easy, to cover a lot of territory. My father beat me, with his fists or whatever was handy. He raped me, countless times. Once is plenty, so why count?"

"Your mother?"

"Gone by then. Junkie whore. I don't

really remember her, and what I do remember isn't any better than him."

"I want . . . I want to say I'm sorry, but people say that easy, too, to cover a lot of territory. Dallas, I don't know what to say."

"I'm not telling you for sympathy."

"No. You wouldn't."

"One night, I was eight. They said I was eight. I was locked in this dump he'd brought us to. Alone for a while, and I was trying to squirrel some food. Some cheese. I was starving. So cold, so hungry, and I thought I could get away with it before he came back. But he came back, and he wasn't drunk enough. Sometimes, if he was drunk enough he'd leave me alone. But he wasn't, and he didn't."

She had to stop, gather herself for the rest. "He hit me, knocked me down. All I could do was pray that was going to be all. Just a beating. But I could see it wasn't going to be all. Don't cry. I can't take it if you cry."

"I can't take it without crying." But she used one of the stingy napkins to mop at her face.

"He got on top of me. Had to teach me a lesson. It hurt. You forget after each time how much it hurts. Until it's happening again, and it's more than you can imagine. More than you can stand. I tried to stop him. It was worse if I tried to stop him, but I couldn't help it. I couldn't stand it, and I fought. He broke my arm."

"Oh, God; oh, Jesus." Now it was Peabody who pressed her face to her knees. And wept, struggling to do so soundlessly.

"Snap!" She focused on the lake, on the calm water, and the pretty boats that glided over it. "It makes a snap, a thin, young bone. And I went crazy from the pain. And the knife was in my hand. The knife I'd been using on the cheese. Fallen on the floor, and my fingers closed over it."

Slowly, face drenched, Peabody lifted her head. "You used it on him." She swiped at her face with the backs of her hands. "I hope to holy God you ripped him to pieces."

"I did. I pretty much did." There were ripples on the surface of the lake, Eve saw. It wasn't as calm as it looked with those little ripples spreading. Spreading.

"I just kept stabbing until . . . well, bathed in blood. There you go." She drew a shaky breath. "I didn't remember that part, or most of the rest until right before Roarke and I got married."

"The cops—"

Eve shook her head. "He had me scared of cops, social workers, anybody who might've stepped in. I left him there, in that room. I don't know how, except I was in shock. I washed up, and I walked out, walked for miles before I crawled into an alley and passed out. They found me. I woke up in the hospital. Doctors and cops asking questions. I didn't remember anything, or if I did, I was too scared to say. I'm not sure which. I'd never had the ID process, so there was no record of me. I didn't exist until they found me in the alley. In Dallas. So they gave me a name."

"You made the name."

"You see it affecting the job, you tell me."

"It does affect the job. It's made you a better cop. That's the way I see it. It's made you able to face anything. This guy we're after, whatever happened to him, whether it was as bad as what happened to you, or somehow worse, he's used it as an excuse to kill, to destroy, and cause pain. You use what happened to you as a reason to find justice for people who've had it taken away from them."

"Doing the job isn't heroism, Peabody. It's just the job."

"So you always say. I'm glad you told me. It says you trust me, as your partner and as your friend. You can."

"I know I can. Now let's both put it away, and get back to work."

Eve rose, held her hand down. Peabody gripped it, held it a moment, then let Eve pull her to her feet.

As much to see Annalisa Sommers again as to grill Morris, Eve made another trip to the morgue.

She found him, removing the brains of a male cadaver. It was enough to put you off, she thought, even without the soy dog in her system. But Morris cheerfully gestured her in.

"Unattended death. Fair means or foul, Lieutenant?"

Morris loved his guessing games, so she obliged by moving toward the body for a closer look. It had already started to decompose, so she put time of death at twenty-four to thirty-six hours before he'd been brought in and chilled. As a result, he wasn't pretty. She judged his age in the upper reaches of seventy, which meant he'd been robbed out of forty or fifty years on the average life expectancy table.

There was some bruising on his left cheek, and his eyes were red from broken blood vessels. Curious now, she walked around the body, looking for other signs.

"What was he wearing?"

"Bottom half of pajamas, and one slipper."

"Where was the top half?"

Morris smiled. "On the bed."

"Where was he?"

"In the Conservatory, with Professor Plum."

"What?"

Morris chuckled, waved a hand in front of his face. "Joke. He was beside the bed, on the floor."

"Signs of disturbance, forced entry?"

"None."

"He live alone?"

"He did, indeed."

"Looks like he stroked out, had a big-ass

brain pop." Since Morris was sealed up, she gestured. "Open his mouth for me, peel the lips."

Morris obliged, shifted aside so she could lean in. "But I'd talk to the domestic and find out if he or she's the one who gave dead guy the laced nightcap that popped his brain. Reddish splotches on the gums and under the lips indicate he downed, and probably OD'd on, an illegal. Booster, or a derivative would be my guess before tox eval. Guy was going to self-terminate for any reason, he'd have finished putting his pajamas on and gotten into bed nice and comfy first. So means are foul. Where's Sommers?"

"I don't know why they bother to keep me around here." But he was grinning as he slid the brain into a tray for scan and analysis. "I expect the tox eval will verify both our suspicions shortly. Sommers is done, and in a cold box. Her family and boyfriend came in together this morning. I was able to block them from seeing her, though it wasn't easy. I had to use official grounds."

"The eyes aren't public yet, and I don't want them to be, not even to next of kin.

Even family and lovers can leak to the media. More so if they're grieving or pissed. No access outside of need-to-know to any of the vics in this investigation."

"You want to see her again."

"Yeah."

"Let me clean up a bit. Our gentleman friend will hold."

He went to the sink to scrub blood, matter, and sealant from his hands. "Her body was more traumatized than the others."

"Violence is escalating. I know."

"So is his pace." Morris dried his hands, then removed his protective gear, dumping it in a hamper.

"We're closer. Every minute, we're closer."

"I have no doubt. Well." He stepped over in his pristine blue shirt and red necktie, offered his arm. "Shall we?"

She laughed, as only he could make her in the company of the dead. "Jesus, Morris, you're some number."

"I am, indeed, I am." He led her to storage, checked the logs, then opened the seal on one of the drawers. The puff of cold vapor steamed out as he drew out the body tray.

Ignoring the marks of Morris's work, Eve studied the body. "Face took more of a beating this time. Face and upper body. Maybe he's straddling her." She put it into her head. "Straddling her while he pounds on her."

"Her jaw wasn't broken, as with Napier, but her nose was, and several teeth. The blow to the back of the head wasn't fatal. She may or may not have come around for the rest of it. My guess is not, mercifully."

"The rape. More brutal this time."

"If there can be degrees of brutality in rape, yes. More abrasions, more trauma. She was a bit small, vaginally. Smaller, that is, than the other two victims in this particular area. And our killer sports one hell of a woody."

"The eyes. Surer cuts than the first, not quite as clean as the second."

"You're very good at what you do, and again cause me some concern about my own paycheck. Yes. They're all three within a range of skill, but this one falls between the others."

"Okay." She stepped back so he could replace the tray, seal the door.

"How close, Dallas? It's beginning to depress me, hosting all these pretty young women in my house."

"It's not close enough," Eve said flatly, "until he's in a cage."

17

Dickie, less affectionately known as Dickhead, Berenski was sitting at a long white counter in the lab, apparently compiling or assessing data on a screen.

When Eve came up behind him she saw the data consisted of a role-playing game involving a bevy of scantily clad, stupendously endowed women battling each other with swords.

"Hard at work, I see."

In response, he waved a hand in front of the screen. The battling beauties laid down weapons, bowed low enough to show considerable cleavage before calling out: "At your pleasure, my lord."

"Jesus, Berenski, are you twelve?"

"Hey, maybe the program's evidence from a crime scene."

"Yeah, one where several adolescent boys masturbated to death. You may not be on the clock, but I am."

"Ten minutes recreational. Got you the shoe, didn't I?"

He had, and she told herself to remember that and not crush his egg-shaped head between her hands. "Annalisa Sommers. Hair anal."

"Work, work, work." He swiveled around on his stool. "Gave that to Harvo, my best hair guy. She's a fricking genius, even if she won't put out."

"I like her already. Where is she?"

He pointed one long, skinny finger toward the right. "That way, then left. Redhead. Hasn't sent me a report yet, so she's not done."

"I'll check it out."

Peabody let Eve get a few strides away, and kept her voice low. "That program come with male characters?"

Dickhead grinned. "Oh yeah."

"Ice."

Eve made her way into one of the glass-walled analysis rooms and saw the redhead. "Harvo?"

"That'd be me." She looked up from her work, studied Eve with eyes the color of spring grass.

Eve figured Harvo was the whitest white woman she'd ever seen still breathing. Her skin was the color of milk powder against those bright green eyes and the thin slash of mouth dyed the same screaming red as her hair.

She wore the hair in a tuft, maybe three inches high and straight up from the crown of her head. She wore a baggy black tunic in lieu of a lab coat.

"Dallas, right?" Her nails were short, and painted in thin, diagonal stripes of black and red.

"That'd be me."

"Peabody, Detective."

Harvo nodded at both of them, gestured them in. "Harvo, Ursa, Queen of Hair."

"What have you got for me, Your Majesty?"

Harvo snickered, scooted a bit to the left on her stool. "Hairlike trace recovered from vic and surrounding scene," she began. Strands of it were secured in a clear, disc seal on the work counter. Harvo popped it in the comp slot, brought its magnified image on screen.

"Hairlike?"

"Yeah, see, it's not human hair or animal hair. Dickhead bounced it to me because when he eyeballed it, he made it as man-made fiber. Guy's freaking brilliant. Too bad he's a complete ass-wipe."

"Hear me loudly not disagreeing."

Harvo chuckled again. "I also serve as Fiber Princess. What you got here . . ." She revolved the image, increased magnification. "Is manufactured."

"As in rug?" Eve tugged her own hair.

"Not so much. Not likely to find this in hair enhancements or replacements. This is more fur than hair. Something you'd find on a toy—stuffed animal, droid pet. It's coated, meeting federal flame retardant standards and child safety laws."

"A toy?"

"Yep. Now, we analyze the makeup, the dye, the . . ." She glanced up at Eve as text and shapes began to flash on her screen. "You want the process and deets?"

"No, though I'm sure they're endlessly fascinating. Bottom line it."

"Gotcha. Through my amazing, almost mystical powers, I've made the manufacturer of the fiber, and its various uses for it with this particular gray dye. Droid pet, feline, common tabby. They do kittens, young cats, full-grown, even your aged family mouser. Manufacturer is Petco. I can hunt up retail outlets if you want."

"We'll take it from here. Fast work, Harvo."

"I am also Goddess of Speed and Efficiency. Oh, and Dallas, fibers were clean. No skin oils, no detergents, no soil. I'd say this little kitty was new."

"Thoughts, Detective?"

"How do you think Harvo gets her hair to stand up like that? It's really jazzed. But that's not what you meant."

"Not even remotely."

"Someone could've given Sommers the droid. We'll need to check with the friends she had dinner with after the play. It's also possible somebody lost the thing in the park before Sommers came along, and she saw it, picked it up. Not so easy to check that out. If we crap out with the friends, we start checking the retail outlets for purchases, and try to match any with the lists EDD is already running on the chance the kitty cat was his."

"Sounds like a plan. Start running with that," Eve said as they started back to Central. "I need to check with Feeney on EDD's progress, then get to Mira's for the you're-beginning-to-feel-sleepy hour."

"You think he'll hit again tonight?"

"I think if we don't lock some names in, if Celina doesn't have a breakthrough, and women don't stay the hell out of the parks in the middle of the damn night, Morris is going to be hosting another guest real soon."

On her way up to Feeney, she snagged a drone from Illegals and had him pump her out a tube of Pepsi from vending. She thought her new method was working out well. The machines didn't balk, and she wasn't tempted to beat them into rubble.

A good deal all around.

She spotted McNab doing the standard EDD pace, dance, chatter when she swung in. He saw her and pranced in her direction.

"Hold program," he said, and tipped down his headset. "Hey, Lieutenant. Where's your curvaceous partner?"

"If you refer to Detective Peabody, she's working. Most of us do."

"Just wondering if you're figuring to split end of duty. We're hoping to finish up with pack-it-up mode tonight and start the haul-it-over mode tomorrow."

He looked so damn happy, she couldn't work up any sarcasm. Any minute, she suspected the words would float visibly out of his mouth in the shape of little red hearts.

Was it something in the air? Peabody and McNab, Charles and Louise, Mavis and Leonardo. It was like a smooch epidemic.

Come to think of it, she and Roarke hadn't had a single spat, skirmish, or spew in . . . well, days. "Can't say when we'll clock out. She's tugging a couple lines right now, and after I talk to Feeney, we'll have more, so . . . What?"

He'd winced. Just a quick flicker, but she'd caught it.

"Nothing. No thing. Man, I gotta get back to this or my ass'll be in the flames. Continue program."

He pranced off, double-time.

"Shit." Eve muttered to herself, and made a beeline for Feeney's office.

Feeney had a headset, and was also running two comps simultaneously, biting out orders, tapping screens or keys in a method she supposed she'd have admired if she understood it. She thought he looked a little like one of those orchestra conductors, in charge, focused, and slightly mad.

Today's shirt was the color of egg substitute, but to Eve's relief was showing some wrinkles and a little coffee stain bloomed between the third and fourth button.

When she stepped into his line of sight, she caught the same flickering wince she'd seen on McNab's face. She said, "Goddamn it."

"Pause all programs." He pulled off the headset. "Doing another run, all data, but what I'm going to tell you isn't going to make you happy."

"How can there not be matches?" She opened the soft-drink tube, violently.

"We got a few—from residential to craft shop, from residential to gyms. But we get nothing on the shoe. None of the purchases of your shoe were made by names on the other lists."

She dropped into a chair, drummed her fingers on the arm. "What about the other matches?"

"Got a couple residents—male, within age parameters, who made purchases at one of the craft shops within the last twelve months. Can't put the red cord in their hands, but they've patronized the establishments. Got you a few more who use or have used the gyms. But we don't get any dupes—no name or names that pop in both places, and none on record as purchasing the shoe."

"Well, he did it all. Ribbon, shoe, gym. I know it."

"Doesn't mean he paid for the murder weapon or the shoes come to that. Guy who rapes and strangles and cuts out eyes isn't going to blush over some shoplifting."

"Yeah, I've considered that. Could be on the murder weapon. Tougher sell on the shoes. Not a snap to slip a pair of shoes the size of airboards out of a store. Hell, he could've lifted them off a delivery van. He might *drive* a damn delivery van. Had to have transpo to take out Kates and Merriweather. Could've gotten the ribbon the same way."

"We can start looking at the delivery services and drivers."

"Yeah, Christ. I'll start that. You still up for some fieldwork?"

"Get me up from this desk? Sure."

She drank contemplatively. "We could split up the matches we've got. Have to check them out. Split them up, move faster through them."

"I can help you out in a couple hours. Got some things to finish up."

"Good. Peabody's running something else. I'd want her with experience if she hits on our guy. She can handle herself, but it'd be better if she had somebody with her who's clocked more field time. You partner with her for this?"

"Sure. What about you?"

"I'll see if my personal expert consultant, civilian's got some time. I've got a session with the psychic and the shrink. Depending on how it goes, I may have a little more data to input."

She pushed to her feet. "Feeney," she said before she started out. "Why would anybody buy a droid cat?"

"Litter box issue?"

"Huh. That's a point."

* * *

"I'm a little nervous."

Celina lay back in a sleep chair, with the lights dim and a whisper of music Eve thought sounded like water flowing into a pool.

She'd left her hair loose and curling lavishly. Around her neck was a silver chain that dangled with several crystals in wand shapes. She wore a dress today, a long straight column in severe black that stopped inches above her ankles.

Her hands gripped the arms of the chair.

"Try to relax." Mira moved around the chair, checking, Eve supposed, the subject's vital and brain wave patterns.

"I am. Really."

"We're recording this, you understand?"

"Yes."

"And you've voluntarily agreed to undergo hypnosis."

"Yes."

"And you've requested that Lieutenant Dallas be present during the session."

"Yes." Celina smiled a little. "Thanks for making the time."

"It's okay." Eve ordered herself not to shift

in her chair. She'd never witnessed a session, and wasn't sure she was going to like it, even as an observer.

"Are you comfortable?"

Celina breathed slowly, in and out. Her hand relaxed on the arms of the chair. "Yes. Surprisingly."

"I want you to continue to breathe, slow and deep. Picture the air coming inside you, soft and blue, expelling, clean and white."

Mira lifted a small screen, and Eve could see the silver star on a deep blue background. The star pulsed, gently, like a quiet heartbeat. "Look at the star. Your breath comes from the star, returns to it. The star is your center."

Uneasy, Eve looked away from the screen, pushed her thoughts back to the case to block out the soothing tone of Mira's voice.

She didn't think you could get hypnotized by accident, but why risk it.

Time drifted—the liquid music, Mira's quiet voice, Celina's deep breaths.

When Eve risked a glance back, she saw the silver star now filled the screen, and that Celina's gaze was riveted on it.

"You're floating toward the star now. It's

all you see, all there is to see. Close your eyes now, and see the star inside you. Let yourself float with it. You're very relaxed, light as air. You're absolutely safe. You can sleep now, and while you sleep you'll hear my voice. You'll be able to speak and respond. You'll keep the star inside you, and know you're safe. I'll count, and when I reach ten, you'll sleep."

As she counted, Mira set the screen aside, and once again moved around Celina to check her medicals.

"Are you sleeping, Celina?"

"Yes."

"And are you comfortable?"

"I am."

"You can hear my voice, and respond to my voice. Will you lift your left arm?"

When she did, Mira nodded to Eve. "And lower it. You're safe, Celina."

"Yes, I'm safe."

"Tell me your name."

"Celina Indiga Tereza Sanchez."

"Nothing can hurt you. Even when I take you back, when I ask you to see something difficult to see, to tell me something difficult to tell, you're safe. Do you understand?"

"Yes. I'm safe."

"Go back to the park, Celina. To Central Park. It's night, a cool night, but comfortable. What do you see?"

"Trees and grass and shadows, streetlights glowing through the leaves."

"What do you hear?"

"Cars passing on the street. Music, a little music through an open window as one goes by. Neo-punk. It's harsh. I don't care for it. Footsteps. Someone's crossing the street. I wish she wouldn't come here."

"Do you see the woman? The woman coming toward you. She has a little dog on a leash."

"Yes. Yes, I see her. It's a little white dog, silly little dog trotting along. She laughs at the dog."

"What does the woman look like?"

"She's pretty. A homey sort of pretty. She has brown hair, light brown hair, straight to her shoulders. Her eyes are . . . I can't see the color, because it's dark. They might be brown, too, but it's too dark to tell. She's white, and looks very fit and healthy. She looks happy as she walks the dog. She talks to the dog. 'Just a quick walk tonight,' she says. 'You be a good doggy now.'"

Her breath hitched, and her voice dropped

to a whisper. "There's someone there. There's someone watching."

"It's all right. He can't hurt you. He can't see you or hear you. Can you see him?"

"I . . . It's dark. Shadows. In the shadows, watching her. I can hear him, breathing—fast—but she can't. She can't hear him. She doesn't know he's watching. She should go back now, go back into the lights, away from the shadows. She needs to go back! But she doesn't. She doesn't know he's there until he . . . No!"

"He can't hurt you, Celina. Listen to my voice. Nothing can hurt you. You're safe. Breathe in the blue, breathe out the white."

Celina's breathing evened, but her voice continued to shake. "He's hurting her. He jumped at her, hit her, and the little dog ran away, trailing his leash. He's hurting her, hitting her. She fights. Blue, her eyes are blue. I see them now, and they're afraid. She tries to run, but he's too big. He's too fast! She can't scream, can't scream when he's on top of her. Crushing her."

"Celina. Can you see him?"

"I don't want to see him. I don't want to. He might see me. If he sees me, he'll—"

"He can't see you. You're floating, and he can't see you. You're safe, and floating."

"He can't see me."

"That's right."

"There's nothing I can do." She shifted restlessly in her chair. "Why do I have to see this? I can't help her."

"Yes, you can. If you look at him, if you tell me what you see, it will help her. Look at him, Celina."

"He's big. He's very big. Strong. She can't push him away, she can't fight. She—"

"Look at him, Celina. Just him now."

"He's . . . Black, he's wearing black. Like the shadows. His hands . . . his hands are pulling and tearing at her clothes. He calls her a whore. 'See how you like it now, whore. It's your turn now, bitch.'"

"His face, Dr. Mira," Eve murmured. "Give me his face."

"Look at his face, Celina."

"I'm afraid."

"He doesn't see you. You don't have to be afraid of him. Look at his face. What do you see?"

"Rage. Rage. Contorted. His eyes are black, black and blind. I can't see his eyes. He's wearing something over them. Shades,

shades over his eyes, with a strap around his head. His head shines. His face shines. Horrible. He's raping her. Grunting and slamming himself into her. I don't want to see."

"Just his face."

"There's something over it. A mask? It shines. Not a mask. Something shiny and slick. Not white. Not white under the shine. Brown. Tanned. I don't know."

Her breathing went rapid, thready as she turned her head side to side. "His face is wide, wide and square."

"Eyebrows," Eve prompted.

"Do you see his eyebrows, Celina?"

"Very dark and thick. He's killing her now. Pulling the red ribbon tight, tighter. She can't breathe. We can't breathe."

"I have to bring her out," Mira said when Celina started to gasp for air. "Celina, turn away now. Turn away from them now and look at your star. Watch your star. Can you see it?"

"Yes, I . . ."

"It's all you see. Only the star. It's beautiful, it's peaceful. It's guiding you back now. Bringing you home. You're floating down now, very slowly. You feel relaxed, refreshed. When I tell you to open your eyes, you'll wake up, and you'll remember everything you saw, everything we talked about. Do you understand?"

"Yes. I want to wake up."

"You're waking up now, coming up through the layers of sleep. Open your eyes, Celina."

She blinked them open. "Dr. Mira."

"Yes. Just stay still for a moment. I'm going to get you something to drink. You did very well."

"I saw him." She turned her head, looked at Eve. "I saw him, Dallas." A smile trembled onto her lips, and she reached out a hand.

Eve rose, gave Celina's hand a brief squeeze, since it seemed called for, then stepped back so Mira could give Celina a cup.

"Would you recognize him?" Eve asked.

"His face." Celina shook her head and sipped. "It's hard. The shades hid his eyes, and whatever was on his face—over it?—distorted it. I know the body type as I'd told you before. I know now he's either mixed race, dark skinned or tanned. And the shape of his face. He's bald. Smoothly, like a man who removes or has his hair removed. I don't understand what he had on his face."

"A sealant, most likely. Thickly applied. What about his voice? Any accent?"

"No . . . No. It was guttural, but that might have been the rage. He didn't shout, though, not even when he . . . He kept his voice down."

"Rings, jewelry, tats, scars, birthmarks?"

"I didn't see anything. Didn't notice. Can we try again, and I'll—"

"Absolutely not." Mira brought up the lights. "I won't authorize another session until tomorrow evening, soonest. I'm sorry, Eve. This sort of thing can't be rushed."

"I feel fine," Celina protested. "Better, in fact, than I did before we started."

"And I want you to continue to feel fine. You're to go home, relax, have a meal."

"Can that meal include a really big glass of wine?"

"Certainly." Mira patted Celina's shoulder. "Do what you can to keep your mind off this, and we'll take the next step forward tomorrow."

"I feel like I did take a step. It won't be as hard tomorrow. Are there photos I can look at?" she asked Eve. "Before the session tomorrow? I might recognize him if I saw his picture."

"I'll see what I can put together by then."

"Well." Celina set the cup aside. "I'm going to go have that wine."

"I'll walk you out."

Mira's admin was closing up for the day, and a check of the time told Eve it was nearly six. Time to get moving.

"Maybe when this is over, we can have a glass of wine together."

Eve led the way to a glide. "Sounds good. This hypnosis thing, does it make you feel like somebody slipped you a tranq? You know, so you're out of yourself?"

"No. Well, maybe a little. But you're tethered, if you know what I mean. There's some part of you that's aware you're being held safe, and you can come back."

"Hmm."

"It was a little strange, but not really unpleasant. The process, I mean, not what I saw during it. Where I had to go was very unpleasant, so I think that colors it somewhat. But, essentially, it's not that different than having visions."

"You got that part nailed."

"I certainly should. I'm hoping this is a

one-shot, this turn my gift's taken. But if it's not, I'll handle it better next time."

"You've handled yourself. You find your way out of this maze from here?"

"Yeah."

"I've got to head back." She gestured toward her sector.

"Haven't you been on since early this morning?"

"That's how it goes."

"You can keep it," Celina said sincerely. "I'll see you tomorrow, at Mira's? Let me know if you want me to come in earlier and look at pictures."

"You'll hear from me."

Eve peeled off, wound her way back to Homicide. She detoured by Peabody's desk, thumped on it, gestured, and headed to her own office. "Got a basic description. Added to ours, he's a really big son of a bitch. Mixed race or—"

"She said white before."

"Sealant threw her off. Sounds like he coats it on thick, probably uses one that's not completely clear. "Mixed race, brown skin or tanned. Bald—smooth dome. Square face, dark, thick eyebrows. No distinguishing marks that she made this time out. He wears dark shades when he does them."

"Jesus."

"Could be something's wrong with his eyes, could be another symbol or part of his pathology. We'll research eye diseases or sensitivities."

"Funky-junkies are light sensitive."

"He's not on the funk. Steroids, maybe, to give the body a boost. What do you have for me?"

"None of the people Sommers spent the evening with gave her or remember her with a droid or a toy. No cat. I've started running purchases, haven't hit anything yet."

"Run it through, then you're going to hook up with Feeney for some OT in the field."

"Feeney?"

"We're splitting his match list, such as it is. I want to cover as much territory as we can, tonight. You saddle with Feeney. I'm bringing Roarke in. He's mostly up to speed anyway. Saves me briefing another badge."

She paused, sat on the corner of her desk. "Listen, if you get lucky, and pop on this guy tonight, remember, he's not going to let you take him down easy."

"You're not going to tell me to be careful, are you?"

"I'm going to tell you to be good. Stay sharp. You pop him, and he goes for either of you, he'll go for you first."

"Female."

"Right. He'll hurt you if he can."

"So don't let him. And right back at you, sir."

"Give Feeney the rest of the description. Keep it in your head. Maybe he wears a rug, so—"

"Dallas, this isn't my first flight out of the nest."

"Right. Right, right." Restless, she got up, but bypassed coffee for water. Overcaffeinated, she told herself as she opened the bottle. "I got bad vibes, is all."

"Want me to call and check in when I get home, Mommy?"

"Scram."

"Scramming."

Eve dropped down at the desk, added her record of the session with Mira to her case file, and organized her notes into her daily report.

Roarke had told her he'd meet her at her office at seven-thirty if not before, so she had time. A little time. She started the research on eye sensitivities, then let the computer hum along while she got up, paced to the window.

Bad vibes, she thought again, and looked out at her city.

It wasn't extrasensory. What she had, what she did was, in her opinion, the antithesis of paranormal. It was elemental, maybe on some level even primitive—the way early man had known when to hunt and when to hide.

She'd say visceral except the word always sounded sort of pompous to her. And there was nothing pompous about cop work.

The vibes, for lack of a better word, were a combination of instinct and experience and a knowledge she had no inclination to analyze.

She knew he'd marked his next target. And could only wonder who, and where, he'd strike tonight.

18

In his elegant dark business suit, Roarke circled Eve's new vehicle while it was parked in her slot in Central's garage. "Haven't had a chance to really examine your upgrade. Long overdue, Lieutenant."

"It does the job."

"Better, one hopes, than your previous one." He tapped the hood. "Release the hood latch."

"Why?"

"So I can look at the engine."

"Why? It runs. What else is there to know? Looking at it doesn't change anything."

He gave her a long, pitying smile. "Darling Eve, your absolute lack of interest and aptitude for mechanics is so female."

"Watch it, pal."

"Wouldn't you like to know what's under here?" He tapped the hood again. "What's getting you where you're going?"

"No." Though he had stirred some mild curiosity. "Besides, I'm getting a later start on this than I'd planned. Let's just move."

"Well, let's have the codes." He lifted a brow when she frowned. "If you won't let me play with it, you can at least let me drive it."

She supposed it was fair. He was giving her the evening for work. She gave him the codes, then walked around to the passenger side. "The department appreciates your time and assistance, blah, blah."

"Please, you're much too effusive in your gratitude."

He settled behind the wheel, adjusting the seat to his preference, scanning the dash. He judged the data and communication system to be middle-range. It baffled him that the NYPSD didn't spring for top-of-the-line for their mobile situations.

He engaged the engine and wasn't displeased by the sound. "You've got more power under you this time, at least." Then he smiled at her. "Sorry I couldn't get here sooner."

"It's okay. I kept busy. And Feeney couldn't wiggle loose until about twenty minutes ago, so he and Peabody are getting a late start with this, too."

"Then let's catch up." He eased out of the slot, drove at a discreet speed to the entrance. Flicked a glance at the pattern of traffic.

And punched it.

"Jesus, Roarke!"

He whipped through, skimming his way around cabs and cars and one-seaters, and nipped through a light a blink before it went to red. "Not bad," he decided.

"If I bung this thing up the first week, I'll never live it down."

"Umm-hmm." He went vertical, maintaining it until he'd swung around a corner. "Could be a bit more elastic on the turns, but it handles well enough."

"And if Traffic lights you up, I'm not flashing my badge to kill the violation."

"Lateral's fairly smooth," he decided after testing it out. "So, where are we going?"

She sighed, long and deep, but at least the question allowed her to relay the first name and address to her map system. "You want the route displayed on windshield or the dash monitor?"

"Dash will do."

"On monitor," she ordered and couldn't suppress the smile when it popped on. "I ditched the vocals. It'll only blab at me if I specifically order it to. Too bad people don't come with the same accessory."

She rattled off the route.

"How did Celina's session go?" Roarke asked her.

"She handled it. We got a few more details, but it's tough going. Mira won't approve another session without a twenty-four-hour break."

"A slow process."

"Yeah, and he's not going to move slow. It's not just women he's after, but women he sees as having control over him."

"Symbolically."

"Maybe I pushed him the wrong way, pushed him when I did the interview with Nadine, then the media conference. He's escalating."

"Whether you push or not, he'll continue to kill until you stop him."

"Yeah, I'll be doing that. I'll damn well be doing that soon."

Her first stop was named Randall Beam, and he wasn't happy about having a cop at the door.

"Listen, I got a thing. I'm just about out the door already. What gives?"

"If we can come in, Randall, we'll tell you what gives, then maybe you can keep your thing."

"Hell. How come a guy has a coupla assaults on his sheet, cops're always yanking him?"

"It's a mystery all right."

Eve stepped in, scanned the room. It was small, man messy without being revolting. There was the faintest whiff of something in the air that could get Randall a little visit from Illegals, but she'd let it pass unless she had to squeeze him.

There were curtains at the windows, which was a surprise, and a couple of nice-looking pillows tucked into the corners of a sagging couch.

Physically, Beam didn't fit her profile. He was about six feet tall, a solid and muscular one-eighty. But compared to a size fifteen, his feet were almost dainty. His complexion leaned toward jailhouse white, and he sported a long brown ponytail.

Still, she'd need to take the time with him. He might have a friend, a brother, whatever, who fit her needs more closely.

"Need your whereabouts, Randall." She gave him the nights of the three murders, waited while he stood looking put-upon and sad.

"How'm I supposed to know?"

"You can't tell me where you were last night?"

"Last night? One of them's last night? Last night, after I got off work? I got gainful employment."

"Good for you."

"So, after work, me and a couple of the guys stopped in at the Roundhouse. Bar on Fourth? Knocked back a few, grabbed some chow, played some pool. LC works the joint. Name's Loelle? I was flush, so I took her up to one of the privates—Roundhouse's got two—for a bang. Had a couple more drinks, got home, I dunno, about two? This here's my day off."

"Loelle and your buddies going to confirm all that?"

"Sure. Why not? Loelle's down there most nights; you can ask her. And you can ask Ike—Ike Steenburg—we work together. He was there last night. What gives?"

"Let's get through the other two nights."

He was clueless about his activities on the night of Napier's murder—but he balked on explaining what he was doing on the night of Maplewood's.

"I had a thing. Was there till after eleven. Went out with . . . with some people after for, you know, coffee. Got home, I dunno, maybe midnight. I really gotta go now."

"What's the thing, Randall?"

He shuffled his feet, stared at them while color came up on his cheeks. "Why I gotta say?"

"Because I have a badge, you have a sheet, I need to know, and if you make me ask again I'm going to be a lot more interested in the Zoner I smell."

"Jesus. Cops. You're always hassling a guy."

"Yeah. It's the part of the job that gets me up out of bed every morning with a big smile on my face."

He blew out a breath. "I don't want the guys to hear about it."

"I'm the soul of fricking discretion."

He shifted his gaze up, ran it over her face, shifted it to Roarke, and hunched his shoulder. "You shouldn't oughta get the wrong idea. I ain't no fairy or nothing. Don't know why guys want to bang each other when there's women around. But you know, live and let."

"That's a touching philosophy, Randall. Spill."

He pulled on his nose, shuffled his feet. "Just that . . . last assault bust, they say I gotta take anger management and shit. So I stop punching people and starting fights. But I never punched nobody didn't ask for it."

Eve supposed the flaw was in her, but she was starting to like him. "I know the feeling."

"So they, shit, they say I should do some therapy kind of deal. Occupational, recreational, relaxational. What all. I sign up for this class in ah, crafts."

"You do crafts."

"Don't make me no fairy or nothing." He gave Roarke a steely look as if daring him to disagree.

"Did you make the curtains?" Roarke asked, pleasantly.

"Yeah. So?" His fists bunched at his sides.

"It's very good work. A nice use, I'd say, of fabric and color."

"Well." He eyed Roarke, eyed the curtains. Then shrugged. "They come out okay. It's constructive and, you know, therapeutic. I sorta got into it. I was working on the pillows there at Total Crafts, they got clubs and shit, and instructors. That's where I was the night you're saying. They give you a break on the supplies and shit, and you can use their machines you need to. And it's kinda interesting is all. I got a class tonight, on needlepoint. You can make all kinds of shit, you know what you're doing."

"Your instructor and classmates verify this?"

"Yeah. But, hey, you go down there asking questions, talking about my sheet, it's gonna mess me up. Coupla skirts in there I'm thinking about hitting on, and it's gonna mess me up."

"You forgot about me being the soul of discretion, Randall. Any of your buddies know about your hobby?"

His face went to stark, stupefied shock. "Hell, no. You think I'd mouth off about fricking curtains and pillows to the guys? They'd rag me till I had to pound on them. Then I wouldn't be managing my anger issues and all that."

"Got a point," Eve agreed.

"You knew it wasn't him when he opened the door." Roarke slid back behind the wheel.

"Yeah, but you've got to run the lap. He says his buddies don't know, but it's possible one does. Or somebody he works with, somebody he's played pool with. A neighbor." She lifted a shoulder. "He nips the cord from Randall, or uses his name to buy it. You can't discount long shots. Let's hit the next."

She went through the paces because it had to be done, but she didn't quibble when Roarke announced it was time for a meal. Nor did she quibble over his choice of a French place with candles on the table and waiters with their noses in the air.

His name got them a corner booth in thirty seconds flat, with the expected fawning service. But the food was choice.

Still, she brooded over it, picked at it, and did more rearranging of it on her plate than eating it.

"Tell me what's troubling you." He laid a hand over hers. "It's more than the case."

"I guess there's a lot going around in my head."

"Give me one."

"I told Peabody about . . . I told her about when I was a kid."

His fingers tightened on hers. "I wondered if you ever would. It would've been difficult for both of you."

"We're partners. You've got to trust your partner. I'm rank, and I expect her to follow an order without hesitation. And I know she will, and that my rank isn't why she will."

"That's not the only reason you told her."

"No. No, it's not." She looked at him through the candlelight. "Cases like this, they get into my gut. I can make a mistake because I'm looking too hard, or I'm looking away because I can't stand to look too hard."

"You never look away, Eve."

"Well, I want to. Sometimes I want to, and the difference is a pretty thin line. She's with me every day, and she's a good cop. She'll see if I'm off, and she's got a right to know why I am, if I am."

"I agree with you. But there's still one more reason you told her."

"She's a friend. The tightest, I guess, next to Mavis. Mavis is different."

"Oh, let me count the ways."

She laughed, as he'd wanted. "She's not a cop and she's Mavis. She's the first person I ever told any part of it to. The first person I *could* tell any part of it to. I should've told Feeney. We were partners and I should've told him. But I didn't know, didn't remember most of it when we were hooked, and besides . . ."

"He's a man."

"I told you. You're a man."

"I'm not your father figure," he said and watched her reach quickly for her water glass.

"I guess. I mean, no, you're sure as hell not. And maybe Feeney . . . in some kind of way. Doesn't matter," she decided. "I didn't tell him. Telling Mira was almost an accident, and she's a doctor. I've never dumped it, in a big lump, on anybody but you, and now Peabody."

"You told her the whole of it then?"

"That I killed him? Yeah. She said something about hoping I ripped him to pieces. She cried. Jesus."

She dropped her head in her hands.

"Is that what troubles you most about this? That her heart hurts for you?"

"That's not why I told her."

"Friendship, partnership. They aren't just about trust, Eve. They're about affection. Even love. If she didn't feel pity for and anger over the child, she wouldn't be your friend."

"I guess I know that. I'll give you one of the other things on my mind, then we have to finish the list. I watched the whole hypnotherapy deal today. Mira's brought it up before, she doesn't push it, but she's told me it might help bring things back to the surface, clear it out of me. Maybe the more you remember, the more control you have over it. I don't know. But I don't think I can go there, Roarke. I don't know if I can, even if it means getting rid of the nightmares."

"Were you considering it?"

"I hadn't ruled it out, completely, for later.

Sometime later. But it's too much like Testing. If you terminate somebody on the job, you have to go through Testing. That's SOP, and you deal. You hate it, but you deal. This is like saying, sure, put me through the wringer, take away my control, because maybe—possibly—it'll make things better."

"If you want to find out more, and you're not comfortable with hypnosis, there are other ways, Eve."

"You could dig details out of my past for me, the way you dug them out for yourself." She picked up the water again. "I've thought about it. I'm not sure I want to go there either. But I'll think about it some more. I guess finding out what we did before, about Homeland surveilling him, knowing about me, knowing what he was doing to me, and letting it happen to preserve the integrity of their investigation—"

Roarke said something particularly vile about Homeland and integrity. Something, she thought with dark humor, that didn't belong in snooty French restaurants.

"Yeah, well. It's played on my head some, finding out other people knew. And it's made me ask myself, would I sacrifice a civilian for a collar?"

"You would not."

"No, I wouldn't. Not knowingly, not willingly. But there are people out there, people who consider themselves solid citizens who would. Would, and do, sacrifice others to get what they want or need. Happens every day, in big ways, in little ways. For the greater good, for their good, for their interpretation of someone else's good. By action, by omission of action, people sacrifice other people all the damn time."

Peabody stepped off the subway and stifled a yawn. It was still shy of eleven, but she was beat. At least she wasn't hungry on top of it, as Feeney had been as happy as she to break for food. Her belly was nicely full of fried chicken strips—at least it had been billed as chicken, and she didn't want to question what else might have been inside the batter.

Dipped into some sort of bright yellow sauce, they hadn't been half bad.

Of course, they'd crapped out on everything else, but that was life with a badge.

She flipped out her palm-link as she trudged up the steps to street level.

"There she is." McNab's face, split by a big, welcoming grin filled the screen. "Heading home yet?"

"Just a couple blocks away. We covered a lot of ground, didn't pick anything up."

"That's the way it goes."

"You said it. Did you get any more packing done?"

"Baby, you're going to give me a really big sloppy one when you walk in the door. It's done, and we're ready to rock and roll out of here."

"Really? *Really?*" She did a little skip-step on the sidewalk. "There was a lot left, you must've worked the whole time."

"Well, I had the really big sloppy one as incentive."

"You didn't throw out any of my—"

"Peabody, I want to live. I didn't ditch anything, including your little stuffed bunny."

"Mister Fluffytail and I go back. I'll be there in five. Be prepared for the sloppy one."

"When it comes to sloppy ones, I'm a fricking Youth Scout."

She laughed, stuffed the 'link back in her pocket. Life was really good, she thought. *Her* life was really good. In fact, just at the moment it was absolutely mag. All the little nerves about moving into a new place, with McNab—signing a lease, blending lives, furniture, styles, sharing a bed with the same guy for . . . well, possibly forever—were gone.

It felt right. It felt solid.

It wasn't as if he didn't irritate her cross-eyed sometimes. It was that she *got* he was supposed to. It was part of their thing, their style.

She was in love. She was a detective. She was partnered with the best cop on the NYPSD—possibly the best cop anywhere. She'd actually lost three pounds. Okay, two, but she was working off number three even now.

As she walked, she looked up, smiled at the lights glowing in her apartment—her old apartment, she corrected. McNab would probably come to the window any minute, to look out, wave, or blow her a kiss—a gesture that might've looked silly on another guy, but gave her such a nice little rush when it came from him.

She'd blow one back, and wouldn't feel silly at all.

She slowed her pace, just a bit, to give

him time to come to the window, fulfill the fantasy.

She never saw him coming.

There was a blur of movement. He was big—bigger than she'd imagined—and he was fast. She knew, in that fingersnap of time that she saw his face—eyes obscured by black sunshades—that she was in trouble. Terrible trouble.

Instinct had her pivoting, reaching for the weapon she wore at her hip.

Then it was like being rammed by a stampeding bull. She felt the pain—crazy pain—in her chest, in her face. She heard something break, and realized with a kind of sick wonder that the something was inside her.

Her mind stopped working. It was training rather than thought that had her pumping out with her legs, aiming for any part of his mass so she could knock him back far enough to give her room to roll.

She barely budged him.

"Whore."

His face loomed over her, features obscured by the thick layers of sealant, the wide, black shades.

It seemed time dripped, slow as syrup. That her limbs were weighed down like lead. She reared up to kick again—all in slow, painful motion—struggling to suck in air to a chest that burned like fire. Ordering herself to remember details.

"Cop whore. Going to mess you up."

He kicked her, so she doubled up in agony as her fingers fumbled for her weapon. Parts of her, separate parts of her went numb, and still she could feel the violent impact of his feet, his fists. She could smell her own blood.

He plucked her up, as if she were no more than a child's doll. This time she heard—felt—something rip.

Someone screamed. She felt herself hurled into the dark as she fired.

McNab put on music. She'd sounded tired when she'd called, so he went for some of her Free-Ager flutey shit. Since he'd finished packing the lot—including sheets—they were going to bunk in her sleepbag. He thought she'd get a bang out of it. Last night in the old place, all cuddled up together on the floor, like kids camping out.

It was just totally frosty.

He poured her a glass of wine. He liked

doing it for her, thinking how she'd do it for him when he caught a late night. It was the sort of things cohabs did. He supposed.

It was the first official cohabitation for both of them. They'd live, he decided, and learn.

He was thinking maybe he'd go to the window, toss her out a noisy kiss as she walked up, when he heard the screaming.

He raced out of the kitchen, leaping over packing boxes and across the living area to the window. And his heart stopped dead.

He had his weapon in one hand, his communicator in the other, without any memory of grabbing either, and was running out the door. "Officer needs assistance! All units, all units, officer needs immediate assistance."

He shouted out the address as he bolted down the stairs. Praying. Praying.

She was half on the sidewalk, half on the street. Facedown, with blood, her blood, staining the concrete. A man and a woman were crouched beside her, and another was huffing toward them.

"Get away. Get away." He shoved blindly at the nearest. "I'm a cop. Oh God, oh Jesus God, Dee."

He wanted to scoop her up, gather her in,

and knew he didn't dare. Instead he pressed shaking fingers to the pulse in her throat. And felt his heart hitch when he felt the beat.

"Okay. God, okay. Officer down!" He snapped it into his communicator. "Officer down. Require immediate medical assistance this location. Hurry, goddamn it. Hurry."

He touched her hand, struggled not to squeeze it. Got his breath back.

"Be on the lookout for a black or dark blue van, late model, heading south from this location at high speed."

He hadn't seen it clearly enough, not enough. He'd only seen her.

When he started to strip off his shirt to cover her, one of the men pulled off his jacket. "Here, cover her with this. We were just coming out, across the street, and we saw . . ."

"Hold on, Dee. Peabody, you hold the hell on." Still gripping her hand, and seeing now she had her weapon in the other, he looked up at the people around him. His eyes went flat and cold as a shark's.

"I need your names. I need to know what you saw."

* * *

Eve's heart was knocking on her ribs when she shoved off the elevator and strode double-time down the hospital corridor. "Peabody," she said, slapping her badge on the counter of the nurse's station. "Detective Delia. What's her status?"

"She's in surgery."

"That's not telling me her status."

"I can't tell you her status because I'm not in surgery."

"Eve." Roarke put a restraining hand on her shoulder before she simply leaped over the counter and throttled the nurse. "McNab will be in the waiting area. We should go there first."

She struggled to draw a breath, even out her terror and temper. "Get somebody to go into surgery and get her status. Do you understand me?"

"I'll do what I can. You can wait down the hall, to your left."

"Easy, baby." Roarke murmured to her, slid his arm around her waist as they went toward the waiting area. "Try to take it easy."

"I'll take it easy when I know what the

hell's going on." She stepped into waiting, and stopped.

He was alone. She hadn't expected him to be alone. Such places were usually filled with people agonizing. But there was only McNab standing at one of the windows, staring out.

"Detective."

He spun around—and the grief and hope on his face shuddered into only grief. "Lieutenant. They took her. They took her into . . . They said . . . I don't know."

"Ian." Roarke crossed to him, laid an arm around McNab's shoulders and drew him toward a chair. "You'll sit a minute now. I'll get you something to drink, and you'll sit a minute. They're taking care of her now. And in a bit, I'll go and see what I can find out."

"You have to tell me what happened." Eve sat beside McNab. He had a ring on each thumb, she noticed. And blood on his hands. Peabody's.

"I was in the apartment. All packed up. I'd just talked to her. She'd tagged me to tell me she was a couple blocks away. She was only . . . I should've gone out and met her. That's what I should've done. Gone out, and then she wouldn't be walking alone. I had music on. Fucking music on, and I was in the kitchen. I didn't hear anything until the screams. Wasn't her. She didn't have a chance to scream."

"McNab."

Roarke turned from the vending AutoChef at the tone of her voice. He was about to step in, draw her away when he saw the change.

She reached out, took one of his blood-smeared hands in hers, held it. "Ian," she said. "I need you to give me a report. I know it's hard, but you have to tell me everything you know. I didn't get any details."

"I . . . give me a minute. Okay? Give me a minute."

"Sure. Here drink . . . whatever he's got here."

"Tea." Roarke sat on the table in front of them, faced McNab. "Have a bit of tea now, Ian, and catch your breath. Look here a minute."

He laid a hand on McNab's knee until McNab lifted his head, met his eyes. "I know what it is to have the one you love, the only one, hurt. There's a war in your belly, and your heart's so heavy it doesn't seem as if your body can hold it. This kind of fear doesn't have a name. You can only wait with it. And let us help."

"I was in the kitchen." He pressed the heels of his hands, hard, against his eyes. Then he took the tea. "Hadn't been more than two, three minutes since she told me she was a couple blocks away. Probably just got off the subway. I heard a woman scream, and shouts. I ran to the window, and I saw . . ."

He used both hands to lift the tea, then drank it like medicine. "I saw her lying, face-down. Head and shoulders on the sidewalk, the rest in the street. Two males and a female were running toward her from the northwest. And I saw—caught a glimpse of a vehicle heading south at high speed."

He stopped to clear his throat. "I ran down. I had my weapon and communicator. I don't know how, I don't remember. I called for assistance, and when I got to her, she was unconscious, and bleeding from the face and head. Her clothes were bloody, torn some."

He squeezed his eyes shut. "She was bleeding, and I checked her pulse. She was alive. She had her weapon out and in her right hand. He didn't get her piece. The son of a bitch didn't get her piece."

"You didn't see him."

"I didn't see him. I got names and partial statements from the three witnesses, but then the MTs got there. I had to go with her, Dallas. I left the witnesses to the uniforms who responded. I had to go with her."

"Of course you did. You get a make on the vehicle? Plates?"

"Dark van. Couldn't tell the color, just dark. But I think black or dark blue. Couldn't see the plates, light was out on them. Witnesses didn't make it either. One of the guys—Jacobs—he said it looked new, really clean. Maybe it was a Sidewinder or a Slipstream."

"Did they see her assailant?"

His eyes went flat again, and cold. "Yeah, they made him pretty damn good. Big, beefy guy, bald, sunshades. They saw him kick her, fucking stomp on her. They saw her lying on the ground and the bastard kicking her. Then he hauled her up, like maybe he was going to heave her into the back of the van. But the woman started screaming, and the guys shouted and started running. He threw her down. They said he threw her down and jumped into the van. But she got a shot off. That's what they told me. She got a shot off when he was throwing her down. Maybe it hit him. Maybe he staggered. They weren't sure, and I had to go, go with her, so I couldn't follow up."

"You did good. You did great."

"Dallas."

And now she saw he was struggling against tears. If he broke, she'd break. "Take it easy."

"They said—the medicals—they said it was bad. We were riding in, they were working on her. They told me it was bad."

"I'm going to tell you what you already know. She's no pushover. She's a tough cop, and she'll come through."

He nodded, swallowed hard. "She had her weapon in her hand. She kept her weapon."

"She's got spine. Roarke?"

He nodded, and, walking out to gather information, left her and McNab waiting alone.

19

He paced and prowled and keened like an animal. And wept like a child as he crossed back and forth, back and forth in front of the staring eyes. The bitch had *hurt* him.

It wasn't allowed. Those days were *over,* and he wasn't supposed to be hurt anymore. Ever. Look at him. He swung around toward the wall of mirrors to reassure himself. Look at his *body.*

He'd grown tall, taller than anyone he knew.

Do you know how much clothes cost, you damn freak? You better start pulling your weight around here, or you're gonna go around naked as far as I'm concerned. I'm not going to keep popping for them.

"I'm sorry, Mother. I can't help it."

No, no! He wasn't sorry. He was glad he was tall. He wasn't a freak.

And he'd made himself strong. He'd worked, he'd strained, he'd sweated, until he'd created a strong body. A body to be proud of, a body people *respected.* Women feared.

You're puny, you're weak, you're nothing.

"Not anymore, Mother." Grinning fiercely, he flexed the biceps of his uninjured arm. "Not anymore."

But even as he looked, as he preened in front of the glass to admire the brawny form he'd spent years building, he saw himself shrink, whittling down until it was a gangly boy with pinched cheeks and haunted eyes staring back at him.

The boy's chest was crisscrossed with welts from a beating, his genitals were raw from the vicious scrubbing she'd given them. His hair hung dank and dirty to his shoulders the way she made him keep it.

"She'll punish us again," the little boy told him. "She'll put us back in the dark."

"No! She won't." He swung away from the mirror. "She won't. I know what I'm doing." Cradling his injured arm, he tried to pace off the pain. “She’ll be punished this time. You can bet your bottom dollar. Took care of the cop bitch, didn’t I? Didn’t I?”

He’d killed her. He was damn sure he’d broken her into a few nasty pieces, oh yeah. But his *arm!* It was hot and numb—the kind of numb that came with prickling needles—from shoulder to fingertip.

He cradled it against his body, moaning, as he was caught between boy and man.

Mommy would kiss it and make it all better.

Mommy would slap him silly and lock him in the dark.

“We haven’t finished.”

He heard the little boy, the sad, desperate little boy.

No, he hadn’t finished. He’d be punished unless he could finish it. Put in the dark, blind in the dark. Burned and whipped, with her voice pounding in his head like spikes.

He shouldn’t have left the cop behind, but it had happened so fast. The screaming, the people running toward him, the shocking pain in his arm.

He’d had to run. The little boy had said: *Run!* What choice had he had?

“I had to.” He dropped to his knees,

pleading with the eyes that floated in silence, that stared without pity. "I'll do better next time. Just wait. I'll do better."

In the bright lights that were never turned off, he knelt and rocked and wept.

Eve couldn't sit. She wandered to the vending area, ordered up more coffee. She carried the thin, bitter brew to the window. Stared out as McNab had done. She ran over in her mind what she'd done, what was left to be done, but she couldn't keep her thoughts from stealing into surgery where she envisioned Peabody's lifeless body on an operating table, and faceless doctors with blood on their hands to their wrists.

Peabody's blood.

She spun around as she heard footsteps approaching. But it wasn't Roarke or one of those faceless doctors. Feeney hurried in, his stylish shirt rumpled from the long day, a flush of anxiety riding on his cheeks.

He shot her a look, and when she only shook her head, he went straight to McNab, and sat—as Roarke had—on the table.

They spoke in murmurs, Feeney's low and steady, McNab's thin and disjointed.

Eve circled around them, and into the corridor. She needed to know *something.* To do anything.

When she saw Roarke coming toward her, when she saw his face, her knees went to water.

"She's not—"

"No." He took the coffee from her because her hands had started to shake. "She's still in surgery. Eve . . ." He set the coffee on a rolling tray so that he could take both of her hands in his.

"Just tell me."

"Three broken ribs. Her lung collapsed on the way in. Her shoulder's torn up, hip's fractured. There's considerable internal damage. Her kidney's bruised, and her spleen—they're trying to repair, but they may have to remove it."

God. "They—if they do, they can replace it. They can replace anything. What else?"

"He shattered her cheekbone, dislocated her jaw."

"That's bad. It's bad, but they can fix—"

"There's head trauma. It's a concern." He ran his hands rhythmically up and down her arms, kept his eyes on hers. "It's very serious."

The attending physician he'd collared in ER had told him Peabody looked as if she'd been struck head-on by a maxibus.

"They . . . they say her chances?"

"They wouldn't, no. I can tell you they have a full team on her, and if there's a need for outside specialists we'll get them. We'll get whatever she needs."

Her throat was flooded, and closed like a dam. She managed a nod.

"How much do you want me to tell him?"

"What?"

"McNab." He rubbed her shoulders now, waited while she closed her eyes, gathered herself. "How much do you want me to tell him?"

"All of it. He needs to know all of it. He—" She broke off, let herself cling for a moment when Roarke drew her in. "God. Oh God."

"She's strong. She's young and strong and healthy. It weighs on her side. You know that."

Broken. Shattered. Fractured. "Go tell him. Feeney's here, Feeney's with him. Go tell them."

"Come, sit down then." Gently, he kissed her forehead, her cheeks. "Wait with them. We'll all wait together."

"Not yet. I'm okay." She eased back, but took his hands, squeezed them before releasing them. "I just need to settle down. And I . . . I need to contact some people. I need to do . . . things, or I'll go crazy."

He drew her to him again, held tight. "We won't let her go."

An hour ticked by, minute by endless minute.

"We get any more?"

Eve shook her head at Feeney. She'd taken to leaning up against the wall outside the waiting area when she wasn't pacing. The waiting room had started to fill with cops. Uniforms, detectives, civilian drones who settled in to wait or stopped by for news.

"Her family—"

"I talked them into staying put, at least until we know more." She sipped from another cup of coffee. "As soon as we do, I'll give them her status. I played it down, a little. Maybe I shouldn't have, but—"

"Nothing they can do, for now."

"Right. If they have to get here, Roarke's already made arrangements for transpo. How's McNab?"

"Hanging on by a couple of greasy

threads right now, but hanging all the same. Helps to have other cops around." His eyes went to slits. "He's meat, Dallas. There's not one badge in the city who won't put in the time to track him now he came after one of ours."

"He's meat," Eve agreed. "And he's mine."

She stayed leaning against the wall, only turning her head when she heard the clip of heels. She'd been expecting them.

Nadine streamed down the corridor, two uniformed officers at her back.

Good, was all Eve thought. She needed the distraction of going a round with someone.

But Nadine stopped in front of them, laid one hand on Feeney's arm, the other on Eve's. "How is she?"

Friendship first, Eve realized. When it came to the wire, friendship crossed the line first. "She's still in surgery. Nearly two hours now."

"Did they give you any idea when—" She stopped herself. "No, they never do. I need to talk to you, Dallas."

"Talk."

"Alone. Sorry, Feeney."

"No problem." He slipped back into the waiting area.

"Is there somewhere we can sit down?" Nadine asked.

"Sure." Eve simply slid down the wall until her butt met the floor. And looking up, sipped her coffee.

After a tap of her foot and a shrug, Nadine sat on the floor beside her. "As far as Peabody's concerned, I won't air anything you don't want aired. That's for her."

"Appreciated."

"She's my friend, too, Dallas."

"I know she is." Because her eyes stung, she closed them. "I know it."

"You give me what you want out there, and I'll get it out. Now let's take a minute to discuss the gorillas you've put on my tail."

Eve looked over at the uniforms, satisfied they were—per her orders—burly guys and seasoned. "What about them?"

"How do you expect me to work with a couple of storm troopers in my shadow?"

"That would be your problem."

"I don't—"

"He went after her, he could go after you. We were on screen together. Little push," she murmured. “A little push. I didn’t expect him to go for Peabody.”

“He was supposed to go for you.”

“Makes more sense, goddamn it. I’m primary. I’m in charge. But he goes for my partner. So he could go after you. Working through the lineup, I get that now. Wants me to see he can take out my people under my nose. Wants me to know it before he comes for me.”

“I can follow the dots, Dallas, but it doesn’t address how I’m suppose to gather data and report same when I come as a trio, and two of that trio are badges. Nobody’s going to talk to me.”

“Deal with it,” Eve snapped. “Just fucking deal, Nadine. He’s not going to put his hands on another friend. He doesn’t get the chance for another.”

Nadine studied the icy rage on Eve’s face, and said nothing. She leaned back, took the coffee out of Eve’s hand, sipped. “Tastes like warm piss,” she commented, then sipped again. “No, maybe a little worse than that.”

“It’s not so bad after the first gallon.”

“I’ll take your word,” she decided, and handed it back. “I don’t want him to get his hands on me. I do want to mention I know how to take precautions. Particularly after my own romp in the park with a homicidal maniac a year or so ago. And I haven't forgotten who got me out of that. I'm also smart enough, and have a healthy enough sense of self-preservation to accept that there might be times I need someone to take an interest in my welfare. So I'll deal, Dallas."

She shifted, looking for comfort on the hard floor. "And actually, the one on the left is kind of hot."

"Try not to have sex with one of my men when he's on duty."

"I'll try to restrain myself. I'm going to go see McNab for a minute."

She nodded. Eve considered pacing again, or just closing her eyes and pushing herself into oblivion. Roarke came out before she'd decided, crouched in front of her.

"It might be an idea to go down, get some food—other than the slop available through vending—for the horde in there."

"Trying to give me something to do with myself?"

"Both of us."

"Okay."

He straightened, took her hand to pull her to her feet.

"It just seems like we should know something more by now. It just seems like—"

She looked toward the elevators and saw Louise and Charles rushing in.

"News?" Charles demanded.

"Nothing. Nothing for over an hour now."

"I'll go into surgery." Louise squeezed Charles's arm. "I'll scrub up, get a look for myself."

"That'll be better," Eve said when Louise dashed off. "We'll know more, and that'll be better."

"What can I do?" Charles gripped Eve's hand. "Give me an assignment—something."

She looked into his eyes. The friendship deal came in a lot of layers, she thought, a lot of measures. "Roarke and I were talking about getting some food for everybody."

"Let me take care of that. I'll just go let McNab know we're here, and I'll take care of it."

"It keeps rippling, doesn't it?" Roarke watched Charles move through the groups of cops to where McNab stood. "All the people, the relationships, the connections.

Lieutenant." He framed her face with his hands, kissed her gently on the forehead. "It wouldn't hurt you to find a flat surface, close your eyes for a few minutes."

"Can't do it."

"I didn't think so."

She waited. And felt she was at the center of a vortex as she contacted or was contacted by Whitney, Mira, Peabody's family. Cops came. Some went, more stayed. EDD and Homicide, uniforms and rank.

"Get McNab," she murmured to Roarke when she spotted Louise. "Keep it low. I don't want the whole department out here when she fills us in."

Bracing herself, she stepped forward to meet Louise. "Roarke's getting McNab, so you only have to say it once."

"Good." She wore scrubs now, pale green and baggy. "I'll go back, observe, but I wanted to give you what I could."

Roarke came out with McNab, with Feeney and Charles. The first circle, Eve supposed, of all those spreading ripples.

"Are they finished?" McNab said quickly. "Is she—"

"They're still working on her. It's going well. She's got a solid surgical team, Ian, and she's holding her own." She reached out, took his hands. "It's going to take a while longer. There was extensive damage, and the fact is she's undergoing more than one surgery. Her vitals are good, and everything that can be done is being done."

"How much longer?" Eve demanded.

"Two, three hours more. At least. She's critical, but she's holding. Now I'm going to suggest you go down and give blood. It's something positive you can do. I'll go back in, observe. The head of the surgical team will give you more details when it's done, but I'll keep you updated as much as possible."

"Could I go in with you? If I scrubbed—"

"No." Louise leaned in, kissed his cheek. "Go down, give blood. Do the positive, think strong thoughts. Those things matter, I promise."

"Okay, I'll go down now."

"We'll both go down," Feeney said, then jerked his chin toward the waiting room. "We'll go down in shifts. Time we're finished, you'll have more cop blood in this place than you know what to do with."

* * *

A little woozy from the loss of a pint of blood—Eve would rather have lost it through injury than by syringe—she sat back in the waiting area. Her hands stayed in Roarke's while her mind drifted.

She thought of the first time she'd seen Peabody, looking efficient in her uniform. There'd been a body between them. There was always another body.

She remembered when she'd pulled Peabody off patrol and into Homicide as her aide. And how Peabody had nearly "Sir, yes, sir'd" her to death in the first hour.

Those days were over.

Hadn't taken the smart mouth long to surface—in, over, and around the "sirs."

Stood up for herself is what she did. Respected the rank, but stood up for herself. Learned fast. Quick brain, good eyes. Good cop.

God, how much longer?

Fell for a detective who turned out to be a wrong cop. Shook her confidence, hurt her feelings. Then McNab had pranced in. Charles had glided. But in spite of the looks of that strange triangle, it has always been McNab.

A couple of hard bumps and they'd

bounced away from each other. Bad feelings, bitter words. Spitting at each other if they were in the same space more than ten seconds. Bounced back together eventually. Maybe that's what people did, bounced back where they were supposed to be, bumps or not.

"Eve." At Roarke's voice, she stirred, blinked her eyes open. And followed his look toward the doorway and Louise.

She got up quickly, joined the group already gathering around Louise.

"She's out of surgery. They'll be bringing her into Recovery, and the surgeons will come through shortly to talk to you."

"She came through it." McNab's voice was hoarse with fatigue and emotion. "She came through."

"Yes. She's critical, and they'll almost certainly put her in ICU for the time being. She's in a coma."

"Oh, God."

"It's not unusual, Ian. It's a way for her body to rest, to recover. The early scans look good, but she'll need more. They'll need to keep a close eye on her for the next several hours."

"She'll come out of it."

"There's every reason to believe so, yes. There are some concerns—the kidney, for instance. But she came through the surgery well. Strong."

"I can see her, right? They're going to let me see her."

"Absolutely. In just a little while."

"Okay." That seemed to settle him. The shakes smoothed out of his voice. "And I can just sit with her, until she wakes up. She shouldn't wake up alone."

"I'm sure you can. No more than two in the room at once. But it'll be good for her to know someone's there. She will know," Louise promised. "She'll know."

Eve took her turn, stepping in with Roarke while McNab hovered just outside the room in ICU. She'd prepared herself, but it wasn't enough.

Nothing would've been enough to brace her for that first look.

Peabody lay on the narrow bed, tethered by more tubes than Eve cared to count. Maybe the steady hum and beep of monitors was supposed to be reassuring, but they made her jittery.

But she could have taken that. She'd visited hundreds of victims, fellow cops, perps in hospital rooms, and knew what to expect.

But none of them had been Peabody lying utterly still with her face so bruised it was barely recognizable.

The sheet covered her to the neck, but Eve imagined there were many other bruises under it. Strapping, bandaging, suturing, and God knew what under that white sheet.

"They'll treat the bruising," Roarke said from behind her. "It wouldn't have been a priority."

"He broke her face. The son of a bitch."

"And he'll pay for it. Look at me. Eve." He turned her, gripped her arms tight. "She's mine almost as much as she's yours. I'm in this until the end of it. I want my chance at him as well."

"It can't be personal. That's the primary rule on any investigation. And that's bullshit." She stepped away from him, stepped toward the bed. "That's just raging bullshit, because it's as personal as it gets. He doesn't get by doing this to her. So yeah." She looked up, met his eyes, then turned her icy gaze to Peabody. "We're both in it, till the end."

She leaned over, spoke quiet and clear. "I'm going to kick his ass for you, Peabody. You've got my word on it." She reached out, then hesitated, unsure where to touch. In the end, she laid her hand on Peabody's hair. "We'll be back."

She waited as Roarke bent to touch his lips to Peabody's bruised cheek, then her lips. "Soon. We'll be back soon."

They went out to where McNab and Feeney waited.

"He messed her up bad." McNab's eyes looked hollow, like caves of anger and anguish.

"Yeah, yeah, he did."

"I want to be there when you take him down. I want to be there, Lieutenant, but . . . I can't leave her. I can't leave until . . . until she wakes up."

"As far as I'm concerned, that's your primary assignment."

"I could do some work from here, while I was sitting with her. If I had the equipment, I could do runs or data searches, anything. We're still trying on the Transit discs. I could keep punching that."

"I'll get your work," Eve promised.

"And I'll get you what you need to do it." Feeney laid a hand on his shoulder. "You go on, son, sit with her. I'll bring you what you need."

"Thanks. I don't think I'd've made it through tonight if . . . thanks."

Feeney drew a long breath when they were alone, and his eyes were bright and fierce. "We're going to burn this bastard."

"Damn right," Eve promised.

She'd start at home, shower off the night, marshall her thoughts and resources. The moment they walked in, Summerset was there.

"Detective Peabody?"

He might be an asshole, Eve thought, but right now he looked like an asshole who hadn't slept, and who was carrying a load of worry.

"She came through it. She looks like somebody tossed her in front of a train, but she came through."

"She's in ICU," Roarke continued. "She hasn't regained consciousness yet, but they're hopeful. McNab's with her."

"If I can be of any help."

Eve had started up the stairs, but now she stopped, looked down on him, and considered. "You know how to run the unregistered?"

"Of course."

"I'm taking Roarke with me, so you're on e-duty. I'm going to get a shower, then I'll tell you what you're looking for."

"Tell me what you're looking for," Roarke prompted when they reached the bedroom.

"I have to think it through."

"Think out loud, while we both grab a shower."

She worked up the energy to narrow her eyes at him. "Shower's strictly for body maintenance."

"I consider sex body maintenance, but we'll catch up with that another time."

She talked it out while the hot water helped rinse some of the fog out of her head. And, though she hated them and the jumpy way they made her feel, she popped a Stay-Up, shoved a couple more in her pocket for later.

"Maybe I'm off, but I want to turn all the stones."

"Whether you're on or off," Roarke replied, "we'll turn the stones and see what's under them. You're going to eat."

"We can chomp a couple nutribars on the way."

"No. Foot firmly down on this one. Fuel. You'll shovel in some fuel. It's barely six in the sodding morning," he reminded her as he programmed the AutoChef. "You want to interview the witnesses, you'll do better when they're awake."

He had a point, and arguing would only slow things down. So she sat, shoveled in what he put in front of her.

"You said something to McNab, about how it feels when somebody—when somebody you love gets hurt. I've put you through that a few times. Maybe not as bad as this, but—"

"Close enough," Roarke replied.

"Yeah. I . . . How do you stand it?" Hints of the fear and the worry of the night eked through. "How do you get through it?"

He said nothing, only took her hand, and, watching her over it, brought it to his lips. It made her eyes sting again, and her throat constrict and burn. So she looked away.

"I can't let go, even a little. It feels like if I let go at all, I'll just break to pieces. And I can't stop. I've got to keep moving, keep going forward, and I have to keep telling myself there's going to be payment. Whatever it takes, whatever it costs, there's going to be payment."

She shoved her plate away and stood. "I'm supposed to say justice. There'll be justice, and I'm supposed to mean it. But I don't know if it's going to be enough. I should step back from it. If I don't know if that's enough, I should step back, but I won't. I can't."

"And will you continue to ask more of yourself than is human?"

She reached down, picked up her badge. She studied it for a long moment before she slid it into her pocket. "Yeah. Let's get started."

She briefed Summerset, kept it short, to the point, then headed out to her car. "I can't believe I'm asking him to commit an illegal act."

"It would hardly be the first of his life."

"*And* that I'm asking him to assist in a police investigation."

"That may very well be a first."

"Ha. No, I'm driving. I'm all buzzed from the chemicals."

"Well now, that inspires confidence in your passenger."

"I gotta do stuff or I'll just rev. You take anything?"

"Not yet."

She got behind the wheel. "Talk about more than human."

"Just metabolism, darling. I'll likely need something by midday if we're still at it."

"You can count on that. Witness lives same block as Peabody. Get me the exact address." Then she looked over at him as he called up the data. "Thanks."

"You're welcome. But this isn't just for you."

"No. I know." Needing the contact, she reached over, gripped his hand as she drove through the gates. "But thanks."

20

She didn't bother to hunt up a parking space, but doubled beside a clunky solar mini that looked as if it hadn't moved in six months.

Flipping the ON DUTY light, she stepped out and ignored the shouted "Cops suck!" from the driver of a rusted compact stuck behind her. If she'd been feeling more chirpy, she'd have taken the time to stroll over and have a little chat with him.

Instead, because she couldn't help herself, she walked across the street and studied the bloodstains on the pavement.

"Laid in wait. That's his style. Maybe he followed her sometime, tracked her home sometime, and she didn't make the tail."

But she shook her head even as she said

it. "You can't just pop a cop's address out. You work at it, maybe you can finesse it, but there are blocks on cops' personal data. Had to tail her, or do some heavy hacking."

She thought about the interview for Nadine, and the media conference. Both times she'd pushed Peabody forward.

"How long would it take a decent hacker to pop a blocked address?"

"Depending on talent and equipment . . ." Roarke was studying the bloodstains as well, and thinking of Peabody. Her steadiness, her sweetness. "Anywhere from an hour to a few days."

"An hour? Jesus, why do we bother?"

"It's a shield against the general populace. Tapping into a cop's data is an automatic flag for CompuGuard. It's a heavy risk unless you don't give a bloody damn, or you know how to get around the blocks and guards. You have any reason to think he's got above-average hacking skills?"

"Just thinking. He knew his victims' schedules, their routes, their habits. Where they lived. And all but one lived without a partner."

"Elisa Maplewood lived in a family unit."

"Yeah, a family unit with the male portion

of that unit out of the country. Maybe he factors that element in. He tailed them, yeah. Had to do some of that. And we've got Merriweather's comment about the big, bald guy on her subway. But he could've done some comp research. Gather as much data as possible. He takes risks, sure—big ones. But they're calculated. And the guy we're projecting doesn't blend. Merriweather spotted him. So I'm thinking he doesn't do extensive fieldwork."

"Preps as much as possible by remote."

"It's possible. Probable. He moved fast with Peabody. Faster, I think, than the others. That's because she wasn't the standard for him. She's an add-on—prove a point because he was pissed. Or threatened."

She stayed as she was, tilted her head to look up at the apartment windows. "And you know what else?"

"He didn't know enough about her to know there was another cop up there. Waiting for her. Or enough about the neighborhood to consider someone might spot him and try to help."

"Didn't do as much research. Too mad, too threatened, in too much of a hurry."

Eve angled back to look down the street.

"She takes the subway most times, and she wouldn't be looking for a shadow. He could've stalked her, like he stalked the others. But I don't think it worked that way because she'd have made him. She'd have made a tail. She's got good eyes, good instincts."

"Hacking her address would cut back on the time, and the risk of being seen."

"Yeah. And she was putting in overtime. You have to log any assigned OT. If he could get her address, he could get her schedule, because when I hooked her with Feeney and brought you in, I plugged it into the system."

He took her chin, turning her head so their eyes met. "Eve."

"I'm not blaming myself." Or was trying not to. "I'm blaming him. I'm just trying to see how it went down, that's all. He nails her home location, knows she'll be late. If he knows all that, he knows she doesn't have a personal vehicle registered in her name, and that she'll most likely be on foot. So he comes here, parks, and just waits. Patient bastard. He just waits until she comes along."

"Still risky. This street's well-lighted, and

she's less than a half a block from her door. And she's a cop, armed and able. It wasn't smart," Roarke said. "It wasn't like the others."

"No, with her—me—he was pissed. Prove a point, like I said. But at the base of it, he doesn't figure she'll give him trouble. Not like she did. She's just a woman, and he's a big, strong man. Take her down, take her down, toss her in the back of the van, and poof."

She crouched down, laid her hand on the stain of her partner's blood. "Where was he going to take her? Same place, same place he took the others, the ones before? The missings and presumeds."

"She'll have gotten a good look at him. She'll be able to describe him more thoroughly, even more than Celina."

Eve glanced up. "If she remembers. Head trauma, she might not remember. But if she does, she'll make him. She's sharp and she notes the details. She'll be the one who takes him down. When she wakes up. If she remembers."

Eve pushed to her feet. "Let's see what the witnesses saw. We'll take the female first."

"Essie Fort. Single, age twenty-seven. Paralegal at Driscoll, Manning, and Fort. Tax lawyers."

Eve worked up a smile as they approached the building. "You're handy."

"We do what we can." He pressed the button for Fort in 3A.

While they waited, Eve turned, judged the distance between the door and the point of attack. A male voice came through the intercom. "Yeah?"

"Lieutenant Dallas, NYPSD. We'd like to speak with Ms. Fort."

"I want to see your . . . oh, there it is," the voice said when she held her badge up to the security cam. "Come on up."

He buzzed them in. And was waiting at the door when they got off on three. "Essie's inside. I'm Mike. Mike Jacobs."

"You also witnessed the incident, Mr. Jacobs?"

"I'll say. Essie, Jib, and I were just coming out, going to head over and pick up Jib's date. And we . . . come on in. Sorry." He opened the door wider.

"I stayed here last night. Didn't want to leave Essie alone. She was pretty shook up. She's getting dressed." He glanced toward a closed door. "The woman who got beat up was a cop, right? Did she make it?"

"She's holding her own."

"Glad to hear it. Man, that guy was *whaling* on her." Mike pushed at his curly mop of blond hair. "Look, I was hunting up some coffee. You want?"

"No, thanks. Mr. Jacobs, I'd like to get statements from both you and Ms. Fort, and ask some questions."

"No problem. We talked to some cops last night, but everything was messed up. Look, let me get this coffee, okay? We didn't get much sleep last night, and I need the jolt. Sit down or something. I'll try to move Essie along."

She didn't want to sit, but she perched on the edge of a chair in bold red. Gave herself a moment to settle by glancing around the room. Lots of strong colors, weird, geometric art on the walls. A bottle of wine and a couple glasses left over from the night before.

Mike Jacobs was wearing jeans and a shirt he hadn't buttoned. Probably what he'd had on the night before. Probably hadn't planned on staying the night.

New relationship maybe, without the understanding sex would follow an evening out.

But he'd stayed. And he had, according to McNab, come to Peabody's aid. Maybe he didn't think cops sucked.

The bedroom door opened. The woman who came out looked fragile and slight. Her hair was a short wedge of glossy, raven-wing black, and her eyes a blue strong enough to fit her decor, though they looked exhausted.

"I'm sorry. Mike said the police were coming up. I was getting dressed."

"I'm Lieutenant Dallas."

"Do you know her? The woman who was hurt. I know she's a police officer. I've seen her walking across the street. She used to wear a uniform, but now she doesn't."

"She's a detective now. She's my partner."

"Oh." Those blue eyes filled—sympathy, distress, fatigue, Eve didn't know. "I'm so sorry. I'm so sorry. Is she going to be all right?"

"I . . ." Eve felt her throat close again. It was harder, somehow harder, to take concern from strangers. "I don't know. I need you to tell me exactly what you saw."

"I—we—were going out." She looked over as Mike brought out two thick red mugs. "Thanks. Mike, would you tell it?"

"Sure. Come on, let's sit down." He led her to a chair, and sat on the arm of it beside her. "We were coming out, like I said. We heard the noise as soon as we walked out the door. Shouts, and well, the sounds you hear from a fight. He was a big guy. Seriously big. He was kicking her and shouting. Kicking her when she was down. She pumped up her legs, knocked him back a little. It all happened really fast, and I think we all froze for a second or two."

"It was just . . ." Essie shook her head. "We were all laughing and joking around, then we heard, and looked over. It was just *bam*!"

"He jerked her up, off the ground, just hauled her up."

"And I screamed."

"It got us moving," Mike continued. "Like holy shit, don't just stand here. We yelled, I guess, and Jib and I started running for them. He looked around, and he just threw her. Like *heaved* her, you know?"

"She went down so hard." Essie shuddered. "I could hear her hit the sidewalk."

"But while she was airborne, there was this flash. I think she fired at him as she was flying." Mike looked at Essie and got a nod. "Maybe she hit him, I don't know. She went down hard, sort of rolled, like she was going to try to fire again, or get up or . . ."

"She couldn't," Essie murmured.

"He jumped into the van. Moved like lightning, but Jib said he thought the guy was holding his arm. Like it was hurt? Anyway, he jetted. Jib chased the van for a few yards. Don't know what he'd've done if he'd caught it. But she was hurt really bad, and we figured that was more important. We were afraid to move her, so I was calling for an ambulance when the guy—the other guy—the cop—comes running out."

Fired at him, Eve thought. Flying through the goddamn air, but she'd fired at him. And had held onto her weapon. "Tell me about the van."

"Black or dark blue. Almost sure it was black. It was new, or really well kept. Lieutenant . . . I'm sorry."

"Dallas."

"It happened really fast. Like—" He snapped his fingers. "And we were all yelling and running, so it's pretty jumbled up. I tried to catch the plate, but it was dark, and I couldn't make it out. It had windows on the side, and in the cargo doors. They might've been blacked out or covered, I couldn't tell, but there were windows."

"You may think it's jumbled, Mr. Jacobs, but every detail you're giving me matters. Tell me about the assailant. Did you see his face?"

"We got a look. When he heard us yelling and turned our way, we got a decent look, I think. Essie and I spent some time last night trying to put it together. Hold on a minute."

"He was like something out of a nightmare," Essie added when Mike went into the bedroom. "I couldn't sleep last night because I kept seeing him, and hearing the way it sounded when he threw her down."

"I think this is the best that we've got." Mike came back in with a sheet of paper, handed it to Eve.

She felt her heart thud when she looked at the sketch. "You drew this?"

"Art teacher." He smiled a little. "We only saw his face for a second or two, but I think that's close."

"Mr. Jacobs, I'm going to ask you to

come into Central, work with an Ident artist."

"Sure. I've got a class at nine, but I can call in. You want me to go in now?"

"It would be a great help if both of you, and Mr. Jibson could go in. This sketch can be used in an ID program. And the three of you can help the police artist create the closest possible likeness."

"I'll get a hold of Jib now, tell him to meet us there. Where do we go?"

"I'll take you. Tell your friend to go to Level Three, Section B. Identification Procedure. I'll have him cleared and escorted."

"Give me ten minutes."

Eve got to her feet. "Mr. Jacobs, Ms. Fort, I want to tell you how much the department, how much I personally appreciate what you did last night, what you're doing now."

Mike moved a shoulder. "Anybody'd do the same."

"No. Not everybody."

Her luck was turning, Eve decided when she was able to collar Yancy as her Ident artist. There were others who were as good with a sketch or a comp-generated image, but Yancy had a way of helping a witness remember details, of talking them through the process.

"What's the latest with Peabody?" he asked Eve.

She couldn't count the number of times she'd been stopped with a variation of the question on her way through Central. "No change."

He looked down at the sketch she'd handed him. "We'll get this fucker."

Her brows lifted. Yancy wasn't just known for his skill with imaging, but for his mild manner. "Count on it. I need you to run me a copy of that, for now."

"Get that right for you." He moved to his imaging comp, slid the sketch in.

"He's got layers of sealant on his face and it distorts it some. You need to factor that. I know I shouldn't ask how long, but I have to."

"I wish I could tell you." He handed her the copy. "How cooperative are they?" He nodded to the anteroom where the witnesses waited.

"Unbelievably. Almost make me want to hang up my cynic's cap and wear the badge of the optimist."

"Then it'll be quicker." He studied the sketch again. "Artist is good. That'll help considerably. I'm pushing everything else aside till we have him for you, Lieutenant."

"Thanks."

She wanted to stay, watch the process, somehow hurry it along. She wanted to be at the hospital with Peabody, somehow bring her back. She wanted to yank and draw on every line and thread at once.

"You can't be everywhere, Eve."

She glanced over at Roarke. "Shows? I feel like I'm running in place. Goal's in sight, but I'm stuck in this spot. Maybe you could contact the hospital again, charm some information out of somebody. I just make them mad."

"People tend to get cross when someone threatens to pull their brains out of their nostrils."

"You'd think they'd give me points for creativity. I'm too wired." She shook herself as they headed toward her division. "Damn chemicals. You take the hospital, check in on Summerset. Talk the e-talk with Feeney, and I'll cut through the rest. Do you need me to find you a space?"

"I'll manage."

"Dallas!" Celina sprang off a bench. "I've been waiting. They said you were on your way in. You haven't answered your voice or e-mail."

"Been busy. Getting to it."

"Peabody." She clamped a hand over Eve's arm.

"She's holding. I'm really pressed, Celina. I can give you a few minutes in my office. You set?" she asked Roarke.

"I am, yes. I'll meet you out here."

"I'm sorry." Celina pushed her hands through her luxurious hair. "I'm upset."

"We all are," Roarke told her. "It was a long, difficult night."

"I know. I saw . . ."

"Let's take it in here." She led the way into her office, shut the door. "Have a seat." Though she knew caffeine wasn't the best idea at the moment, she wanted coffee. Ordered two. "What did you see?"

"The attack. On Peabody. God, I was in the tub. Hot bath before bed to relax me for today. I saw her walking—sidewalk, buildings. He—he just leaped out at her. It was like a blur, and the next thing I know I'm floundering around in the tub like a damn trout. I tried to contact you."

"I was already in the field, and went straight to the hospital. I haven't gotten to a lot of my messages."

"He knocked her down. He was kicking her, and she was fighting him. He hurt her. It was terrible. For a minute, I thought she was dead, but—"

"She's not. She's holding."

Celina clutched the coffee in both hands. "She's not like the others. I don't understand."

"I do. Just tell me what you saw. I want the details."

"They're not clear. It's so damn frustrating." She set the mug down with a snap. "I talked to Dr. Mira, but she won't budge on the time element for the next session. I wanted to go under immediately. I know, I *know* I'd see more. But I saw—I heard—screaming, shouting, and he threw Peabody down. I saw him jump into . . . It was a van. I'm sure it was a van. Dark. But everything seemed dark. He was hurt. There was pain."

"She got to her weapon."

"Oh. Good. Good. He was afraid. I feel . . . it's hard to explain it, but I feel it. His fear. And not just of being seen, or caught, but of something else. More. Of not finishing? I want to know, I want to help. Can you convince Dr. Mira?"

"She won't budge for you, she won't for me." Sitting on her desk, Eve tapped her fingers on her knee. "If I could get a personal item from someone I believe was a victim, a previous victim, would you get anything from it?"

"Very possibly." Excitement shone in Celina's eyes as she leaned forward. "It's more what I do. That connection. If I could link, I might see something."

"I'll work on that. I don't know if I can be there for your session today. We've caught a break and I'm following it through. The witnesses from last night got a pretty good look at him."

"Thank God. If you can identify him, this will be over. Thank God."

"I'll work on getting you something as soon as I can."

"Anytime. Absolutely anytime. I'll come in as soon as you want me. I'm sick about Peabody, Dallas. Just sick about it."

Some time during the endless night, McNab dropped off in the chair beside Peabody's bed. He'd lowered the guard so he could reach her more easily, and when fatigue won, he rested his head beside her breast with his hand under the sheet and linked with hers.

He didn't know what woke him—the pings of the monitors, the shuffle of feet outside the room, the light that spilled through the window. But he lifted his head, winced with the crick in his neck, rubbing it out as he studied her face.

They hadn't yet treated the bruising, and it broke his heart to see her face so damaged. It twisted his belly to see her so still.

"It's morning." He cleared the worst of the hoarseness from his voice. "Morning, baby. Ah, sun's out, but it looks like we might get some rain. You, ah, had a lot of people in and out, checking on you. If you don't wake up, you're going to miss all the attention. I was going to get you flowers, but I didn't want to leave you that long. You wake up, and I'll take care of that. Want some flowers? Come on, She-body, rise and shine."

He slipped her hand out, pressed it to his cheek. There were nasty abrasions down the arm where it had skidded over the sidewalk.

"Come on, come on back. We got a lot to do, you know. Moving day."

He kept her hand there as he turned his head and watched Mavis come in.

She said nothing, only walked to him, laid a hand on the back of his head.

"How'd you get by the dragons?"

"Said I was her sister."

It made him close his eyes. "Close enough. She's still out."

"Bet she knows you're here." Mavis leaned over, touched her lips to his cheek. "Leonardo's down getting her some flowers. She'll like having them when she wakes up."

"We were just talking about that. Oh, Christ." He turned his head, pressed his face into Mavis's side as he fought to hold on.

She waited, stroking his hair until the tremors passed, and he was able to draw a steady breath. "I'll sit with her if you want to take a walk, get some air."

"I can't."

"Okay."

He shifted, but stayed close so they watched the steady rise and fall of Peabody's chest together. "Louise checked on her a few times. I think she and Charles stayed most of the night."

"I saw him in the waiting area. Dallas?"

"She's going after the bastard. She's hunting the animal who did this to her."

"Then she'll get him." After giving him a pat, Mavis turned away to pull over a chair.

"Wait, sorry, let me get that. You shouldn't be hauling stuff."

At best, the folding chair weighed four pounds, but she let him move it over for her. "McNab, there isn't a lot we—me and Leonardo—can do. But we can move your stuff, set up your new place."

"It's a lot of stuff. I don't want—"

"We can do that, if you let us. Then when she's better, you can just, you know, carry her in. It'll be done. You need to be here, with her. We can do this for you. For both of you."

"I . . . that'd be mag. Thanks, Mavis."

"Hey, we're going to be neighbors."

"You, ah, don't go lifting anything heavy. With that bun in the oven."

"Don't worry." She rubbed a hand over her belly. "I won't."

"I feel like I'm going to fall apart any second. Then the second passes, and it's the next, and I . . ." He jerked straight in the chair. "I think she moved. Did you see that?"

"No, but I—"

"She moved. Her fingers." He turned over the hand he held in his. "I felt them move. Come on, Peabody. Wake up."

"I saw it that time." With her fingers gripping his shoulders, she leaned forward. "Look, she's trying to open her eyes. Do you want me to get somebody?"

"Wait. Wait." He pushed up, leaned over. "Open your eyes, Peabody. You can hear me. No sliding back under again. Come on, you're going to be late for your tour."

She made some sound—part gurgle, part moan, part sigh—and he'd never heard sweeter music. Her lids fluttered, and her swollen, blackened eyes opened.

"There you are." The tears flooded his throat; he swallowed most of them and grinned at her.

"What happened?"

"You're in the hospital. You're okay."

"Hospital. Can't remember."

"Doesn't matter now. You hurt anywhere?"

"I . . . everywhere. God, what happened to me?"

"It's okay. Mavis."

"I'll get somebody."

When she dashed out, McNab pressed his lips to Peabody's hand. "It's going to be okay now. I promise. Dee. Baby."

"I was . . . coming home."

"You'll get there. Soon."

"Can I have drugs first?"

He laughed, as tears rolled out of his eyes.

Eve caught herself leaning over Yancy's shoulder, and eased back.

"It's okay. Used to it. Let me tell you first, if everybody brought me witnesses like yours, my job would be a hell of a lot easier. Maybe a little boring."

Then he glanced back at Roarke. "This is one of your programs."

"So I see. It's one of the best image programs on the market though we're working on some upgrades. Still, it's only as efficient as its operator."

"I like to think so."

"Can you guys get back to your admiration session later?"

"Well, take a look. Here's the sketch your

wit brought in, and here's my revised image, after the session. See? We got a little more detail, subtle alterations, but they can boost time on an ID match."

"Less Frankenstein," Roarke commented.

"Yeah. The behavior of the subject tends to influence the witness's memory of his physicality. They see this big guy pounding on a woman, and he takes on giant characteristics. Monster shit. But your wit had the basics, and he had them down. Square face, lots of forehead, shiny dome. Knowing about the sealant lets me program that element. The shades hamper the ID—eyes are the best element for a match. But from here, we start building, using the program."

He initiated, took the sketch through the building stages. "Profile. Adding dimension, skull shape."

Eve watched Yancy use a stylist to prompt the program, section by section, on the image.

"Ears, line of neck. Revolve to back view, other profile. Full face. Shape of the mouth, nose, angle of bone. Get it to three dimensions, add skin tone. Okay, this is the best probability, given current data. To take it the last step, you have to go with a combo of your own judgment and the comp's. Remove shades."

Eve stared at the eyeless face, felt a shudder run through her.

"Apt," Roarke stated.

"Yeah."

"His eyes could be damaged, but for ID purposes, we're going to try the highest probabilities for the shape. Color's not an option, though I'd lean toward dark with this skin tone and the eyebrows. Highest percentage. Going that direction, this is what I get."

Eve studied the finished image. The hard, square face, soft mouth, thick eyebrows over small, dark eyes. The nose was large, slightly hooked, the ears prominent against the bald skull.

"There he is," she said quietly.

"If it's not damn near close as a photograph, you can spank me," Yancy said. "I'll toss this to your office unit. Got you plenty of hard copies. I'll pass some out myself. You want me to run the ID match?"

"Shoot it to Feeney in EDD. Nobody's faster." Then she glanced at Roarke, saw him smile. "Hardly. That's a hell of a job, Yancy. One hell of a job."

"Your wits were gold." He handed her a stack of hard copies. "Tell Peabody we're pulling for her."

"Bet your ass." She punched him lightly on the shoulder, a sign of affection as much as appreciation, and hurried out. "Going to run for a match myself. Feeney'll probably beat me to it, but we'll get this started. And once we—shit, shit, shit."

She yanked out her beeping communicator. Seeing McNab's code on the readout, she stopped short. Instinctively, she reached for Roarke's hand as she answered. "Dallas."

"She's awake."

"On my way."

Eve all but sprinted down the hospital corridor, and when an ICU attendant held up a hand, she only snarled. "Don't try it."

She surged through the door and straight into Peabody's room. And stopped short.

Peabody was propped up in bed, a vague smile on her battered face. The short counter under the single window had been transformed into a garden, with flowers jammed together in such abundance their scent overpowered even the hospital scent.

McNab stood beside her, holding her hand as if he'd been glued there. Louise was on the other side. And perched on a chair was Mavis, doing some blooming of her own in florid purple and green.

"Hey, Dallas." Peabody's voice was slightly slurred and absolutely cheerful. "Hello, Roarke. Jeez, he's just so gorgeous, what're ya gonna do? You gotta think about it."

Louise chuckled. "And who could blame you? You'll have to excuse her," she said to Eve. "They gave her something for the pain."

"Something really, 'specially good." Peabody grinned. "Totally iced drugs."

"How's she doing?"

"Very well." Louise gave Peabody a light pat. "She's got more treatments in store. Tests, scans, therapy—all that fussy medical business. And she'll need to be monitored carefully for a while yet. But they've bumped her all the way down to stable. She'll move to a standard room within a few hours if she stays stable. I expect her condition will be deemed good by the end of the day."

"You see my face? I mean, whoa shit! Messed me up good. They had to—what was it—reconstruct my cheekbone. I don't know why they couldn'ta done both while they were in there, and given me some. Cheekbones, you know? And he dislocated my jaw, so I'm talking funny. But it doesn't hurt a bit. I love drugs. Can I have more?"

"Can you cut them back a little?" Eve asked.

"Aw." Peabody poked out her bottom lip.

"I need to talk to her, get her statement. I need her a little more coherent for that."

"I'll check, see what I can do. But you'll need to keep it short."

"She's in a lot of pain without them," McNab said when Louise stepped out.

"She'd want to do this."

"I know." He sighed, smiled as Peabody examined the fingers of her free hand. "She's really wonked."

"How come we don't have six fingers, you think? Six would be frosty. Hey, Mavis!"

"Hey, Peabody." Mavis moved across the room, slid an arm around Eve's waist. "She says, 'Hey, Mavis,' about every five minutes," she whispered. "It's cute. I'm going to go out, sit with Leonardo and Charles while you do this part. Anybody you want us to tag to update them?"

"We spread the word, but thanks. Thanks, Mavis."

Louise and Mavis passed, going in and out. "I'm going to cut her IV down a little and give you ten minutes tops. She doesn't need to deal with pain right now."

"Can I kiss Roarke first? Come on. Please, please, please!"

Though Eve rolled her eyes, Roarke laughed and walked to the bed. "How about I kiss you, gorgeous?"

"Not so pretty right now," she said. Coyly.

"You're beautiful to me. Absolutely beautiful."

"Awwww, see? What're ya gonna do?"

He leaned down, laid his lips softly on hers.

"Mmmm." She patted him on the cheek when he lifted his head. "Better'n drugs even."

"Remember me?" McNab asked.

"Ah, yeah, skinny guy. Crazy about the skinny guy. He's just so cute. Got the cutest little butt. Oughta see it naked."

"Louise, cut them back. Have mercy," Eve demanded.

"Takes a minute."

"Stayed with me all night. Sweet boy. Love the sweet boy. Heard you talking to me sometimes. You can kiss me, too. Everybody can kiss me because . . . oh-oh."

"Give me some room," Eve demanded. "Peabody."

"Sir."

"You get a look at him?"

"Yes, sir." She drew a breath, shakily. "Jesus, Dallas, he messed me up. Came at me like a hell-god. I kept feeling stuff breaking and tearing inside me. Hell of a thing."

Her fingers moved restlessly on the sheet, then dug in as she struggled with the pain. Eve covered it with hers, stilled it.

"I got to my weapon, though. I hit him. I know I did. Arm, shoulder maybe, but I nailed one in him."

"You see his vehicle?"

"I didn't. Sorry. I just—"

"Forget it. He say anything to you?"

"Called me a whore. Whore cop."

"You make the voice if you hear it again?"

"Bet your ass. Sir. I think I heard him. . . . It sounds weird, but I think he called for his mother. Or called me Mother. Maybe it was me, calling for mine because, I can tell you, I wanted her."

"Okay."

"I can give you a full description."

"I'm going to show you a picture. Tell me if it's him."

She held it up, adjusting the position so Peabody could study it without moving.

"That's him. He had a lot of sealant on his face, but that's him. You got him?"

"Not yet. We will. Can't take you on the bust because you'll be having your drug party, but we'll take him, and you're part of it."

"Will you tell me when you've got him?"

"You'll be the first."

She stepped back, nodded to Louise. "You want to get sprung from here, you can recoup at our place if you need to."

"Appreciate it. I . . . whee!" She laughed as the drugs bumped up. "That's more *like* it."

"We'll be back," Eve promised. McNab was on her heels as she went out.

"Dallas? We're crapping out on the Transit discs. Since you got your ID, you won't need me on that anyway. Anything else you need me to do?"

"Get some sleep."

"Not until."

She nodded. "Stick with her. I'll let you know if anything comes up. I'll be back in a minute."

She strode away, headed straight for the woman's bathroom. Inside, she just sat on the floor, pressed her hands to her face, and cried.

Her chest hurt with it, heaved with it as the pressure finally broke free. Her throat was raw, her head thumping as the emotions she'd stifled took over, poured out in a hot, violent flood.

And sucked her dry.

She started to spring up when she heard the door open, then stayed where she was when she saw Mavis.

She just lifted her hands, let them fall. "Shit, Mavis."

"I know." Mavis settled down beside her. "Scared everybody. I had my jag already. You can go ahead, finish yours."

"I think I did." But because she could, she let her head lean on Mavis's shoulder a moment. "Maybe after she's better, Trina could give her the full works. Peabody'd like that. She can be a real girl."

"Good thinking. We'll have a complete girl party."

"I didn't mean . . . sure, whatever. You got any sunshades on you?"

"Do monkeys screw in the jungle?" She reached into the purple fringe worked into her shirt and drew out a pair of purple shades with green lenses.

"What the hell." Deciding they were marginally better than going around with red, swollen eyes, Eve put them on.

"Uptown!"

"No, I'm thinking down." Eve got up, helped Mavis to her feet. "Thanks for the loan. I've gotta go bust this bastard."

21

Roarke said nothing until they were back in the car, Eve behind the wheel.

"Not your usual fashion accessory."

"Huh?"

He tapped a finger on the frames.

"Oh. Mavis. I, ah, borrowed them because . . . She blew out a breath.

"You don't need to hide them from me." He slipped the glasses off, leaning over to lay light kisses on her eyelids.

"Aw," she said with a half smile. "What're ya gonna do?" She threw her arms around him, burrowing in. "I didn't want to break down and start blubbering all over McNab. I got most of it out, so you don't have to worry about me blubbering all over you."

"I never worry. You were due for a breakdown, and you timed it until you were sure our girl was going to be all right."

"Yeah, I guess." It was so good to hold, to be held. "Now we're going to take care of business." She eased back. "Eyes bad?"

"They're beautiful."

She rolled them. "This is not Peabody on drugs."

"By the time you get to Central, good as new."

"Okay." But she stuck the sunshades back on. "Just in case."

They weren't even out of the parking garage when her communicator beeped. "Dallas."

"Got him."

"Oh Jesus, Feeney. Send it through to my vehicle's unit. I want to see him. We're on our way to Central now. Can you meet me in my office?"

"I'll be there. Take a look."

Quickly, she programmed the vehicle for Central's garage and shifted to auto so she could give the image her full attention.

"There you are, you son of a bitch. Blue, John Joseph. Age thirty-one. Damn it."

Since auto didn't allow her to exceed

speed limits or outrun reds, she switched back, hit the sirens. "I don't want audio," she said to Roarke. "I don't need to hear it all. Just give me the salient."

"Single, mixed-race male. No spouse, no legal cohabitation partner. No offspring on record. No criminal on record."

"He's got something. Juvenile, I'll bet your ass. And sealed. We'll worry about that later."

"Residence listed as Classon Avenue, Brooklyn."

"Brooklyn?" She shook her head as she screamed through traffic. "No, that's not right. Can't be."

"That's what's here. Resided that address eight years. Owner, operator Comptrain, Inc.—same address. Want the details on that?"

"Yeah." But he didn't live in Brooklyn. Not now.

"Ah, small data analysis company. There's your hacking skills, Lieutenant. He'd do most of the work right out of his home for this. Tech support and the like."

"Cross with the customer and member lists."

"Moment. You've got him as a member,

ten years standing, at Jim's Gym downtown."

"And he didn't pop because of the Brooklyn addy. We'd've gotten to him, but he wasn't in the first layer. He's not coming to the city from Brooklyn to stalk and kill. I don't buy it. And they've got gyms in Brooklyn, for Christ's sake."

She flew into the garage, cut speed seconds before she arrowed into her slot. Roarke, made of sterner stuff than Peabody, never flinched. He was out of the car with her, moving double-time to the elevator.

"A second residence in the city then. One he hasn't listed, or rents, has bought under another name."

She jumped off the elevator on the first floor and dashed to a glide, hot-footing it up, elbowing passengers aside on the way.

Ignoring protests, she hopped off, jumped on another. "I'm going to put this op together, fast. Two tactical teams. One to Brooklyn."

"And the other?"

"I've got an idea on that."

She streamed up the glide at a run, pivoted, and rushed through her bull pen without acknowledging any of the calls or questions.

"Full data up," she snapped at Feeney.

"Up. What's with the shades."

"Hell." She yanked them off, tossed them on the desk. "Mother. Ineza Blue, age fifty-three. Address listed on Fulton. Bingo, you rat bastard."

"Ineza Blue," Roarke said, working rapidly on his PPC. "Retired licensed companion. One child, son."

"You get me the mother's image from, say twenty years ago, I bet you get me a white woman with long, light brown hair." She slapped Feeney on the back.

"Lieutenant?" Roarke held out his palm unit. "She's a hit on your customer list for Total Crafts."

"Get me details on her purchases, last six months. Look for the cord."

She snapped back to Feeney. "Let's get started," she said and turned to her 'link to contact the commander.

Fifteen minutes later, she was in a conference room briefing her tactical teams. "Team One takes the target in Brooklyn. Briscoll goes in as delivery to ascertain if the subject is on the premises. Target is to be surrounded at all points. We're also looking for a black van, now identified as registered to subject's mother. Last year's model, Sidewinder. If said van is spotted, lock it down. Baxter, you're heading this team.

"Team Two will deploy to the Fulton Street residence. The same procedure applies, with Ute taking the delivery position. I head this team. In both locations, we go in fast and we go in hard. Warrants are coming through. If the subject isn't located, we wait for him. I don't want this asshole making a cop. He makes any of you, I fry you. We take him down, and we take him today. If there are any screwups on this one, any screwups in procedure, in chain of evidence, if somebody fucking sneezes at the wrong time, I will personally put their neck in a wringer and hit go. Questions?"

"Just one." This from Baxter. "The subject is a large individual with considerable muscle. It may take some extreme measures to restrain him. Just want to make sure everyone on my team is prepared to take these measures, whatever they may entail."

Eve angled her head. "I want him conscious for Interview. Other than that . . ." She let it hang. "Don't let those measures get out of hand. Move out. Feeney, round up Team Two."

She ordered her team to strap on protective gear. Though she didn't see it as an issue, she wasn't taking chances. She didn't want to visit another cop in the hospital.

"You don't figure the mother's in on this," Feeney said as they waited inside the surveillance van.

"No. We got the cord, twenty-yard length of it, delivered to the Fulton Street address five months ago. I'm saying she had some in stock previous to that, and the new supply was ordered by the son. She didn't have any deliveries listed before that, or after. She always picked up her supplies. I figure she's dead or incapacitated."

She shifted to the balls of her feet, back again. Squatted and straightened to be sure the gear didn't hamper movement. "If he offed her, maybe that's what set him off on the rest. Maybe she just kicked, and that set him off, but I'm betting he helped her out."

She looked over at Roarke. "You and I are going in the front, once we've determined he's inside. Feeney and his man in the back.

Communications remain open, at all times. I want everyone with a badge, and the civilian consultant, to know where everyone is. Good-sized house," she commented, studying it through the screened window of the van. "One floor down below street level, two above. Two men take the below, and we go in on my signal. I want every door, every window covered. He moves fast, and he's not going to fall down and surrender. He'll run."

"Team's in position," Feeney told her. "Go to Ute?"

"Go."

She watched Ute zip down from the east corner on a compact jet-bike. He secured it at the curb, bounced off, and up to the door with his misdirected package. He rang the bell, bounced his head around as if bopping to the beat of music through headsets.

And she heard, clear as a bell, the answer from the securitycom. "What?"

"Delivery, man. You wanna sign. Shit. Starting to rain."

The first thin drops splat the streets and sidewalks when the door opened.

"Hold positions."

"You got the wrong place," Blue said. "This is 803, not 808."

"Hell, it looks like a three. Are you—" The door slammed in his face. Ute made a business out of turning his back, pointing at his ass, and making a kissing sound before bouncing back to his bike.

"Subject verified. No visible weapons."

Eve jerked her head, and slipped out the side door of the van with Roarke. He hefted the small battering ram. She crouched behind a parked car as Feeney drove off.

"Gonna get wet," she murmured. She rolled her shoulders, rocked back and forth on the balls of her feet.

"You know, Lieutenant, I can get through the door nearly as quickly myself as with this ram. And with more finesse, and considerably less noise."

"Not looking for finesse." She nodded when Feeney's voice came through her earpiece. "Move in! Go, go, go!"

Still crouched, she dashed across the street, noting the movements of her team out of the corners of her eyes as she charged up the steps. "Take it down!"

He reared back, slammed it twice, then

let it fall as the door crashed open. They were through, weapons drawn.

Every light blared on full, and she could hear the fast and heavy rush of feet. She veered right toward the sound and caught sight of Blue streaking up the stairs.

"Police! Stop where you are." She was already running up behind him. "You're surrounded. You've got nowhere to go. Stop or I will fire."

He swung back, his face red with exertion and what she took as panicked temper. She knew, though she couldn't see his eyes, she knew in that instant from the stiffening of his body, he recognized her.

And he lunged.

She fired a stream midbody that crossed with the stream Roarke fired. The combination knocked Blue back three staggering steps.

To her amazement, he shook it off like a man hyped on Zeus. Lunged again. "Bitch! You hurt me!"

She didn't question herself, the need, the motive, but rather than firing on him, she got a running start, pumped her legs, and slashed into a flying kick that landed both feet in his face.

Blood erupted from his nose, spilled out of his mouth, but he was still on his feet when she dropped back to hers. "Don't fire," she shouted at Roarke, and whoever was pounding up the steps behind them.

"Screw this," she muttered as he came for her again. "Let's see how *you* like it." And she curled down, locking her hands around her weapon. Brought them up with as much force as she could muster, into his balls.

He screamed, a high-pitched sound that made her heart sing. He dropped to his knees and rolled.

"That seems to have done it. Subject is secured! I need extensions for these restraints," she called out as she pressed her weapon to his cheek. "You're a big boy, Blue, big, strong boy, but if I fire this weapon from here, you're going to lose a chunk of your face. While I might consider that an improvement, you may not."

"See if these work." Feeney stepped over Blue, muscled his arms behind his back, and fought extended restraints into place as the man began to cry like a baby. "Barely. Maybe hurts a little, but gee, what can you do?"

"Get him in the tank, read him his rights."

When she started to get to her feet, she winced, crouched down again.

"Give you a hand, Lieutenant?"

"Thanks." She took the one Roarke offered, and stretched her left leg. "Might've pulled a little something on that kick. It was a little high for me."

"Well placed, though I did enjoy the second maneuver."

"First was for Peabody. Second was . . ."

"I know. For all of them." He knew it embarrassed her, but he couldn't help himself. He leaned down, kissed her. "You are my hero."

"Get out."

"Lieutenant?" One of the team called out from below. "You're going to need to see this. Basement level."

"On my way."

It was a horror she'd never forget. No matter how many she'd already witnessed, how many were yet to come.

The basement had been converted, some years before from the look of it, into a small warren of rooms. His primary living space,

Eve concluded, with some recent adjustments.

His office was tidily and efficiently set up. Three complete d and c units, a wall of discs, minifridgie, miniAutoChef. And lights so bright they almost burned the eyes.

He'd set up a personal fitness center, equipment, mirrors, a sparring droid nearly as big as he was. The lights seared.

In the third room, the walls were also mirrored, and the lights burned bright, bouncing their reflections everywhere. She could see the fitness area from that position.

It was his bedroom—a young boy's room with toys on a shelf, Space Invaders paper on one of the walls. The bed was narrow and neatly made with a cover that boasted interplanetary warriors in full battle.

There was a chair, child-sized, fit with restraints. Wrist and ankle shackles. Tied on one of its arms was a bright red cloth.

She'd cast him into the basement, Eve thought. And despite the toys, the touches of youthful decor, had made it his prison.

He'd kept it as one.

But he'd made an addition.

There was a single long shelf bracketed

into the wall. New from the looks of it, and the metal brackets shone clean and silver.

On it were fifteen clear jars filled with a pale blue liquid.

Floating in the pale blue were fifteen pairs of eyes.

"Fifteen," Eve said and forced herself to look. "Fifteen."

Eve stood with Roarke in Observation. Inside Interview A, Blue was shackled to the table—hand and foot.

He'd screamed like a madman—mad child—when they'd muscled him down, snapped them on. Had only calmed when at his terrified demands, they'd boosted the lights in the room to full.

She imagined, if he got riled enough he could lift the whole shebang and do some damage.

"You're not going in alone." It wasn't a question Roarke asked, it was a statement with the subtle edge of warning.

"I'm not stupid. It's me, Feeney, and two uniforms built like Arena Ball tackles. You sure you want to watch this?"

"I wouldn't miss it for worlds."

"Patching it through to Peabody's hospital room, so she and McNab can watch. They'll put him away in an institution. Mental defectives. It's not the cage I'd choose for him, but it'll have to do."

"You need him to tell you where the bodies are."

She nodded. "He'll tell me."

After one last look, she moved out of Observation. Signaling to Feeney, she unlocked the door, stepped inside ahead of him and the two guards.

"Record on." She recited the data, smiled. "Hello, John."

"I don't have to talk to you. Bitch."

"No, you don't have to talk to me." She sat down, hooked an arm around the back of her chair. "And that's Lieutenant Bitch to you. You don't want to have a chat, we can send you back to a cage. You're booked, John. All those murder charges. Rape, murder, mutilation. Got you cold, and you're smart enough to know it. Crazy as a shithouse rat, maybe, but you're not stupid."

"You shouldn't call him crazy, Dallas."

"Oh, yeah, right." She smirked at Feeney. "Probably got a bunch of sob stories to tell. Traumas and emotional scarring. Shrinks'll eat that up. Me, I don't give that shithouse rat's skinny ass. You're going down, John. Fact is, you are down. We got evidence flying out our butts on you. You go and leave us the eyes. What's with that? What's with the eyes, John?"

"Fuck you."

"Rape isn't fucking. Didn't your mother ever tell you that?"

He reared back, face contorting. "You shut up about my mother."

Got your trigger, she thought. "I don't have to shut up about anything. See, how it works is I'm in charge here. I'm the boss. I'm the woman who busted your balls and locked you up. You messed up my partner, John, so I'm not going to shut up until you squeal like a pig."

She slapped her hands on the table, shoved her face into his. "Where are they, John? Where are the rest of the bodies that go with the eyes?"

"Fuck you, whore bitch."

"Sweet-talking me isn't going to work."

"Come on, Dallas." Feeney patted her shoulder. "Ease back a little. Listen, John, you want to help yourself here. You got trauma, I can see that."

Eve made a rude noise.

"We saw the shackles, John. We saw how it must've been for you when you were a kid. I bet you've been through a lot, and maybe you didn't know what you were doing. Not really. You couldn't help it. But you need to help yourself now. You need to show us some remorse. You need to tell us where the others are, John. You do that, you volunteer that, and it's going to make a difference with the PA."

"She says you're going to lock me away for killing a bunch of whores. How's telling you where anything is going to help me?"

"Listen, the police officer's going to be okay."

"Her name's Peabody," Eve interrupted. "Detective Delia. She got one into you, didn't she, John. Gave you back some pain."

She arched her eyebrows when he drew one of his arms toward his chest. "Stings like a bitch, doesn't it, when the stream hits."

"Doesn't bother me." His gaze tracked to the mirror, and his shoulders relaxed again. "Look at me. I can take anything."

"Ran, didn't you? Ran like a rabbit."

"Shut up, you bitch! I did what I had to do."

"Let's calm down." Feeney gestured down with his hands, keeping the tone and rhythm of good cop in play. "The important thing for you, John, is Detective Peabody's all right. That counts a lot. Maybe we couldn't help you out if she'd taken a downturn, but she's okay. There are things we can do for you, John. You cooperate, you show remorse, you give us the information we need to bring some closure to the families of those other victims, we're going to put in some good words for you."

"I did what I had to do. Why do you lock a man up for doing what he has to do?"

Eve pulled a red cord out of her pocket. "Why did you use this?" When he only stared, she wrapped it around her own throat, watched his eyes go glassy. "You like how it looks on me? Want to get your hands on the ends, John, and pull?"

"Should've killed you first."

"Yeah, you got that right."

His gaze was locked on the cord, and beads of sweat were popping out on his face, on the dome of his head. "Where's your mother, John?"

"Shut up, I said, about my mother!"

"She liked to do crafts. We got her account from Total Crafts. But you know what, word is nobody's seen her around, in months. Damn near a year now. You kill her first, John? You take some of her ribbon, like all that red ribbon we found in the house, and wrap it around her neck? You rape your own mother, John? Did you rape and strangle your mother, and take her eyes?"

"She was a whore."

"What did she do to you, John?"

"Deserved what she got." Breathing shallow, he stared at the mirror again. Nodded slowly. "Deserved it. Every time."

"What did she do?" There was nothing wrong with his eyes. She could see that, and she'd checked his medicals. And she thought of the bright lights. Sunshades and bright lights. Eyes in jars.

"It's a little bright in here," she said conversationally. "Lights, fifty percent."

"Turn them back up." The sweat was rolling now. "I'm not talking to you in the dark."

"You're not saying anything I want to hear. Lights, thirty percent."

"Turn them on, turn them on! I don't like the dark. Don't leave me in the dark. I didn't mean to see!"

His tone had gone high. A boy's voice in panic and plea. It touched something in her, but she tamped it down. "See what? Tell me, John. Tell me, and I'll turn the lights up again."

"Whore, naked in bed. Letting him touch her, touching him. I didn't mean to see."

"What did she do to you?"

"Put the cloth over your eyes. Tie it tight. Little prick, got no business spying on me when I'm working. Lock you in again. Lock you in the dark. Maybe I'll poke your eyes out next time, then you won't see what you're not supposed to see."

Chains rattled as he struggled in the chair. "I don't want to be in the dark. I'm *not* weak and puny and stupid."

"What happened in the park?"

"Just playing, that's all. Just playing, me and Shelley. I just let her touch it. It hurts, it hurts when Mommy hits it with a stick. Burns, burns when she scrubs it with the powder. Pour acid on it next time and see how you like it. In the dark, can't see, can't get out."

He fell against the table, weeping.

"You got strong, didn't you, John? You got strong and paid her back for it."

"She shouldn't have said those things to me. She shouldn't laugh at me and call me names. I'm not a freak. I'm not good-for-nothing. I'm a man."

"And you showed her you were a man. A man who can rape whores when he wants to. You shut her up."

"Shut her right up." He lifted his head, and madness rolled in his eyes even as tears streamed out of them. "How do you like it now? She only sees what I tell her to see now. That's what. I'm in charge now. And when I see her again, I know what to do."

"Tell me where she is now, John. Where the rest of her is."

"It's dark. Too dark in here."

"Tell me so I can turn the lights back up."

"Buried. Decent burial, but she kept coming back! It's dark in the ground. Maybe she doesn't like it there. Put her outside, put her in the park. Make her remember! Make her sorry."

"Where did you bury her?"

"Little farm. Granny's farm. She liked the farm. Maybe she'll live there one day."

"Where's the farm?"

"Upstate. Not a farm anymore. Just an old house. Ugly old house, locks on the doors. She'll lock you in there, too. Maybe leave you there for the rats to eat you don't do what she says, when she *damn* well says it. Granny locked her in plenty, and that'll teach you to mind your p's and q's."

He was jerking on the chains as he spoke, rocking back and forth in the chair, teeth bared, skin shining with sweat.

"But she won't sell it. Greedy bitch won't sell it and give me my share. She won't give me anything. Not giving her hard-earned to some freak. Time to take it, take it all. Bitch."

"Lights on full."

He blinked against them, like a man coming out of a trance. "I don't have to say anything to you."

"No, you've said enough."

22

She ordered droids and dogs, a search unit, and the equipment necessary for multiple remains location, identification, and removal.

And knew it would be a very long, very difficult procedure.

She requested Morris personally, and asked that he select a team. She expected and was unsurprised when Whitney and Tibble arranged to make the trip upstate.

For the moment, for a small window of time, they would keep the media at bay. But it would leak soon enough, she knew, and the ugly carnival would begin.

Because she wanted time to prepare, to think, without the distraction of cop chatter or questions, she traveled upstate in one of

Roarke's jet-copters, with him in the pilot seat.

They flew through a steady, dreary rain. Nature's way of weighing in, she thought, to make a hideous job more so. She saw a little burst of lightning bloom on the horizon, far to the north, and hoped it stayed there.

Roarke didn't ask questions, and his silence throughout the flight helped steady her for what was to come. This sort of procedure would never be routine. Never could be routine.

"Nearly there." Roarke glanced at the comp map highlighting their destination, then nodded toward the windscreen. "At two o'clock."

It wasn't much of a house. She could see that from the air as they started the descent. Small, ill-kept, poorly maintained, if she was any judge. It looked to her as if the roof sagged—probably leaked, and the lawn fronting the steep, narrow road was weedy and littered with trash.

But the back was blocked in with trees, and in front of them ranged a high fence. The lawn, such as it was, spread up, dipped down, following the rise and fall of land.

There were other houses, and the curious

would come out of them before long. None of those houses were close, not to the bumpy land back of the house. A man with a mission, she thought, a man with a job to do, could carry it out in relative privacy in such a place.

Uniforms would knock on doors and ask about the Blues, and a dark van, and any odd activities.

They set down. Roarke killed the engines.

"You feel some sympathy for him. John Blue."

Through the rain, she stared at the house, the dark, dirty windows, the scabs of paint puckering its skin. "I feel some sympathy for a defenseless child tortured by a parent, by a woman who most certainly was vicious and cruel. We know what that's like."

She turned her head, looked at him. "We know how it can twist and scar. What it can drive you to. And I feel a twinge, maybe more than a twinge, at the way I played the child in Interview. You saw how I went after him."

"I saw you doing what needed to be done, even when it hurt you. Hurt you, Eve, as much as him. Maybe more."

"Needed to be done," she agreed, and

would live with that. "Because a child didn't kill these women. A child didn't rape and beat and strangle them, mutilate their bodies. A child didn't put Peabody in the hospital. So no, when it comes down to the line, I don't feel for John Blue. We had as bad."

"You had worse."

"Maybe." She breathed deep. "Maybe. And like him, I killed my tormentor."

"Not like him, Eve. Nothing like him." It was that point, that vital point he'd wanted to make to her. "You were a child, in desperate terror and pain. Defending yourself, doing whatever you could to make it stop. He was a man, and had the choice of walking away. However she twisted him, he was a man when he committed these acts."

"The child lives inside. I know that's shrink pap, but it's true enough. We've both got that lost child in us."

"And?"

"And we don't allow that lost, damaged child to strike the innocent. I know. You don't have to soothe me. I know. We use, I guess, that child to stand for the innocent. Me with my badge, you with places like Dochas. We could've gone the other way, but we didn't."

"Well, I had a few detours."

It made her smile, and thank God for him. "And we haven't finished the trip yet. Roarke." She touched a hand to his. "You don't know how hard this is going to be."

"I have some idea."

She shook her head, and her face was already bleak. "No, you don't. I've done this before. It's worse than you can imagine. I'm not going to ask you to go back or hang around the edges, because you won't. But I'm saying, if you need a break from it, take it. Walk away for a while. Others will, believe me. There's no shame in it."

She, he thought, would never walk away. "Just tell me what you need me to do."

She had the back of the house cordoned off. While the dogs and droids were sent in, she took a team into the house. It was dank and foul inside, dark as a cave, but when she called for lights, the place illuminated like a torch.

No dark rooms for John Blue, she thought.

He'd killed them in the bedroom, the smaller of the two. His room, Eve assumed, whenever they'd made the trip here. There were locks on the outside of the door—old locks. Locks she'd undoubtedly installed to keep the boy inside. Lock him in the dark, as her mother had locked her.

So he'd killed her there, on the stained mattress, lying naked on the floor. Killed others there, in her image.

She saw lengths of red cord, remnants of women's clothing, and the smears and stains of blood that had dried on the mattress, on the floor.

"Everything bagged and tagged," she ordered. "I want a full sweep. Personal items of some of the vic's may include their identification. When it's done, I want the porta-lab and tech in here to get samples of the blood. We're going to ID every victim he brought here."

"Lieutenant?" One of the team stepped up. He wore his full protective suit, but had yet to attach the mask and filter. "We're locating them."

"How many so far?"

"Dogs just found number seven, and it doesn't look like they're done."

"On my way."

Feeney hustled over to join her. His Mrs.

Feeney suit was smeared with cobwebs and muck. "Found a Robo-dig in the basement. Looks fairly new. Been used."

"Why use a shovel when you can use a machine? And one that makes a manly hum. Neighbors could've heard that."

"I'll dispatch some uniforms, start the knock on doors."

"Get it started." She pulled on her protective suit, carried her mask out into the rain.

Found seven, she thought. No, they hadn't finished yet. She knew exactly how many more would be found.

Droids scooted along the uneven ground. One of the dogs barked, and his body went into a shiver of wagging as he snuffed along the ground. At his handler's signal, he sat, waited.

He'd done his job. And they put up the marker for number eight.

Eve walked to Whitney who stood under a wide, black umbrella. "Sir. Do you want me to begin evacuation?"

"Eight." His face was set like granite as he stared out at the scene. "This is your procedure, Lieutenant."

"Evac can confuse the dogs. It would be

my choice to leave that until we believe all remains are located and marked."

"Do so. There's nine," he murmured.

They worked, inside the house, outside in the rain. Dozens of cops moving like ghosts in their gray gear. Dogs barked, droids signaled, and flags were marked on the ground.

"Call them off," she ordered when thirty minutes passed without an alert. "Move in the evac team. Let's have some lights," she called out as she started across the spongy ground. "Two evac teams, one far west, one far east. Morris."

"I'm with you."

"I need IDs as soon as possible. Sooner."

"I've got dental for the missings on the city list, and those we've culled from this area. It doesn't come up to this number." He scanned the ground where the evac units were beginning to dig. "But I've got equipment in the portable that will match the dentals for what we have. Others are going to take a little longer."

"Ground's rocky under this sponge," Roarke commented. "Muddy now as well. It'll take awhile for the robot diggers to get through this muck."

"Can you operate one?"

"I can, yes."

"Get this man a machine," Eve shouted out, and turned to Roarke. "Start due south. Morris, assign one of your guys to Roarke. Let's get this done."

She shoved on the mask, engaged the filter, and strode toward the first marker. She stood, much as the search dog had, and waited.

"Got remains," the operator announced. The robot was shut down. It was handwork now, a careful excavation with sensors beeping, reading out hair, flesh, bone beneath the thin layer of dirt.

She saw hands first, fingers laced—or what was left of them. The filter couldn't mask the full impact of what death slowly does to flesh. But still she crouched, came closer, as the shell of a woman was unearthed.

Her hair was long. Longer than it had been at death, Eve thought. In one of those mysteries, hair continued to grow after life winked out. It was dark with dirt, but it would be light brown.

You're found now, Eve thought. We'll give you back your name. The one who did this to you is boxed and caged. That's all I can do.

"How long she been in there?" Eve asked Morris.

"Few months, maybe six, I'd say. I'll tell you more when we get her in."

"Get her out," Eve said, and, straightening, moved to the next marker.

The false twilight the rain brought deepened toward night. The air was cold, damp, and carried the pitiful stench of death. Tagged bodies lay bagged beside gaping holes in the earth until they could be transported. Remains lay on tarps shielded by tents while the ME's team worked to identify.

The yard took on the look of a mass grave.

Overhead, the media copters circled, spun out their lights. Word was more reporters were camped on neighbors' lawns. It hadn't taken them long. Even now, she assumed, the scene where she stood, the misery and horror of it was being relayed to screens all over the state—the country. The damn world.

And people sat in their homes and

watched. Grateful to be warm and dry and alive.

Someone brought her coffee, and she drank it without tasting it, without thought. Snagging another, she walked to Roarke.

"This is the third I've done." Absently, he wiped rain from his face. He shut down the machine, boosted it aside so the hand team could work. "And you were right. It's worse than anything I could imagine."

"Take a break." She handed him the coffee.

He stepped back and shoved up the mask as she had done. It barely helped now in any case. Beneath it his face was pale, damp with sweat. And grim as a grave.

"I won't be put in the ground when my time comes," he said, quietly. "Ashes to ashes, dust to dust, whatever the hell, I won't make that transition in the bloody dirt. I'll take the fire, quick and clean."

"Maybe you can bribe God and live forever. You've got more money than He does."

He managed a small smile to please her. "It's worth a try in any case." He drank coffee, and looked, was unable not to look at the horror surrounding him. “Sweet Jesus, Eve.”

“I know. His personal cemetery.”

“I was thinking his private holocaust.”

And she stood with him for a moment, in silence, listening to the mournful sound of rain pattering on the bags.

“Morris has ID’d a few, through dental. Marjorie Kates, Breen Merriweather—from the city. Lena Greenspan—thirty-year-old mother of two from three miles away. Sarie Parker, twenty-eight, adult ed instructor, worked at the local school. Some of them are going to be street people, or LC’s. But we’ll ID them all. However long it takes, we’ll ID them all.”

“It matters, who they were, where they came from, who loved them. You have to make it matter or they’re just rotting flesh and bone after all. They’re only what he made them. Isn’t that so?”

“Yeah.” She watched as another was bagged. “And they’re more. Much more than he made them.”

When it was done, as much as could be done then and there, Eve stripped off her gear, tossed it into the pile for sanitizing and disposal. She wanted a shower. She wanted hours in hot water, as hot as she could stand, then more hours in oblivion.

But she wasn't finished. Not yet.

She dug in her pocket for another Stay-Up, dry-swallowing it as she walked to the copter where Roarke waited.

"I'm going to ask you for one thing," he began.

"You're entitled to more than one after the night you put in. Above and beyond, Roarke."

"We see that differently, but I will ask for one thing from you. When this is done, when you've closed it down, I want two days. Two days away from this, from all of it. We can stay at home, or go anywhere you like, but I want that time—for both of us. To—I'd say to get this out of our system, but we never will. Not really."

He pulled off the leather strap he'd used to tie back his hair. "To rebalance ourselves, I'll say."

"It's going to take some time yet. I need to be around until Peabody's on her feet."

"That goes without saying."

"Yeah." Because she understood it did,

she pointed, then walked to the other side of the copter. Maybe it was silly to need it as a shield, but there were still a lot of cops on scene. She'd given her official statement to the media, though a few lingered, hoping for more.

They'd get no more from her tonight, and she wanted private moments to stay private.

She slid her arms around his waist, pressed her cheek to his. "Let's just hold on here a minute."

"Gratefully."

"It shakes me. You can never get yourself ready for something like this. No matter what. And you know they'll never be enough payment made for it. There can't be. I'm sick. I'm sick in every part of myself."

She turned her head so it rested on his shoulder. "So yeah, I'll give you two days—and take them. Somewhere away, Roarke. Away, where it's just us. Let's go to the island."

She tightened her grip, tried to envision the sugary sand, the blue water, and erase the vision of the muddy ground and body bags. “We don’t even have to take any clothes.”

With a small sigh, he rested his head on top of hers. “I can’t think of anything more perfect.”

“I got to finish up tonight’s work. A couple days more, maybe after that. Then we’ll get the hell out.”

He gave her a boost into the copter. “You sure you’re up to the rest of this tonight? You’re running on chemicals.”

“I sleep better when I tie off the ends.” She strapped in, then used the ’link to check on Peabody while the copter rose into the rain.

Celina opened the gate to the elevator in her loft. “Dallas, Roarke. You both look exhausted.”

“You’re not wrong. I know it’s late. I’m sorry.”

“Don’t worry about that. Come in and sit.” She gestured them in. “Let me get you something. Have you eaten?”

“Not thinking about food for some time yet. But wouldn’t say no to a chair.”

“And some tea, I think.”

"She could use it," Roarke said before Eve could speak. "We both could."

"Just give me a minute."

She hurried away on bare feet with her lounging robe floating around her ankles. "Peabody?" she asked from the kitchen.

"She's pretty good, considering. In a regular room—well in the hospital palace Roarke finagled for her. She'll need a couple more days in anyway, then maybe she can switch to at-home care until she's a hundred percent again."

"I'm so glad to hear it. I don't know if you've talked to Mira, but we made more progress today, and I think I could work with a police artist tomorrow."

She carried a tray back in, hesitated when she saw Eve's face. "What?"

"We ID'd him this afternoon. We got him."

"My God." Celina set the tray down with a little thunk and rattle. "You're sure? I can't believe it."

"We're sure. It's one of the reasons we came by. Guess you haven't had the screen on."

"No, I haven't. Clearing the mind, and all that. How? When?"

"I figured I'd left you out of the loop, but

everything moved fast once it started moving."

"That's not even an issue. He's locked up? It's done." She breathed out slowly, then reached for the teapot. "I don't even know how to think, or feel. It's such a relief. How did you find him?"

"Witnesses who saw him assault Peabody got a decent look at him, and his ride. We worked from there. Picked him up. He broke in Interview in less than an hour."

"You must be not only exhausted but very pleased." She passed cups of tea around. "It came down to straight cop work, after all."

"And some luck."

"I guess I didn't contribute much, at the end of things."

"Not so. You did quite a bit."

"You have a gift," Roarke continued. "You've utilized it."

"It's not something I have a choice over."

"Oh, I disagree." Eve sipped tea. "You certainly chose to use it when you murdered Annalisa Sommers."

"What?" Celina's cup rattled in her saucer. "What did you say?"

"You must've been watching John Blue—

visioning him—for months. Did you see him kill his mother, Celina? Did it go back that far? Is that when you started to plan how you could get rid of your competition?"

As she stared, her face went stark white. "This is horrible. This is hideous and horrible. You're accusing me of murder? Of killing poor Annalisa? You have the man responsible. How could you say this to me?"

"I have the man responsible for murdering fifteen women. Fifteen, Celina. He had their eyes on display. Over the past few hours we've been disinterring bodies from the backyard on his mother's place upstate. Bet you know about that place, too. We have thirteen bodies. Thirteen—including his mother whose remains have been positively ID'd. Thirteen women he practiced on."

Eve's face wasn't pale. It was hard as stone, cold as ice, but a faint flush of rage tinged it. "Did you watch him kill them, too? Add Elisa Maplewood, add Lily Napier, and you've got your fifteen."

Celina's hands fluttered up, crossed over her breasts. "I can't believe what I'm hearing. I think you must have pushed yourself over some edge."

"Right up to it, but not over. If I'd gone over, I'd be breaking your face right now, the way Blue broke my partner's."

"You'd accuse me, after I came to you, after I've tried to help, because you have one too many bodies to fit your case? For God's sake. I want you to leave my house. I want you—"

When she started to rise, Roarke simply reached out, shoved her back into place. "You want to sit quietly, Celina." And his voice was deathly calm. "We've both had a miserable few hours and may be less courteous than you're accustomed to. So I'd sit still if I were you."

"Now you're threatening me. I'm calling my lawyer."

"Haven't read you your rights yet, so you don't get any. I'll read them to you, Celina, and you can call your lawyer, but right now, we're just having a conversation."

"I don't like the tone of this conversation."

"You know what I don't like? I don't like being used. I don't like being hosed by some selfish bitch with a sixth sense so she can kill her boyfriend's new woman."

"*Listen* to yourself! I was at home, all

night, when she was killed. I took a tranq. I never left the house."

"Not at all true," Roarke commented. "Oh, you've got the security discs that'll prove you didn't go out the front, use the elevator. But interestingly enough, you've no tenants down below and haven't for the last few months."

Summerset's little contribution, Eve thought. "You didn't renew their lease."

"It's certainly my choice—"

"And that made it very simple," Roarke went on. "You went out the door there—where you shut down the security cams—down the stairs, into 1-A, and out the emergency evac. I checked it myself, and you didn't think to seal up first. We've your prints on the door, on the window, on the evac mechanism."

"It's my property." But her hands were moving restlessly now, from her lap, to her throat, to her hair. "My fingerprints might be anywhere."

"Annalisa didn't fit. She was close," Eve considered. "In the ballpark, but she didn't quite fit Blue's vision. Hair's too dark, too short. Then there's the kitten. He didn't use props with the others. But you needed that moment of distraction. You're not a two-hundred-eighty-pound man. You needed to distract her, to get her down so she didn't have time to fight."

"For heaven's sakes. He *raped* her. In whatever fantasy you've dreamed up, for whatever reason, you can hardly accuse me of raping another woman."

"Couldn't have been pleasant for you. What appliance did you use? They make all kinds. Some of them are so realistic, you can hardly tell them from the real McCoy."

"Please."

Eve patted Roarke's knee. "Sorry."

"You'll never prove this."

"Oh, Celina, I will." Eve leaned forward so Celina could look directly into her eyes. "You know I will. Just like you knew I'd get John Blue, with or without you. You wanted me to, just not before Annalisa. You have the right to remain silent," she began.

"This is insane," Celina said when Eve finished the Revised Miranda. "Why would I come to you, to help?"

"Always better to be in the inner circle, closer to data, if you can. That was clever of you."

"I'm going to call a lawyer."

"Go ahead." Eve gestured toward the 'link. "Once you do, I'll make it my mission in life to take you down harder. I'm tired. I want to close this down. Because I'm tired, I'm inclined to work with you on this, see what we can manage."

She saw speculation, just an instant of it, flicker over Celina's face. "Blue's got no reason to lie, Celina. He knows how many women he killed, and what he did to and with every one of them. The number is fifteen. He wasn't in Greenpeace Park the night Annalisa was killed. He's alibied."

"Then it was—"

"Someone else?" Eve suggested. "Yes, it was. Someone who knew the details, details not released to the media. Someone who could use them, copy them. But that someone wasn't a man. Because there was no man that night. Only you. He left you. Lucas left you, and ended up with her."

"We left each other, and he wasn't seeing her when we were together."

"No, he wasn't. Decent guy, honest guy. He didn't two-time you. But he'd met her before you split. He confirms that, by the way. He'd met her, and he'd felt something click. I bet you knew he was interested, maybe before he really knew it himself. I bet you read him every chance you got."

"I told you I don't intrude."

"You're a liar. Up till now, your gift's been more a game to you than anything else. Entertaining, interesting, lucrative. You told me once you were shallow, and that's one absolute truth. Lucas wasn't in love with you anymore, he was pulling away. Had to save your pride and make it seem amiable. And now, look at this, his new lady meets with a terrible death, and there you are, arms open to comfort. Did you weep a few tears when you went over to comfort him this afternoon?"

"I had every right to see Lucas. Decency—"

"Don't tell me about decency." The whip of Eve's voice had Celina's head snapping back. "You knew what John Blue was, where he was, what he was doing long before you came to my office. You watched him kill, over and over again. And you used them, used him, used me. One of the clerks uptown—you were smart to go uptown—at a craft shop remembers you, Celina. You're a striking woman, and she remembers you coming in four months ago. Four months ago, and buying three yards of red corded ribbon."

Her cheeks weren't pale now. They were going gray. "That—that doesn't prove—"

"You think it's all circumstantial, and maybe. But it adds up so nice. Means, motive, opportunity." She flipped out three fingers. "You knew the victim, you knew the details of the other murders, you had the murder weapon in your possession. We can trace it back to that uptown shop. It'll take a little time, but we can do it. When we do, it's as good as around your neck."

She waited a beat to let that factor sink in. "You're the only one who could have killed her. You're boxed. Stand up to it, Celina. One thing you're not, is weak."

"No, I'm not." She picked up her tea, wrinkled her nose in distaste. "I'd rather a brandy, I think. Would you mind?" She gestured vaguely. "On the shelf by the kitchen. A double."

Roarke obliged her, walked across the room.

"You love him very much," Celina said to Eve. "We could say outrageously."

"You can say whatever you like."

"What would you do, how would you survive if he fell out of love with you? If you knew you'd become an obligation, a duty he didn't quite know how to avoid, because being a decent man, he didn't want to hurt you. To hurt you. How could you stand it?"

"I don't know."

"I let him go." She closed her eyes a moment, and when she opened them again they were clear. Steady. "I tried to let him go, to be reasonable and sophisticated. But it hurt." She pressed a fist to her heart. "So much. Unbearably. Worse when he fell in love with her. I knew he'd never come back to me, there was no chance he'd love me again as long as he loved her."

She looked up at Roarke as he brought her the brandy. "Men enslave us, even when they don't mean to. I sought the first vision. I was grieving, and I sought it out. I don't know what I intended to do, but I was so unhappy, so angry, so lost, and I opened myself up. And I saw him, as clearly as I see you. John Blue. I saw what he did."

She swirled brandy, sipped. "It wasn't his mother. It wasn't the first. I didn't know how many before. It was Breen Merriweather. I didn't see him take her from the city. But I saw him lifting her out of a van. It was dark.

Very dark. Her hands and feet were bound and she was gagged. I could see her fear. He took her inside, and all the lights, so many lights came on. So I saw everything he did to her in that horrible room, and I saw him bury her in the backyard."

"And you started to plan."

"I don't know. That's sterling. I didn't know what to do, what I would do. I almost went to the police. It was my first instinct, I swear it. But I . . . didn't, and I wondered who he was and how he could do the things he did."

"So you watched him," Roarke finished. "To find out."

"Yes. I was fascinated and repelled, but I was able to link to him, and I . . . studied him. And I wondered: Why doesn't he kill Annalisa? Everything would be the way it should be again, if he'd kill Annalisa. I wondered if I could pay him to do it, but that was too risky. And he's mad, so he might've hurt me. And I realized, maybe, there'd be a way for me to do it. Then he killed Elisa Maplewood. Right here in the city, and I knew how it could be done."

She let her head fall back. "I didn't just come to you for information," she said to

Eve. "I needed to know how you would handle the investigation, how quickly you would find him, what you thought of me. And a part of me, I swear to you, a part of me hoped you'd find him quickly, before I . . . But you didn't. I gave you information hoping, in some part of myself, that you'd find him, stop him, before . . ."

"So you could put the blame on the investigation, on me, when you killed her."

"Maybe. I agreed to the hypnosis before Annalisa," she reminded Eve. "I volunteered for it. I asked Mira to start it right away, but she was so cautious."

"Her fault, too."

"It plays in, certainly. If any one factor had gone differently, it all would be different. I told myself if the information I gave you led you to him quickly, that was what was meant. If she, if Annalisa didn't walk into the park that night, I'd stop the whole thing. If she didn't take the shortcut, I'd walk away from her, that I was meant to. I'd tell you everything I saw. But she did. She did, so it seemed *that* was meant, and I let myself become him, in a way, so I didn't have to think about what I was doing. I let myself become him so I could stand apart and watch, with a kind of horror. Then it was too late to go back."

She shuddered, drank more brandy. "She saw me, just for an instant. And she was so confused. But it was too late to go back. I couldn't stop myself. Well." She breathed out. "When did you know?"

"When I learned her connection to Lucas Grande."

"Please." She waved that away. "You're a very clever woman, but you had no idea at that point. I read you in Mira's office, and after the attack on Peabody just to cover myself."

"You're not the only one who can block." Eve angled her head. "I told you Mira has a daughter who's Wiccan and a sensitive. She gave me a few pointers."

"You played me."

"That's right. But not well enough, not fast enough, or my partner wouldn't be in the hospital."

"I didn't know he'd go after her. By the time I did, it was too late. I tried to contact you. I *like* Peabody."

"Me, too. Guess you didn't have the same sensibilities about the other women he butchered."

She lifted her shoulders a little, let them fall. "I didn't know them."

"I do."

"I did it for love. Whatever I did, it was for love."

"Bullshit. You did it for yourself. For control, for power, for selfishness. People don't kill for love, Celina, they just like to pretty up the mess they've made by saying so."

Eve stood. "On your feet."

"I'll make a jury understand. It was a kind of madness, that's all. And that madness took me over—my gift makes me all the more susceptible—until what he was got inside of me and killed Annalisa."

"You go on believing that. Celina Sanchez, you're under arrest. Why don't I give you a rundown of the counts?" She nodded to Roarke who moved to the elevator. "First degree sexual assault, first degree murder, mutilation of Annalisa Sommers, a human being. Accessory to sexual assault, murder, and mutilation, before and after the fact. Fifteen counts."

"Fifteen . . . You can't blame me for what he did." She tried to swing around when Eve snapped on the restraints.

"Oh yeah, we can. We do. And I'll bet

mine against yours we'll make a jury understand why." Eve looked over as McNab and Feeney got off the elevator. "Additional counts, accessory before and after the fact, attempted murder, assault and battery on a police officer. Take her in, Detective. Book her."

McNab took Celina's arm. "My pleasure."

"List Detective Peabody as arresting officer, in absentia."

He opened his mouth, then cleared his throat. "Thank you, sir."

"Go home, kid," Feeney told her as he took Celina's other arm. "We've got it from here."

Eve listened to the elevator start down. "Should get a team in here tonight, see what we can dig up. Add a few bars to her cage." Then she rubbed her tired eyes. "Screw it, we'll lock it down. Tomorrow's soon enough."

"Music to my ears." He recalled the elevator. "That was well done, Lieutenant. Giving the collar to Peabody."

"She earned it. I'm still buzzed." She rolled her shoulders and stepped into the elevator. "My eyes want to close, but my body's still jumping."

"I believe we can fix that when we get home. You can close your eyes." He leaned down, kissed her, long and deep. "And I'll jump your body."

"Sounds like a deal."

She walked outside, fixed a police seal to the door. "Rain's stopped," she commented.

"Still a bit misty yet."

"I like it."

"You liked her," he added.

"I did." She stood in front of the door, looking out at the street, the wash of puddles as a Rapid Cab slewed through. "I did like her. Still do on some level, even knowing what she is."

He slung an arm around her shoulders, she hooked hers around his waist. "Do you think she loves him? Lucas?"

"No." She knew what love was now. "But she thinks she does."

Eve dropped into the passenger seat this time, yawned comfortably when Roarke took the wheel. She leaned back, closed her eyes, trusting he'd get her home.

Yes, she knew what love was.